BARBARA
NADEL
ON THE BONE

headline

The right of Barbara Nadel to be identified as the Author of
the Work has been asserted by her in accordance with the
Copyright, Designs and Patents Act 1988.

First published in Great Britain in 2016
by HEADLINE PUBLISHING GROUP

1

Cataloguing in Publication Data is available from the British Library

ISBN 978 1 4722 1379 2 (Hardback)
ISBN 978 1 4722 1380 8 (Trade paperback)

Typeset in Times New Roman by Palimpsest Book Production Limited,
Falkirk, Stirlingshire

Printed and bound in Great Britain by CPI Group (UK) Ltd, Croydon, CR0 4YY

MIX
Paper from
responsible sources
FSC® C104740

Headline's policy is to use papers that are natural, renewable and recyclable
products and made from wood grown in well-managed forests and other
controlled sources. The logging and manufacturing processes are expected to
conform to the environmental regulations of the country of origin.

HEADLINE PUBLISHING GROUP
An Hachette UK Company
Carmelite House
50 Victoria Embankment
London EC4Y 0DZ

www.headline.co.uk
www.hachette.co.uk

To Alex and Lia

Acknowledgements

This book would not have been possible without help from the following people:

Earl Starkey and his wonderful assistant Gonca Özküçük who introduced me to the spectacular Zenne Segah. Leigh Turner CMG, Consul General for Trade and Investment for Turkey, Central Asia and the South Caucasus, who gave me tea and 'the tour'. For perspective on the 'Syrian situation', Revd Canon Ian Sherwood, OBE, and, as ever, to my friend and fellow traveller Pat Yale. Plus I've also watched a lot of television cookery shows!

Cast List

Police:

Inspector Cetin İkmen – middle aged İstanbul detective

Inspector Mehmet Süleyman – İstanbul detective and İkmen's protégé

Commissioner Hürrem Teker – İkmen and Süleyman's boss

Sergeant Kerim Gürsel – İkmen's sergeant

Sergeant Ömer Mungun – Süleyman's sergeant

Arto Sarkissian – Armenian police pathologist

Constable Halide Can – police officer

Others:

Fatma İkmen – Cetin's wife

Kemal İkmen – one of Fatma and Cetin's sons

Gonca Şekeroğlu – Süleyman's mistress

Sinem Gürsel – Kerim Gürsel's wife

Peri Mungun – Ömer Mungun's sister, a nurse

Boris Myskow – American celebrity chef at the Imperial Oriental Hotel

Chef Tandoğan – chef at the Imperial Oriental Hotel

Bülent Onay – chef at the Imperial Oriental Hotel

Aysel Gurcanli – chef at the Imperial Oriental Hotel

Tayyar Zarides, also known as Cyrus – a Greek pork butcher

Imam Özgür Ayan – a cleric

Burak Ayan – the imam's son

Mustafa Ayan – the imam's son

Radwan – a Syrian refugee

Azzam – a Syrian refugee

Uğur İnan – originator of the Art House squat

İsmet İnan – Uğur's son

Birgül İnan – İsmet's wife

Ziya Yetkin – a biker

Zenne Gül – a male belly dancer

Meltem Baser – Gül's friend

Ahu Kasap – Gül's friend

Pembe Hanım – Gül's friend

Celal Vural – a waiter

Selma Vural – Celal's wife

Aylin Hanım – Imam Ayan's neighbour

Ramazan – Aylin's son

General Abdullah Kavaş – murder victim's father

Belgin Kavaş – murder victim's mother

Major General Deniz Baydar – retired soldier

Defne Baydar – the Major General's wife

Father Bacchus Katsaros – Greek Orthodox priest

Cüneyt Civan – Internet trader

Mimi – prostitute

Could guilt kill? Scientifically that had to be bullshit. But dying as a result of guilt, well, that could be possible, couldn't it? The stress of carrying guilt could put pressure on the central nervous system, which could in turn affect the heart. Long-term stress could result in damage to the heart muscle. And heart disease was in the family.

He felt hot, then cold, then hot again. His chest hurt. Indigestion, his body rejecting food it hadn't been designed to eat. Or had it? Of course it hadn't. He'd known it was wrong. But at the same time, he'd been curious. And it had looked good. Now he knew what Hagop meant when he talked about 'crackling', although he doubted whether his Armenian friend had ever had it like he had.

He felt sick. It wasn't good to be out on İstiklal Caddesi on a Saturday night when he felt so rough. Istanbul's principal party street was buzzing with noise, food smells, tobacco smoke and a cross-section of humanity that made his head swim at the best of times. Now everyone looked frightening and disapproving. He felt they *knew*, and his chest tightened again. But how could they know? Sweat poured down his face. Years ago, when his family had taken holidays, he'd got food poisoning in Sicily. He'd thought he was about to die. But then he'd also had the shits. He gagged. Maybe it was coming out of the other end? He'd have to get to a side street or a shop doorway. He wasn't far from the church of St Antoine. If he could stagger through the gates and on to the steps, he could sink down on the ground and maybe start to feel a bit better. But as he began to walk towards the church, he felt the world turn upside down and he hit the road with his shoulder.

He saw people come. He heard them ask him if he was OK. But then he entered a blackness that he had, and hadn't, been expecting.

Chapter 1

'Does this have to be done now?'

Fatma İkmen looked up at her husband. Surrounded by tins, she was sitting on the floor in front of the food cupboard. She was uncomfortable and angry.

He answered his own question. 'I see it does.'

He lit a cigarette.

'Out!'

Cetin İkmen loved his wife. They'd been together for over forty years and he had never regretted a day of it. But there were limits.

'No.' He sat down at the kitchen table.

Fatma's plump face turned red. 'Nobody smokes indoors now,' she said. 'Only in brothels and drug dens.'

'Is that so?' He drank the tea she'd made for him before she started cleaning out the food cupboard. 'Can't say I really notice cigarettes when I'm raiding a bonzai factory in a godforsaken suburb full of hopeless addicts.'

Synthetic cannabinoid, or bonzai, had been popular in Turkey for almost five years. Cheaper than cannabis or heroin, it was highly addictive and deadly. And although Inspector Cetin İkmen's task in the Istanbul police force was to apprehend murderers rather than drug dealers, sometimes his quarry was one and the same.

'Anyway, all that's nothing,' Fatma said as she wafted his smoke out of her face. 'Are you going to help me sort out these tins?'

'I'm going to work in a minute.' He smoked.

3

'Ah, what am I to do! It's all over the television,' she said. 'Anatolia Gold.' She looked at the tins and shook her head. 'How could they?'

İkmen rolled his eyes. Product giant Anatolia Gold had owned up to selling tinned products that contained traces of pork. Actually they'd been found out by government scientists, who had checked their white beans after people had complained that they tasted odd. They'd found the beans contained pork products, and in a Muslim country, that was headline news. All over Turkey, women just like Fatma İkmen were clearing out their food cupboards and wondering how much pork they'd already unwittingly eaten. Most of them feared for their souls and the souls of their loved ones. Expressly forbidden in the Koran, consumption of pork was considered a sin in Islam. Eating this unclean animal, either by accident or design, was a very serious infringement of Islamic law.

'Are you not just a little worried that you might've eaten pork?' Fatma said.

'No.'

She shook her head again. 'I will never understand you, Cetin.'

He smiled. 'Well you haven't done badly after forty years of marriage,' he said. 'Putting up with an atheist. But then I've not always found you easy to live with either. Now, I think, is one of those times.'

She scowled.

'Fatma, you're one of the most genuinely pious people I have ever met,' Cetin said. 'You are the real thing, and that is rare these days. These women covering themselves in black . . .'

'That's not Islam. That's an Arabian custom.'

'I know that, and so do you, but sadly, certain young women who wear far too much eye make-up do not,' he said. He leaned down towards her. 'You're not going to eternal damnation, Fatma.'

'How do you know? You don't believe in anything.'

He shrugged. 'Because it doesn't make sense. If your God is as kind and loving as you always say he is, why would he condemn good people? Now if you're talking about the God of the jihadis . . .'

'Ah, don't even think about them! It's madness!'

'Maybe.' He stood up. Put his cigarette out and then lit another. 'It looks like it to me, but not to everyone, and also you can't arrest someone for talking out of their backside, can you? Or rather you shouldn't.'

Fatma stopped looking at tins. She frowned. 'I think maybe you should, sometimes,' she said. 'All I see is hatred spreading.'

'Some people don't mind that.'

She looked up at him. 'Well they should.'

He bent down to kiss her. 'I agree.'

The youngest of the İkmens' eight adult children, Kemal, had just told his mother he was gay. His father had known for some time. Fatma had not been happy, but she had accepted what, deep down in her soul, she had known was coming anyway. Now all she had to do was reconcile her son's sexuality with her faith. She seemed to be making a start by condemning religious fanatics.

'If it were up to me, I would lock them all up,' she said. Then she went back to her tins.

Her husband smiled, said, 'Yes,' and left.

'Human flesh? Are you sure?'

'Absolutely,' the doctor said. 'And what is more, it has been cooked and was accompanied by an apple and plum sauce. Makes one wonder how that combination was arrived at. Was the apple included because it is claimed by some that human flesh is similar to pork?'

'God knows.'

'But I'm afraid, Commissioner, that someone died to provide Mr Ümit Kavaş with his last meal,' Dr Arto Sarkissian said. 'Which means that his body is now a crime scene.'

Commissioner Hürrem Teker ran her fingers through her thick dyed hair. The pathologist was right. Kavaş's body, although he had died of natural causes, couldn't be released to his family.

'The general will not be pleased,' she said.

'General Kavaş can be as displeased as he likes,' the doctor said. 'I can't release the body.'

'No.'

It was easy for Sarkissian to say. As an Armenian Christian, he couldn't understand the frantic need Muslim families had to bury the bodies of their loved ones. Christians didn't believe a soul was in torment until its body was in the ground. Not that Hürrem Teker thought that General Kavaş believed in such things for a second. He had been a shaven-headed committed secularist, a follower of Atatürk, in his youth. He probably still was. But since he'd served a term in prison for alleged involvement in a plot against the Islamically rooted AK government, his public stance had altered. Now he prayed. Now he was on the phone every five minutes demanding the return of his son's body.

The Armenian said, 'The meat was rare. But that didn't contribute in any significant way to Ümit Kavaş's death. Though only thirty-five, he had advanced coronary artery disease.'

'Like his father. He had a heart bypass years ago.'

Hürrem was from a military family. Her father had known General Kavaş.

'Pity the son didn't,' the doctor said. 'What are you going to do, madam?'

She leaned back on the side of a sink.

'Well we can't start yelling about cannibals. The more lurid media outlets will have the public hiding under their beds. It will be a zombie apocalypse, a left-wing plot, an attack on family

6

values. Every testosterone-fuelled kid will be out on the street with a gun.'

'That's why I called you directly.'

'Which I appreciate,' she said. 'It's not easy. The area where Kavaş was found is jammed with restaurants and bars.'

'I doubt that what Mr Kavaş ate had been served commercially,' he said. 'If anyone is trying to pass human flesh off as animal meat, then it can only be as pork. And as far as I know, there's only one pork butcher left in this city.'

'An Armenian?'

'No, a Rum.'

Rums, or Istanbul Greeks, were rare in the city now. Even rarer was one who butchered pigs.

'Tayyar Zarides,' the doctor said. 'To his friends he uses his Greek name, Cyrus.'

'Are you this man's friend, Dr Sarkissian?'

He smiled. Accustomed to the idea that all Turks thought that all non-Muslims knew each other, it still mildly amused him. 'My brother is a fan of pork,' he said. 'Mr Zarides's product is very good. He rears at a small farm in Thrace, and I am told his butchery skills are second to none. So why he would want to taint his product with human flesh . . .'

'He probably doesn't,' she said. 'But we must start somewhere. I imagine you've heard about this Anatolia Gold scandal?'

'Pork fat in the beans. Yes.'

'Tensions are running high. One of their factories in Kayseri has already been attacked.'

'Exactly. If you go into Tayyar Zarides's place under these circumstances . . .'

'Oh, I won't,' she said. 'I'll send your friend Cetin.'

Arto Sarkissian frowned. His childhood friend Cetin İkmen was one of the best-known policemen in the city. Scrupulously honest and fair, Istanbul's quirkiest cop had been helping to

7

make the city a safer place to live for decades. Everyone from street sweepers to millionaires knew him. Love him or loathe him, İkmen was very visible. Surely if Teker wanted to keep a lid on this thing, using İkmen wasn't going to help her?

'I can't help thinking that's not entirely a good idea . . .'

'No?' she said. 'Because he's a known face? He is. But he's also known as an out-and-proud atheist. Not many of those about in public life any more. But İkmen remains. And when people see him in a pork butcher's, they won't think, "Oh there go the police persecuting minorities". They'll think, "If İkmen's with Mr Zarides then they're probably friends". They might not like it, but I think they'll accept it. At least I hope so.'

'Oh. I see.'

She had a point.

'We'll need a team to investigate this situation,' she said. 'And I can't think of anyone better for that job than İkmen. Can you?'

People went missing in Istanbul all the time. Children and teenagers ran away from home, tourists got lost or fell in love and then tumbled off the radar, and elderly demented people wandered. Few were never found. But occasionally a body would turn up. In the waters of the Bosphorus, behind some dustbins in a quiet, pious suburb, dumped on the metro tracks. And it was then that a select few officers would be assigned to what was possibly a murder. But they usually had some visual clues or formal ID to go on.

Cetin İkmen was still frankly reeling from the case Commissioner Teker had presented to him. Apart from the contents of a cadaver's stomach, there was no physical evidence that his victim had ever lived. His sergeant, Kerim Gürsel, was checking missing persons records, and the only other officers who were going to be assigned to this very low-key investigation were out. There was, however, always Arto. And as happened so often, the doctor was way ahead of him. İkmen's phone rang.

8

'I can get you into Tayyar Zarides's place with no problem at all,' Arto said in answer to İkmen's question about the pork butcher. 'Although as I said to the commissioner, I don't think it's an entirely good idea at the present time.'

İkmen laughed. 'You think.'

'What I've done is ordered some further DNA tests on the meat,' Arto said. 'With a city full of unnamed and unaccounted-for Syrian refugees, it could be useful to know the ethnicity of the victim if we can.'

'I wonder if the diner knew what he was eating,' İkmen said. 'I don't know much about General Kavaş and his family, but I don't picture them on the outré side of the tracks. Especially not now.'

'Mmm. But remember that lurid stories circulated about them for a couple of years.'

'When he was public enemy number whatever it was,' İkmen said. 'But he was exonerated last year, Arto. And according to Teker, who knows him, he and the rest of the family have been keeping their heads below the parapet ever since.'

'Maybe Ümit was tired of being a good boy.'

'Bit of an extreme way to break out, wouldn't you say?'

'We live in extreme times,' the doctor said. 'Why do otherwise perfectly civilised young men go to Syria to fight for something they barely understand? Why are they persecuting completely benign groups like the Yezidis? And beheading? In 2014?'

The rise of ISIS, or the Islamic State of Iraq and al-Sham, was as worrying as it had been rapid. Born out of al-Qaeda in Iraq, it had hacked its way across Iraq and Syria and was now at the Syrian border with Turkey. Young Muslims had gone to join ISIS from all over the world, hoping to build a modern caliphate out of countries artificially created by the old imperialist powers of the twentieth century.

'I think we have to destroy ISIS completely,' İkmen said.

'They're people who have been brainwashed. I've seen them in districts like Çarşamba.' Çarşamba was home to many of the ultra-religious. 'I've listened to them. As a liberal, I have to defend their right to talk absolute nonsense, but I can't condone what they do. I don't want my children to have to live around them. There is no circumstance under which it is right to kill innocent non-combatants.' He shook his head. 'Anyway, Teker tells me that she's going to see General Kavaş to try to get him off your back.'

'He wants his son's body.'

'Of course. She is going to tell him about the, you know, the eating . . .'

'Is that a good idea, do you think?'

'I don't know,' he said. 'As long as General Kavaş and his wife keep it to themselves. Ümit was their only child. Tragic for them, but maybe, from our point of view, it will make it easier for the story to be contained.'

'The commissioner is very keen to keep this low-key,' Arto said.

'And with good reason. Imagine what some of the tabloids would do with a story like this. It would go, what is it? Viral, online. Teker knows it has the potential to spawn all sorts of conspiracy theories and mad quasi-religious violence. She wants it solved yesterday.'

'I pity you, my friend.'

İkmen smiled. 'Luckily I won't be alone,' he said.

'Well, you have Sergeant Gürsel . . .'

'And my dear friend Mehmet Süleyman, and Sergeant Mungun,' İkmen said. 'The best.'

What stuck in the craw almost more than the crime itself was the man's own attitude to what he'd done.

'She was a whore,' he said. 'It's not my fault you people don't do your job with such women any more.'

10

Inspector Mehmet Süleyman bundled the man, Musa Şahin, into the custody van and slammed the door. One of the constables standing guard outside the Şahins' apartment frowned.

'What do you want me to do?' Süleyman said. 'He killed his wife.'

'He admitted it,' the constable said.

'Which makes it OK?' Süleyman walked over to the boy, who coloured. 'He phoned us because he's proud of himself,' he continued. 'Now, after years of beating the poor woman, he can congratulate himself on becoming man enough to stab her in the stomach.'

He walked back to the custody van and banged on the door to let the driver know he should go.

Süleyman's sergeant, Ömer Mungun, shook his head. 'What are we supposed to do with this, sir?'

'Charge him, wait for forensics to deliver their results, just in case he's covering for one of his sons, and then let him have his day in court,' Süleyman said. 'It's obviously what he wants.'

They'd been called out to a crime scene that was apparently a formality. Fifty-year-old Musa Şahin, a resident of Ayvansaray, had phoned the police to say he'd killed his wife of thirty years, Melda. When they'd arrived, they'd found Şahin in a state of what appeared to be righteous rage and the body of a woman in her forties. She'd been stabbed in the stomach, but a preliminary examination had revealed that she had also sustained heavy bruising over what could be a long period of time. Şahin had admitted he'd beaten her. Apparently she habitually looked at other men.

'We saw a lot of this in Mardin,' Ömer Mungun said. 'I didn't think I'd see it here. Don't know why.'

'Nor I,' Süleyman said. 'Sadly.'

Mardin, a wonderful ancient honey-coloured town, had always been a melting pot of races and creeds from all over the region. However, it was also the wild east, where men were men and women frequently lived in fear. Now on the very edge of the new ISIS caliphate, it was a place Mungun still felt connected to because his ageing parents lived there. In recent months he had asked them to move to Istanbul, but they had refused. They had said that many of the horrors that happened around Mardin happened in Istanbul too. And if this case was anything to go by, they were right.

They began to walk back to Süleyman's car. The inspector's phone had buzzed a couple of times when they were in the Şahin apartment. Now he looked at who might have contacted him.

'Commissioner Teker wants to see both of us as soon as we get back to the station,' he said. 'I wonder what we've done wrong, Ömer.'

Life had never been easy for Mehmet Süleyman. As a member of the former Ottoman royal family, he'd grown up in the 1970s under a rampantly secular administration that had openly derided people like him. Tall, handsome and clever, he had quickly made a name for himself in the police, and under the tutelage of Cetin İkmen had found a way to largely erase the handicap of his background. And then the world, as it will, had turned. Now under the religiously inspired AK government, the Ottoman Empire was back in favour, but Süleyman was still uncomfortable. Neo-Ottomanism, with its emphasis on religion and 'right' behaviour, was not something a man given to many vices could approve of. In the last year he had been criticised for his romantic involvement with a gypsy artist who he continued to see. But then if Teker had called both himself and Ömer into her presence, it was unlikely to be about that. Nevertheless, as he got into his car and fired up the engine, he couldn't help feeling a little anxious about what might await them.

Chapter 2

'Rare? Are you sure?'

'That's what Dr Sarkissian told me,' İkmen said. 'If you want to argue with an expert, then go ahead.'

'No, of course not.' Süleyman sat down.

Crammed into İkmen's small, untidy office, two of the officers had had a chance to get over the shock of their new case, while two, who had come straight from Commissioner Teker's office, had not.

'Why would anyone eat another person unless he was starving?' Ömer Mungun said.

İkmen shrugged. 'I don't know. I find some of the food in these new gourmet restaurants in the city quite incomprehensible without bringing human flesh into the equation. You know what my son Orhan had the other day? Textures of tomato with a goat's cheese foam. Fifteen lira. What the hell is that?'

'But no one is going to serve human flesh in a restaurant, high end or otherwise,' Süleyman said. 'Are they?'

'The fact that you're thinking like that, Inspector, may be their best defence,' İkmen said. 'As a first reaction I thought exactly the same way. But now it's sunk in, I wonder, why not? Of course we'd discount restaurants, but we shouldn't. Even though I can't come up with any plausible reason why any restaurant would want to sell human flesh, it doesn't mean they're not.'

İkmen opened his office window with his foot and offered

Süleyman a cigarette. Neither of the two younger men smoked, but Kerim Gürsel dutifully locked the office door when the senior officers lit up. Not smoking in enclosed spaces, which had been illegal since 2008, was not easy for İkmen and Süleyman.

'It's about as niche as it gets, though,' Süleyman said. 'I mean, what would you say if someone invited you to eat human flesh?'

'I'd say no,' Ömer said. 'Why would you want to?'

'Curiosity?' İkmen suggested. 'For the thrill of breaking one of the oldest taboos we have? If you put religion aside, even the completely secular won't go there. I'm sure that certain religious types would like to accuse the secular of such behaviour . . .'

'Isn't there some sort of notion that the Yezidis eat human flesh?' Kerim said.

'That's nonsense,' Ömer replied. 'They're not devil-worshippers either.' Then he added awkwardly, 'I knew some. Back home.'

'People like to believe myths about people who are different, as we know,' İkmen said.

'Isn't cannibalism a way of dominating your enemy?' Süleyman said.

'Or ingesting his power and taking it into yourself,' İkmen added. 'But we're not on a battlefield here, much as it might feel like it sometimes.'

'And yet we're talking about a warrior's son,' Kerim said.

'Indeed. Who collapsed outside the church of St Antoine last Saturday night and died of a heart attack and whose last meal was human flesh. An e-mail from Dr Sarkissian half an hour ago enlightened me further. Apparently meat is not easily digestible in humans, and in his opinion, Ümit Kavaş's body had barely begun to digest his last meal.'

'So he ate it in or around İstiklal Caddesi?'

'Unless he got a taxi to İstiklal,' İkmen said. 'He lived in Karaköy, Hoca Tahsin Sokak, so he may have been on his way home when he collapsed outside the church. We'll need to try and find out when he left his apartment. So far we've only got CCTV picking him up a few metres from the church. As you know, all you need is one broken or non-functioning camera and you're screwed. People appear and disappear as if by magic.' He rolled his eyes. A city bustling with CCTV cameras was only safe if said instruments worked.

'Kapıcı.'

'Yes,' said İkmen, 'though you know what gossips they are about the people in their buildings.'

'So . . .'

İkmen looked at Süleyman. 'We'll have to inform the kapıcı Mr Kavaş is dead. But I also think we'll have to invent a small crime in the vicinity of Kavaş's apartment. To justify our presence in the absence of the dead man's family.' He turned to the two sergeants. 'A job for you two, I think.'

'That's a very chic area these days. Some drink-related anti-social behaviour?' Ömer suggested.

'Perfect. Oh, and Kerim, what about missing persons?'

'Discounting historicals, we've currently got five Turks and three foreigners, which includes one Syrian,' Kerim said. 'But there could be more Syrians because they don't report things, as we know. The other two foreigners are tourists, one American, one French. All three are male.'

'Male.' İkmen looked up at the ceiling as the smoke from his cigarette curled against the light fitting before disappearing out of the window. 'You know, that's odd. Hard as I try, I can't perceive of this unknown victim being anything other than male.'

Süleyman put his cigarette out. 'Do we know what gender it is?'

'Not yet, no. Maybe I can't bear the thought of a woman being eaten. Or perhaps, given that cannibalism can be an act

15

of dominance, I don't see why a man would eat a woman. It's not that kind of male–female dominance, to my mind.'

'No, Ömer and myself have just come from one of those,' Süleyman said. 'So what now?'

'Now we begin with the obvious and proceed to the obscure,' İkmen said. 'Commissioner Teker is with the Kavaş family to explain the situation. It's going to be a terrible thing for them to have to take in. But then we will have to interview them – quickly. We'll have to trace Ümit's movements, inasmuch as we can on Saturday night, and I must meet Istanbul's last pork butcher.'

'The Greek in Nişantaşı?'

İkmen had known that Süleyman would know. His brother Murad had been married to an Istanbul Greek until she'd died in the earthquake of 1999. Murad's daughter had a Greek family and so the Süleymans knew most members of the community.

'Tayyar Zarides.'

'Why a pork butcher, sir?' Kerim asked.

'Because human flesh is said to taste more like pork than anything else,' İkmen said. 'So it's possible Ümit Kavaş bought that meal as pork.'

'He was a Muslim,' Kerim said.

'Who may have been curious to taste pork,' Süleyman said. 'Perhaps it was sold to him on that basis.'

'As pork.'

'Maybe.'

Kerim shook his head. 'My wife and a friend have been throwing out Anatolia Gold tins all day. Is this a time to go to a pork butcher's shop? People are wound up about this.'

İkmen smiled. 'If I go, most people will see not a policeman but an atheist, and who else would they expect to see at a pork butcher's shop? Anyway, it's in Nişantaşı, where people don't worry about such things.'

'Which leaves me, I imagine, with the Kavaş family,' Süleyman said.

'When Commissioner Teker calls you, yes,' İkmen said.

There had been a time when Hürrem Teker had called General Abdullah Kavaş 'uncle'. She remembered the colourful little orchid greenhouse he'd had on the balcony of his palatial Nişantaşı apartment. It was still there. But like the general and his wife, 'Auntie' Belgin, the greenhouse was old and neglected and broken.

'I am sorry that you never got to know Ümit,' the old man said. He sat in the same chair Hürrem remembered him sitting in when she was a child. He'd fallen out with her father during the 1980 coup. Commander Recep Teker had opposed the military tribunals that had taken place in the wake of the coup, and the two families had become estranged. Ümit had only just been born.

'I too am sorry,' Hürrem said.

The Kavaşes had not had their one child until late. Hürrem didn't know why. It wasn't something people talked about.

'Had you known him, you would realise that he could never have done such a thing,' Kavaş said. 'For better or worse, my son was a liberal, Hürrem Hanım. Against his mother's advice he took part in the Gezi protests.'

He didn't say that he himself had been in prison at the time and so unable to advise his son. Hürrem didn't allude to that time either.

'General, I wish I could say that my pathologist's findings are a mistake, but they're not,' she said. Auntie Belgin sobbed.

'He has checked his results, and also, I trust him implicitly.'

'He must have an agenda,' the old man said. 'What is he? One of these new men?'

She knew what he meant. There was a certain type of person who would do anything to discredit the old secular elite.

'Why won't they leave me alone, eh? I was exonerated. Why can't I die in peace now?'

'My pathologist is an Armenian,' she said.

'Ah. Them.'

She'd forgotten how anti-minorities the general and many of his friends had been. Something else he'd fallen out with her father over.

'And so he has no agenda,' she said. 'If that is what you fear, sir.'

'My son did not eat human flesh. Why would he?'

Belgin Kavaş left the room.

'I don't know,' Hürrem said. 'It's very possible he didn't know that was what he was eating. We know it was cooked.'

'And so what type of meat would it have been mistaken for?'

Hürrem cringed. She knew that the general was a secularist, but she also knew he was trying to behave as if he'd changed his life.

'Biologists reckon it's closest to pork,' she said.

He nodded his ash-grey head. 'And so the slander continues.'

'No. No,' she said. 'General, everyone involved in this investigation, scientists and police officers, is sworn to secrecy. Istanbul is as volatile – if not more so – as it was back in the bad old days of the leftist and rightist conflicts of the 1970s. I have no idea where it's all going to end. Nobody does. But what I do know is that this story, if it gets out into the public domain, will not help. People of all sorts could use it to their advantage, and believe me, the last thing I want is more trouble in this city. What I need from you—'

'You'll get nothing from me,' he said. 'They killed my son and now they make up lies about him!'

'Who? Who does this, General?' She'd known he'd be distressed and angry, but now he was doing what she feared others would do too if the story was made public. He was making a political point.

'Ümit died of natural causes,' she said. 'He had a heart attack. Sadly for him, he suffered from heart disease. Just like you.'

He looked down his long broken nose at her with disgust.

'Our pathologist confirmed that before he received the results of the tests on Ümit's stomach contents. What he ate and his death are unrelated,' she said. 'But look, you're a soldier, and so I will be blunt. The task at hand is not to see who killed Ümit, but to find out who he ate for his last meal.'

She saw him flinch.

'I need your help. I need you to tell one of my senior investigators everything you know about Ümit, his work, his friends, his relationships . . .'

'No,' he said. And then he turned away from her and looked at the empty chair where his wife had been sitting.

There was no kapıcı at the building where Ümit Kavaş had lived on Hoca Tahsin Sokak. But there was a landlord. Ponytail-wearing, Gauloise-smoking and at most twenty-five, Samat Rahmi owned two small buildings on the street. One of them incorporated a café called Kappucino, which was where Sergeants Ömer Mungun and Kerim Gürsel met the young entrepreneur. When they told him about Ümit Kavaş's death, Rahmi was shocked.

'He was a really nice guy,' he said. 'What happened?'

Ömer told him about the heart attack. 'We don't know what brought it on, but there were a few complaints about alcohol-fuelled behaviour in the area on Saturday night,' he said.

'He died here?'

'No, on İstiklal Caddesi. But if he got involved in anything down here before he went out, that might be good to know,' Kerim said.

Samat Rahmi's face darkened. 'What, so a few anti-alcohol nuts can get us all closed down? There's always "behaviour" here, as you put it. Karaköy's buzzing these days. Bars, cafés, galleries, boutique hotels, restaurants. And there are four churches. It's a noisy area.'

'Did you see Mr Kavaş go out on Saturday night?' Kerim said.

'No. I liked him, but we weren't friends. Ümit came and went as he pleased. I rent out six apartments in these two buildings. He had the one directly above the café. Last time I saw him was probably last Thursday. Surely if he died of natural causes you don't need to be here. Don't I have to give his stuff to his family?'

'You do. But as I'm sure you know, Mr Kavaş's father is a controversial man.'

'Oh.' Samat Rahmi looked down into his coffee cup.

'We'd like to keep things discreet for the general's sake,' Ömer said. 'But we do need to look at Ümit's apartment. We also need you, Mr Rahmi, to keep this to yourself.'

Both Ömer and Kerim knew that Samat Rahmi was bursting to say all sorts of things about police oppression, about corruption and intimidation, and Kerim in particular could sympathise with that. But Rahmi kept his counsel.

'I'll get the key,' he said.

There was no sign outside to let potential customers know what was inside. Looking through the front window, it was easy to see meat. But none of it was labelled. The unwary could easily just walk in and find themselves somewhere that, in some cases, could make them feel queasy. But not Cetin İkmen.

'Mr Zarides?'

An overweight, heavily mustachioed man of about fifty looked over from his place behind the counter. 'Yes?'

İkmen held up his police ID.

Tayyar Zarides put his hands on his hips and sighed. 'If this is about Anatolia Gold, I've never supplied them in my life. I sell licensed pork products to a few businesses, which I can

20

prove. My books are immaculate. They have to be. And then there's passing trade. A chop or a few rashers of bacon.'

İkmen began to walk towards the counter.

Zarides narrowed his eyes. 'Oh, it's you. Cetin Bey. Sorry, my sight is so bad these days. I've seen you on the TV. You're Krikor Sarkissian's friend.'

İkmen bowed his head slightly. 'His brother, Arto, is our pathologist.'

Zarides came round the side of his counter and washed his hands in the sink on the wall. 'I'd forgotten you were coming,' he said. 'Ever since this Anatolia Gold story broke, I've had all sorts in here shouting abuse, asking when I'm going to close down, telling me I deserve to hang.'

'You must report it,' İkmen said.

'Which would achieve what?' He shrugged, dried his hands on a paper towel and then offered one of them to İkmen.

İkmen shook Zarides's hand and then said, 'Tayyar Bey . . .'

'Oh call me Cyrus,' the butcher said. 'All my friends do. I know you, Cetin Bey. I know you have a good heart.'

'That's very kind of you to say, Cyrus Bey.'

'You want tea?' Zarides asked. 'What can I get you? Krikor said something about you wanting to talk about where my product goes. Like I say, I have all my records. Is this about Anatolia Gold? Because if it's you, I don't mind—'

'Cyrus Bey, it isn't about Anatolia Gold,' İkmen said. It wasn't easy to get a word in. The butcher was clearly nervous, but then why wouldn't he be? He'd received death threats. 'It isn't even about you. I simply need a list of organisations that place regular orders with you. I'm not interested in individuals who buy the odd slice of ham.'

'Mmm.' He frowned. 'I'll get my son to watch the shop and I'll take you through to my office.' He called out, 'Alexis!' Then he turned back to İkmen. 'You see, Cetin Bey, I spend my life worrying about not if but when I will be closed down. Don't misunderstand me, I don't know any Muslim personally who objects to what I do. My daughter is married to a Muslim. But these fanatics . . .'

'Lots of us feel oppressed by those,' İkmen said. 'I have a new neighbour in my building who, when he first moved in, felt the need to tell my daughters to cover their heads whenever they visited. I had to have words. He doesn't do that any more. I can have words with whoever is threatening you, Cyrus Bey.'

A young man with heavily lidded eyes came out of a door behind the counter.

'This is my son, Alexis,' Zarides said.

İkmen and the young man nodded at each other.

'Alexis, this is Inspector İkmen from the police. We have some business. If you can watch the shop . . .'

'Sure.'

But before his father and İkmen left, Alexis Zarides said, 'You're not going to close us down, are you?'

'No,' İkmen said. 'I just need to look at your father's books, and I will also have to take some samples of your product, Cyrus Bey.'

He smiled. 'Take the pork chop of your choice, Cetin Bey. Take ham, chorizo, leg or belly. My product is disease-free and as clean as a virgin. Whatever else may be wrong, it isn't my pork.'

'This is harassment,' the old man said.

'General, this is an investigation into an illegal act,' Süleyman replied. 'No one is saying, as yet, that your son knew what he was eating. We have no proof either way. However, at the moment, your son is the only connection we have to this offence. We have to start with him because we don't have anywhere else to begin. Can you understand that?'

General Kavaş said nothing. Süleyman had come to the Kavaşes' apartment fully aware of the fact that the old man had told Commissioner Teker he wasn't going to co-operate with her investigation. But he also knew that he'd have to.

'Sir, I'm sure you don't want your wife—'

'My wife has already been through more than most women could endure.'

'Then talk to me,' Süleyman said. 'I know your son was educated in London. I know he worked as a translator for publishing houses and I am aware of his involvement in the Gezi protest movement. What I don't know is anything about his social life.'

'You think I do? He was a thirty-five-year-old man who lived alone. He was an adult. We had our differences.'

'What differences?'

'Ümit was a liberal,' he said. 'He believed that if women want to cover themselves, they should be allowed to do so. I've always thought that was dangerous. Not in itself, of course, but I fear what it represents. This nation threw the Ottoman system away because it used things like religion to impede progress. Ümit talked about freedom without any knowledge of the fact that it comes at a price.'

'You think the price is too high?'

'I do. My views are well known.'

'As is your retraction of those views.'

'Ha!' The old man stared fiercely into his eyes. 'You've been inside prisons, I imagine, Inspector. What wouldn't a man do to get out of those places? But now that my only child is dead, what do I care? As long as you leave my wife in peace, you can take me back any time you like. I am tired of playing games. I am what I am, and if I could shift this notion I have that this is just another attempt to slander me, I would help you.'

There was a pause. Then Süleyman said, 'Who were his friends?'

General Kavaş sighed. 'You're not leaving until I tell you something, are you?'

'No, sir. And as I'm sure Commissioner Teker has already told you, this is not political. I give you my word of honour on that.'

'As an Ottoman?'

'As a Turk,' Süleyman said. 'My background is well known, General. But it is irrelevant. What *is* relevant is that someone has died and been eaten by at least one other human being. My job is to discover the identity of that person, find out who, if anyone, killed them and whether that person also cooked that body. And why. In addition, my colleagues and I have to do this discreetly. I'm sure I don't have to tell you how hard policing this city has become in recent years. Panic about something as sensitive as this is the last thing we need.'

General Kavaş sighed again. He had one of those hard, spare faces that characterised a lot of professional soldiers. It wasn't easy to read. But he could hold Süleyman's gaze, which was not something many people could do. Still fewer could get the Ottoman to look away.

Eventually the old man spoke. 'If I tell you what I know, can you assure me that none of those I name will end up in one of your prisons?'

'Only if they are guilty of a crime,' Süleyman said.

General Kavaş continued to think.

Chapter 3

He called it his charity work. Sending soup and bread over to the people who lived in the Art House. They weren't all poor – in fact most of them came from well-off families – but getting out wasn't always easy and Samat Rahmi wanted to do his bit. Squatting wasn't something İstanbullus did. He'd seen squats in Paris and Berlin but never in his home city. The post-Gezi Park protest movement had spawned a lot of new ways of thinking about living in the city. Ever since what had begun as a sit-in against the urbanisation of one of Istanbul's few parks had started in May 2013, a lot of İstanbullus had become socially active.

When the two plain-clothes police officers had come to the café to talk to him, Samat had feared it was going to be about the Art House. The law had been hovering around the old building for a couple of weeks. But instead, they'd come about Ümit Kavaş. Poor Ümit had died and they were trying to tie his death, which by their own admission had been natural, to rowdy behaviour in Karaköy. He'd let them search the dead man's apartment – as if he had a choice. But they'd left saying nothing.

What did they expect from the city's newest hip quarter? The romance of the old maritime buildings coupled with the proximity of Istanbul Modern had been bringing locals and tourists in for some years. Now cafés, bars and clubs had followed. There were even on-trend loft apartments for wealthy professionals attracted to the alternative liberal culture of the district. One of Istanbul's first squats had obviously been created in Karaköy. Where else would it be? Over in conservative Fatih? Samat scowled. A squat in Fatih would really stick it to those who wandered into Karaköy telling people to stop drinking and avert their eyes from uncovered women. If anyone caused trouble in Karaköy, it was the religious fanatics. But he hadn't told the policemen that. How was he to know they weren't fanatics themselves?

Samat filled a basket with bread and gave it to his cook to take to the squat with the soup. He couldn't stand them. The old ones were OK, but some of the young men were angry and volatile. One of them had berated Samat's sister Pinar for ten minutes outside Istanbul Modern about her clothing. Eventually she'd been rescued by a security guard, who'd told the furious boy to go and join Islamic State. Only Ümit Kavaş had ever given such people the time of day. Nobody knew why. His father had been imprisoned for a supposed plot against a government that wanted to promote religious values. Ümit himself had been heavily involved in Gezi and, more lately, in supporting the squat. Why and how had he even listened to such people?

There were six buyers of pork from the Zarides shop within a five-kilometre radius of İstiklal Caddesi. All were hotels, except for one restaurant in Nişantaşı. The closest place to where Ümit Kavaş had died was a very smart and discreet guest house just off Taksim Square. It didn't advertise that it offered bacon as one of its breakfast options, but the owner was happy to talk about it.

'I don't buy much,' he'd told İkmen when he'd shown him the fridge where a few bacon rashers were kept. 'But the Germans particularly like it, so why not? Our cook's from Romania, so he doesn't care.' İkmen asked if he could take a sample of the meat. The owner said, 'Yeah. Of course.'

The restaurant bought small quantities too and was happy to

provide samples. Also, like the guest house, the owner of the restaurant was content to let İkmen check his CCTV tapes from the previous Saturday evening. Only two of the hotels bought in bulk, and only one of their owners proved difficult. When asked whether İkmen could come and talk to him, Boris Myskow of the Imperial Oriental Hotel stated that he had a very busy service that evening and so he couldn't possibly talk to anyone until the following morning. He said he knew nothing about CCTV inside or outside the hotel. İkmen responded by telling Mr Myskow he'd meet him in half an hour. Myskow, who was a celebrity chef in his native America, did a lot of screaming down the telephone until he suddenly stopped and said, 'Come tonight as my guest. Bring a friend. Then I will sit at your table and I will talk food.'

'Oh good,' İkmen said. 'It's food I want to discuss.'

Then he phoned Süleyman.

'How do you like the idea of a meal at the Imperial Oriental's restaurant?' he said.

'That crazy American's place?'

'You've seen him?'

Süleyman laughed. 'You can get his US TV show on Fox,' he said.

İkmen shook his head. 'I can't believe you watch that.'

'I don't. It's just on sometimes.'

Süleyman lived for part of his time with his gypsy mistress in her chaotic house in Balat. A successful modern artist, Gonca was addicted to daytime television almost as completely as she was to her younger lover.

'So what is Mr Myskow like?' İkmen asked. 'On the phone he sounds deranged.'

'Yes, I think he is,' Süleyman said. 'He's totally besotted with food; one of those chefs who makes dishes no one sane would think of.'

'Does he?'

'Oh, I don't mean like, well, what we're looking for. At least I don't think so. He won't take criticism. He is maestro and that is the end of it. If you don't like something he puts on your plate, he will have a tantrum.'

'Oh well. If you don't want to come . . .'

'But I do,' he said. 'Actually, and in spite of myself, I am thrilled. His dishes are so strange. I mean, a hamburger sorbet . . .'

'I can feel the indigestion now,' İkmen said. 'All I want to do is look at any CCTV he may have, find out how he stores and cooks his pork, take some samples for analysis and then get out of there. It's Myskow who wants us to eat.'

Cetin İkmen had always known he had to eat to live. But smoking was more to his taste. And tea.

'It will be an experience,' Süleyman said. 'In the same way that meeting Ümit Kavaş's friends may be.'

'Oh?'

'According to General Kavaş, one of them lives in a vast yalı I remember visiting as a child, while the rest are apparently Karaköy squatters.'

'No!'

Belgin Kavaş ripped the phone out of her husband's hand and threw it on the floor.

'They're recording everything we say!' she said. 'You can't breathe a word about this. You heard what that policeman said.'

General Kavaş picked the phone up and put it back on its stand. 'People should be warned,' he said.

'People? What people? Our son is dead!' she said. 'I don't care about anything else. I don't even care that he was found with human flesh in his body!'

'Keep your voice down!'

28

'Why?' She'd been ripping at her own face with her fingernails, like a peasant. It disgusted him.

'Take control!'

Through her tears, she laughed. 'Take control? Take control of what? Take control of my life, which is now childless and entirely without meaning?'

'You have—'

'I have nothing!' she said. 'They can find a way to take this apartment away from us at any time. But then again, you don't mean that, do you, Abdullah? You mean that I still have you. The problem with that is that I don't want you. I have never been unfaithful to you and I never will, but I don't want you either. You are a bull-headed man who has brought misfortune to this family, and I cannot and will not find it in my heart to forgive you.'

He looked at her for a moment, his face blank and colourless. Then he struck her so hard she collapsed on the floor.

It was the same boy. Long black shirt, black şalvar trousers, kufi on his head. If he'd covered his face, he would have looked like an IS militant. As it was, he always appeared to be a bit half-hearted and slightly embarrassed. But he still managed to unnerve the residents. Including Birgül.

She opened a window and shouted down to him. 'What do you want?'

He looked up at her with an expression of incomprehension on his face. He never spoke.

'Look, if you can't speak Turkish, I can't help you,' Birgül said. And then Barış began to cry, so she shut the window and went to him.

Moving into the Art House squat had been the right thing to do, even if it had happened only a few days after she'd given birth. But İsmet had proved to be a great father. She'd always known he would be. They shared the childcare just as everyone in the house shared chores.

Birgül picked her son up and smiled at him. He stopped crying. Such a good little boy! But then there was so much to interest him in the squat. Not only did he have other children to watch, but the place was always buzzing with people creating art and making music. Everybody loved him, especially Uğur, İsmet's father, who had found the building and started the squat. He was a textile designer and had created the most beautiful wall hangings for what had become the new family's room. Birgül's only sadness was her parents' disapproval. Her father was a member of the Republican People's Party and an avowed secularist who believed that political protest should only be expressed via traditional methods. That meant, in his case, some sort of military intervention. The residents of the Art House, some of whom were practising Muslims and Christians, didn't want that. Military coups belonged to the old Turkey, and Birgül didn't want to go back there.

She cradled Barış in her arms and went back to the window. The boy was still out there. She wondered whether he was one of the refugees from Syria who had come to the city to escape the war. One of the covered girls had gone out to try and talk to him once, but he'd run away. Sometimes he appeared with a couple of other boys, who shouted abuse. They were definitely Turkish, but of the religiously obsessed variety, calling everyone 'infidel'.

She walked away from the window, sat down and began to feed her son. Samat in the café, who gave them soup and bread, had come over and told Uğur that Ümit Kavaş had died. They were going to have a little memorial to his life later on. It was very sad. She hadn't known Ümit well, but she knew that he and a couple of the other squatters had been close. Ümit's father had been in prison for a while, which had given him something

30

in common with several people in the Art House. Even Ahu, one of the covered girls, had a brother in prison. He too had been in the military.

Samat had told Uğur that apparently Ümit had died from a heart attack. But then he'd also said that the police had come to talk to him about Ümit, which seemed strange if he'd died from natural causes. Maybe it was because Samat's place was opposite the Art House? The police did periodically sniff around, but they never did anything. Uğur said that Samat had told them nothing about Ümit's involvement with the squat. Apparently they'd tried to connect his death with so-called rowdiness that had taken place in the street. In Uğur's opinion they were just fishing. But Birgül had noticed that he'd put a sign up in the meeting room about visitors. They were to be carefully vetted.

Cetin İkmen had not been to the Imperial Oriental Hotel since its refit in 2012. He'd never been to it before that either. But Süleyman had.

'It used to be like the Pera Palas and the Londra,' he said.

'Faded opulence.' İkmen adjusted the napkin the waiter had draped dramatically over his lap and looked around. The new Imperial Oriental restaurant was very modern. Comfortable but minimalist, it was decorated in matt white and patent black and was full of the type of people who dressed for dinner. This did not include Cetin İkmen, who rarely made concessions to dress codes. But his companion had made an effort.

'New suit?' the older man asked.

'No, just don't get to wear it very often,' Süleyman said.

İkmen drank some water. 'I'm not comfortable with this,' he said.

'This place?'

'No. Well, yes, of course. But I'm not happy about being given this man's food. We should pay.'

'Then we will.'

'Have you seen how much this tasting menu he wants us to eat costs?' İkmen said. 'I'm still paying for the central heating my wife had put in. I can't afford this!'

Süleyman smiled. 'I'll put it on my credit card.'

'Oh yes, and you're *loaded*, aren't you! When are you going to pay it off? When you're dead? Why this bastard won't talk to me unless I eat his food . . .'

'That is Boris Myskow,' Süleyman said. 'He's obsessed.'

'He's mad.'

A waiter arrived. Smiling, he said, 'Gentlemen, are you ready for your tasting experience?'

İkmen looked at Süleyman. 'I'm ready for my dinner . . .'

There were sixteen courses on the tasting menu, each one accompanied by an appropriate wine. The first three dishes were apparently starters and, as the waiter solemnly explained to them, the entire menu consisted of Ottoman-inspired modern Turkish molecular gastronomy. Cetin İkmen was tempted to ask 'What the fuck is that?' but managed to restrain himself.

Dish one, like all subsequent offerings, came with an explanation. Something hot and, by the smell of it, spicy in the middle of a vast plate was described as 'Albanian calves' liver in sumac, red, green and black pepper topped with a hummus foam'.

İkmen picked the whole thing up on his fork and shoved it into his mouth. Süleyman cut his tiny morsel into even tinier morsels and practised restraint.

When he'd finished chewing, İkmen said, 'Delicious. Don't know what the foam added, but very nice. What a pity the partially sighted would never be able to find it.'

'That's why we're having sixteen courses.'

İkmen drank some wine. 'Thank goodness for alcohol.'

The second course was beetroot soup, which came in a tiny

white jug and which they were instructed to pour over their 'textures' of beetroot – three different-coloured slices of the root vegetable at the bottom of a vast bowl. Tiny star-shaped filo pastry börek followed, filled with tulum cheese and mallow leaves. İkmen was just about to declare that ordinary when a tiny middle-aged man approached their table and Süleyman's eyes widened.

'Inspector İkmen?'

If anything, Boris Myskow was even thinner than İkmen, although he was far better dressed. He looked at least sixty, in spite of extensive plastic surgery, and had dyed black hair and hands that looked way too big for his body.

İkmen stood up, but Myskow waved him down. 'Please don't,' he said. 'I never shake hands.' Then he saw Süleyman and smiled. 'Ah, your guest . . . .'

'Inspector Süleyman,' İkmen said.

'Hello.' Myskow sat down.

Süleyman smiled. İkmen resumed his seat and said, 'It's very kind of you to invite us for this, er, experience, Mr Myskow.'

'Everyone needs educating about food, Inspector,' the American said. 'Even the police. Now your friend here, he speaks English?'

'Yes,' Süleyman said.

'Ah, good, because I'll be honest with you, Turkish is beyond me. My wife tried, and went running back to Los Angeles a broken woman. But the food, tell me about it. Tell me how it made you feel. People report that the textures of beetroot teamed with the soup make them think about soil and what it consists of. The liver is iron, it's metal, industrial. With the chickpeas in the hummus there is some rooting back into the earth again, but in the form of a cloud that elevates an essentially humble ingredient to something quite nebulous, almost ethereal. Yes?'

It was food. What there had been of it had been nice. But İkmen knew that he couldn't condemn with faint praise. Not with this man. It would be better to say it was vile. He took a deep breath and said, 'Yes.'

For a moment he wondered whether Myskow had heard him. But then the American said, 'Yes, what? Yes, those descriptions have resonance for you, or the food made you have different experiences, or what?'

İkmen looked at Süleyman, whose English was not as good as his own. He appeared bemused. Panic started to set in, but then İkmen had a brainwave. Make it up. Myskow obviously did, unless of course he was indeed deranged.

'The soup, for me, was about . . . well, the miracle of the natural world. The nobleness of growing vegetables and herbs and . . . It was visually stunning.'

Thank goodness Fatma watched food programmes on TV!

Myskow said nothing.

İkmen's panic came back. He'd have to say more. 'As for the börek, well, this is a food I grew up with. The mallow leaves inside grow everywhere here in Turkey. The poor take them from the side of the road. But with the cheese, it becomes luxurious. A poor man and a rich man in a blanket of wonderful filo pastry.'

The American shook his head and İkmen felt his heart sink. But then Myskow smiled. 'You know, that is exactly how I feel about those dishes,' he said. 'All that BS about the soil . . . It's all about elevation. Elevating the humble, marrying the luxurious to the everyday. Food democracy, as you have so insightfully put forward. If I shook hands, I'd shake yours.'

'Ah.'

'And now, pork.' Myskow changed the subject. 'That's what you wanted to talk about, wasn't it?'

'Yes, Mr Myskow. How you store, cook, present the meat.'

'I could give you some to try, but of course it isn't on the Ottoman tasting menu. Here I'm going for an almost central Asian vibe. You know, the steppes where you people come from.'

34

'Of course.'

'So it's gonna be meat you won't have heard about here a whole lot. Kind of a Turkish–Mongol fusion. I was so excited when I was told we could source yak meat. New food experiences just jazz the hell out of me. But basic, you know. Peasant food.'

'Like pork in Christian countries,' İkmen said.

'Oh yeah, the pork, right. So do you want to come and see it now, or when you've completed your food journey?'

İkmen said, 'Well now if it's not too much trouble, Mr Myskow. Then we can come back to our meal with our job done and really concentrate on your food.'

'Perfect!'

In spite of all the assurances he'd been given, he'd always known that somebody would come. What he hadn't counted on was that it would be the police. Wouldn't it have been more logical to send someone from the health ministry?

'I keep all the paperwork associated with pork products separately,' he said.

'Good.'

The policeman called İkmen smiled. The other one didn't. Nor did he speak. Were they doing a good cop, bad cop routine on him?

'I buy everything from Mr Zarides.'

The paperwork was immaculate. It gave him confidence. But would they actually want to know what was in the fridge? Or the freezer? Would they want to examine it? Weigh it? He soon found out.

'We'll need to check your paperwork and your stocks,' İkmen said.

'You want to look at the meat?'

'Yes. Inspector Süleyman will inspect the paperwork.'

Boris knew he'd coloured up. He always did. His face was like a Mexican carnival and he could see that they'd noticed it.

There wasn't much paperwork. Invoices and receipts from Tayyar Zarides, the Imperial Oriental's licence to sell pork products. Zarides was always careful to accurately record the cut of meat provided, together with its weight.

Boris hadn't asked what this was about. Now he said, 'Is there a problem with my pork licence?'

'No.'

He led them into his office and pulled out the correspondence from Zarides.

'And your licence?' the younger cop asked.

'It's in with the receipts,' Boris said.

'May I sit at your desk, Mr Myskow?'

'Yeah. Of course.'

Inspector İkmen put a hand on Boris's shoulder. He winced. 'Let's see the meat.'

It didn't take long. There wasn't much for the policeman to see. Boris wondered whether İkmen and the other one, whose name kept escaping him, would check what he'd bought against what he'd used. İkmen picked up frozen meat and looked at the bottom of the freezer. Then he said, 'Forgive me, Mr Myskow, but I didn't think chefs like yourself used frozen meat. Does it not come in fresh every day?'

Boris took a deep breath. 'Yes. Except the pork,' he said.

'Why?'

'Because demand is sporadic. Sometimes we have a lot of guests from Europe and the States, sometimes all our guests are Arabian.'

'I see.'

Should he ask him what this was about?

'We will need to take copies of your paperwork and samples of the meat,' İkmen said.

36

'Samples . . .'

'Yes.'

'You want me to get . . .'

'I want to take a random sample of my choosing,' İkmen said.

'Why?'

He smiled. 'For testing.'

'What for?'

Boris knew he was coming across badly. Even he could hear desperation in his voice. Christ knew how İkmen was interpreting that!

'To make sure that the meat is disease-free and of good quality.'

'But don't you have other police to do this kind of stuff? We've had them here before. They're in uniform . . .'

'The Zabıta, yes,' İkmen said. 'Our market police do usually deal with issues like this. But they are principally concerned with weights and measures, ensuring that the public receive the right quantities of, for instance, pure gold in a jewellery product. I am confident that weights and measures are not an issue at an Istanbul institution like your hotel.'

'So what are you . . .'

'As I said, Mr Myskow, I am simply making sure that the conditions of your licence are being fulfilled and that the meat you are serving is free of disease.' He picked up a frozen leg from the bottom of the freezer.

'I'll take this if I may.'

Back in the restaurant, a frozen leg of pork resting on İkmen's feet under the table, the two men were offered something that looked like a pomegranate but tasted of lamb. Once Boris Myskow had received their praise for this dish, he left. Clearly they were all friends again.

İkmen, smiling, whispered to Süleyman, 'Did you see how his face coloured?'

Chapter 4

Burak and Mustafa Ayan had been his only Turkish friends. He knew they'd always laughed at him, but he hadn't cared. They could speak Arabic.

They'd let him hang about with them and they'd asked him lots of questions. They hadn't thought he was a freeloader. Whenever they'd seen him, they'd always come over and talked. Not like the people in the squat.

He'd been told about the Art House by a woman he'd met at a local market called Mina. She was Syrian too, but he suspected, even though she'd never said, that she was a Christian. She didn't cover and she was educated. They were all educated, the Christians. The Turks in the squat were educated and they had given Mina food and a place to stay until she got a room of her own. Now she was working and he didn't see her any more. Radwan had no business with the squat. But he kept on going there, standing outside, suffering abuse, or so he thought, from the people inside. How could he know what they were saying when he didn't speak Turkish?

The Art House people probably did think he was strange. He knew they found him threatening. Boys dressed like him hung around the streets in that area all the time. Mainly they reminded people of their religious obligations. Most of them, like Burak and Mustafa, were Turks from the Fatih district, which was where Radwan stayed, in a park that was in an old empty reservoir known as a cistern. It was quiet there at night and he could generally sleep undisturbed. Burak and Mustafa used to play basketball there most mornings before they all went over to the Karaköy squat. But now they'd gone.

The last time Radwan had seen the boys had been outside the Art House. There were a couple of covered girls in there who Burak was always keen to speak to. Why were these sisters living in a place of sin where people danced and drew representations of the human body? All three boys had thrown stones at the building until a man had come roaring out carrying a baseball bat. They'd run away, but later they went back. It was then that Burak and Mustafa had disappeared. They'd told Radwan to go and steal some cakes from behind the café opposite, but when he'd come back, they'd gone. He'd looked for them but to no avail. He knew the Art House weirdos had them.

Beyond knowing that their mother, who they said had been Syrian, was dead, Radwan didn't know anything much about Burak and Mustafa. He had no idea where they lived or what they did when they weren't hanging around the streets. They prayed, but he didn't know which mosque they attended. All he knew for sure was that they were religious and they cared about his country.

There were days when all they spoke about was Syria. In his heart, Radwan just wanted to forget. He'd seen his father shot by one of Assad's soldiers. Then they'd raped and killed his mother. He'd had two sisters and a brother, but he had no idea where they'd gone. Not that he'd talked to Burak and Mustafa about his family. All they'd wanted to know about was Islamic State. They were obsessed with the idea of the caliphate the ISIS fighters were building. But Radwan had never seen any of them. When the boys had asked him about ISIS men, he'd just made things up. When he'd fled from his home city of Aleppo, there hadn't been any ISIS fighters in the area. But Burak and Mustafa

39

had believed him, and as time had gone on, Radwan had taken to making up more and more elaborate stories about his adventures with ISIS. And what he didn't know, the boys got off the Internet. Their dearest wish had been to go to Syria to fight with ISIS. Especially Burak. On the day the boys had disappeared, as far as Radwan knew, they'd gone back to the Art House to have it out with the baseball bat man. And he had killed them. He must've done, because he was still in the house and the boys had disappeared. But how was Radwan going to make anyone understand that? All he could do was wait for an opportunity to go inside and look for their bodies.

'We grew up and grew apart.'

Mehmet Süleyman knew of the Lalebahçe mansion in Tarabya. Built by a minor Ottoman prince in the 1880s, it had been home to the once powerful Tanır family since the beginning of the Republic in the 1920s. But time and events had changed the Tanırs' lives, and the patriarch of the family, Admiral Faruk Tanır, had been imprisoned for a supposed plot against the current government, just like General Kavaş. The difference was that the admiral, in spite of his family's many costly campaigns to have him released, had died in prison.

Now his son and heir sat in the mansion he was obliged to sell in order to pay his debts, and told the policeman about his old friend Ümit Kavaş.

'I think if anything I became more firmly rooted in what they now call the "secular elite" as my father's problems multiplied,' he continued. 'But Ümit was different.'

Cengiz Tanır was a thin, bald man in his mid thirties. He'd aged badly.

'I'm not saying that he embraced what some call the new Turkey. He was involved in Gezi, but he sought a future that accommodated the realities that have emerged in recent years.'

Süleyman knew what he meant. He also knew that Tanır would say no more than that. He would view Süleyman, as a police officer, as part of that new reality. So he would be guarded.

'He was very involved with people who have set up a squat in Karaköy,' Süleyman said.

Cengiz smiled. 'Ümit believed that all and any ways of life could and should be accommodated. He looked with horror at what had been done by the secular elite in the past. Of course, he didn't want what had been good about that to entirely disappear, but he accepted that it needed to change while at the same time in no way believing that his own father had done anything wrong. Which we now know, of course, he hadn't.'

'When did you last see Ümit Kavaş, Mr Tanır?'

'Not for a while. Why, may I ask, are the police so interested in Ümit? He died naturally.'

General Kavaş had given Süleyman Tanır's contact details, and although the old soldier had assured him that he wouldn't tell anyone about what had been found in Ümit's stomach, he couldn't be certain about precisely what, if anything, this man knew.

'Although, as you say, the death was natural, we want to make sure that nothing unnatural precipitated it,' he said.

'Like what?'

'That is what we're trying to determine,' Süleyman said.

'But if you don't know—'

'So you were a friend? Not close, these days?'

'No. As children we were. And as students. We both went to university in London. But then I married, and when our fathers . . . when the investigations into our fathers' affairs began, we drifted apart. Nothing personal, just life.'

'Did you know he was living in Karaköy?'

'I didn't know he was living there but I had heard he was involved with the squat down there.' He smiled. 'Typical Ümit, getting himself in with the local unconventional arty types.'

41

Unconventional enough to eat human flesh? Süleyman wondered. 'Some of the squatters are quite militant.'

'If violence is involved, then Ümit won't have been part of it,' Tanır said. 'Not directly. Whatever you might think about Gezi, there were a lot of peaceful people involved in it. Ümit was one of them.'

Süleyman knew. He'd been there when the protest to save Gezi Park had started in 2013. He'd also been in the park when his colleagues had attacked. Even now, talk of Gezi left him feeling uneasy and conflicted. A lot of the protests had indeed been peaceable.

'But I suppose that if you want to blacken Ümit's name after his death, you can just go right ahead and do so.'

'What?'

'You, the police,' Tanır said. 'Isn't that what you do to people like Ümit these days? Blacken the names of the old regime, that's your brief, isn't it?'

Süleyman knew that this was exactly how some of the old elite felt, but he hadn't expected to hear one of them articulate it so openly. Had Ümit felt like this underneath all his liberal feelings? Had eating the flesh of one of the new conservatives been his one and only act of violence against those he sought to embrace but who, by their very existence, rejected his kind?

'I can assure you—'

'Oh spare me,' Tanır said. 'My father, an innocent man, died in one of your prisons. I have to sell this house to a millionaire builder who can hardly read to pay the legal fees I still owe for trying to get justice for my father. I know who you are, Inspector Süleyman. You're a member of that family my family thought we had consigned to the dustbin of history. Now climbing aboard a shiny new train that will take you back to power again. But it won't. Those in power now use the notion of the Ottoman Empire to puff themselves up, not you. I may not have been close to

42

Ümit Kavaş in recent years, but he was a decent man and I resent you sullying his death with your so-called investigation. Be honest and the good Muslim you people always talk about being, and let his family have his body.'

So he had been speaking to General Kavaş.

'Because if he died naturally, he needs to be buried, and if he didn't, then find out why and take action. Do something,' Cengiz Tanır said. 'Because I may not have seen Ümit for quite some time but I still love him and I feel pain for him. Blacken his name and I will use whatever money I have left after the sale of this house to do the same to you.'

Whatever he might have been, Süleyman thought, Ümit Kavaş evoked strong emotions, even in death.

Pembe Hanım breezed in bearing tins. She held them up so that Sinem could see them from her bedroom.

'Guaranteed non-pig beans,' she said.

'Oh, thank you.'

It was one of Sinem Gürsel's bad days. The pain in her joints was so bad she could hardly move. Feeding herself anything but tablets was impossible. Preparing food for her husband, Çetin İkmen's sergeant, Kerim, was unthinkable. But then that was why Sinem and Kerim had Pembe – in part. When necessary, Pembe cooked, cleaned and did anything else that Sinem could not. She also made the invalid Sinem laugh, which wasn't easy sometimes. Sinem had had rheumatoid arthritis since she was a teenager, and so her life was small and full of pain. People had been surprised when handsome, clever Kerim had asked Sinem's father if they could marry. What had a catch like him wanted with a cripple like her?

'I'll make kuru fasulye,' Pembe said. 'I know Kerim likes that.'

'His mother used to make it,' Sinem said.

'I know.'

All three of them talked about everything. But Sinem couldn't remember saying anything about her mother-in-law's white bean stew to Pembe. Kerim must have mentioned it. She wondered if his mother's cooking formed part of their pillow talk.

'How's your pain, kitten?'

Pembe used lots of endearing names for all those close to her. Madame Edith, her oldest friend, was by turns 'sugar syrup', 'chicklet' and 'honey cake'. Sinem was often 'kitten' but could also be 'princess'. It depended how Pembe felt. The pet names weren't always complimentary, especially when Pembe felt Sinem was alone with Kerim. But then Sinem knew Pembe had to resent her on some level. In law at least she was Kerim's wife, and she was a woman. She was everything Pembe had to want to be.

'Zenne Gül said he saw Kerim Bey in Karaköy yesterday,' Pembe said.

'Zenne Gül?'

'The dancer. Lives in the squat they call the Art House.'

'I know who he is. I thought he lived in Fener.'

'He did, but it got too uncomfortable,' Pembe said. 'All those districts covered by Fatih municipality are getting difficult. Gül lived on Sultan Selim Caddesi, which is absolutely heaving with piety. Those people don't appreciate a pretty young guy in sequins.'

'How did he end up in a squat? Male belly dancers make good money at clubs and restaurants, not to mention at henna nights. Everyone wants a zenne at their party these days. All that old Ottoman stuff is all the rage.'

'But "decent" people don't want to live around them.' Pembe rolled her eyes. 'The squat was started by Uğur İnan, the textile designer.'

'Why does *he* need to live in a squat? He's got money too.'

'Yeah, but he's also really pro the spirit of Gezi. I admire him.

44

He puts his money where his mouth is. Someone who designs fabrics for Madonna could cosy up to the state, but he's on our side.'

Sinem moved uncomfortably in her bed. While she was having a bad day, Pembe was having one of her bouncy, breezy days.

'Our side?'

'The side of the gypsies, fags and generals.'

'I don't see it as a "side" . . .'

'Because of the soldiers? Sinem, sister, we've been pushed together in an arranged marriage. Get used to it. There's them and us and some of us are fucking strange. But it is what it is. Anyway, how did we get here? Oh yes, Kerim Bey was in Karaköy. Asking questions about a man who had a heart attack, according to Gül. Makes you wonder if that's not allowed now. Heart disease not permitted beyond this point!'

'Pembe Hanım!'

'Well, the world's gone mad! When police start asking questions about a man who dies of a heart attack, there's something wrong. Some man murdered his wife the other day for apparently looking at other men. What are they doing about that? I tell you, Sinem Hanım, Kerim Bey is courting disaster working for today's police. Even if he does work for Cetin İkmen. He'll have to choose a side one of these days. Either he's with us or he's against us. There's no such thing as a queer policeman. At least there shouldn't be.'

'Oh, and what do you think Kerim should do instead? Become a zenne?'

Pembe looked at her without smiling. 'He has the body for it,' she said.

'We have to say something,' İkmen said.

Commissioner Teker shook her head. 'What can we say? That isn't a rhetorical question. I mean it. What can we say?'

'I don't know,' he said. 'But carrying on asking questions about a natural death is weird. Inspector Süleyman had a very awkward interview with one of Ümit Kavaş's old friends and is now on his way to the squat where Kavaş spent most of his time more recently. People aren't stupid, they'll know this isn't normal. Any one of these people could have been with Ümit Kavaş when he ate human flesh. But unless we can ask them more specific questions . . .'

'So we tell them their friend ate human flesh?' She sat down.

'Well, there is an argument that in a world where people behead each other and drink their blood, what harm can the knowledge of a little local cannibalism do?'

Teker said nothing.

They called themselves a commune.

'I know the word has negative associations for some,' Uğur İnan said. 'But that isn't my problem. We live communally and so we are by definition a commune.'

Süleyman had seen İnan on television and so he wasn't surprised by the dreadlocks. The state of the squat was another matter. Although decorated with fabrics more suited to a Hollywood mansion, the actual material of the building was dire. There were holes everywhere, and in some rooms water from damaged pipes ran down the walls.

'I'm only here to talk about Ümit Kavaş,' Süleyman said. 'Not to discuss how you live.'

'Yes, but your colleagues will come and try to shut us down.'

They were in a large room with, Süleyman counted, five other people. One covered girl, a woman with a baby and two young men.

İnan sat on a floor cushion. 'What do you want to know?'

There was nowhere to sit except on the floor, and so Süleyman sat.

46

'I understand Mr Kavaş had friends here,' he said.

'Ümit was a great supporter of the commune, yes,' İnan said. 'We're all really sorry that he's dead. But he died naturally, right?'

'Yes.'

'So why are you here?'

He'd had a brief telephone conversation with İkmen after he'd left Cengiz Tanır's house, where he'd been asked the same question. İkmen said he'd speak to Commissioner Teker about what was becoming a real problem, but so far, Süleyman had to stick to his previous story.

'We want to make sure that no external factors may have precipitated Mr Kavaş's heart attack,' he said. 'Do you have any idea where he went on the night he died?'

'Up on to İstiklal,' İnan said. 'That was where he was found, wasn't it?'

'Yes.'

'So up there.'

'He didn't come here?'

'He lived across the road. He dropped in from time to time. We're all creative people here. Ümit appreciated that.'

The young woman with the baby said, 'Everyone here was at Gezi. Ümit too.'

Süleyman was surprised she had mentioned it. He knew that Ümit Kavaş had been involved in the Gezi protest, but as a rule, people avoided the subject.

'And in answer to your next question, yes, we talked politics,' İnan said. 'Urban development, gay rights and freedom of expression are political issues in this country. You know it and I know it. Ümit was passionate about the notion of not allowing the spirit of Gezi to die. He also had personal issues with the current administration. I'm sure you're aware of this.'

'Yes.'

'Ümit and ourselves, we were all in the same place politically, so if you're looking for someone he might have argued with before he died, you've come to the wrong place.'

'The only trouble we get round here, apart from the police, comes from the kids from Fatih who like stoning the place and calling us infidels,' one of the young men said. He was tattooed, pierced and had wild, unkempt hair.

'Did Ümit get any trouble from them?' Süleyman asked. Although it was irrelevant to the investigation, he was curious – kids like this seemed to be becoming ever more visible in the city.

'A lot of people do when they come to visit us.' Uğur İnan narrowed his eyes as if thinking. 'Alone on the street, he may have done.'

'Those boys give you a hard time, don't they, Meltem?' the woman with the baby said to the covered girl.

For a moment the girl looked confused, then she said, 'They have. Sometimes.'

'You should complain,' Süleyman said.

Uğur İnan laughed. 'To whom?'

'Well . . .'

'You?' He laughed again. 'And have you come and pat the boys on the head? Look, if you're here to try and connect us in some way to Ümit's death, then let me make your job easy. We liked Ümit and he liked us. Ask anyone round here. Ask the jihadi kids! Even they will back me up. And while you're there, you might ask them what they were up to before Ümit died. They don't just hang about round here, you know; they're every-where these days. Could even be in your neighbourhood, Inspector. People like us here in the Art House are swimming against the tide. Personally, I call this place my last stand.'

Chapter 5

Çetin İkmen had almost given up hope of getting an answer from the pork butcher when someone picked up the phone.

'Cyrus?'

'Yes.'

He relaxed. 'Çetin İkmen here. Can I ask you some questions about your meat?'

'What do you want to know?'

İkmen had his feet up on his desk and was half hanging out of his office window so that he could smoke.

'Do you ever sell wild boar?' he said.

There was a knock at the door followed by the entrance of Mehmet Süleyman. İkmen silently offered him a chair.

'No,' Cyrus Zarides replied.

'Never?'

'No.'

'I don't suppose you know where to get it, do you?' İkmen asked.

'I know where they're killed,' he said. 'Anatolian wild boar hunts are really popular with foreigners. There's a couple of firms do it in the Kayseri area and up round the Black Sea. Anatolian boars are huge. But in this country they're only hunted for trophies.'

'What? Tusks?'

'And heads. Germans like that sort of thing.'

'So what about the meat?'

'I don't know,' Cyrus said. 'They're not allowed to sell it. Whether the foreigners eat it, I don't know.'

'But you can't get it?'

'No, and I wouldn't try,' he said. 'I know it can be got. But not from the type of people I'd like to do business with.'

'Criminals.'

'I don't suppose they think they are, but . . .'

'Thanks.'

İkmen put his mobile on his desk and threw his cigarette packet at Süleyman. 'Help yourself.'

He did. 'What was that about, Çetin?'

'Boris Myskow's so-called pork has turned out to be wild boar,' he said. 'I just called Zarides, the pork butcher, to see whether he sells it, and he doesn't. And yet, as we saw last night, Myskow only gets his pork from Zarides. All his paperwork relates to Zarides's shop, which is, according to its owner – and, by the way, borne out by the samples I took from the shop myself – a boar-free area. Clearly Myskow is getting boar meat elsewhere, Makes you wonder whether he's *only* getting boar.'

'Does Zarides know where boar could have come from?' Süleyman said.

'He implied the source was not strictly legal,' İkmen said. 'Did you know that there are tour companies in Anatolia that offer boar-hunting expeditions to foreigners?'

'I have heard of it. But they don't eat them, do they?'

'No idea. Be interesting to find out. I'm beginning to wonder whether Mr Myskow knows . . .'

They both became silent for a few moments. Then Süleyman said, 'I spent some time with Ümit Kavaş's squatter friends.'

İkmen put one cigarette out and then lit another. 'And?'

He sighed. 'They were hostile . . .'

'Which is to be expected.'

'Didn't understand why I was investigating a natural death. They accused me of cooking up some sort of conspiracy against them using Kavaş as a pretext.'

'Again, to be expected.'

'Did you tell Teker that people aren't buying into the story about a natural death having been precipitated by some sort of conflict?'

'Yes, I did.' He looked at Süleyman. Then he shrugged. 'But she's not budging. We carry on in spite of any difficulties – like veracity. We don't talk about cannibals, but we have to find out who served the meat to Mr Kavaş.'

'So we have two odd meat products to investigate?'

'It would seem so, yes.'

İkmen spoke quietly and, largely, with a smile on his face. Only those who knew him very well, like Mehmet Süleyman, would realise how close to the edge of fury he was.

'Simple, eh?'

Süleyman changed the subject. 'Now I know we're not looking for anyone in connection with Kavaş's death, but the squatters did tell me that their place gets attacked with stones from time to time by kids from Fatih. They call them "jihadi" boys, but I think they're probably just pious kids from Çarşamba district.'

İkmen raised his eyes.

'I asked Uğur İnan, the squat's apparent leader, whether anyone had reported these incidents, and he laughed at me. He calls the Art House his "last stand". A reference I imagine to how he feels about the place of the secular in modern life.'

'And we too are the enemy,' İkmen said.

'Yes, which is something I want to change,' Süleyman said. Then, even though they were alone, he lowered his voice. 'We both know that the two of us have more in common with the squatters than we can say. I'm going to look out for those kids and try to put a stop to it. People like Uğur İnan are becoming very hostile to us. It's not right. I hate being at odds with sections of the community like this. I want to regain their trust.'

'Good luck with that,' İkmen said. 'Post-Gezi.'

Not only was he angry, he was also down. Even before Gezi there had been a polarisation evident between people who wanted one particular kind of lifestyle and those who did not. It wasn't as simple as the difference between those who were religious and those who were not, as some believed. A considerable number of the Gezi protesters had been devout Muslims. The split was much more to do with politics, and specifically development policy. And in that regard, what was going on was reflecting what was happening the world over. The rich were getting richer and the poor and their allies were not prepared to be quiet.

'At the very least they should behave,' Süleyman said.

İkmen shrugged.

Süleyman had never seen him so deflated. Had something happened, beyond the case, to bring him down?

'Cetin . . .'

'Oh, you have to excuse my mood,' he said. 'Or rather, I ask you to.'

'Of course.'

'It's the kids themselves that worry me,' he said. 'Old bastards like us can be as set in our thinking as we like, but for youngsters to be so polarised in their beliefs I find especially depressing. They are our future. And at the moment, our future looks bleak.'

'Dad!'

İsmet İnan stood between his father and the boy lying on the floor and held up his hand.

'What are you doing?'

Uğur İnan, worn out by his recent exertions, pulled back his clenched fist and let his arm fall to his side. 'The little shit was in the kitchen,' he said. 'Poking around.'

İsmet looked at the boy on the floor. His lip had already started to swell where Uğur had hit him. A big, livid bruise was developing. He must have really belted the kid.

'There was no need to hit him that hard,' İsmet said as he raised the boy to his feet. 'Are you all right?'

The boy said nothing.

'He was trying to steal from us,' Uğur said. 'After throwing stones at us!' He put his face close to the boy's. 'What do you want our food for, eh? Aren't we infidels? Aren't we unclean?'

The boy still said nothing.

'Can't answer that, can you?'

'Maybe he doesn't speak Turkish,' İsmet said.

'All the others have been able to.'

'Yes, but maybe he can't. Maybe he's Syrian. The streets are full of them.'

Uğur shrugged. 'Just get him out of here,' he said.

İsmet took the boy out into the garden, but not before he'd grabbed a bottle of ayran for him out of the fridge. Once they'd both sat down in the sunshine, İsmet mustered his very basic Arabic. 'You from Syria?' he asked.

The boy didn't seem to know what to be most frightened of – İsmet or the ayran.

'Drink.'

But he didn't.

'What's your name?' İsmet asked. 'I not hurt you. Drink.'

Still he didn't speak, or drink.

'You can have ayran. It's OK.' The boy looked at the bottle. It seemed he understood İsmet at least.

'My Arabic is not good,' İsmet continued. 'Sorry.'

Still he remained silent.

'You are Syrian, aren't you?'

The boy looked at him for a long time before, slowly, he nodded.

'I am sorry my father hit you,' İsmet said. 'You are hungry. You can come here for food. But not throw stones. No.'

'You are infidels.' The boy's voice croaked, as if he hadn't used it for a long time.

İsmet shrugged. It was sad to hear such a word used by a young boy. Kids should be brought up to be race- religion- and colour-blind. He was going to make sure that Barış was.

'You do something bad with Burak and Mustafa,' the boy said.

'Who?'

But the boy said nothing. Then he threw the bottle of ayran on the ground and ran across the garden to the wall.

'Hey!'

İsmet only half-heartedly pursued him. The kid was much more agile than he was and was up and over the wall almost before İsmet had got to his feet. Alone with the smashed bottle of ayran, he wondered who Burak and Mustafa were. He imagined they were two of the other kids who came and threw stones and shouted abuse at the squat from time to time. But which ones? And why did the Syrian boy think that the squatters had done something with them?

Cetin İkmen had been expecting Ümit Kavaş's last meal to be male. And he had been proved right. Arto Sarkissian looked at the report just e-mailed to him by the forensic laboratory and sat back in his chair to consider its implications.

The carefully prepared gourmet body had been that of a male, but as yet, the ethnicity of this person was unknown. It wouldn't stay that way, but it would take a bit longer for those results to come through. Whether the nationality of Kavaş's dinner made any difference to who had prepared and possibly killed him, and why, was moot, and fortunately for Arto, finding that out was beyond his remit. But he knew it would be giving Cetin a headache. Commissioner Teker wasn't allowing anyone outside the investigation to know any details, and certainly the word 'cannibal' wasn't even to be breathed. But how long, realistically, could that continue?

Boris Myskow shrugged. 'I don't know what to say.'

Cetin İkmen looked down at him. Sitting at his desk, he looked vulnerable and not at all the prima donna he portrayed in his TV programmes.

'Our results are unequivocal. Tell me where the boar comes from,' İkmen said.

Kerim Gürsel had accompanied him this time. He'd never been to the Imperial Oriental Hotel before and kept on, rather annoyingly, looking around as if he were in Wonderland.

The hotelier shrugged again. 'I have a man involved in the trophy shoots,' he said.

'What man?'

'I know him as Domuz,' he said.

İkmen raised his eyes. Had no one on Myskow's staff had the balls to tell him? Or was he lying? 'Domuz is the Turkish word for boar,' he said.

'Is it?'

When he looked up, Myskow bore a slight resemblance to Barry Manilow. Fatma İkmen would have been enchanted. Her husband was irked.

'Well if you don't know that's what the word means, then either you are suffering from the sin of omission or, sir, someone has been playing a game with you,' İkmen said. 'Either way, you must tell me how I can contact this person.'

Myskow put his head in his hands. 'Why?'

He had a good point. Selling boar instead of pork wasn't

exactly the crime of the century, but if he were selling human flesh too, that could be.

'Boar is not covered by your licence,' İkmen said. 'It's a wild meat that is untested. Unlike Mr Zarides's meat. Wild pigs may carry diseases like toxoplasmosis. And no, I didn't know what that was until I looked it up on the Internet, but it's bad.'

'God.'

'Where do you get the boar, Mr Myskow?'

'From Do—'

'What part of the country does this man work in?' İkmen said. 'Boar range all over Anatolia. Where do you get yours from?'

'I don't know.'

'Oh come on, you must know!' İkmen sat down. 'Don't insult my intelligence, Mr Myskow. I know that boar are hunted for trophies by foreigners. It's quite legal in this country. But eating their flesh is another matter. They're not screened. Who knows what could be getting into the food chain if they're consumed? The only way out of this for you is to tell me. Who do you get it for?'

'Customers.'

'Well clearly you get it for customers. But who? Do people ask you for it? I haven't seen the words "wild boar" on any of your menus. Do you get it for particular customers who pay you specially to obtain it for them?'

He didn't reply.

İkmen sighed. 'Well if you won't tell me, I'll have to arrest you,' he said.

Myskow raised his head. Oddly, he was calm. 'I do have the right to an attorney in this country,' he said.

'Of course.'

'Then I will exercise that right.'

Chapter 6

Radwan hid in the bushes. What had happened at the Art House had unnerved him. His lip was still swollen and painful. What if the weird people from that place came after him? Murdered him? There weren't many places to hide in the park because most of the area inside the old cistern was taken over by basket-ball and football courts. But it was night-time now, and all the boys who usually played in the park were elsewhere. Only Radwan remained, or so he thought.

'What you doing?'

He was probably older than Radwan. He was certainly thinner and more dirty. When Radwan had come out of the bush, this boy had let himself down from a tree.

'Where you from?' the boy continued. He spoke Arabic well, which probably meant that he was an Arab brother. Turks didn't speak it well, in Radwan's opinion. Not like this.

'Who are you?' he countered.

'You tell me who you are first.'

He had a knife. Radwan could see it shining in the moonlight, half in and half out of a scabbard on his hip.

'Radwan.'

He jerked his head upwards. 'Azzam of Damascus.'

He was a bit grand about himself.

'Do you sleep here in this park?'

'Sometimes,' Radwan said. 'Why?'

'Don't lie,' Azzam of Damascus said. 'I see you here all the time. Talking nonsense to those jihadi Turks.'

He had to mean Burak and Mustafa. They had other friends who sometimes tagged along, but since the brothers had disappeared, they had given Radwan a wide berth.

'What do you want?' Radwan said.

'What've you got?'

'Nothing.' Azzam frisked him. He only stopped when he was satisfied Radwan was telling the truth. Then he said, 'You didn't meet ISIS in Aleppo. I heard you bragging. It was bullshit.'

'How do you know?'

'What, apart from the fact that your dates don't add up? My father fought with the Free Syrian Army. He's dead now, but he told me all about ISIS.'

'They've started a caliphate.'

Azzam grabbed him by his shirt collar. 'So? What's a caliphate, eh? You know what the ones who caught my dad did? They made him dig his own grave and then they shot him. In the back. How brave are they, eh? How noble?'

Radwan had never thought that ISIS were anything other than killers. But Burak and Mustafa had idolised them, particularly Burak, and he'd needed those boys. They'd brought him food. Would this Azzam give him food if he agreed with him?

'I know ISIS have done bad things,' Radwan said.

'Then why did you boast that you knew them?'

'Because Burak and Mustafa liked them.'

'Like that's a reason?' Azzam slapped him.

His face was already sore. Radwan winced. 'Ow!'

'You got in with them because you don't speak Turkish,' Azzam said. 'I do.'

Radwan nursed the cheek Azzam had slapped and mumbled, 'Good for you.'

'Yes, good for me. But bad for you now that your friends have gone to Syria.'

'What? Burak and Mustafa Ayan? No, they haven't gone to Syria,' Radwan said. 'Some infidels in a house in Karaköy have kidnapped them. Last time I saw them was at that house. Why do you say they've gone to Syria?'

'Because that's what their dad, the imam, is telling everyone,' Azzam said. 'He is crying all the time now because his only sons have gone to join ISIS. And it's all your fault.'

When he'd been a child in the 1970s, people had lived in the Aetius Cistern. There'd been a village in what was then called the Sunken Garden. Gonca and her sisters had told fortunes door to door and people had dried red peppers on their rooftops. The area had been a traditional Turkish district, like a little piece of Anatolia in the city. But then it had first been abandoned, then redeveloped, and now it was a sports park in a district that was like a little piece of Arabia in the city.

Mehmet Süleyman knew that as a man in a suit, smoking a cigarette, he stood out. Almost all the other men on the street wore şalvar trousers or dishdashas, and every one of them had a beard. He didn't. A neatly trimmed moustache, yes, but he had been brought up to associate beards with men from the country-side, peasants working on the land and those of a fanatically religious turn of mind. None of these stereotypes was attractive to a man from the old Ottoman elite. He didn't have much in common with the secular, working-class republican Cetin İkmen, but a dislike of beards was one area where they concurred.

In contrast to the part of Balat where Gonca and her huge family of gypsies lived, this area was quiet and shuttered. He had no doubt that the eyes of women and children were on him from behind closed windows. But only their men stood in the street, looking at him and at the old cistern, which was now dark and silent. No more smoke from open fires in little wood and terracotta-tiled shacks, no more children running around in loose summer clothes, playing in the moonlight in front of Mehmet and his brother, jealous in their tight-fitting school uniforms. Had their father taken them to such rough parts of the city to see what real life was about? Or had he made those journeys to show the boys what was in store for them when they grew up? Because although the scion of princes, Mehmet was just a policeman now. It was all, with the exception of his army service and his student years, he had ever been.

If kids from Fatih went over to Karaköy to threaten the squat, it was probably from this area. Youngsters in Balat and Fener were more culturally diverse than these children of the pious, and kids in Sultanahmet were too busy making money from tourism to think about anything else. Now it was dark, were they indoors, or out on the streets somewhere, staring at unbelievers? It was difficult for him to think about people like this in anything but negative terms. And although in recent years the Ottoman Empire had come back into favour along with strict religious observance, he couldn't get behind it. In spite of his Ottoman blood, he felt it wasn't real. The Ottoman Empire was something from the past. To try to repeat it would devalue everything it had been, good or bad.

His job now was to try and protect the Art House and give the squatters some reason to believe in the police. He also had to catch a person who had cooked another human being. He didn't know which task was harder.

'This is bullshit!'

Cetin İkmen and Kerim Gürsel followed Boris Myskow and his lawyer out into the station car park.

'Your client is guilty of obtaining unlicensed meat! Don't you care about that? And it's porcine!'

The lawyer opened the door of his car and ushered Myskow inside. Then he turned to İkmen. 'My client is not your concern, Inspector İkmen. As I have told you, anything concerning Mr Myskow and his activities is under the auspices of a higher authority.'

'Oh, so it disappears into James Bond land. Great. You know this could be connected to an investigation I'm involved with . . .'

The lawyer moved towards İkmen, quickly. He lowered his voice. 'Your cannibal case has nothing to do with Mr Myskow,' he said.

İkmen felt his face wrinkle into a sneer. 'I don't suppose I have to ask how you know about that, do I?' he said.

'You don't and you won't,' the lawyer said. Then he walked back to his car and drove away.

İkmen and Kerim Gürsel watched the car leave. İkmen lit a cigarette.

'What do the security services have to do with Boris Myskow?' Kerim said.

'What have they to do with so many things they get themselves involved with?' İkmen replied. 'I don't know. But I don't suppose Mr Myskow per se is the cause of their concern. That's more likely to be what he's serving.'

'The boar?'

'Contentious, theologically unsound and possibly contaminated. Not that we will ever know now,' İkmen said. 'National security, Kerim. Oh, how very important and dangerous that catch-all term is! Is Myskow selling contaminated boar to enemies of the state, or is he feeding those he shouldn't with his porcine delights? Has he now in fact turned his attention to the delights of human flesh? Who knows?'

Kerim moved closer to his boss. 'His lawyer knew about our case.'

'Yes. But only because our spooky colleagues told him. Just in case we made life a little difficult for him. Arsehole.'

İkmen began to walk back to the station. Kerim followed.

'Do you really think Myskow was also serving human flesh, sir?'

'If I hadn't thought that, I would've probably left him alone with his wild boar,' İkmen said.

'Would you?'

'Yes. But now, with higher powers in tow, Myskow would seem to be a dead end. I'll gripe and bitch to Commissioner Teker and we'll have to see what she says. I'm certainly not going to let Dr Sarkissian's unknown male be eaten in vain.'

He needed carbs.

'I need carbs!' he said as he bounced into the kitchen and headed for the fridge. Two henna parties one after the other had shattered him.

'What the fuck are you doing?'

It was Ziya, the tattooed biker, whose dad had been a major in the army before he'd been put in prison for crimes against the state.

'I'm getting myself some food,' Gül said.

Ziya came through the doorway that led out to what he'd been told was an old washroom.

'What are *you* doing?'

'Chasing rats,' Ziya said.

'Oh God, do we have rats down here?' Gül cringed.

'There's droppings in the garden,' Ziya said.

'Is it OK to get something from the fridge?' Gül said. 'I need carbs after all the dancing, and I've got some leftover pasta in there.'

'There won't be rats in the fridge, Gül.' Ziya smiled.

Gül opened the fridge door. Every shelf was packed with food labelled with its owners' names.

'Oh my God, I don't believe Meltem Hanım has got something as wicked as lokma!'

Ziya laughed. Then he looked over his shoulder, nervously.

'I'll just take my pasta and go to my room,' Gül said as he took his food out of the fridge. 'Leave you to your macho animal-hunt thing.'

'A rat is hardly a tiger.'

'No, it's worse,' Gül said. 'If a tiger bites you, you just die. If a rat nips you, you die too, just a long time afterwards. Filthy little bastards! Night.'

And with a swish of chiffon and a rustle of sequins, he was gone. Ziya waited for a moment before he went back into the old bathhouse and took out the knife he'd been holding behind his back.

Sometimes the only thing to do was to drink.

'I don't want to go to one of those designer bars in Beyoğlu,' Teker told Cetin İkmen as they got into the taxi he'd ordered.

'Don't worry,' he said. 'No chance of that.'

They ended up walking the last half-kilometre because the driver wouldn't take them any further than the Syriani church on Karakurum Sokak. The district of Tarlabaşı still had a reputation for violence and drug dealing, even though it was currently under redevelopment.

As they walked through streets populated by disaffected kids, transgender prostitutes and addicts high on bonzai, Teker was surprised at how many people İkmen acknowledged.

'You're popular.'

He smiled. 'What's the point of alienating the sick and the desperate?' he said. 'They want happy lives, just like we do. Why should we be part of their very considerable problems?'

The bar İkmen took her to was the front room of what had once been a considerable Greek mansion. It was dark, filled with smoke and the smell of rakı – the only drink on offer. Prostitutes, both male and female, and soldiers mixed with bonzai addicts keen to get even higher and a few old men all of whom claimed to have met Ataturk when they were children.

İkmen called over to a middle-aged Kurd to bring them a bottle of rakı. 'And clean glasses, Lütfü,' he said. 'My guest's a lady.'

'This must've been quite a place at one time,' Teker said as she looked at the blackened classical friezes on the ceiling.

'Many of our Ottoman Greek and Armenian citizens were wealthy business people and artisans,' İkmen said. 'Tarlabaşı was the place to live back in those days. Even as recently as the 1960s, some clung on. Inspector Süleyman's Armenian nanny used to live in Tarlabaşı.'

'How very Ottoman,' she said. 'I'm surprised he's not parading around in a kaftan. Won't he and his kind be ruling us all again soon?'

İkmen smiled. 'Now you know that's not the point of the new Ottomanism, madam,' he said. 'That's just window-dressing.'

The rakı and a carafe of water arrived. The waiter gave the glasses a quick polish on his dirty apron and left.

'As good as it gets here, I'm afraid, madam,' İkmen said as he poured them both a large measure and then topped each glass up with water. The spirit became cloudy, just as it should be.

Teker took a big slug. 'You can drop the madam here,' she said. 'It's Hürrem.'

He smiled and offered her his hand. 'Cetin.'

She shook it.

'We can talk in this place?'

'Everyone's too high, too old or too horny to care about us,' İkmen said. 'I come here a lot.'

'To old Istanbul.'

He knew what she meant. The ungentrified city that he loved. 'Absolutely.'

She drank some more rakı and lit a cigarette. 'Talk to me, Cetin.'

'I want to know why an American who breaks the law by sourcing illegal meat is being protected from on high,' he said. 'I'd also like to know how I'm meant to find whoever prepared, cooked and possibly murdered our unknown victim if I'm not to be allowed to follow up what could be a lead.'

'Just because Myskow serves boar doesn't necessarily mean he serves . . . other things.'

'No, it doesn't. But it might.' İkmen drank. 'It's a well-known fact that a person's latitude for acceptance of criminal behaviour often begins small, with wild boar for instance, and then gets bigger and more ambitious. Whoever prepared this "meat" did it well and will almost certainly have been paid handsomely for it. Mr Myskow is well known for breaking culinary boundaries; why not the ultimate taboo?'

'Where are you in the investigation?' she said.

'CCTV footage places Ümit Kavaş on İstiklal, but there is no evidence of his visiting any café or restaurant. Not that I can categorically state that he didn't. I just don't have any evidence to support a restaurant visit. We're focusing on Kavaş's past at the moment, speaking to his family and friends. He was a Gezi supporter, very involved with alternative movements, particularly that squat in Karaköy.'

'The Art House.'

'Yes. Bunch of hippies and arty types, as far as I can tell. The only thing to come out of that is an allegation of intimidation. But it does involve Ümit Kavaş.'

'How do you mean?'

'The squatters and their friend Ümit have been targeted by kids they call "jihadis". They reckon they come from Fatih . . .'

'Would make sense.'

'Hurling abuse – and stones. Giving the girls in the squat,

particularly the covered ones, a hard time. They call them infidels and unbelievers and say that they'll cut their heads off. The usual shit. Inspector Süleyman is investigating. Whatever one thinks about squatting, the squatters are intimidating no one. The kids from Fatih are. And, I'll be honest, it's a public relations exercise. A considerable proportion of the population feels, rightly or wrongly, abandoned by the police. We need to do something about that, in my opinion.'

A thin boy sitting in a dark corner wound an arm around his transsexual companion's neck. His skin was covered with sores. A sign of heavy bonzai use.

Teker leaned across the table. 'You will need to be careful,' she said.

'Hate crimes are illegal in this country,' İkmen said.

'Mmm.'

Her lack of comment spoke volumes. Crimes based on hatred of someone's race or religion were illegal. But crimes against some groups were not taken quite as seriously as they should be by certain officers. And some of those were senior to both İkmen and Teker.

'You are walking on dangerous ground, Çetin,' Teker said.

'Where you put me, Hürrem.'

The sound of a siren outside made everyone run to the one small window. İkmen checked it wasn't their colleagues and then returned.

'Ambulance,' he said.

Teker finished her first glass of rakı and poured herself a second. 'You can't touch Boris Myskow. Not with the kind of muscle he's got behind him. And I doubt, to be frank with you, whether those who are protecting him are eating human meat.'

'Do you? I don't.'

She smiled. 'Can you imagine what would happen if they were?'

66

'Yes, I can,' he said. 'I fantasise about similar scenarios all the time.'

'Well you mustn't,' she said. 'It's important for all of us to be objective. Something like this could blow up in our faces and the faces of those people in the squat. You wish to win their trust. Do so. But be careful who you alienate at their expense.'

'I won't—'

'A lot of offences are now considered to be acts of terrorism,' she said. 'Those squatters could be considered terrorists by certain pairs of eyes. I believe an old colleague of yours has been ingratiating himself by discovering a lot of terrorist activity on the south-eastern coast.'

Both İkmen and Süleyman had worked with Inspector Metin İskender in the past. Always a stickler for procedure, he'd come from a poor background but had married a wealthy and successful woman, and at one time he'd looked set to become one of the department's better detectives. But then he and his wife had moved, first to Ankara and then Metin alone had gone to Adana. There he'd been promoted. He'd worked hard, got in with what many regarded as the 'right' people. It was then that his wife had divorced him. Since that time he'd been the scourge of dissent in all its forms in the Adana area. Had he had some sort of ideological epiphany, or had he just lost his mind when his wife deserted him?

'Tread carefully with the jihadi boys of Fatih,' Teker continued. 'These days they may not be simply zealous kids. And watch Boris Myskow, but from a distance.'

'How do I do that?'

'Carefully,' she said. 'It's not up to me to tell you how to do your job, or even to know what you're doing every minute of every day.'

'So if I . . . we get caught . . .'

'Don't. Do what you have to do discreetly. Even within the department. I know you're better than Mr Myskow's protectors.'

67

'I don't have their power.'

'But you are in charge of *this* investigation. If there is a trade in human flesh going on in this city, we need to know who's doing it and arrest them. Irrespective of who they are, who they might know or how much money is involved. But we have to be cleverer than they are, and that is not as easy as you might think. Retain your contempt, that's your right, but don't show it. Play the game, but don't. You know what I mean.'

İkmen looked around the room at the lost souls of old Istanbul. 'I'll try.'

'I will help you,' she said. 'Just don't push your luck. In the meantime, I'll think about other avenues we might explore.'

'What kind of avenues?'

Teker narrowed her eyes. 'I'll let you know,' she said. 'When I know.'

Chapter 7

His wife had gone to her sister's house, and so he'd had to call her on her mobile.

'They're releasing our son's body for burial tomorrow,' he said. 'You'd better come back. Arrangements will have to be made.'

She exhibited no emotion. 'I'll be an hour,' she said, and then she cut the connection.

Abdullah Kavaş turned to the old man at his side. 'You'll come to the funeral.'

'Of course.'

The general shook his head.

Brigadier Erol Korkmaz put a hand on his friend's shoulder. 'You mustn't blame yourself.'

'How can I not?' There were tears in his eyes. 'Ümit was vulnerable. I should have protected him.'

'He was also a man,' the brigadier said. 'And an idealist. A liberal. Not a nationalist.'

'No, but . . .' The general lit a cigarette. 'We should not have been joking. We made light of it, which was wrong. There are no jokes now.'

'You shouldn't be smoking.'

'Why not? What do I have to live for?'

'Abdullah Bey, some comments were made, I believe, in a light-hearted manner, relating to the excavations at one of the Neolithic sites in Anatolia,' the brigadier said. 'About culinary practices amongst the early Anatolians.'

'Ümit was not amused.'

'No.'

'Deniz Bey . . .'

'Abdullah Bey, what's done is done. Deniz Bey . . . well, he did what he did. I know he upset your son.'

'He's too strident. Always has been.'

'Well, I don't know about that . . .'

'I do.'

'What was the point in prolonging the family's agony? Especially once the commissioner had given her consent. We retain the stomach contents, which are our real interest.'

Çetin İkmen looked red-eyed at his friend Arto Sarkissian. It had been many years since he'd had such a thundering hangover. When the Armenian had first seen him, he'd laughed. Now, however, they were being serious.

'You've still got some DNA tests pending, right?'

'Yes,' Arto said. 'Racial profile. Hopefully the meat wasn't in Kavaş's stomach too long to get a result. We'll see. God, Cetin, were you drinking alone last night?'

'Yes.'

Even Arto didn't need to know about his conversation with Teker, and he certainly needed to be spared the details about what had happened after their alcohol binge. İkmen had ended up sleeping in the bar under a table. When he'd woken up, Teker had been nowhere to be seen. He'd only encountered her, bright as spring and clean as mountain dew, when he'd arrived at the station. Either she had a powerful hangover cure or she was an awesome drinker.

'You know you shouldn't do it,' Arto continued. 'Not with your history.'

'Yes, yes, yes. Can we please get back to Ümit Kavaş and his stomach contents?'

That İkmen had experienced problems with alcohol in the past was well known. But that had come under control years ago.

Arto shrugged. He'd said his piece. There was nothing to add. 'What about missing persons?' he said.

'What about them? We have some, most of whom are male, and we're working through them. Any one of them could be our victim at the moment. If or when you get me some more information . . .'

'I know, a narrower field.'

'What we can't find is a connection to Ümit Kavaş,' İkmen said. 'Not that he would necessarily know who he was consuming the night he died.'

'Or even the true nature of what he was eating,' Arto said. 'From what I could make out, the sauce accompanying the meat was piquant to say the least.'

'Strong?'

'Interesting.'

İkmen shook his head. 'You go to some of these fancy new restaurants sometimes, don't you?'

'Not if I can help it, but yes, Maryam would like to go to places like Fish and Leb-i derya. Her friends go to those restaurants; they like to show each other pictures on their phones of the food they've eaten.'

'Have you ever been to the restaurant at the Imperial Oriental Hotel?'

'The one run by that American chef? No,' he said. 'Why?'

İkmen wondered what to say next but then decided on nothing. What could he say? Not a lot. But Arto had known him all his life and so he would have got the hint.

'Oh.'

'Yes, Boris Myskow is the American's name,' İkmen said. 'Celebrity chef. Very innovative and very well connected.'

'Is he?'

71

'Yes.'

'Mmm.' Arto sat back in his chair.

Had he picked up on the gossip that some sort of celebrity had been brought in the previous evening? Did he know that some meat from a high-profile restaurant had been tested at the forensic laboratory? He almost certainly knew the latter, and he usually talked to everyone he came across when he visited police headquarters. And he knew a lot of people. Moreover, some of them were the type who noticed things. Bored constables like Yıldız, who had worked for the department for years, might not know who this or that famous person was, but he'd know a celebrity when he saw one, and he'd seen Myskow. When İkmen had shouted at the chef and his lawyer in the car park, a lot of people had seen Myskow.

'Well then perhaps I should take Maryam to the Imperial Oriental to sample Mr Myskow's food,' the Armenian said.

Of course he'd picked up the gossip.

It was a warm day, but the imam was cold. The Twisted Boy came to give him his lunch and found him hunched over a fire.

'Imam Ayan,' he said as he put the bowl of lentil soup his mother had prepared for the old man down on a table. 'If you want to be warm, you should go outside.'

'If I go outside, I have to talk to people.'

'No you don't.'

'People ask for guidance.'

The Twisted Boy manoeuvred himself into a chair beside the imam. Born with spina bifida, his real name was Ramazan, and his main job in life was to support his widowed mother. She cooked for those who couldn't, like the imam, and received small sums of money for her labours. Ramazan delivered her food.

72

'There's a policeman talking to people in the coffee house,' the boy said. 'The simitçi says that he wants to know about some boys who come from here and make trouble in other places.'

'What boys?'

'He didn't say. I thought that you could tell him about Burak and Mustafa.'

'Burak and Mustafa don't make trouble in other places!'

Ramazan didn't comment either way. The imam knew that the boy was as aware of his sons' shortcomings as he was.

'Because they're missing,' Ramazan said. 'Maybe . . .'

'Where they've gone, nobody else can follow,' the old man said. 'What good would it do to get the police involved?'

'I don't know. I'm just saying.'

'Well don't. There's two lira on the sideboard for your mother; take it and go.'

With difficulty, Ramazan stood and left.

Alone with his fire and his soup, the old man looked at the text he'd received that morning from Burak. All it said was 'Mustafa is dead.'

Ömer Mungun recognised the type. He saw them everywhere. A woman in her mid twenties, who looked older and was way too hot. She staggered into Süleyman's office under a heavy burden of small children, baby buggies, shopping and toys. She wore a thick woollen headscarf and a long black coat.

Ömer offered her a chair, but she said she preferred to stand. Instead, some of the children clambered on the chair. Others ran around Ömer's superior's desk. The woman let them.

'My husband's gone,' she said.

Ömer took a pen out of a young girl's hand just before she scribbled on Süleyman's office chair. He'd really drawn the short straw when he and Kerim Gürsel had divided up their workload. Kerim was out interviewing the families of missing persons in their own homes. He was probably being given glasses of tea, cakes . . .

'Mrs . . .'

'He's called Celal Vural,' she said.

She appeared to be entirely oblivious to the chaos her five children were causing. Another kid, a boy this time, had one of Süleyman's cigarette packets in his hand.

Ömer gave up. 'Look, I can't do anything with your children destroying my office,' he said. 'Let me explain: I share this office with my boss, who is a very particular individual. Can you please get them to sit down?'

He sat and waited for her to arrange her children on the floor with bags of sweets. But even when they were settled, she still stood.

'He's been gone for nearly a week,' she said.

Ömer opened a new page on his computer screen. 'Can you please sit down, Hanım.'

She perched on the edge of the chair, her handbag on her lap like a shield.

'What's your husband's name again?'

She told him. 'He's thirty,' she said. 'We live in an apartment in Kağıthane.'

Right next to the upmarket Etiler district, Kağıthane was only starting to experience gentrification. Traditionally it was working class, like this woman.

'Tell me what happened.'

The smallest child, little more than a baby, blew a large snot bubble.

'He went to work and he didn't come back,' the woman said.

'When?'

'Saturday.'

Ömer typed.

'When was he due to come home?'

74

'Sunday morning.'

He looked at her. 'Your husband works nights?'

'More evenings,' she said.

'What does he do?'

'He's a waiter,' she said. 'He works in Beyoğlu mostly, although he does do a few hours at a nargile place in Tophane on Thursday evenings, covering for his brother on his night off. He's not been there this week and so his brother's been angry.'

Ömer looked up. She was worried, and so going into detail he didn't need. 'Where was your husband working when he disappeared?'

'At the hotel,' she said. 'I've spoken to them but they haven't seen him. He left on Saturday night after work and they thought he'd come home. But he didn't. He'll lose his job, I expect.'

'What time did he leave?'

'Just after midnight, when his shift finishes.'

'Which hotel does he work at?' Ömer asked.

'The Imperial Oriental,' she said. 'In the restaurant.'

Holding on to Pembe Hanım's bags after a shopping spree was not something that was alien to Zenne Gül. In spite of the fact that Pembe was so much taller than he was, he remained the man and so was eligible for the task of pack mule. Now they were drinking coffee in the Sugar and Spice Café and gossiping.

'You know we've got rats,' Gül said.

'Ugh!' Pembe waved a hand. 'You should leave, darling. I told Sinem Hanım where you were living and she was stunned. I mean, you can do so much better than a squat.'

'I like the people.'

'Mmm?' She raised an eyebrow.

'Don't be vulgar!' Gül laughed. 'I don't fancy any of them. But I do believe that what Uğur Bey is doing is good. He's created a communal arts centre. Nobody cares what your background is as long as you are creative and have a basic appreciation of the values that informed Gezi.'

'So no holy people.'

'You know we have covered girls, Pembe.'

'Yes, but they're not covered girls like the ones you see trailing behind their men in Fatih. Your girls all want to be doctors and have parents who live in Nişantaşı. The veil's just their teenage rebellion.'

Gül shook his head. 'They're not teenagers, they're my friends. But let's not argue. I like the squat because you get all sorts of people in and out. From covered girls to old ex-con generals. And they accept me just as readily as I accept them.'

'Yes, but what about the fact that it's temporary?' Pembe said. 'I mean, you said yourself that my Kerim Bey has been sniffing around Karaköy. Believe me, I've tried to find out why, but he won't say – whatever I do . . .'

Gül laughed. 'You are so cruel to that man.'

Pembe touched Gül's hand. 'Don't be mean,' she said. 'I look after his wife, who I do love dearly, and he gets the most spectacular sex. But he won't talk about his work.'

'The police will come, we know that,' Gül said.

'And then they'll smash the place up and take all your stuff. You'll probably get beaten up into the bargain. Then you won't be able to work.'

Gül drank coffee. 'Uğur Bey gave me a room when I was desperate,' he said. 'I owe him, and if I'm honest, I think we need to make a stand against the way the city's being taken over by tower blocks. Gezi isn't finished, and it won't be until that stops. I mean, that place I lived in on Sultan Selim Caddesi should've been fine. I always liked that area, but it's changed.'

'The religious—'

'Look, Pembe, I don't have a problem with religious people. Not in the ordinary way of things.'

'Yes, but they're *lunatics*!'

'No. No they're not,' he said. 'I know you can't stand anything like that, but I feel differently. My mum was religious. My sisters cover. My problem was with the young boys. A lot of them are high on bonzai and know nothing about religion, but they jump on board the train because some of the carriages carry people who promise them a world of excitement. They call it jihad and it comes at them through the Internet. They are the reason I moved, not because of a lot of old men mumbling unhappily into their beards every time they saw me.'

Pembe felt a little put down. But she ignored it. 'So the rats . . .'

'The rats are in an old bathhouse out the back of the kitchen,' Gül said. 'Ziya, the biker with the tattoos, was in there last night with a very large knife. I swear he believed I hadn't seen it, but it was all too visible. They're probably all dead now. He's a pretty thorough guy.'

'Good. You don't want vermin.'

'No. But . . .' Gül shook his head.

'What?'

'I don't know,' he said. 'The building's dilapidated and we're near the water, but I've never seen any rats. Ziya went in there with a knife the size of a small scimitar.'

'Oh, you know what those macho types are like, darling,' Pembe said. 'Everything's a tiger in the bushes to them.'

Chapter 8

Cetin İkmen felt both elated and nervous. While Ömer Mungun's investigation into the disappearance of Celal Vural provided an opportunity for further monitoring of Boris Myskow's restaurant, with the American under official protection, how was that going to look?

Commissioner Teker said, 'We'll have to come clean.'

'What do you mean?' İkmen asked.

'I'll have to contact his lawyer,' she said. 'Let him know what's happened.'

'Thereby alerting Myskow, who for all we know may have something to do with Vural's disappearance.'

'Mrs Vural said that her husband was happy in his job,' Ömer Mungun said.

'Maybe he was,' İkmen said. 'Maybe he's run away with another woman and his employers have nothing to do with his disappearance. But knowing what we know about Mr Myskow's activities, we also know that he breaks the law. And he gets protection while he does it. If it's Vural's flesh that was in Ümit Kavaş's stomach . . . But then it can't be. He didn't go missing until the Saturday night.'

Teker sighed. 'No, he didn't. All right, not the lawyer,' she said. 'But I'll have to contact someone.'

They all knew who she meant.

'And yes, I know you hate spooks,' she said. 'I do too. But we don't know what interest they have in Boris Myskow, or why.'

'They're protecting him. He knows they're protecting him!'

'Of course. But he may not know why,' she said. 'Perhaps he thinks their interest is in his wild boar activities. But they may only want him to think that. They move to the sound of a different drum.'

'Usually to our detriment,' İkmen said.

The rivalry between the police and the security services was well known and long-standing. It was at its most intense when their investigations overlapped. With countries on almost every border with Turkey in states of conflict, this happened more often than ever.

Teker said, 'Sergeant Mungun, you're working with Inspectors İkmen and Süleyman on the Kavaş case, aren't you?'

'Yes, madam.'

'How did you come into contact with this Vural woman?'

'Along with Sergeant Gürsel, I've been assigned to assess our missing persons file,' he said. 'Because our victim could be almost anyone male who went missing any time from one week ago to, well . . .'

'Yes, I know what freezers can do, Sergeant Mungun.'

'When we're working together, we split tasks. Today Kerim, Sergeant Gürsel, was out interviewing friends and relatives of the missing and I was working in the office. Mrs Vural came into the station and was directed to me.'

'I see.' She looked at İkmen. 'How many missing persons do we have at present?'

'More than we thought,' he said.

'Once you'd taken into account a possible historic element?'

'Forensic have assured me that frozen meat can be pleasantly edible for up to a year,' İkmen said.

She nodded. 'Sadly, that is a phrase that will not pass quickly from my mind, but I know what you mean.' Then she said, 'Leave it with me. Somehow we will have to find a way of getting back into the Imperial Oriental Hotel without upsetting Mr Myskow or his friends. Thank you, Sergeant Mungun, you may go.'

'Madam.'

Mungun left. İkmen made to follow him, but Teker held up a hand.

'Not you, Cetin Bey.'

He closed her office door and sat down.

'Have you put anyone in place at the Imperial Oriental yet?' she asked.

'I've sent texts,' İkmen said.

'To an informant?'

'I listened to what you said last night, and how even here we have to be careful. He works in the tourist industry. He's not got back to me, but he will.'

'I assume you can trust this person?'

'I could finish his career,' İkmen said. Then he added. 'I'm not proud of that, but . . .'

'Frightening times make spooks of us all,' she said. 'Let me know when he gets back to you. If he doesn't, I have an idea.'

Everyone in the Çarşamba area of Fatih district had perfect children. Mehmet Süleyman had been expecting it. Had he asked the same questions of fathers in the upscale secular district of Nişantaşı, he would have got the same answers. As it was, the kufi-wearing religious denizens of the Çarşamba coffee houses were quite certain that their kids would never cause trouble in other parts of the city.

One elderly man who apparently had a twelve-year-old son had said, 'Why would they? We don't bring our children up to stray. Here our boys have their mothers, their mosque and the friends they will have for the rest of their lives. Why would they want to go somewhere else?'

Süleyman could have made more than a few suggestions, but he hadn't. He saw the contempt in the eyes of some of the teenage boys he came across – and the envy. It was all very well for those youngsters who were content with the simple life of the neighbourhood, but a lot were not. When he'd sat down outside the first coffee house he'd come to, he'd seen the way some of the kids looked at his mobile phone. They had them too, but few had the latest models. They were carried by slightly older men in their twenties and thirties who otherwise gave the appearance of sober, traditional piety. Along with the stylish phones went beards, black şalvar trousers and tunics that in some cases strained to cover their well-developed chests. Some were Syrian refugees, but a lot weren't. Long gone were the days of skinny migrant men from Anatolia living in shacks in old Byzantine cisterns. These men were connected. What they were not were the stone- and abuse-throwers the squatters had described. There were plenty of candidates for that, running around the streets being 'perfect'. But now they'd been warned, maybe the harassment would stop. For a while.

He was about to walk back over the hill to his mistress's much more convivial district when he noticed that a man was staring at him. Not unusual behaviour in a district like Çarşamba. Süleyman was about to ignore it when the starer, an old man, walked over.

'I need to speak to you, bey efendi,' he said, addressing the policeman formally.

'Of course.'

'But not out here. Would you come to my home?'

'Yes. What is your name?'

'I am Imam Özgür Ayan,' he said. And then he began to cry.

Meltem was conflicted. On the one hand, she loved living at the Art House, because she could pursue her writing in peace. She was also able to share a room with her best friend, Ahu. They'd been to school together at Notre Dame de Sion. Ahu shared her views on everything, including covering. But there were down sides. The house could get very noisy on occasion, a lot of the residents smoked, and there was alcohol. However, at the present time, Meltem was more concerned about food than anything else. The Anatolia Gold scandal didn't seem to bother anyone in the house except Ahu and her. She'd spoken to Uğur Bey about it many times and he had assured her that the kitchen was guaranteed pork-free. But then she'd seen a tin of beans in one of the larders. It had been an Anatolia Gold product from the previous year. It had to be contaminated. Either Uğur Bey had missed it or he'd lied. Either way, she knew she couldn't trust him.

Now it was dark and most of the residents were out. Uğur Bey had taken his family over to Üsküdar to visit his mother, Ahu was at a study group evening and most of the others were out at local bars. She had the kitchen to herself.

The fridge contained bottles of beer, but there was nothing she could do about that. As long as she wasn't drinking alcohol herself, that was all right. Alcohol was *contained*. What was so frightening about pork was that it could be anywhere. Ziya had some slices of something meaty on his shelf, which was directly above hers, but she didn't dare touch it. Instead she moved her food towards the back of the fridge so that it didn't sit underneath his stuff. But it wasn't really the fridge that bothered her. It was the larders.

She'd just seen one tin of beans and that had freaked her. How many more were there? What if there were a lot and she threw them all out? Would people be angry, or wouldn't they notice?

But whatever happened, there was no point prevaricating. She either looked or she didn't. She knew the one tin she had found was in the cupboard nearest the back door. She started there. The offending tin was still there and, now that she looked more carefully, it wasn't the only Anatolia Gold product on the shelves. There were lots more behind. Meltem shook her head. Was it all right to touch tins that contained pork? If only her parents had been religious, she would have grown up knowing such things. But her entire family was secular and so she, like Ahu, knew very little. Maybe when Ahu returned from her study evening she'd be able to advise her.

Meltem opened the back door. If she threw the tins straight into the bin and then washed her hands, that had to be OK. She could carry four tins at a time, and as far as she could see, she'd need to make about five trips.

It was on her fourth trip that someone grabbed her from behind.

'Why didn't you tell us before?' Süleyman said.

Imam Ayan shook his head. 'The shame. I know it's ridiculous, but I felt that if I just ignored it, they'd come back and all would be well. I told people they'd gone to visit their uncle, my brother, in Afyon. But then it became unbearable and so I told the truth. Some people here applauded, said the boys were martyrs. And in spite of all my learning, my years and years of study devoted to Islam, I wondered. I tricked myself into believing that if I told the police, I would be committing a sin. I deluded myself.'

Süleyman sat down beside the old man. 'Do you have any idea where Burak was texting from?'

'I have my phone.' He held it out. 'You can take it.'

'Thank you.'

Imam Ayan was not of a generation that could easily deal with mobile phones. Süleyman quickly scrolled through the text register.

'So the text came first. When did you receive the call from your son?'

'About two.'

'Any other calls since?'

'A couple. Local people.'

There was a number unknown at 2:23.

'I'll have to get our technical people to try and trace it,' he said.

'He called from Syria.' The imam shook his head. 'From that terrible place they all go. What did I do wrong, bey efendi? I have always tried to live by the Holy Koran. I have spoken out about the horrors that people commit in the name of our religion. These are people I warned my sons about every day!'

'You've done nothing wrong,' Süleyman said. 'Do you know who Burak and Mustafa might have been associating with in recent months? How old are they?'

'Burak is nineteen, Mustafa seventeen – he is the larger of the two. They have no work. That has been a problem. Too much time spent in that park.'

'The one in the cistern.'

'Yes, all sorts hang around there. I have nothing against the refugees who have come from Syria, but not all of them are good people. Some of the boys who beg in the streets also steal.'

'Your sons befriended these Syrians?'

'Some. But what do I know? My wife, a Syrian herself, died many years ago, and I haven't been there for the boys like a mother can. I've had to work.' He shook his head.

'Did your sons have some curiosity about their mother's country?' Süleyman said.

He shrugged. 'Not that I know about. All that interested them, apart from being in the park, was that computer I got them.'

Süleyman looked around the room, but he didn't see a computer.

'It's in their bedroom,' the imam said. 'Oh, they nearly drove me mad asking and asking for that thing.'

'When did you get it?'

'Last year,' he said. 'An Apple. I paid so much money for it! But they were delighted. On it every night.'

Süleyman began to feel cold. Hanging around with a few Syrian refugees probably hadn't done the boys too much harm. Even mixing with local austere and pious youth probably wasn't enough. But if the Ayan boys had been radicalised, then the Internet had probably been their greatest influence.

'Can I see the computer?' he asked.

'Yes.'

The old man took him to a small room upstairs where two neat beds were overshadowed by a very large computer screen.

'I bought the best and biggest one that I could afford.'

'Can I switch it on?'

'Yes.'

Süleyman sat down on one of the beds and started the machine.

'Is it password-protected?'

'Oh yes, my neighbour Imad Bey set that up for us. It is the name of my late wife, Zanubiya.'

He spelled it out while Süleyman typed.

A sound like the opening chords of a military march heralded the coming of the screen saver, which was ghastly.

She didn't know who was speaking. He didn't introduce himself. He just arrived in her office.

'You see the difficulty we have,' Commissioner Teker said.

'I do.'

He was younger than her, probably forty, and looked as if he had a drink problem. Unshaven and, by the look of his eyes, sleep-deprived, he stank of cigarettes and cheap aftershave. His whole demeanour was that of a man who hunted and was hunted for a living.

'We thought, begging your pardon, that Boris Myskow had

entered our jurisdiction when we discovered wild boar in his freezers,' Teker said. 'We were clearly wrong. But a missing person is most definitely under our jurisdiction.'

'I can see you'd think that,' he said.

'Well, isn't it?'

He scratched his head.

'One of his employees has gone missing,' she continued. 'His wife has contacted us expecting that we fulfil our duty and look for him. She says that the last time she saw him was on Saturday evening, when he left for work at the Imperial Oriental. No one called her from the hotel to say that he hadn't arrived, and so she, and we, have to assume that he completed his shift. If we don't look for Celal Vural, it will seem odd.'

'Myskow is not your business.'

'Maybe not, but he is Vural's employer. We have to question him. Can you see my problem?'

'Yeah.'

His hands fidgeted. She knew the score. He needed a cigarette. But she didn't open her window and offer him the chance to smoke, as she routinely did with Cetin İkmen. Whoever he was, he marched to the kind of drum that could damage her for breaking the rules, even in a small way.

'So what do I do?' she said.

She hated having any sort of contact with people like him. Spooks made her blood boil. She knew that sometimes they were needed. But she didn't have to like it.

The man sighed. 'I'll get back to you,' he said.

'And will that take long?'

It wasn't easy not to shout at him. A woman and her children were without their breadwinner. For them it was serious, and if Celal Vural's body turned up in a rubbish bin somewhere in the meantime, it could be as serious as it got.

The man stood. 'I'll be in touch,' he reiterated.

Teker wondered how long it would take. The man's organisation could be very quick to move when they wanted, but they could also be glacially slow when they didn't. She remained seated. 'I need an answer.'

'You'll get one.'

'Soon.'

He looked down his nose at her, barely suppressing a sneer. She knew what he thought of her. She was an old bag who should have retired years ago. She looked into his eyes and could see that he'd marked her in his head. A troublesome woman.

Fuck it. 'Unlike you, I have to deal directly with the wife and the wider public,' she said. 'Make sure it's soon, and close my office door on your way out.'

She very pointedly looked at her computer.

He slammed the door when he left and she cursed him. 'Arsehole!'

'You!'

Meltem had recognised the boy who hurled abuse at them immediately. Small, dark and dressed in dirty black clothes, he was one of the kids from Fatih district. But he wasn't usually on his own.

'Where are the other boys?' she asked.

She'd had to fight him off. He'd come in through the kitchen door and put his hand over her mouth. She'd bitten it. Then she'd punched him. Now he was crouched in a corner beside the washing machine, holding his hand up to staunch the bleeding.

'Well?'

She towered over him. He didn't meet her gaze. Nor did he speak. But then she remembered that he probably didn't understand what she was saying. İsmet Bey had tried to talk to him and found out that he only spoke Arabic. Meltem had studied Arabic at university. She said, 'OK, let's get down to business, shall we? What do you want? And what's this rubbish about İsmet Bey doing something bad with your friends?'

The boy's eyes widened, but he didn't say anything.

'What's your name?' she said. 'That easier for you? Or are you so surprised that you've just been bitten by a covered woman that you need some time to absorb the shock?'

Still he said nothing.

'Lost your voice, have you?'

'No.'

He mumbled into his own hunched chest. Meltem shook her head.

'So you now know I can speak your language,' she said. 'Then let's talk, shall we? What do you want? Why won't you leave us alone, and what do you think we've done with your friends?'

'I don't know. Killed them.'

'Killed them?' she laughed. 'Why would we do that, eh? They're just kids like you. Honestly, if you think you and your loud-mouthed friends are anything other than an annoyance to us . . .'

'They came here and then they disappeared,' the boy said.

'What, inside the building? That's stupid. No one would just let people like them in here. This is the second time you've broken in here, isn't it?'

'Some man hit me.'

'I don't know about that,' she said. 'But I do know those boys you hang around with. They're not here.'

Slowly, the boy stood. He was very small.

'I thought that because you are a sister you would understand, but you don't.'

Meltem clicked her tongue. Why did men and boys with any sort of Islamist agenda think that she would automatically agree with anything they said?

'If you weren't talking rubbish then I might,' she said. 'If your

88

friends have disappeared, it's nothing to do with us. Maybe they've run away to do what they think in their twisted little minds is jihad.'

Meltem had had quite enough of these kids.

'And anyway, you assaulted me,' she said. 'I think your story about your friends is nonsense. You just wanted to get in here so you could steal from us.'

'No!'

'Oh I think the young lady is right.'

Meltem recognised the voice; it made her smile.

'Deniz Bey.'

He was old enough to be her grandfather, but Major General Deniz Baydar was charming, handsome and possessed the most exquisite manners. He was also a friend of Uğur Bey.

'I didn't know you could speak Arabic,' Meltem said.

'Ah, there is a lot that isn't known about me,' Deniz Bey said.

'All good?'

'Of course!'

They both laughed.

Deniz Bey changed to Turkish. 'So what is . . .?'

Meltem saw his face drop.

'Bey efendi?'

'Wasn't there a boy here just now?' the old soldier said.

Meltem turned her head and saw that the Syrian had gone.

Chapter 9

One of the Ayan boys' favourite websites was entirely in English.

'Think they just liked the pictures?' Cetin İkmen said.

Mehmet Süleyman winced. On the screen, men dressed entirely in black nailed a man already covered in blood to a cross. The victim's screams were hard to bear. He turned the sound off.

İkmen leaned back in his chair.

'If the Ayan boys have gone to Syria, what does the imam want us to do about it?' he said.

Süleyman sighed. 'I think he has some notion that we can get the surviving boy back.'

'Well we can't. If he's in Syria, then that's that. All we can do is find out whether these particular boys radicalised any other kids and warn their parents. Why wasn't the imam on top of this?'

'To be fair to Imam Ayan, his sin, for want of a better word, was not one of radicalisation but of omission,' Süleyman said. 'The boys' mother died when they were small, and he didn't spend much time with them. She was Syrian, by the way.'

'Ah. Family still in the country?'

'I doubt it,' Süleyman said. 'She was a Christian. She converted to Islam when she married the imam.'

'Mmm, few Christians in Syria now. Unless the family were from Damascus, I suppose.'

'Yes, but even if they are still in the country, the boys wouldn't have gone to them, would they?' Süleyman said. He pointed to the computer screen. 'They've gone to be with this lot. We'll have to see what else the technicians can get off this machine and from the imam's phone.'

İkmen shook his head. 'I take it you got a less than enthusiastic greeting in the neighbourhood?'

'If the Ayan boys were sharing this material with their friends, it probably found some willing viewers,' he said. 'But then maybe that's my cynicism speaking. Not all bored young boys will be attracted to this.'

'But a proportion will be.'

'Yes. Sadly. I did ring Uğur İnan at the squat, and he said they'd had no trouble from kids in the last few days. I wonder if a whole group have gone.'

'Did you ask the imam if he knew of any other cases?'

'Yes, and he said he didn't. I know you don't like clerics . . .'

'It's not that I don't like them.'

'You have issues,' Süleyman said.

'Well, yes.'

'But Imam Ayan did do quite a brave thing by talking to me. Maybe it'll lead to others coming forward.'

'Or trouble for the imam?'

He shrugged. 'I don't think so. Say what you like about that area, people do respect their religious leaders. If Ayan is vocal about his disgust for what his boys have done, maybe others will follow.'

İkmen turned the computer screen off. 'I can't take any more of that. How has the world got into this state, eh?'

'I don't know.'

They sat in silence for a few moments, then İkmen said, 'And this isn't even part of our investigation, which may have got rather more complicated in light of a finding from the forensic laboratory that Dr Sarkissian has promised to talk to me about tomorrow morning.'

'What's that?'

'Our cannibalised victim was a carrier of a rare disease, apparently.'

'Which one?'

'He wanted to be a hundred per cent certain the results were correct before he told me,' İkmen said. 'But apparently, according to the doctor, if the lab is right, we could have even more problems with this investigation.'

'Arto?'

He looked up. Had he really been staring at his napkin?

'What's the matter?' Maryam Sarkissian said. 'Are you not feeling well?'

Cetin İkmen had suggested he come to this very prestigious restaurant and keep his wits about him, and he was drifting off into space. But then that too was indirectly because of Cetin İkmen. Waiting for the kind of phone call he was expecting was hard. If that first test on the consumed human flesh was confirmed by a second, then they were in an even more bizarre world of possibilities than they'd been in to begin with. Every part of him wanted it to be wrong. But every part of him also knew that it wasn't.

'I've decided on the scallop tartare with nasturtiums,' his wife said.

Arto looked at the menu. Unlike Cetin İkmen, he enjoyed food. But this wasn't his kind of meal. Things like scallops and foie gras didn't excite him. A large bowl of lentil soup, or even tripe, was more his sort of thing. Eventually he settled on prawns.

When the waiter had taken their order, he got on with the job at hand and looked around. He could remember when the Imperial Oriental had been called the Kazanjian Hotel, after its one-time owner, Zenor Kazanjian. Arto's parents had often dined at the old restaurant, not that Zenor Kazanjian had been running the place even then. He and his family had left the city for the USA by that time. When he looked around, Arto could see only one man he recognised as Armenian. He wondered if he, a local car dealer, came because the restaurant had once been Armenian-owned.

'How clever of you to get a cancellation,' Maryam said.

'Thank you.'

Oddly, it had been easy. He had wondered whether maybe Istanbul had fallen out of love with Boris Myskow's revolutionary cooking. But the place was full. He must've just got lucky. He smiled at his wife. 'You look lovely.'

She turned her head away slightly. Going out in public was still a strain for Maryam Sarkissian. An innate feeling of inferiority had plagued her all her life. This had not been helped by multiple plastic surgery operations designed to improve what she considered to be her flawed looks and thereby bolster her self-esteem. None of it had ever contented her, and for years she'd been almost a recluse in the huge Sarkissian house on the shores of the Bosphorus. Now she was getting out a few times a month. She had been delighted when her husband had booked this meal.

'I've seen Chef Myskow on the BBC,' Maryam said. 'Do you think we'll see him in here tonight?'

'I don't know.'

There were plenty of other celebrity types on show. Arto could see one talk-show host and several footballers. However, there was also, behind a pillar nearest to the service area, a table featuring a very incongruous group of men. Although quiet and well behaved, unlike everyone else they were not dressed for dinner. They weren't dirty, but their clothes were ordinary, cheap, and not one of them wore a tie. They looked a bit like a group of un-uniformed security guards on a cigarette break, though obviously they weren't smoking.

But then Arto's phone rang and he forgot about the tie-less men in the corner.

* * *

93

'Don't be silly!'

Meltem pushed Gül away, but she laughed as she did so.

'I'm telling you, the old man has the hots for you,' Zenne Gül said.

'Deniz Bey is very proper,' Meltem said. 'He always behaves like a gentleman, and anyway, he's married.'

'To a much older woman than you.'

Gül threw himself down on the biggest floor cushion in the room and leaned his head back. 'I am exhausted!'

Meltem sat down beside him. 'What have you been doing?'

'Carrying Pembe Hanım's shopping,' he said. 'Never again. I am half her size. You know, when she was a man, she was actually in the marines.'

It was dark outside now, and Meltem was tired. But she was anxious too. The appearance of the Syrian boy had unnerved her. Deniz Bey had told her the child was simply an unfortunate derelict, maddened by war. But until very recently he had always turned up in the street with others. Two boys who spoke Turkish. Older than the Syrian, they'd been rude and aggressive. One of them had called her a whore. She'd ignored him. Why did the Syrian boy think that anyone in the squat would want to invite such people inside? She hadn't seen them. But what he wasn't deluded about was the fact that the other boys seemed to have gone somewhere.

Gül nudged her. 'You're thoughtful. Anything the matter?'

She leaned against his shoulder. It was nice having a gay friend. She liked being able to be close to a man without feeling threatened.

'Oh, I saw one of those boys who hangs around here sometimes,' she said.

'Was he rude to you? I hope you managed to get it together to tell him to fuck off.'

Meltem said nothing.

Gül hugged her. 'Honestly, he's just a moron,' he said. 'Uneducated and stupid. Did he say anything to you?'

'Yes.'

'Well tell Uncle Gül and he'll make it better.'

She laughed. 'He's got this idea that the two friends he hangs about with came in here and we killed them.'

'He's off his head!'

'Of course, but he was so worried. He kept on at me about it until Deniz Bey came and rescued me.'

'Where was this?'

'In the kitchen.'

'The little horror got in?'

'I left the back door open. I was throwing out old Anatolia Gold tins.' She shook her head. 'I know he's probably mad or ill or something, but that boy was determined to get in here. And he was upset. Whatever I may think about the things he said, he believes them.'

Neither of them spoke.

Then Gül laughed, pulled Meltem on to his lap and hugged her even tighter.

'Stop it, Meltem Abla, you're giving me the creeps!'

The park was dull without Burak and Mustafa, and because it was in an old water cistern built by Christians, it gave Radwan the creeps. Were there ghosts of priests in the walls? Would ancient artisans suddenly appear amongst the trees? He closed his eyes tight. It was hardest to bear at night, which was when he'd always been alone, ever since his family had gone. Back in Aleppo in the old days, he'd never had a moment to himself, and he'd loved it. Even that boy from Damascus, Azzam, would be some sort of company, but he hadn't seen him since he'd told him off about supporting ISIS.

Not that he did support ISIS. Radwan didn't support anyone.

He'd come to Turkey to survive. That was all. And now he had no family, he didn't even know why he was doing that. Stealing and begging were not things he'd done before. His parents had always taught him that those activities were wrong. But if he didn't steal and beg, he went hungry . . .

He'd managed to grab a piece of bread from the kitchen of the squat when the old man had come in to talk to the girl. Then he'd just run. Now the bread was long gone and Radwan was hungry again. He missed Burak and Mustafa, and now that it was the depths of the night, he wished he had their company to look forward to in the morning.

Why had Azzam told him that the boys had gone to Syria? He'd said their father was telling everyone that story, but how was Radwan to know? He didn't speak Turkish. He knew they had said they wanted to go there at some point, but he'd thought it had just been a boast. On the day the two of them had disappeared, they'd all gone to the squat together and thrown stones, and then the man with the baseball bat had come out. They had run away, but then Burak had said he was hungry. Mustafa said that there was sometimes unused food dumped in the alleyway behind the café opposite the squat, and so Radwan, as he often did, volunteered to help. He spent a good ten minutes gathering old bits of cake and börek from bins. When he'd returned, the boys had gone. It had been a hot early afternoon and the street had been silent, as if they had never existed.

Radwan had stood and looked at the squat for some time before moving on. He reckoned the boys couldn't be far away and wondered whether they were playing a hiding game with him. Although they were a bit old for that.

He'd gone down to the shore of the Bosphorus and the Karaköy ferry pier, but they hadn't been there. While he'd looked, he'd eaten all the cake and börek he'd taken from the bins, which he had felt was fair enough. If the boys had gone, who else was there to eat it?

Now he wondered whether Azzam hadn't been right and the boys had gone to Syria. They'd both known that Radwan always volunteered to do whatever they wanted. Had they sent him to the bins just to get him out of the way? Had they then run off to catch a bus to take them to the Syrian border? And if they had, how much had his made-up stories about the bravery and courage of the ISIS fighters influenced them?

Chapter 10

'It's called Bloom syndrome,' Arto said.

'I've never heard of it.'

'Oh, it's rare,' the doctor continued.

Cetin İkmen flicked his cigarette ash out of the window. He knew his friend didn't like him smoking, but it was his office. 'You must've run every test under the sun.'

'I did. When you've got no actual corpse, you need to obtain as much information as you can from what you have got.'

'Yes, and I thank you for that. How significant is this?'

'Our man was not a victim of Bloom syndrome, but a carrier,' Arto said. 'He didn't have the disease himself, but he could have given it to his children. He would have inherited the gene from one or both of his parents. It's rare, but it does occur more frequently in Eastern European Ashkenazi Jews. It's characterised by short stature, a receding chin, extreme light sensitivity and an increased propensity to diabetes and cancer. A nasty little disease. Thank God it's not widespread.'

'Ashkenazi Jews are uncommon here. Most Turkish Jews are Sephardic.'

'Like your son-in-law.'

He nodded. One of İkmen's daughters had married a Sephardic Jew, a goldsmith called Berekiah Cohen.

'But some of the Ashkenazim settled here during and after the Second World War,' Arto said. 'I would say that maybe our man was a tourist, but then his genetic profile would seem to suggest, at least in part, a Turkish background.' He leaned across his friend's desk so that he could whisper. 'In the current climate in this part of the world . . .'

'Oh, I know,' İkmen said. 'A Jew is cannibalised in a Muslim city. Believe me, this news brings me a heap of problems. I'll have to tell Teker.'

'You will.'

İkmen shook his head. 'Good job we kept it under wraps.'

'Difficult for you.'

'Downright impossible.' He put one cigarette out and lit another. Then he said, 'How was your meal last night?'

'Overpriced.'

He laughed.

'But Maryam enjoyed it,' Arto said.

'That's the main thing. I'm glad you got her out.'

'So am I. As for myself? Well, we didn't see Mr Myskow, much to Maryam's disappointment, and the clientele were almost exclusively celebrity faux gourmets and footballers. There were a few real food aficionados who seemed to know what they were talking about. But there was also a lot of nonsense about provenance and molecular gastronomy. Went right over my head, if I'm honest. Then there was a rather odd table.'

'What do you mean?'

'Well, everyone, including Maryam and myself, was dressed for dinner as befits a venue like the Imperial Oriental. Such places tend to be very unwelcoming if you turn up in a cheap suit. But there was a table of men who had done just that. Over by the service area, just out of the main body of the restaurant, eating what we were eating but looking like a bunch of off-duty cab drivers or security guards. Not a necktie amongst them.'

'Really?'

Knowing who was protecting Myskow's boar trade, İkmen wondered whether they were spooks or, perhaps, bodyguards.

'You asked me to report anything odd, and so I have,' Arto said. 'Could they be boar hunters, do you think?'

So he'd definitely heard about the wild pig. Of course he had. The forensic lab was his second home.

'I looked for it on the menu, but sadly it wasn't there,' Arto continued.

'That's a pity.'

'I do know that the Imperial Oriental doesn't have a licence for boar. No one does. Putting two and two together with your recent outburst in the car park . . .'

'Which I can't talk about.'

They looked at each other in silence for a few moments. Arto would know that if Cetin couldn't talk to him about something, it had to be very serious.

'Don't get me wrong,' İkmen said. 'I am grateful that you went to the Imperial Oriental last night and I'm glad that Maryam had a good time, but it has been pointed out to me that Mr Myskow's establishment is beyond my investigation and so we need to abandon that line of enquiry.'

'I see.'

'Mmm.'

He didn't have to say any more.

Soon afterwards, the doctor departed, leaving İkmen to ponder the implications of Bloom syndrome and wondering why his informant in the tourist trade hadn't got back to him.

Most nights Celal Vural walked back from the Imperial Oriental Hotel in Beyoğlu to his home in Kağıthane.

'Around six kilometres,' Kerim Gürsel said. 'Every night!'

Ömer Mungun shrugged. Back in his home town of Mardin, that was nothing. People, especially older folk, walked everywhere, sometimes all day long out in the olive groves and vineyards.

The men had got together to share lunch in Gülhane Park as

they criss-crossed the city chasing up male missing person cases from up to three months ago.

'What choice did he have at that time of night?' Ömer said. 'It's get a taxi or walk, and he wasn't earning a whole lot of money.'

He'd been to the shabby home Celal Vural shared with his wife and children in Kağıthane. Even his illiterate great-uncle, who lived in the middle of nowhere, had a better standard of living than the Vurals.

'True.'

'He caught the metro to work, so he only walked one way,' Ömer said. He took a small bottle out of his pocket and poured a sticky syrup on to his egg sandwich.

Kerim shook his head. 'You know you have to forgive me for saying so, but I just don't know how you can put that stuff on egg.'

'Pomegranate molasses?' Ömer put the bottle back in his pocket. 'It's how you know you're from the south-east. If you have a desire to put it on everything, then you are; if you don't, you're not. My sister puts it on fish. I draw the line there.'

'Right.'

Kerim had bought lahmacun, which he'd folded into a roll and topped with parsley.

'How was your morning?' Ömer asked.

'I saw two relatives of missing men,' Kerim said. 'An old man in Cihangir and a woman in Etiler. She was frightening.'

'Why?'

'I think they call them cougars . . .'

Ömer laughed. 'She came on to you.'

'Just a bit.'

'What was she like?'

'Oh, attractive. Tall, slim, blonde.'

'Sounds good.'

'And wearing some very fake breasts and old enough to be your mother,' Kerim said.

'But well preserved.'

He shook his head. 'Artificially so, yes. And really pushy. As soon as I walked in there, she made it very apparent what she wanted, and it wasn't her missing husband.'

'Ah,' Ömer said. 'Think she had anything to do with the husband's disappearance?'

'She has to be a candidate. Mind you, she was in Ankara when he went missing and so you can't jump to conclusions.'

'No, but you can also never underestimate the sneakiness of the human mind,' Ömer said, 'especially where unwanted spouses are concerned.'

Kerim shrugged. 'Find out anything more about Celal Vural?'

'His wife told me he was under a lot of pressure. As well as looking after her and the kids, Celal sends money home to Trabzon to keep his ageing parents.'

'A lot of men have to do that,' Kerim said. What he didn't say was that he knew that Ömer was one of them.

'And although his wife told me initially that he liked his job at the hotel, this time she admitted he actually hated it. According to Mrs Vural, there were problems with pay – as in he didn't always get paid on time – and his boss didn't like him.'

'What, the American?'

'No. His manager.' Ömer finished his sandwich and opened his notebook. 'Ali Buyuk. Vural's wife claims this Buyuk treated her husband like a dog. On his only night off, Thursday, he covered for his brother at a nargile place in Tophane. So Celal felt trapped. He could have done a disappearing act . . .'

'Or . . .'

Ömer's phone rang. He looked at it. 'İkmen.' He answered, 'Sir.'

İkmen didn't speak for very long. When he ended the call,

Ömer said to Kerim, 'Our victim could be Jewish, apparently. At least partly so. He's a carrier of a rare disease called Bloom syndrome, which is more common amongst Jews.'

Kerim frowned. 'What does that mean? Do we have to ask people whether they're Jewish, or if Bloom syndrome is in the family?'

'So he says. I wonder if they'd even know.'

'Why?'

'Because a lot of people keep their ethnicity dark,' Ömer said. 'You know how it is. There was a family I knew well, I went to school with several of them. They all worked in the bazaar. Nobody knew the mother was Jewish until she died. Then they brought her body up here for burial. People said she was probably the last Jew in Mardin.'

The call Burak Ayan had made to his father had come from Syria. The old man shook his head.

'Did Burak say how his brother had died?' Süleyman asked the imam.

'No,' he said. 'He just said that he was dead. He told me that he would become a martyr for both of them.'

Süleyman frowned. 'Which implies to me that Mustafa didn't die in battle.'

'I don't know,' the imam said. 'He didn't say. But if Mustafa died in some other fashion, then maybe a little of what I taught my boys got through.'

'What do you mean?'

'Martyrdom is, to me, a very specific thing. People use the term thoughtlessly these days, but to die in a street brawl or a house fire is not martyrdom. When a person dies for his faith, only then can that term be used. Simply to be a Muslim and to die is not enough, and that, I think, is what Burak was saying.' He looked up. 'Can you get Burak back for me?'

He could soften the blow. But what was the point? 'Not under current circumstances,' he said.

Kurdish fighters were beginning to take on ISIS on the Iraqi border, but no Turkish troops were involved.

'I'm sorry, there's nothing I can do.'

'No. No.' The imam's eyes watered. 'I know the Kurds are there. I've seen them on the television. I have Kurdish friends, I could go.'

'I wouldn't recommend it,' Süleyman said. It was all so bleak for the old man. Was it wise or stupid to leave him with some hope? In the end he said, 'Do you have a photo of Burak? I can circulate it to officers near the border. Maybe if he comes back . . .'

The old man shook his head, but he also stood. 'I have never heard of anyone coming back from that so-called caliphate. But I'll see what I can find.'

He went to a room at the back of the house and returned a few minutes later holding a photograph.

'It's a little out of date,' he said as he handed it to Süleyman. 'The boys stopped taking photographs, except on their phones. I think this was taken last year.'

It was unusual to see a real photo as opposed to a virtual one. It showed a small, thin boy with a beard holding a puppy. He looked about as warrior-like as the little animal in his arms.

The young woman was attractive, but in a spiky, angular sort of way. She reminded İkmen a little of Ömer Mungun's sister, Peri.

'This is Constable Can,' Commissioner Teker said.

Had he seen the young woman before? Probably. İkmen saw lots of people in the course of his day. He smiled.

'Constable Can has a friend who works at the Imperial Oriental Hotel,' Teker said.

'Her name's Aysel,' Can said. Her voice was light and very

feminine, like a little girl. İkmen resisted the temptation to think about how that voice would work in a riot scenario.

'What does she do, this Aysel?'

'She's a chef,' the constable said. 'Only a junior one. At the moment.'

'But extremely well placed to see what goes on in the Imperial's kitchen,' Teker said.

İkmen's informant hadn't got back to him and Teker had said she'd had an idea if that failed.

'So, what, we'll coach this—'

'No, sir,' the young woman said. 'I'll go in.'

'How?'

'They want people to clean up,' she said. 'Restaurant kitchens always need them. It's a terrible job. People do it for a short time, get sick of it and just leave.'

'How do you know that you can get in?' he asked.

Teker and Can shared a look that İkmen didn't understand.

Then Can said, 'I sometimes go to meet Aysel from work. I've met some of her colleagues a few times. I can have a job there if I want.'

'You've already discussed it?'

How did this lowly constable know that they even needed a presence inside the Imperial Oriental Hotel? Even if she had seen the fracas with Boris Myskow, only a very few officers knew that İkmen was continuing to pursue the chef.

'I took Constable Can into my confidence,' Teker said.

Seemingly before İkmen had approached his informant. If indeed this had been her big idea. But if it had been, how had she known to approach Can? Did she somehow know this Aysel too? And how did a commissioner of police even know the name of a constable?

But he had another question. 'Do they know you're a police officer?'

'Aysel does, but no one she works with, no. Whenever I go to meet Aysel, it's to go out to a club, so I'm always dressed up. No one knows anything about me.'

'Are you sure?'

If the women were such good friends, wouldn't Aysel talk about what the constable did?

'I'm certain.'

'And so am I,' Teker said. 'Now, Inspector, if you would brief Constable Can, she is due to start at the restaurant tonight.'

It was a fait accompli. It was quite a benign one, as it meant he didn't have to try and find another way in to the Imperial Oriental himself. But it still didn't feel exactly right.

'If you would leave us for now, Constable, I'd like to speak to Inspector İkmen alone.'

'Madam.'

She left.

Teker opened her office window and offered İkmen a cigarette.

When they'd both lit up, she said, 'I expect you feel a little overridden. I know I would, but Constable Can had this contact and I would have been negligent had I ignored her.'

'Of course.'

But how had she known? He didn't want to ask her, but curiosity simply took him over. 'Madam, Constable Can—'

'Inspector, I have given my life to policing,' she said. 'I've made little impact. But . . .' She raised a hand to silence his protest. 'But if I manage to achieve anything in this current role, I want it to be for the benefit of my officers, particularly the women. Now I know that you and I think alike in lots of ways, İkmen. You are a republican, you drink, you smoke, you make up your own mind . . . But what we can't share is our gender.'

'No.'

'If women are to progress, we need to help each other. One of the things I do is actively look for female officers with what

106

I perceive to be the ability to lead. Constable Can was brought to my notice by Sergeant Bayrak. Do you know her?'

Hatice Bayrak was a hard-as-nails multiple linguist who worked for the tourism police. İkmen had a lot of time for her.

'Yes,' he said.

'Sergeant Bayrak encouraged Constable Can to join the service,' Teker said. 'I've known the sergeant for many years.'

'Me too.'

She smiled. 'I told Constable Can everything.'

'About the cannibalism?'

'Yes.'

'Mmm.'

'You think I made a mistake?'

He knew she'd be expecting him to say something like *that's not for me to say*, but instead he said, 'In view of who is involved in protecting Mr Myskow, I am surprised . . .'

'And yet I imagine even you have to accept that under these circumstances it is difficult to know who to trust,' she said. 'I would even extend that to ourselves, Cetin Bey.'

She wasn't wrong. The security services had a way of recruiting the most unexpected people. That was why they were who they were. And of course money helped.

'I believe that Constable Can will be an honest and accurate informant. I hope her friend Aysel can be trusted,' Teker said. 'And Boris Myskow is all you've managed to come up with so far. That said, he is Jewish.'

İkmen raised his eyebrows.

'Dr Sarkissian has told me that the cannibalised body could be Jewish,' she said. 'Why would Myskow prepare one of his own for the table?'

'Why would Myskow cook wild boar?'

'True.'

'He's nervous, in spite of his protectors,' İkmen said.

'Yes.'

She told him to go. As he walked along the corridor back to his office, İkmen wondered whether the old rumours about single woman Hatice Bayrak were true, and whether Constable Can suffered from the same speculation. Then he wondered about Teker.

'Do you know who I am?'

Kerim knew her surname was Baydar. She was the sister of a missing man called Volkan Doğan. He'd just asked her, tactfully he thought, whether any of her antecedents had been Jewish.

'My husband served his country in the military for all his working life,' she said. 'Not that such a thing means anything to people any more.'

'I'm sorry . . .'

'Do I look Jewish to you?'

Did Jews have a particular look? Kerim remembered going to school with the Nabarro sisters, who, it was said, had been Jewish. But they had just looked like all the other little girls at his school. Except they'd been twins.

Defne Baydar looked into his eyes. She was a small woman in late middle age, thin and severe. She wore no make-up and had met him at the door to her apartment in a pair of rubber boots. 'Well?'

'I don't know, hanım,' Kerim said. 'I've simply been asked—'

'My brother has been missing for three months,' she said. 'And after the first flurry of interest from your department, we have heard nothing. Why this sudden interest in a man with learning difficulties, eh? The policeman who came here when Volkan went missing behaved almost as if he thought my brother's disappearance was some sort of blessing.'

A lowly constable had turned up in the first instance. Defne Hanım clearly thought she was 'someone', and had been offended.

'I'm very sorry, hanım.'

'And now you come and ask me about some sort of Jewish connection.' She shook her head. 'Another attempt to taint our name?'

'Hanım, I assure you . . .'

'My husband has been to prison,' she said. 'He has served time for who knows what, some non-existent felony. And now this.'

She sat down on a vast red sofa.

'I don't know what this Jewish business is about, and quite frankly, I am not interested. My only question is whether or not you have found my brother.' She looked up at him. 'So have you?'

Once again, Kerim didn't know what to say.

Chapter 11

Mehmet Süleyman had employed a zenne at his first wedding, to his cousin Zuleika. But that had been a long time ago. Back then, the zennes had not been as glamorous as they appeared to be if Zenne Gül was anything to go by.

'I'll tell Uğur Bey you're here to see him,' the young dancer said as he led him into the communal room that Süleyman had been to the first time he'd visited the squat.

'Thank you.'

'And sorry to meet you like this,' he smiled. 'I'm just about to go to work and it's only two streets away.'

His outfit was purple. A tiny bolero above a shimmering sequin-encrusted skirt. There was a big pink rhinestone in his navel.

'It's no problem.'

Süleyman sat down. He could hear people in other rooms. Maybe they were getting ready for evenings out in bars and clubs. He picked up a listings magazine that had been flung on a cushion and began to look at what was on in Istanbul. It was only seconds later that he felt the hair on the back of his neck rise. Someone was watching him. He was sure of it. He lowered the magazine and looked around the room. But nobody was there. It took him a few moments to realise that his watcher was outside the building.

A face at the window, small and dirty, with dark, terrified eyes. As he looked into them, their owner appeared to take fright. He – Süleyman was sure it was a boy – disappeared.

'Inspector Süleyman.'

Uğur İnan walked into the room and Süleyman stood. The two men shook hands.

'What can I do for you?'

'Well, I thought I could do something for you, but maybe I can't,' Süleyman said.

'Oh?' He gestured for Süleyman to sit. 'Please . . .'

'I came to tell you that I hope you may be given some respite at least from the boys from Fatih. I have spent some time in the district talking to parents of apparently perfect children . . .'

Uğur İnan, smiling, sat down.

'I have even made contact with one of the local imams. So I was going to say that I hoped you were not going to experience any more incidents. However, I've just seen a rather dirty little face at your window.'

'Just one?'

'Yes.'

'Oh, one we can deal with, I think,' Uğur İnan said. 'Thank you for doing that, Inspector. I can imagine it wasn't easy.'

'It is trite to describe what divides certain parts of this city as a clash of cultures, but we all experience people and situations that are alien to us in what has become a truly vast conurbation in recent years.'

'True. When I was a boy, there weren't even two million people in Istanbul.'

'And now we are fourteen million,' Süleyman said. 'We all have to adapt, and that is the line I took up in Fatih. We don't even know for sure whether the kids came from there. Although it is a fair assumption.'

'It's a poor district. I think religion is only part of their problem with us.'

'Oh?'

'I think they believe we have money and the technology they

crave. Money we do have, a little, but technology is something we actively eschew. The surveillance society is not for us. Some of us have even actively come offline. But thank you anyway.'

'No problem. And next time, call us,' Süleyman said. 'We are here to serve everyone.'

The artist smiled. 'I heard that Ümit Kavaş was buried today.'

'I believe so.'

It had been reported that his father's military friends had attended in force.

'So your investigation into his death is over?'

'It never really began,' Süleyman said. 'Mr Kavaş died of natural causes; all we wanted to do was find out whether any external factors had contributed to it.'

'But you found none.'

'No,' Süleyman said. 'We didn't.'

'When service starts, you are going to have to be quick like the wind, canım,' Aysel said.

She'd helped Halide Can find her locker and put on her apron. Now they were in the kitchen, with service set to start in less than an hour.

'Chef Romero will let it be known if he's not happy with your work,' Aysel said.

'Is he a bit of a monster? I know you've said—'

'Oh, Chef Romero doesn't do anything except create dishes and tell Chef Tandoğan when he's upset about what's going on in his kitchen. He doesn't speak Turkish, canım. He tells Chef Tandoğan what he wants in Spanish and then Tandoğan yells at us.'

'Oh God.'

Aysel shook her head. 'You deal with worse, much worse than him on the streets.'

'Don't say that!'

'Well, you know! Tandoğan is nothing compared to drug dealers and—'

'Shut UP, Aysel!' She lowered her voice. 'I'm nothing to do with the police, all right?'

Aysel shook her head. 'No.' She was a pretty, plump girl with dimpled cheeks. But now she looked serious. For a moment. Then she smiled. 'But it IS exciting—'

'Shut up!'

This time Halide put a hand over her friend's mouth.

'I'm not taking my hand away until you stop behaving like a school kid,' she said.

She felt ragged, excited breathing underneath her hand and waited until it slowed.

'OK?'

Aysel nodded and Halide removed her hand.

'Yes.' Aysel took another calming breath. 'OK, so Chef Tandoğan does shout but he's only Chef Romero's servant really. He can dismiss you on the spot, though, and so you have to keep your wits about you. Chef Myskow will hardly ever come, but when he does, you mustn't look at him.'

'Why not?'

'He doesn't like it,' Aysel said. 'If you do look at him, he might dismiss you.'

Halide muttered under her breath, 'This is a minefield.'

Aysel gave her a packet of plastic gloves. 'It can be,' she said. 'Come on, let's go out the back for a quick cigarette. We've got time.'

They went through the staffroom and out through a door that led on to a terrace. Outside, the air was choked with petrol fumes but the view was amazing. The Bosphorus and the Golden Horn illuminated by the lights of a million homes and hovels. Out on the water, ferries sailed from Europe to Asia and back again. Halide was a born-and-bred İstanbullu, often infuriated by the dirt, the smell and the size of her city. But she never tired of the views.

Both girls lit cigarettes.

'What about the other people in the kitchen?' Halide asked.

'Well, you know Muammer and Serra. They wait at table. Then there's Zerrin, who is also a cleaner. She's a bit slow in the head, if you know what I mean.'

'If she's slow, why hasn't Chef Tandoğan got rid of her?' Halide said.

'Because she's the mother of a friend of Mr Myskow,' Aysel said. 'Don't worry about her, she doesn't speak. All the sous-chefs and the waiting staff are fine apart from Ali Buyuk, who's the front-of-house manager. He's a prick, but you won't have to get involved with him. Except for Chef Romero and Chef Tandoğan, the only people you have to worry about are Mr Myskow's friends. Or rather his guests. I don't know.'

'Who are they?' This was the first time Halide had heard anything about Myskow actually entertaining personal guests. 'What are they like?'

'They vary,' Aysel said. 'Some of them are celebrities, but you don't have to worry about them because they rarely notice us. Some are rough, look like gangsters to me, but I don't know that they are. They don't bother us really, except some of the younger girls don't like the way they look at them. The smartly dressed men who sometimes come are really creepy, though. Muammer said he thinks they might be businessmen. But they don't often come to the kitchen. They may walk through occasionally, but Mr Myskow always entertains them in a private room up in the conference suite, so there's a limit to how much time you have to spend being disgusted by them.'

'Ugh. But you have to cook for them.'

'Oh no,' Aysel said. 'Mr Myskow always cooks when that lot come.'

Was that perhaps where the wild boar was cooked? Or something worse? Halide felt her heart begin to race. Were these parties for friends significant?

'How does that work?'

'There's another kitchen on the first floor,' Aysel said. 'It's a service kitchen for the conference rooms. You can cook there, but it's just a bit of a pain because it has no freezers. You're up and down the back stairs all the time. But when Mr Myskow cooks for these people, he makes sure that everything he needs is already in place.'

Halide smoked and thought. Aysel knew that Celal Vural, a waiter she was acquainted with vaguely, was missing. She didn't know what Mr Myskow had in at least one of his freezers, and who was making sure he was able to keep it a secret.

Cetin İkmen knew that he should probably be more adventurous when it came to places to drink, but the Mozaik Bar was close to home, and if he went there, people always knew where to find him. This evening those people were Ömer Mungun and his sister Peri, who had just taken a new job at the Armenian Hospital in Yedikule.

'I've always wanted to work with elderly mentally ill people,' Peri said.

'You're brave,' İkmen said. His own father had suffered from dementia at the end of his life, and he'd found living with him very hard.

Peri looked at her brother. 'Our grandfather developed Alzheimer's disease,' she said. 'It was very tough for our mother. Whatever can be done to make life easier for their families has to be a good thing. And the Surp Pirgiç Hospital takes people from all communities.'

'The staff used to be mainly Armenian, though,' İkmen said.

'Oh yes, many still are,' Peri said.

Ömer looked up. 'The grandfather Peri speaks of was Armenian,' he said. 'Mardin has always been a mixed city.'

'Yes. Inspector Süleyman worked down there for a few months some years ago,' İkmen said. 'There are some ancient and very diverse sects in that area.'

Neither of the Munguns said anything. Had he hit on a raw nerve? ISIS fighters were just across the border from Mardin in Syria.

İkmen raised his glass. 'Well here's to your new job, Peri. Şerefe!'

'Şerefe.'

Their glasses met and everyone smiled. Ömer's phone rang and he excused himself from the table.

Alone with Peri, İkmen said, 'Ömer tells me that you now have cats.'

She smiled. 'Yes, two Vans.'

'Ah, the swimming cats.'

'Yes, but Zeytin and Aslan don't really get the chance to do that.' She lit a cigarette. She was a striking young woman with her slanted green eyes and long, slim legs. A lot of men also seated outside the Mozaik looked at her.

'My cat's wandering around here somewhere,' İkmen said.

'Oh? What's its name?'

'Marlboro,' İkmen said. 'A huge ragged male.'

Peri laughed.

'He's just a street cat. My wife can't stand him, although she should be used to him by now.'

'Have you had Marlboro long, Inspector?'

'This one, about five years,' he said. 'We've had, I think, six or seven Marlboros over the years. All street cats, all loud, all oddly devoted to me.'

'Well if you feed them . . .'

Ömer returned and sat down. He looked at his sister. 'Excuse me, Peri, I need to talk about work.'

'It's OK.' She snuggled into her gin and tonic and watched the world go by. She was used to her brother's work breaking into their lives.

'Sir, that was Celal Vural's wife,' Ömer said.

'Didn't you go to see her this afternoon?'

'Yes,' he said. 'When apparently, so she says now, she lied to me.'

İkmen frowned.

'I asked Mrs Vural whether her husband had any Jewish ancestors,' Ömer said. 'She became quite flustered . . .'

'Yes, that question does cause some people trouble,' İkmen said. 'Kerim was virtually thrown out of one property for asking it. But what else can we do?'

Ömer shrugged. 'Anyway, Mrs Vural told me that no, her husband had no Jewish antecedents. Now, however, she phones up telling me that she lied.'

'Celal Vural is a rabbi?'

He laughed. 'No, sir, but his father was a Jew, and what's more, he was Ashkenazi.'

'Interesting.' İkmen lit a cigarette.

'The family's original surname was Bronstein,' Ömer said. 'Celal's father came to Turkey as a refugee from Germany during the Second World War. Once here, he changed his name, his religion and his past.'

'A lot of Jews fleeing the camps did that,' İkmen said.

'And he was old when Celal was born,' Ömer said. 'He died soon after that, so Celal was brought up by his Turkish mother, Bronstein's second wife.'

'How sad.'

'How typical,' Peri said. 'Sorry, I couldn't help overhearing. It is sad, Cetin Bey, it's also terrifying. If people can't be honest about who they are—'

'Mrs Vural says there are some papers relating to her

father-in-law in her husband's possession but she can't read German,' Ömer said.

He'd cut very rudely across his sister. He usually showed her a great deal of respect. Why had he done that?

'I speak German,' İkmen said. 'But if Mr Bronstein did have Bloom syndrome, it's unlikely he would have known about it. I looked it up, and it wasn't discovered until the 1950s. And anyway Vural only went missing on Saturday night so the timings don't work unless his wife is lying, which is unlikely. But then if our victim is a relative of Vural's . . . Are there photographs?'

'I don't know,' Ömer said.

'I'll go and see her.'

'Yes, sir.'

Peri Mungun finished her gin and tonic quickly and with a furious expression on her face. It didn't disappear when she asked her brother for another drink.

'And make it a large one,' she said as she handed him her empty glass.

Ömer said nothing.

They hadn't touched each other for decades. Defne Baydar had only stayed with him because he'd been to prison and because she believed he was innocent. How could he be anything else if he was her husband? She didn't even like him. And now she was angry with him too.

'The effrontery of it!' she said. 'Coming here asking whether my brother was a Jew!'

The major general said nothing.

'If it wasn't for you, the police would never have asked such a question!'

Still he didn't reply.

'Deniz Bey!'

'What?' Finally he looked at her. 'I don't know why the police would ask you whether your brother was Jewish. Why would I know that? I wasn't here!'

'No, you were getting drunk with Abdullah Bey . . .'

'Because he buried his son today,' her husband said. 'You know, a child? Something you could never give me . . .'

She tried not to react, but she failed. A sound like a growl came out of her mouth.

'Oh don't spit your poison at me,' he said. 'I don't know why the police asked you anything about Volkan. I thought they'd stopped looking for him months ago.'

'Apparently not. Apparently even they care more than you do!'

'And since when were you so concerned?' he said. 'You were the one who locked him in his room whenever we had guests. No wonder he got as far away from here as he could, whenever he could.'

'We don't know where my brother has gone, or even if he's alive.'

'No, because you're too busy worrying about inane questions from policemen to go out and look for him.'

'I have looked for him,' she said. 'Why do you think I go out every day scouring the parks?'

He shook his head. 'Because you've nothing better to do?'

'I wish you'd just die, and I do mean that,' she said.

He shrugged.

'Anyway, you should be grateful I didn't tell him about *you*.'

'What about me, Defne?' he said. 'Going to give him a list of affairs I've had with other women? An account of my drinking habits? Your so-called fear for my sanity?'

'You talk such nonsense!'

'Ach!' He waved a dismissive hand.

She didn't say anything for a moment. Then she blurted out, 'I could've told him about your mother.'

119

'My mother?' He leaned forward and spoke into her face. 'My mother is dead. She never liked you. What are you going to do about it?'

'Your mother was a Jew!' she yelled. 'Not my brother! Not me! Your mother!'

Major General Baydar raised his hands in a gesture of exasperation. 'Oh for God's sake, Defne, how many times do I have to tell you? My mother was Austrian.'

'An Austrian Jew! What was her name?'

'You know what it was!'

'Bergfeld,' she said. 'Berg-feld.' She snapped her fingers in his face. 'Jewish!'

Deniz Baydar stood. 'One more time, Defne,' he said. 'And only one more. My mother's father, Heinrich Bergfeld, was seconded to the Ottoman Army in 1915. He was a Christian. Her mother was a Turkish Muslim from Antep. My mother was not a Jew . . .'

'And yet you believe lies about our ancestors!'

'What lies?' he said. 'If you mean do I believe that our ancestors caused the deaths of over a million Armenians, then you're talking nonsense. I do not. Don't accuse me of *that*!'

She waved a hand across her face. 'No, not that! I mean the rubbish you talk with your friends about how our forebears did things, terrible things . . .'

'Oh, you mean the fact that the early Anatolians were bloodthirsty pagans who worshipped idols and murdered people? They did. It's how they survived. Those were tough times – just like now.'

Defne Baydar shuddered. Her husband, though not a traitor, often talked about ancient Anatolia and how their ancestors had committed barbarous acts. She didn't want to hear it. As far as she was concerned, her ancestors were nice law-abiding Muslims who occasionally drank alcohol and never had sex outside marriage. She was not alone in this belief. A lot of people subscribed to the notion of saintly forebears. Just not her husband.

She walked towards the door. As she left the room, she heard him say, 'At least our ancestors got laid without guilt.'

Chapter 12

'Oh dear.'

Meltem and Ahu were used to just walking into Zenne Gül's bedroom. He never had anyone with him, but he was sometimes hung-over. This was one of those occasions.

Meltem put a glass of water down beside the bed. 'I'm sorry, Gül,' she said, 'but you don't look fabulous this morning.'

'Then why did you wake me?'

Actually he did look cute, even if he reeked of alcohol. Zenne Gül was, in many ways, the brother Meltem had never had.

'Because Ziya and Bülent are going to knock down the old bathhouse behind the kitchen today,' she said. 'The noise and the dust are going to be terrible. The boys want us out by ten.'

'Ten!' He looked at his clock. It was already nine. He flopped back on to the bed. 'Why?'

'Because the bathhouse is falling down,' Meltem said.

'No. Why is it happening so early?'

'To get it done in one day, I imagine.'

'God!'

He put a hand over his eyes.

'You can stay here if you want,' Meltem said. 'But they're going to use power tools and so it'll be loud and really dusty.'

Gül sipped some water. 'But where shall I go? What are you doing? Are you at college today?'

'No. Ahu and I thought we'd go to Yıldız Park and have a picnic. You can come too if you want.'

He didn't look impressed. The outdoors wasn't really Zenne Gül's thing. But he said, 'As long as I can lie down.'

She laughed. 'I don't see why not.'

He flopped back on his pillows again. 'And we must get a taxi. I'll pay. I made good tips last night.'

'Then I won't say no,' Meltem said.

'I should think not, young lady.'

Halide Can was one of those women who had a naturally sallow complexion. Now she also had dark purple circles underneath her eyes, which made her look ill. Cetin İkmen indicated that she should sit.

'You look tired, if you don't mind my saying,' he said.

She shook her head. 'I've never worked so hard in my life.'

He smiled. 'One of my sons worked in a professional kitchen when he was a student. His mother used to wait up for him to come home so that she could make up a bowl of lavender water for his feet.'

'I must remember to do that,' Can said. 'But I'm not here to talk about my feet . . .'

'No.'

'I didn't see Myskow last night. But I did find out that he sometimes hosts private dinners for selected guests in one of the conference rooms. It's on the first floor, and there's another kitchen up there, which is where he goes to prepare and cook these meals.'

'Do you know who comes to these private dinners?'

'Men who Aysel says make some of the girls feel uncomfortable whenever they walk through the main kitchen.'

İkmen considered whether young women were the only weakness these men had. Sequestered away from the main restaurant with experimental chef Myskow, they could be doing anything. Maybe eating anything.

'Local?'

'Turkish. Some are apparently celebrities. But no names were mentioned. I have to be careful what I say even to Aysel, so I didn't push it. But nothing like that was on last night. It was just the main restaurant service. I did find out that Celal Vural was not popular with the management, though.'

'We know he didn't get on with his manager, Ali Buyuk.'

'One of the waiters told me that Vural tended to be a bit mouthy.'

İkmen frowned. 'Meaning?'

'It sounds like he's a bit of a socialist,' she said. 'Very keen on getting people to unionise.'

'I don't suppose that went down well.'

'He'd been up on a disciplinary, but that was some months ago. Lately, apparently, he'd toned it down. They know what we know.'

'That he's missing?'

'Yes. The day he disappeared, he did his shift as usual and said he was going home. What I did see was a group of incongruous men who sat at a table in the restaurant away from everyone else. They were dressed very casually, and if you'd asked me, I would've been inclined to say they were undercover cops.'

'Would you?' İkmen thought he knew who they were, which was not a million miles away from Can's observation. Or Arto Sarkissian's.

'Aysel reckons they come often.'

'Do they eat?'

'Yes,' she said. 'And they're very quiet. Looking at them, I'd expect them to be noisy and drink lots of beer, but they don't drink at all.'

If they were on duty, which they almost certainly were, they wouldn't drink.

'Did you see the freezers?'

'I saw them, but I didn't have any reason to go anywhere near them,' she said. 'I'll try to have a look tonight. But all my job consists of is washing up, sweeping the floor and cleaning down after the chefs. It's constant. Service begins and it's chaos until it finishes.'

'Then what happens?'

'Then I have to clean up. There's three of us. Me, Zerrin, who is an older lady and the mother of a friend of Myskow's – don't know who – and a student called Birce. The cooking staff go out the back for a smoke; the cleaners try to go but don't always make it. I'll see if I can have a look around tonight, but I had to work myself in first, sir.'

'Of course. You did the right thing,' İkmen said. 'If you'd gone digging around in freezers when you didn't need to, it would have looked odd. In the meantime, I have some news for you, which is that Celal Vural was, or is, half Jewish.'

'Oh. So's Myskow.'

'Yes, I know, and so is our unknown victim,' İkmen said. 'It may mean nothing and it may mean everything, I really don't know. But you should be aware of it.'

'Yes, sir.'

'Hopefully I will find out more later today when I go and see Mrs Vural. And you should go home and rest up for your shift tonight.'

There had been spite behind the old woman's words. It was entirely irrelevant whether or not her husband's mother had been Jewish, and yet she seemed to have delighted in making a special phone call to tell him.

Kerim remembered when her husband had been arrested, but there hadn't been anything in the press about Jewish antecedents. And given that Deniz Baydar had been up on charges of treason, it would almost certainly have been common knowledge. Kerim wrote a quick note about it and then went back to the photograph Süleyman had given him.

Although according to his father, the imam, the photograph of Burak was a year or more out of date, Kerim doubted whether the kid had changed much in that time. Small, thin and wearing a straggly beard, he was an unsmiling youth by the look of him. He also wore a lot of clothes. Religious kids did tend to, but Burak Ayan looked as if he was kitted out for winter. Maybe he was. But the picture was bright and full of sunshine.

Inspector Süleyman had told the boy's father that there was nothing they could do to try and get him back, but Kerim had been told to circulate this picture to police and jandarma posts near the borders with Iraq and Syria. He suspected that Süleyman felt sorry for the old imam and so felt obliged to do something even if it was futile. Kids like Burak Ayan were trying to get to the caliphate every day. Stopping them was difficult largely because ISIS had handlers all over Europe and the Middle East who were skilled at getting the youngsters to the front line.

At forty, Kerim Gürsel was hardly an old man, but he'd seen the world change out of all recognition. On a personal level he'd seen acceptance of gay lifestyles grow in Turkey to the extent that, at one time, he'd almost felt able to come out in public. Sinem had shared those feelings. But then, almost out of the blue, conservative voices had begun to attract attention – and power. Of course this hadn't really happened out of the blue at all. With sectarian violence endemic in neighbouring Iraq, and the devastating arrival on the international scene of al-Qaeda in 2001, new forces had been rising for some time. None of them tolerated homosexuals.

Why were kids like Burak Ayan attracted to such illiberal ideologies? When Kerim had been that boy's age, he'd been ragingly left wing. Why would anyone want less freedom? But then he looked at the photograph again. A small boy in thick, shabby clothes clutching his puppy. Neither of the Ayan brothers had been able to find a job. And so, decent upbringing aside, what did they have to look forward to?

The reality was that the boys had been an easy mark for the extremist recruiters. The caliphate had probably given them something to live for even if it had sent Mustafa to his death. They would never get Burak home.

Radwan watched the imam. He was sure the old man didn't see him. But Azzam did.

'You should tell Imam Ayan what you did,' he whispered. 'Only then will you feel at peace with yourself.'

But Radwan was scared. If the imam knew what he'd said to his boys, he'd kill him.

'I don't speak Turkish,' Radwan said.

'But the imam speaks Arabic,' Azzam said. 'You know this. The boys' mother was Syrian.'

Radwan began to sweat. Who was this boy and why did he keep bothering him?

'Go away!'

Azzam laughed. 'If you don't tell the imam, then I will.'

'Why? What business is it of yours?'

He wanted to tell him to fuck off, but he didn't dare. Azzam was bigger than he was, and there was no one else in the park. It was midday and hot and the whole area looked dead.

'Why do I think you should tell the imam?' Azzam swung from a tree branch and then dropped expertly to the ground. 'Well, it's the right thing to do,' he said. 'And I know that you made it all up and so you do need to be punished. But most of all I think you should tell him because you were with Burak and Mustafa on the day they went missing. I saw you. You came back alone. Did you watch them get on a bus to the Syrian

127

border? If you did, you should tell their father. He cries all the time now, just like I did when I had to come to this country without my family.'

'I haven't done anything to your family! Leave me alone!'

'Making you feel guilty?'

He was. Radwan knew he should have been to see the imam as soon as he'd realised the boys had gone off somewhere. Except that all this business about Syria was nonsense. The boys had been taken by the weirdos in the squat. He'd been trying to get them out so that their father didn't have to. But he'd failed. He knew that the imam would go crazy at him when he found out, but what choice did he have? If he didn't do something, then Azzam would, and if that happened, the imam would probably kill him.

'My husband wasn't a real Jew, bey efendi.'

The woman's apologetic demeanour made Ömer Mungun cringe. If Peri had been with him, she would have screamed. But Cetin İkmen was more conciliatory, at least on the surface.

'Nobody is saying that your husband is a Jew, Selma Hanım,' he said. 'Not that being a Jew is a bad thing. It isn't. But you told Sergeant Mungun yourself that his father was.'

Selma Vural sat down. 'Yes.'

She had some papers in her hand. Two of her children clung to her legs as she sweated in the heat of one of the hottest days of the year. The poor woman had to be worried. Alone, she couldn't pay the rent or even feed her kids.

She showed the papers to İkmen. 'I don't know what these are,' she said. 'My husband said they were in German.'

'I can speak German, let me see.'

İkmen sat opposite the woman. She placed the papers in his hands. 'There's a photograph as well,' she said.

İkmen scanned the documents and the photograph while Ömer

looked over his shoulder. According to his co-workers, Celal had been something of a socialist, which was no wonder given where he lived. Just minutes from upmarket Etiler, the Vurals' apartment block was a run-down sewage-scented disgrace.

İkmen said, 'Your father-in-law was Leo Bronstein, born 1910 in Berlin. His father was a goldsmith and so I imagine the family were well off. This,' he held up a yellowing document, 'is a letter of recommendation to the University of Berlin from a Herr Doktor Stahl. Seems Leo wanted to study medicine. Dated 1930. I'm assuming that as a Jew, he didn't get the chance.'

'He wasn't a doctor,' Selma said. 'Celal said he worked on the ferries.'

'Yes, well one does what one can when one is a refugee. And then there's this . . .'

He held up a photograph of a thin, dark young man with a prominent nose and thick glasses.

'Celal is tall, like his mother and one of his brothers,' Selma Vural said. 'His father was small.'

'His brother who works in a nargile salon?' Ikmen said.

'Oh no, another one,' she said. 'Celal said he died.'

Once outside the building, the two men looked at the photograph of Leo Bronstein more closely. Street kids tried to see what they were doing, but they shooed them away.

İkmen said, 'Bloom sufferers don't tend to live long lives. But Leo was seventy-five when he died.'

'Celal is tall,' Ömer said.

'As a carrier, he can be. If he's a carrier. His mother was tall . . . His supposedly dead brother . . . But the fact remains that Celal disappeared on the Saturday night, so the timings don't work,' İkmen said. 'And yet he has Ashkenazi antecedents, which is rare in this city. There was also some money in Celal Vural's family at one time. Looking at the shit hole they live in, it makes me wonder whether they could be entitled to reparation from the German government. They must have owned property in Berlin.'

'But Leo left all that behind,' Ömer said. 'People do. To forget is the only way forward. Sometimes.'

'I know. I just think that that poor woman doesn't need to live like that.'

Ömer knew that İkmen was proud of his working-class roots, but he had less understanding about what it was to be part of a displaced minority. Discrimination could rot a person's soul and make them cower into the comfort of any new situation that appeared to be benign. Or it could make a Peri Mungun. He wondered what she'd told her new employers about her background. Was there a reason other than professional development why she had applied to an Armenian hospital?

İkmen sighed. 'We won't be able to tell whether Leo had Bloom syndrome just from this photograph,' he said. 'Go back inside and ask Selma Hanım if she has her husband's hairbrush and whether she'll lend it to us. Our budget will protest, but now I don't think we have a choice. Vural is missing. DNA can't be put off any longer.'

Chapter 13

The building looked weird without the little domed bathhouse outside the kitchen. In recent years it had been used mainly for storage and had contained a very antiquated chest freezer. That now sat in the garden, surrounded by rubble.

Ziya the biker looked ripped in just a pair of jeans, a cement cutter in one big tanned fist. Bülent looked less impressive, but the girls just ignored him.

'Why'd you have to knock it down?' Ahu asked. 'It was old, wasn't it? Aren't there laws about demolishing things?'

'What, in a squat?' Ziya laughed. He had very white teeth for a man who smoked so many cigarettes. 'This place has been up for total demo for months. Uğur Bey reckoned it was unsafe. We had rats in there. And now that we've got kids in the place, who can have that going on?'

'It fell down easily. All we did really was push it,' Bülent said.

Zenne Gül saw Ziya give Bülent an evil stare. Easy demolition didn't sit well with Ziya's macho image.

'What about the freezer?' Meltem asked.

'Dunno.'

'We'll sell it,' Bülent said.

'Does it still work?'

Meltem had never had anything to do with anything in the old bathhouse.

'Yeah, but it's locked,' Ziya said.

Meltem frowned. 'You can't leave it unplugged like that,' she said. 'It'll rot.'

Ziya drew himself up to his full height. 'I know that.'

'We're going to plug it in through the kitchen window,' Bülent said.

'Yeah, but—'

'Look, we're selling it, Ahu Hanım, it's OK.'

'If you say so.'

'I do.'

But when the two boys went indoors, the three friends looked at each other with raised eyebrows.

'They've made a real mess out here,' Gül said as he surveyed the rubble-strewn garden. 'I think I'd rather have the rats.'

Sometimes Gül liked to sunbathe in the small garden. Now, at least temporarily, that was going to be impossible.

'If there *were* rats,' Meltem said.

Ahu frowned. 'What do you mean?'

'Well, did you ever see any?' her friend asked.

They wanted to come again so soon! Boris had dreaded it from the start, but now he'd had the police sniffing around, it made him even more nervous. And only one of them could speak English well.

He'd made his misgivings known to Ibrahim, who had answered that all would be well.

Boris Myskow thought the Turks were weird. In retrospect, he regretted buying the Imperial Oriental Hotel. But it had seemed so glamorous at the time! Istanbul had definitely been the next frontier in gastronomy. The whole place was literally hungry for new and exciting food experiences. What Boris hadn't realised was that at least half the population were very picky about what they ate. He knew that Arabs, just like Jews, didn't eat pork, but he'd thought that Turks did. He'd soon found out that they didn't, and that wasn't a tragedy. He'd worked around the ban just as he worked around the way that not everybody drank wine. But then he'd discovered that not everything was what it seemed in the land of the Turk, period. And not so long ago, he'd had the police at his door.

Ibrahim had laughed when he'd told him that nothing had actually happened. He'd said that because of his private guests, it couldn't. It was impossible. But it had shaken Boris. When his first private guests started coming, he'd been happy to accommodate them. But then Ibrahim and his boys had come along too, and Boris had felt overwhelmed. If only he'd been able to get his head around the language! People spoke and he didn't know what they were talking about. All he knew was that these men were vital to his professional survival. He just cooked.

That was what he told himself.

The imam looked at the boy through eyes full of tears. 'What do you want me to say to you?' he asked.

The child, Radwan, didn't speak. Imam Ayan had seen him with his sons in the cistern park. They'd told him the boy was a refugee, but he'd never asked them for any more information. And now here he was, giving him hope or talking malicious nonsense. How could he know which?

'I know nothing of this squat,' the old man said. 'What is it?'

The boy shrugged.

'And where? I have to know where it is if you're telling me my sons are there.'

'It's by the water,' Radwan said.

'What water? Where?'

'I can take you . . .'

'Take me where? You don't know where anything is!'

133

He saw the boy cringe. Only God knew what the child had been through in his own country. When people shouted, maybe it brought it all back. The imam lowered his voice.

'Radwan,' he said, 'the police have traced a call that Burak made to me. It was from Syria. I know you are wrong about my boys being in this squat. But I have to check out everything. Do you understand? I am their father.'

'I will take you.'

The boy Azzam, who the imam knew was a thief, had brought Radwan to his door. He'd said that the child knew where Burak and Mustafa had gone. He'd clearly been expecting some sort of monetary reward, but Imam Ayan had sent him away empty-handed. At some point he'd be back and he'd take something from the house or the garden, but the imam didn't really care.

'Take me to this place,' the old man said.

'It was the last place I saw the boys,' Radwan said.

'If you are lying, I will punish you.'

'I know.'

The old man stood. 'That boy Azzam told me that you talked to my sons about ISIS.'

'Yes.'

'And you encouraged my sons to worship them.'

'They liked them,' Radwan said. 'They wanted to be fighters. I just told them stories. I didn't tell them that I'd run away from ISIS.'

The imam looked down at the child and sighed. 'You lied to them.'

'Yes.'

General Abdullah Kavaş wasn't proud of himself. This was the second day he'd been drunk. He'd started even before his son was in the ground. The imam who had led the prayers had noticed, he was sure. He'd looked down his nose at the whole affair. But the general didn't care. His son was gone and his life was over. Who gave a damn if he drank himself to death?

All the old fossils had come out to bury Ümit. Admirals, brigadiers, generals. Their careers finished, their names discredited, when they all walked through the cemetery it had been like a parade of the condemned. It had been good of Ümit's friend Cengiz to come. He had troubles of his own. Also his views were not the same as those of the general. Cengiz Tanır felt that Ümit's friends from the squat should have been invited. He hadn't been alone in that view.

Deniz Baydar had brought a bottle of whisky to the apartment. Belgin had almost thrown him, and it, out. But a civilised exterior had to be maintained, and so Deniz Baydar had attended the funeral and then come back to the apartment, where he'd got drunk. Like most of the men. Now that he was out of prison, Abdullah was supposed to be serious and meticulous about his religious observance. Belgin even covered her head when she went out sometimes. But Abdullah had stopped caring the moment he heard that Ümit had died. Was that really less than a week ago?

Liberal and soft, his son had hardly been a credit to him, but he had been his only child. General Kavaş drank another glass of whisky. He'd died of natural causes, but how could his death have been truly natural with what he'd had in his stomach?

No one had said a thing, but Abdullah knew where the blame lay.

He looked at the pile of newspapers on his desk. Full of terrifying conspiracies juxtaposed with inane celebrity gossip. What was happening? Was everyone in the world becoming insane? He wanted nothing to do with it, or with his wife, who had gone to stay with her cousin in Ayvalık. Everyone had betrayed him. Just as he, in his turn, had betrayed his son.

* * *

135

'Do you know anyone at the Jewish hospital in Balat?'

Peri looked up. Her evening meal lay in front of her, hardly touched, and she was smoking. 'Why?'

'Well, you know we have an interest in Bloom syndrome . . .'

'I know a Pink Angel,' she said.

He frowned. Sometimes it was difficult to know which conversations were strictly real and which sprang from a belief system that was alien to everyone outside a few families from the area around Mardin called the Tur Abdin. In common with the Christians of the area, Peri and Ömer's native language was Aramaic. Like their Muslim neighbours, they were deeply religious, and they revered the sun, as did the sect called the Yezidis. But they gave their hearts to a deity called the Şarmeran, the snake goddess, whom they, with their parents, had both seen on the Mesopotamian Plain, where man and god had first made contact. It was not something they spoke about to others, and it was this silence that divided them from the rest of the city.

'You should try and do something for your own people occasionally,' she said. 'Jews and Christians are protected.'

'In law, yes,' he said. 'But you know how things are at the moment. Young men leaving to join radical groups every day. I wish our parents would come here.'

'Why should they?' Peri put her cigarette out and lit another.

'I wish you'd eat.'

'Don't change the subject! ISIS are nowhere near Mardin,' she said. 'And it is Mum and Dad's home. You know why they stay.'

'There are Syrian refugee camps . . .'

'Yes, they're nearby and I know you fear that they may harbour radicals. They might, but what can we do about it? Until people like us can be ourselves . . .'

'We never can.'

She shook her head. 'Until there is recognition that we even exist, nothing will improve. We need to stand up, join with the Yezidis and maybe even the Christians and fight.'

'So why do you work in an Armenian hospital in Istanbul, then?' he said. 'Why aren't you on the front line with the Yezidi militias?'

'I ask myself that every day,' Peri said. 'More so since Gezi. But you can't support Mum and Dad on your own. You'd have no money for yourself.'

Ömer put his fork down on his plate. Suddenly bulgur wheat and lamb chops looked unappealing.

'Dad is not going to get better,' Peri said. 'He needs his medication, and his condition has to be monitored.'

'He can get treatment here.'

'Yes, but he doesn't want to come here. Neither of them do. Why should they be separated from their culture? Why should they have to lie?'

'We do.'

'We chose to,' she said.

They sat in silence. Then Peri said, 'So what's this about the Jewish hospital?'

'It's a long shot, because most of their patients are Sephardic Jews,' Ömer said. 'This genetic disorder, Bloom syndrome, affects Ashkenazis. But most of them left the country a long time ago.'

'You want to know if there's anyone at the Or-Ahayim Hospital who has this disorder.'

'Yes.'

'So ask. You're the police.'

'It's a problem.'

'What is?'

'What we're investigating isn't straightforward,' he said. 'I can't tell you any more than that.'

Peri had been in the dark about Ömer's work before. She'd never got used to it. When they were kids, they'd shared everything. It was what had kept them strong.

She shrugged. 'I'll speak to Rosa. As it's you.'

'Thanks.'

'But don't hold out too much hope. She's not a doctor or a nurse,' Peri said.

'What is she then?' her brother asked.

'I told you, she's a Pink Angel.'

He'd heard about this place. A squat called the Art House. Full of intellectuals and, some said, atheists. Why would Burak and Mustafa spend time at such a place? Imam Ayan looked at Radwan and said, 'I don't understand. Why did you all come here?'

The boy, who was probably damaged beyond repair, was extremely frustrating to talk to.

'Radwan!'

Barely clad young people danced outside a bar across the street, smoking cigarettes, drinking alcohol and talking loudly. It was almost midnight, but Karaköy was humming with noise and colour.

'We used to throw stones,' Radwan said.

'At that building?'

'And shout at people. They're all infidels.'

Imam Ayan had never liked that word, 'infidel'. People had used it about his Zanubiya, even when she was dying. People never forgot . . .

'Well what you have told me has made me ashamed,' he said. 'If those people had thrashed the lot of you, I wouldn't have blamed them.'

'This is where I last saw Burak and Mustafa,' the boy said. 'They told me to go round the back of that bar, and when I returned, they had gone.'

The imam looked at the brightly lit bar again. 'Why did you go to the back of this place? Were you stealing?'

'No! They throw food away,' Radwan said. 'It's a sin. The boys were hungry.'

'Were they?' The picture this child was painting of his sons was not one that Imam Ayan liked.

'I went and I found cakes. But when I came back, they'd gone. I looked everywhere, but I couldn't find them.'

'And this you interpret as evidence that the people in that house killed my Mustafa.'

'The last time I saw him—'

'Yes, was outside a house where the three of you had mis-behaved,' the imam said. 'I accept that you looked for my boys, but you couldn't ask anyone because you don't speak Turkish. And the fact remains that Burak called me from Syria.'

'Maybe they killed Mustafa . . .'

'And maybe they did not.'

'One of the men had a baseball bat!'

Green and pink light from a sound system lit up the boy's eyes, which were not fanatical but were in what looked like shock.

'Radwan, my boys went to Syria,' the imam said. 'They tricked you into looking for food and then they left.'

'Yes, but you must tell the police . . .'

'Oh, I will. I will.' He put a hand on the boy's shoulder. 'But only because maybe the people inside saw my sons go. I imagine they would remember it if they did. They must have been relieved.'

Chapter 14

She needed sleep. But Halide Can knew she wasn't going to get any until she had spoken to Cetin İkmen. She lay back on her pillows and put her phone to her ear. As it rang, she looked at her feet. Were they swollen, or did she just think they were?

İkmen answered, and Halide launched straight in.

'Boris Myskow was in last night,' she said. 'So the atmosphere was tense to say the least.'

'Did he spend much time in the kitchen?'

'No. But just having him in the building seems to make most members of staff quake. I suppose it's because he's the boss. But he doesn't shout or act up like a lot of celebrity chefs. At least he didn't last night. The restaurant's head Turkish chef, Tandoğan, does, but then he speaks the language, so he has to keep the staff in line.'

'Do you know why Myskow was there last night?'

'Taking delivery of some equipment for his kitchen upstairs,' Halide said. 'No idea what it was because I was pretty much chained to the restaurant kitchen. But I did take a look in the meat freezers.'

'Is there more than one?'

'I saw two. One was well ordered and neat, each joint clearly labelled. The other one was a mess,' she said. 'Unlabelled meat, some bagged up, some not, just flung everywhere.'

'Do you know why?'

'I heard Tandoğan talking to the head chef, Romero, in

English,' she said. 'The meat had come in for the kitchen upstairs, but it wasn't staying.'

'Where was it going?' İkmen asked.

'I don't know. Aysel led me to believe that nothing was stored in the kitchen upstairs, but it must be.'

'Mmm. Did it look different in any way, this meat?'

'No. But I took a piece,' Halide said. 'Part of a leg of something. I've put it in my freezer.'

'Good girl. Can you get it over to forensics, or shall I send someone?'

'I just need an hour's sleep and then I can do it myself, thank you, sir,' she said.

'You sound shattered.'

'I am. Because Myskow was in the kitchen, it had to be scrubbed so it squeaked,' she said. 'I didn't get home until five.'

'Oh God!'

'It's OK.'

'No it isn't! Stay where you are and go to sleep,' İkmen said. 'Don't worry about for how long. When you wake up, call me and I'll send someone round to pick up the meat. It'll wait.'

She was too tired to argue.

'Thank you, sir.'

'You're welcome.' But then he said, 'Just out of interest, does the meat look like wild boar, do you think?'

She smiled. He was desperate to know about it. But unfortunately she couldn't help him.

'I'm sorry, sir,' she said. 'I can't tell one type of meat from another.'

Once she'd put the phone down, Halide snuggled into her duvet and thought about how disappointed her mother would have been if she'd heard her talking about her lack of knowledge. A girl who didn't know meat would never get a husband.

*   *   *

'Oh!'

Zenne Gül would have been the first to accept that he had a penchant for good-looking middle-aged men, but this was just ridiculous. It was the second time he'd opened the front door to this man in what had to be only just over twenty-four hours.

'You again?'

'I fear so,' Inspector Mehmet Süleyman said. 'I need to speak to Uğur Bey again.'

'Well he's in but I don't know whether he's up yet,' Gül said. 'Have you seen the time?'

It was just before nine.

'Yes.'

He was clearly unbothered by it.

'Come in,' Gül said. 'I'll get him.'

The policeman didn't mind that Gül hung around once Uğur Bey was up.

'We've found out the identities of a couple of the boys who've been abusing you,' the policeman said.

Uğur Bey smiled. 'Good.'

'Trouble is, they're missing.'

'Oh?'

'Yes,' Süleyman said. 'Apparently they were outside this building when they were last seen by their friend who also liked to bring trouble to your door.'

'When was this?'

'The twenty-fourth. In the afternoon, at about five. The boy who was with these two apparently went behind the café to go through their bins for food. While he was gone, the others disappeared.'

Uğur Bey shook his head. 'What do you want me to do, Inspector?'

'Let me know if any of your residents saw anything suspicious going on outside that afternoon.'

'Like what?'

'Like two teenage boys being bundled into a car, perhaps? Two boys talking about running away from home? One is nineteen, the other seventeen. One small and thin, one medium height, well built.'

He passed Uğur Bey a picture of a thin boy with a dog. Gül squinted at it over Uğur's shoulder. He really needed glasses now, but he recognised the face.

'That boy called me a fucking bastard,' he said. 'You don't want to know what I called him back.'

Süleyman smiled. 'Did you see anything untoward involving that boy on the twenty-fourth?'

'Who can say?' Gül said. 'I can't really remember yesterday that well, let alone the twenty-fourth. Those kids were always persecuting us. Missing or not, I'm just glad you know who they are.'

When the policeman left, Uğur Bey said that he was going back to bed. He'd promised Süleyman that he'd speak to all the residents about the two missing boys, but then to Gül he said he only might.

'Why should we give a shit about religious nutters?' he said.

'Because they're kids?'

But he didn't reply.

Uğur was usually such a caring man, it wasn't like him. But then Gül knew he'd had a big session on the beer the night before. He had to be hung-over.

Gül went to the window to see if he could spot Süleyman in the street. He saw him immediately. He was looking at the pile of rubble where the bathhouse used to be.

His mother had always said he had a big mouth. His wife, too. Not that her opinion counted for anything. Just because one member of his staff had shown that he had a brain . . .

It wasn't even as if he was fucking him. He didn't like men. Not like *that*.

Boris put his head in his hands. Not even Ibrahim would let this go if he found out. And he was going to. Though even if he did, wouldn't he just make the problem, and the troublesome man, go away? Probably. But then who else knew? He shook his head. That'd teach him to be careless and curious. Ibrahim, if he found out, would go insane. After all, it wasn't Boris he was actually protecting. He didn't give a shit about him.

But then Boris Myskow had a little play around on Google, and very quickly he saw a possible way out.

What made a person eat human flesh?

Hürrem Teker looked down on the city from one of its best vantage points, outside the church of St Mary of the Mongols in Fener. Below, what had been the old Greek quarter and Balat, the Jewish part of Istanbul, tumbled down to the Golden Horn like a dirty heap of children's building blocks. It all looked so authentic and untouched. But Hürrem knew that a few large bulldozers would make short work of this area, just as they had in the gypsy quarter of Sulukule. The memory of the once crazy streets of that neighbourhood, alive with dancers, whores and musicians, made her remember that Mehmet Süleyman's gypsy lover lived nearby. But she hadn't come to see her.

'Commissioner Teker?'

Even in his ecclesiastical robes, Father Bacchus Katsaros looked athletic. She hadn't expected that. But then Halide Can hadn't told her anything about Father Bacchus's appearance. Halide had never met him, but she had read his books, which was how she knew about his interests – which were out of the ordinary. They could also, Hurrem had felt, move the Ümit Kavaş investigation in a new direction. If Halide was right, there were scenes in society that almost beggared belief.

144

She shook his hand. 'Good of you to meet me, Father.'

He took her to a house down a nearby slope so steep she felt as if she might tumble head first to her death.

'I didn't know how to direct you,' he said as he opened the front door. 'As you can see, there is no way one can get a car down here.'

'No.'

The priest's house was in the middle of a terrace of elegant, if battered, nineteenth-century buildings. Outside, it was filthy, but inside was characterised by clean wooden floors and many small rooms lined with books. It had the look of a place where a man lived alone, although apparently Father Bacchus had a son.

He offered her tea, which they took in his main drawing room. His ikons and books on Orthodox Christian theology sat in stark contrast to his large range of cheap Greek paperbacks. When they had settled down, he took one off the shelf.

'I don't know if you read Greek . . .'

'No. Father Bacchus, this conversation has to be off the record . . .'

'Of course.' He smiled, looking at the book. 'This one is called *Dead on Arrival?*. It has a question mark after it because we don't know whether one particular character is dead when he arrives at a hospital in Thessaloniki.' He smiled. 'My mother came from that city, I know it well.'

Teker shook her head. 'I have to say, I was . . . well, not shocked, but surprised to find out what you do.'

'Mmm. Priest and archaeologist are not pursuits that are so far apart . . .'

'Priest, archaeologist and author of zombie fiction, however, does make your job title both long and strange,' she said.

He laughed. 'Ah, but in the world of fiction, I am not Father Bacchus but Kostas Onassis – like the shipping magnate.'

'Is that deliberate?' She sipped her tea.

'Oh yes,' he said. 'Aristotle Onassis was not a pleasant man, and neither is Kostas. He writes about dead people eating live people. What's to like?'

'You seem to be very nice, if that helps,' Teker said.

He laughed again.

'And you're also an expert on cannibalism.'

'What can I say?' He shrugged. 'In the past, in some civilisations, the eating of human flesh was part of everyday life. In some cases human body parts were used in medicine. For instance, crushed Egyptian mummy was thought to get rid of headaches in places like Italy and Britain. That's why some people plundered tombs, to get hold of a mummy to render to powder and make some money. Ancient Romans drank the blood of dead gladiators so that they could in some magical way obtain their strength. It's all nonsense. And it can be dangerous. There are a range of illnesses called Prion diseases, which cause dementia amongst other things. These can be directly traced to cannibalism. The image of the zombie is I think so frightening because there is the element of contagion within the myth. Both the creature eating human flesh and the victim contain a sickness for which there is no cure.'

'But zombie fiction is very popular.'

'Ah, zombie fiction can be fun!' he said. 'Because it is fiction. The deep roots beneath the image of the zombie are not seen by everyone.'

'You see them.'

'I do, yes. I trained as a scientist, before I was called to God. Cannibalism is taboo in all major religions, but it was not always the case. Blood sacrifice was common in ancient South American religions; in the Middle East, warrior races like the Assyrians and the Hittites are thought to have consumed the blood of their enemies. As in ancient Rome, this was in order to absorb their strength. Religions like Judaism, Christianity and Islam developed rules to put a stop to this because by that time, people were more informed. It's my belief that the very strong taboos against cannibalism in these religions come from an understanding, albeit basic, of how the consumption of human flesh can harm. That said, as a Christian, I have to accept that in my religion, the notion of ingesting – in our case the divine – remains.'

'Do you mean the wine and the bread?' Teker said.

'Transubstantiation,' he said. 'The wine and the bread become the blood and body of Christ. And Christ himself ordered this. I know scholars who will swear an oath that this is simply the replaying of a custom that early converts to Christianity, pagans, would have found familiar and comfortable. I don't believe that, but . . .'

'What about cooking and eating a human body?' Teker asked.

He nodded. 'In Papua New Guinea into the nineteenth century.' Then he paused. 'You know, Commissioner, I am happy to talk about these things to you, but if you're a fan of zombie fiction . . .'

'I'm here on business.'

'Ah, of course.'

'I can't give you any information at all,' Teker said. 'As I said before, I must insist that our conversation goes no further.'

'It won't.'

'All I can say is that we have a certain situation and we need some expert guidance. I came to you, Father, because one of my officers – a female – reads your books.'

'Ah. In Greek?'

'No, English.'

She'd seen Halide Can with her head in more than one Kostas Onassis book over the years. More recently, they'd had a conversation about them. Halide had explained that Onassis was actually an Istanbul priest. Then she'd looked him up online.

'Why would someone cook human flesh with a fruit sauce?' she said.

Father Bacchus crossed his legs. 'It's said it tastes like pork. We frequently cook pork with apples and cider . . .'

'But why cover up the taste like that?'

'Why not? If you're thinking that whatever you can't tell me about was some sort of experiment with human flesh, then I admit that is odd. But if you're describing a meal . . . Was there rice, vegetables?'

'Yes.'

'So a banquet?'

She shrugged.

'If it's celebratory, it could be part of a ritual. Maybe a cult? Rare, though. Modern cannibals tend to work alone.'

'Like that German case?'

'Armin Meiwes, 2002, yes. He found his victim – who was willing, by the way – online. There was a community, now no more, called the Cannibal Café. It was for people who fetishised cannibals and cannibalism. Meiwes cooked his victim's penis in wine and garlic before killing him and hanging him up on a meat hook. Celebratory? Maybe.'

Teker shook her head.

'These days, those sorts of sites are not so easy to find,' the priest said. 'Now, I think, if you want to find serious people, you will have to explore what they call the Dark Web. I expect you've heard of it.'

'Oh yes.'

The Dark Web was a part of the Internet inaccessible to standard search engines and web browsers. It was where sensitive inform-ation lurked and where crimes were instigated and in some cases committed by groups such as terrorists and paedophiles.

'I'm sure you have a department that monitors such sites,' he said.

'We do.'

Although in Teker's experience, even the most skilled technical people were not always as thorough as they might be. An old technical officer, who had left the force, had once told her that the most reliable people to consult about the Dark Web were actually criminals themselves.

Father Bacchus underlined this observation. 'And I'm sure they're very good,' he said. 'But the best people to access the Dark Web, I have found, are hackers. They know the twists and turns, the tricks and subtleties of the system. I consulted a, shall we say, reformed hacker when I was researching one of my books some years ago. He is entirely above board these days, but he was very helpful. If you like, I'll contact him and ask if he might be interested in helping you.'

Teker knew of old that sometimes in order to get a result, one had to figuratively hold the hand of the devil.

'Yes,' she said, 'that might be useful. But no details, eh?'

'No. Of course not.'

Chapter 15

Thin, dark and nervous, the boy reminded him of his Zanubiya. She too had come from Syria as a refugee. But twenty years ago, it had not been because there was a civil war. Then Assad Senior had been in control and there was no dissent. Minorities had flourished in Syria at that time – with one exception. That was why Zanubiya had left, and why the imam always told people that she had been born a Christian. It was easier.

The child slept. When they had returned from Karaköy, the imam hadn't had the heart to throw him out on to the street again. He'd made up a mattress on the floor. Then, once Radwan was settled, he'd called Inspector Süleyman. The policeman had been to the squat but had reported only bemusement on the part of the residents. The imam had expected as much. Now a second night had passed and Radwan was still in his house. This had raised some eyebrows. The mother of the Twisted Boy had said that he was playing with fire letting a refugee into his home. But it was hard for the imam to care. If Radwan stole from him, he stole from him. He was pretty sure that that other boy, Azzam, had taken his bicycle from the yard. But a bicycle was only a thing, and things were replaceable. People weren't.

His sons had been seduced away from him by the Internet. Other boys, he knew, supplemented attendance at his mosque with 'educational' meetings at the offices of organisations that called themselves charities. But the imam knew they were something else, everybody did. No one spoke – except for the Twisted Boy. But he wasn't listened to, except by Imam Ayan.

'They discuss Syria,' he'd told the old man months ago. 'Then they send boys over there. They tell them they'll make lots of money, but they lie. They keep all the money they collect for themselves.'

The imam had warned his sons about the charities, and they had kept away. But ISIS had still reached them. Via the Internet, they were in homes all over the world, promising martyrdom with images that had killed Mustafa and would kill Burak. In the meantime, the imam wondered whether either of his sons had already killed anyone. Specifically, had they inadvertently killed one of their compatriots.

He should have told them about their mother when she died. He, personally, should have laid her to rest with her own kind.

'Word in the Imperial Oriental is that Boris Myskow is giving one of his private parties tonight,' Cetin İkmen announced.

'Be interesting to see who comes,' Commissioner Teker said. 'I'm sure that Constable Can, now she is a more familiar figure in the hotel, will be able to find out more. But I feel we should also move this investigation along in a more obscure direction.'

'Are these the other avenues of investigation you once talked to me about?' İkmen said.

Süleyman sat down next to İkmen and lit a cigarette.

'Indeed. Yesterday I had a conversation with someone who knows about cannibalism,' Teker said. 'I mean that in an academic sense.'

'I'm glad to hear it,' İkmen said.

She nodded. 'There are many reasons why a person might eat human flesh. They may include belief in its medicinal properties, a desire to ingest the strength of an enemy, or just curiosity. But the person I spoke to believes that human flesh cooked and prepared in the way it was found in Ümit Kavaş's stomach could point towards some sort of celebration, possibly connected to a fetish, probably sexual.'

İkmen looked at Süleyman. 'How Freudian.'

Mehmet Süleyman's ex-wife had been a psychiatrist. He rolled his eyes.

'A few years ago, you may remember, a modern-day German cannibal called Armin Meiwes killed and ate a man for his own, and his victim's, sexual gratification.'

'Yes.'

'Meiwes and his victim met on the Internet . . .'

'Whence all horror and deceit flows,' İkmen said.

Teker smiled. 'Which is precisely why that part of the investigation is going to be performed by a contractor. Have you gentlemen heard of the Dark Web?'

'Where terrorists meet.'

'Where, as you said, Inspector, all horror lives,' she agreed.

Süleyman said, 'Don't the techs monitor the Dark Web?'

'Yes, but I am assured that if I want to get as deep inside it as I can, which is where those interested in cannibalism are more likely to operate, I need an expert.'

'So you're contracting this cannibal . . .'

'We have a hacker,' she said. 'Reformed, of course. He's coming here this afternoon. His name is Erol Bilici and I want you to brief him.'

'Everything?'

'Everything. I have made very clear what could happen if he opens his mouth outside this building. I spoke to him last night and made him a financial offer he was unable to refuse. He sounds very intelligent.'

'He'll be hugely overweight and obsessed with computer games,' Süleyman said.

Teker smiled. 'You may be surprised.'

The old man was admitted on to the ward while his nurse from the Balat Jewish hospital and one of the Pink Angels, or volunteer carers, looked on.

Although well cared for at the Or-Ahayim Hospital in Balat, Sarkis Aznavourian wished to die amongst his own people. Luckily, the Surp Pirgiç Armenian hospital had a bed.

Nurse Peri Mungun took Mr Aznavourian's notes from Nurse Turkan Polat and then invited her and the Pink Angel, Rosa Nabarro, to tea in the hospital's garden. It was a beautiful day and so the women readily accepted.

Peri had known Rosa, a woman at least twenty years her senior, for some time. They'd met when Peri and some other nurses from the German hospital, where she'd worked at that time, had been given a guided tour of the Or-Ahayim. Peri had been impressed by the dedication shown by the volunteer Pink Angels and had kept in touch with Rosa.

A student brought their tea. Peri didn't know Nurse Polat, and so various niceties had to be exchanged before any serious conversation could begin. But she knew she couldn't miss this opportunity to talk about that strange disease Ömer had an interest in. How did she broach the subject?

Eventually she said, 'You know, I've been wondering ever since I came to work here about how prevalent genetic diseases are in other minority hospitals. I mean, we now take anyone who needs us. But our core work still involves people of Armenian origin. And that population is small.'

'Yes, but genetic disorders generally arise as a result of inter-marriage,' Nurse Polat said. 'And speaking just for the Jewish population, I have to say that they appear to be marrying out.' She looked at her colleague. 'What do you think, Rosa?'

'It's true,' she said. 'I'm not ancient, I'm fifty, but marrying out was just not done in my day. Now my eldest son has a Muslim wife, and my daughter is married to a Greek. What can you do?'

A slight expression of disapproval crossed Nurse Polat's face. Maybe she was one of those Turks who thought that the minorities should be grateful to be able to marry out.

'But then it's a good thing too,' Rosa continued. 'Because of the genetic diseases. One of our neighbours back home in Karaköy suffered from beta thalassemia. Terrible anaemia she had. She died. And that's a Sephardic disease. She was pure, she was, her family hadn't married out ever. Thank God my father married an Ashkenazi, so please God, me and my brothers will have missed that particular bullet.'

'Yes, but Ashkenazis have genetic disorders too.'

'Everyone does, Peri love,' Rosa said. 'Even you lot.'

Peri smiled.

'I know. But because so many of our patients here are old people from pure, small minority populations, I've been doing some reading about genetic diseases we may or may not come across. Have either of you heard of Bloom syndrome?'

Nurse Polat frowned. 'No. What's that?'

'The worst part about it is that it predisposes sufferers to both cancer and diabetes,' Peri said. 'And there's an appearance thing . . .'

'Is that the one where they're short but have long faces?' Rosa asked.

'Yes.'

'That's an Ashkenazi disease. Your Armenians won't get it.'

'No. But I found it interesting,' Peri said. 'Have you ever come across it?'

Peri knew that Rosa knew what her brother did for a living. She watched the Pink Angel narrow her eyes. Rosa plumped pillows, washed floors and prepared food, and she knew everyone and everything that happened in the small community of the Or-Ahayim Hospital. She'd also worked Peri out.

'Only once,' Rosa said. 'A good decade ago now. A young woman, pretty little thing. She was dying when she came to us. She had tumours all over her.'

'What happened?'

'She died,' Rosa said. 'But it was a strange business. She was just dumped on our doorstep. Timür, who works in the kitchen, said he saw a man and a covered woman leave her, so we assumed she was Muslim. Then she started raving in her sleep, and one of our doctors recognised it as Yiddish. He came from France originally, that doctor, and so he had a bit of an idea she might have Bloom syndrome and did a test. We never knew who she was, but when she died, we had her buried in the Ulus Ashkenazi Cemetery. The hospital paid. What else could we do?'

'You did your best,' Peri said. 'But you've seen no cases since?'

'Not that I know about,' Rosa said. 'There are very few Ashkenazim left here. Most of them moved on to Israel at the end of the forties. Also, she was a strange one, that little lady.'

'In what way?'

'Well, Ashkenazis generally look a lot more sort of Western than Sephardis. My mum was blonde, would you believe! But this lady, if I'd had to put a nationality to her, I would have had her down as a Kurd. All sparkly bright clothing underneath a full-on abaya. She was the strangest ethnic mix you've ever seen in your life.'

Zenne Gül sat outside the office he'd been told to go to. It was clinical, and slightly squalid at the same time. He hadn't been in places like this often. Thank God.

He'd toned the whole zenne thing right down. No jewellery, no make-up, very conservative, male clothes. The only thing he hadn't compromised on was fragrance. But then some of the men he'd seen since he'd arrived had smelled nice. That whole macho man thing was, in some places, going out of style. That look had always made his flesh crawl. His best friend Zenne Menekşe had a liking for the hairy-chested, sweaty type. Gül couldn't understand it. Those men played rough, and they were usually married with umpteen kids. Menekşe had dated loads of them, and all he'd ever got for his pains was a black eye and a broken heart. But then Gül was wary of love and he knew it. He'd only ever had one real boyfriend, who had quickly ditched him when his parents made him marry a girl from their home village. Now he hung out with the girls at the squat, but that suited him. Getting another broken heart was not in his life plan. What Gül wanted was money, so that he could buy his own little club on the Mediterranean coast and get away from the insanity of the city.

The door he sat beside opened. A grizzled head emerged.

'Erol Bilici?'

'Yes.'

It wasn't often that people used his real name. It was a bit weird.

'Inspector İkmen?' Gül said.

'Yes.'

The small, grizzled, tobacco-scented man shook his hand.

There was only one copy of the menu, and that was just for those who were curious. When the meal was over, it would be burned. Such a ridiculous amount of nonsense about a perfectly safe meat. Although was it? Safe? Of course it was. Boris Myskow hammered the steaks thin. Schnitzel of boar was on the menu, and he could hear his mother turning in her grave.

He'd never even seen pork until he was an adult. Most kids

in Boro Park were the same. People said it was the biggest Orthodox Jewish enclave outside Israel, and he could believe it. Even the rest of New York had been a mystery to him until he was sixteen. Then he'd got out. He clearly remembered thinking, 'I don't buy this shit.' So why did the Turks? Not that the people he gave his little parties for did. He couldn't understand what they said, but they said it drunk with pig inside their bellies, so they had to have contempt for their religion. Didn't they?

He hammered the steaks until they were almost see-though and then stopped. Such massive slabs looked far from elegant, and he was tempted to trim them down and throw the excess meat away. But did he dare do that? Should he eat the leftovers himself? He was tempted. It would be an experience. He decided to make mini schnitzels. Garnished with stuffed olives and anchovies, they would look elegant, which was what diners expected from him. Even these diners with their hairy knuckles and ill-fitting tuxedos.

Boris had cooked for the cream of Turkish society. Academics, captains of industry, politicians, even princes. But this lot were different. Most of them straddled several worlds in their pursuit of material gain. At bottom they were opportunists and chancers, small-minded misogynists, in love with diamond-studded mobile phones and impossibly powerful cars. Boris allowed himself a chuckle as he remembered his first wife, Mary. She'd been one of those horsey British aristos whose whole family was mad. She'd called people like Boris's diners 'nouveau riche'.

Why did they come to him? Was it because his food was better than anyone else's, or was it because he was expensive – and a foreigner – and a Jew? It was all of the above and Boris knew it. They thought he didn't understand the politics of their weird country, but he did. They were using him to show off. To each other. And he used them. Having them around meant that his business was safe.

* * *

'You don't have a record. I checked,' İkmen said. 'You must've been good.'

Zenne Gül smiled. 'I was lucky,' he said. 'And remember, Inspector, I did a maths degree. I was surrounded by geeky people who routinely shared tips about computers, the Internet, all that stuff. I stood on the shoulders of giants.'

'And now I want you to do that again.'

'It's odd.' He shook his head. 'I mean, if you'd said to me even yesterday morning that the police would come to me . . .'

'As I'm sure you're aware,' İkmen said, 'we have our own team of techies who I would not presume to criticise. However . . .' He opened his office window and offered Zenne Gül a cigarette.

'Oh, can we . . .?'

'I do,' İkmen said. 'And so does Commissioner Teker. Please . . .'

Zenne Gül took a cigarette and lit up.

İkmen, smoking too, said, 'We, Commissioner Teker and myself, know that you have, in the past, accessed parts of the so-called Dark Web for the author Kostas Onassis.'

'Do you read zombie fiction, Inspector?'

'No,' İkmen said. Although he knew that several of his children indulged.

'Oh, it's great fun.'

İkmen didn't really understand the amusement to be had from the idea of the dead chomping on the bones of the living, but he consoled himself with the notion that it was probably a generational thing. He was just too old.

'Well I'm sorry, Mr Bilici,' he said, 'it doesn't do a lot for me. But that's beside the point. We've got you here because we seem to have a real cannibal situation in the city.'

For a moment the zenne said nothing. Teker hadn't given him any details.

'A man known to residents of your squat, Ümit Kavaş, died of natural causes.'

'Yes, I know,' Gül said. 'He was a nice person. But when he died, the police started asking questions. Uğur Bey reckoned you were trying to smear his name. After what happened to his father . . .'

'We weren't,' İkmen said. 'What we were trying to do was find out why a man of apparent integrity like Ümit Kavaş had human flesh in his stomach when he died.'

Once again Gül was silent.

İkmen smiled. 'This is not pleasant, Mr Bilici,' he said. 'Or would you rather I called you Gül?'

'Gül.'

He was slightly in shock.

'Not only had Mr Kavaş eaten human flesh, but it had been cooked,' İkmen continued. 'We know some things about the victim – his gender and his possible ethnicity, for instance – but we don't know his identity. Basically, we want you to help us find out what sort of cannibal activity is going on in Istanbul. Was this a one-off incident, or do we have a cult of some sort on our hands? Tell me, do you think from your experience of him that Ümit Kavaş might have been involved in anything like that?'

'I don't think so. Ümit never struck me as a dark soul. He was very straightforward and honest.'

'Can you help us?'

'I can try,' he said. 'But there are two problems. First, since the Armin Meiwes case in Germany, people who like this sort of thing have gone even further underground, and second, I've never performed any of my research on the Turkish scene. Father Bacchus sets his books in Europe. I can speak English and German, and so I concentrated on those countries, plus the US.'

'We haven't, as yet, discovered any sort of Turkish scene,'

159

İkmen said. 'The only recent case I've been able to discover is that of Özgür Dengiz in 2007.'

'The Ankara Cannibal.'

'Yes. A lone psychopath who was committed to a mental institution. I've read some of the case notes. He acted apparently on a whim. He didn't cook his victim. What Mr Kavaş consumed, however, was part of an elaborate meal. Commissioner Teker has spoken to me about the conversation she has had with Father Bacchus, and it seems to us, if indeed we have anything here at all, that it's probably a sexual fetish.'

'Which is far removed from straightforward zombie fiction,' Gül said.

'So I gather.'

'Kink scenes can be dangerous. I know that may seem strange to you, coming from a man who does what I do now. But I've always kept away from that stuff. Doing research for Father Bacchus was one thing. I could look at what I found and not get involved. But he never wanted me to make contact. I assume you do.'

'You will be protected at all times. I give you my word.'

Gül put his cigarette out. 'I had a friend who met a guy online in a very ordinary chat room about a year ago. This man seemed really nice. It was only when my friend got to his house that he discovered what a mistake he'd made. OK, he didn't hurt my friend, but he did want him to lie in a coffin and play dead while he had sex with him. My friend made his excuses and left.'

'You won't have to get involved with any of these people,' İkmen said. 'We just need you to find them and make contact.'

Gül nodded. He said nothing.

'Zenne Gül?' İkmen said.

'I'll do it, because to be honest with you, I want to clear Ümit's name. If he ate human flesh, then it had to be by some sort of accident. I can't believe he was . . .' He shook his head.

'Just so you know, accessing sites, should they exist, is the least of a job like this.'

'So what's the most of it?' İkmen asked.

'If you want to find these people, I'll have to enter chat rooms,' he said. 'And if I want to be believed, that means opening myself up to a lot of people's fantasies.'

'I know that's a risk.'

'And how. Also, there is a practical problem.'

'Which is?'

'I haven't done any work for Father Bacchus for a long time,' Gül said. 'My computer is ancient. I am most definitely an ex-hacker these days. That's one of the reasons I like the squat so much. No one there really does tech.'

'Don't worry about that,' İkmen said. 'We will supply everything you need.'

'OK.'

Zenne Gül felt his heart beat a little faster.

Chapter 16

It was so hot, she felt as if she might pass out. She went to the freezer room to get cool as much as anything else. It had been a very long night, but at least she'd finally met someone who had liked the missing Celal Vural.

'What are you doing in here? Again?'

Halide Can turned her wet red face towards Chef Tandoğan. 'I'm so hot . . .'

'You work in a kitchen. It's one of the down sides,' he said. Was there an up side?

'You get to eat some of the finest food in the world and we pay you,' he said. 'But in return you have to work in heat. What's the matter with you? Got a heart problem or something?'

'No, Chef.'

'Then stop hanging about round the freezers,' he said. 'I know what you people do.'

What did he mean? And who were 'you people'?

She stood up. But she must have looked confused, because he said, 'We know you all steal. Why do you think we get through so many of you?'

He meant cleaners, and as far as Halide could tell, they got through so many because no one could stand such a dismal, poorly paid job for too long. But she didn't say anything.

'You chose to do a double shift, no one made you,' he said.

Halide left the room. He wasn't wrong about that. She had offered to stay on once the restaurant had closed at midnight to stack the dishwashers after Mr Myskow's dinner in the conference room ended. That hadn't been until three in the morning. Now it was almost four, and, having loaded one dishwasher with dirty plates, glasses and crockery, she knew she had to face the long walk to the upstairs conference room to clean up there. She'd also assumed that the job included the upstairs kitchen. Being in Myskow's kitchen, alone, was an opportunity she had to take. When Tandoğan had found her, she really had just been way too hot to go on, and she was lucky she still had the job. She couldn't take a risk like that again.

When she arrived at the conference room, she found the door closed. She opened it and went in to find a table littered with empty wine bottles, petits fours and ashtrays overflowing with cigar stubs. So much for no smoking in enclosed public spaces. But because anyone could come in and disturb her at any time, she made straight for the kitchen.

Originally conceived, she imagined, as not much more than a service kitchen, it had two ovens and a six-ring hob, one large fridge and a chest freezer. Compared to the vast facilities downstairs, it was little more than a domestic kitchen. And unlike the restaurant kitchens, it was not as hot as hell. The floor was clean and the work surfaces had obviously been washed down before she got there.

'What the fuck are you doing?'

The English words caught her unawares, and for a moment, she had no idea what had just been said.

'What are you doing?'

He wore bright pink rubber gloves and had pieces of what looked like burnt paper in his hair. He'd been cleaning one of the ovens.

'Oh, you don't speak English,' Boris Myskow said.

Weirdly he was still wearing all but the jacket of his tuxedo. Cleaning an oven in a white shirt didn't seem sensible.

'I can speak English,' she said.

'Well, what are you doing here? Why didn't you answer me? You're just supposed to clear the table. Didn't Tandoğan tell you that?'

'No.'

Tandoğan hadn't mentioned the kitchen.

'You just clear the table,' Myskow said. 'Understand?'

'Yes, sir.'

'I always clean down my own kitchen, capisce?'

Halide had no idea what 'capisce' meant, but she just said, 'Yes.'

'Then go clear the table,' he said.

As she left, she saw him stick his head back inside one of the ovens again. Hadn't Aysel said that the upstairs kitchen didn't have a freezer?

'Gül?'

He was sitting on his bed with what Meltem recognised as a brand new laptop.

'Oh, hi.' He looked up.

Meltem walked into his room. 'I thought you'd stopped all that ages ago,' she said.

She'd got up to go to the bathroom. It was only 6 a.m., and Gül was deep in a computer. It was weird.

'I'm just looking stuff up.'

'Yeah, right,' she said. 'This from the reformed hacker who once called the web "evil".'

She sat down beside him and looked at the machine. It was clearly new.

'Where'd you get that?'

'Bought it.'

'From the Apple shop in Beşiktaş?'

He stopped what he was doing. 'Why? I know we don't really do tech here, but I felt like it.'

She shrugged.

'I make good money now,' he said. 'And I've missed having a decent machine. We've got Wi-Fi for the phones, so why not this? I'm not going to hack MIT, if that's what you think.'

She laughed, but then her face became solemn again. She put a hand on his arm. 'I don't want you to get into trouble.'

He took her hand and squeezed it. 'That's all behind me now,' he said. 'This is just me having a bit of fun.'

'You have to make sure it doesn't become a problem,' she said. 'You will tell me . . .'

'Yes, I'll tell you,' he said. But then he went back to looking at the screen again.

Usually Gül worked late and rose late too. Meltem knew he'd been out working most of the night and had probably not even been to bed. She feared that if he had such a hypnotic computer in his hands, he'd miss an entire night's sleep. She hadn't spent much time with him when he'd been a hacker. But he'd told her stories – about staying up all night on sites he shouldn't have been able to get to, living on coffee, cigarettes and amphetamines. He'd been really good at what he did and had never got caught. But that was then. Now, with the coming of increased national security, the extension of police powers to search and arrest people perceived to be enemies of the state, usually on terrorism charges, hacking had become a very dangerous hobby.

Meltem stood up. 'I hope you've told Uğur . . .'

'I'm not hacking,' Gül said. 'Trust me. I'm not putting the squat at risk. I love this place.'

All Meltem could do was trust. Gül was a good friend who believed in the ethos of the squat. She had to hold on to that.

As she left, she said, 'Oh, Uğur Bey and Ziya are levelling off the ground where the old bathhouse used to be today.'

'Do you know what they're going to do with it?'

'Flower garden,' she said. 'Eventually. But I'll just be glad when we're not all falling over bits of old concrete.'

What would Gonca have done if the boy her daughter was in bed with *had* been Roma?

The girl, Arsena, was not backwards in asking that question. 'Well?' she said as her mother pulled her from the bed of her lover. 'Would you have been doing this if I was with Metin the truck driver's son?'

'Just get up and get home,' Gonca said.

The naked young man in the bed looked terrified.

'All the way down here to hipster land just to make sure you don't ruin your life,' Gonca said. 'What a mean woman I am!' She looked at the boy and said, 'Eh?'

'No!'

'No,' she said. 'Right answer. You know who I am, young man?'

'Yes.' He pulled his duvet up to his chin.

Arsena looked down at him while she put her clothes on. 'Oh please! Don't inflate her ego.'

'You're Gonca Hanım, the artist,' he said. 'You make collages out of things like horsehair and blood. Your work sells at Christie's in New York.'

Arsena groaned. He was obviously impressed. They always were.

'That's it, kid,' her mother said.

'You're the only Roma artist—'

'What did I tell you about inflating her ego?'

The boy shrugged.

'Go and get in the car,' Gonca said to her daughter.

Arsena put her shoes on. 'I bet it was that little shit Harun . . .'

'Your brother was out all night,' Gonca said. 'Don't worry about your siblings, madam! Out!'

The girl walked slowly towards the apartment door and let herself out.

Gonca looked down at the boy. 'Fuck my daughter again and I'll chop your balls off,' she said.

His face went white.

'She's the only girl in my family to get to university, and you are not going to screw it up for her. Understand?'

Out in the street, a glazed Mehmet Süleyman waited beside his car. Some cousin of Gonca's who worked in a bar in Karaköy had phoned to tell her he'd seen Arsena going into an apartment building opposite the Turkish Orthodox church at five that morning. Gonca had pulled Süleyman out of bed, and now, at just before six, they were in Karaköy and the girl was getting into the car.

But he wasn't really taking much notice. He was too busy looking at who had just gone into Uğur İnan's squat.

Ömer Mungun didn't understand.

'My sister's friend said they'd had one case of Bloom syndrome at the Or-Ahayim about ten years ago,' he said.

Arto Sarkissian shrugged. 'Mario Politi says he's never seen a case in his life. What does your sister's friend do at the Or-Ahayim, Sergeant?'

'She's one of the helpers, a Pink Angel.'

'With respect, Mario Politi is a surgeon,' the Armenian said. 'A very clever man. I can't see him passing up an opportunity to observe what is a rare disease by anyone's standards.'

'The woman, Peri's friend said, looked more Kurdish than Ashkenazi . . .'

'Mmm. Has the ring of an urban legend to me. A strange disease, undiagnosed.'

'Oh, it was.'

'Or was it? Closed institutions like hospitals are notorious rumour mills,' Arto said. 'A woman is dumped on a hospital doorstep. She's clearly dying. She's also dark and exotic-looking. On top of that, she appears to speak Yiddish. Why not also give her a very outré disease?'

'But she did speak Yiddish.'

'Maybe she'd learned it from a friend or neighbour as a child. Doesn't mean it was her native tongue.'

And yet it was well known that people close to death would usually revert to their native tongue.

Arto Sarkissian put a hand on Ömer's shoulder. 'Mario is a very old friend,' he said. 'Why would he lie?'

Ömer knew it was unlikely that a respected man like Dr Politi would lie. But what if he just didn't know?

Burak hadn't called him again. Waking or sleeping, that silence echoed in his head all the time. Did this absence mean that his only remaining son was dead? Imam Ayan put the kettle on to make more tea and then sat in the sunshine waiting for it to boil. How could he carry on being a leader of his community when he had failed so badly in his own life?

He'd let the boys down and he'd let their mother down too. What would she have thought had she lived to see the day her sons went off to die in her old country for a cause she would have despised? Maybe even killing some of her relatives? Who knew?

'I can take you to Burak if you want.'

The Syrian child Radwan had returned from only God knew where. Since he'd taken the child in, he'd noticed that when alone he wandered, speaking to no one that the imam could see. When the imam came round from his waking dream, Radwan was standing in front of him.

'Do you know where Burak is?'

'In Syria.'

The imam shook his head. 'This is more nonsense, isn't it?' he said. 'Don't you believe that my boys are in that house in Karaköy any more?'

'Mustafa is. But Burak is in Syria. I know that now because of the phone call he made. I can take you.'

The old man put his head in his hands. 'God help me.'

'What?'

He looked up. 'Boy, I cannot help my son. I couldn't help his mother. I'm an old man who has lived a life underneath too many secrets. I am a bad person, Radwan.'

The boy thought for a moment, then said, 'Maybe you should do jihad to make up for it.'

'I don't want to kill anyone. I—'

'No, just come to Syria, with me,' the boy said. 'I can't live in this city any more. I have to go home now.'

The imam shook his head. 'But Syria is a place of death. You can't go there.'

'I can't stay here,' Radwan said. 'I can't live in a park . . .'

'Live with me.'

'No,' he said. 'Come with me to Syria and we'll find Burak. I know we will.'

The old man put his arm around the boy and cuddled him.

'And will we find your family too, Radwan?'

'Oh no,' the boy said calmly. 'They're all dead. Their ghosts are here now and I just can't stand it.'

Major General Baydar had not suffered as much as some of his colleagues when he'd been in prison. He'd managed to keep relatively fit and healthy and had never given any indication that he had endured physical abuse. But the stain it had put on his good name was one, or so Mehmet Süleyman felt, that would never go away. Every interview with Baydar he'd ever read or seen on TV had been characterised by a bitterness that was visible. A veteran of the 1974 Turkish invasion of Cyprus, Deniz Baydar was an old-style patriot who was a Turkish soldier first, everything else in his life coming a very far-away second.

Childless, he regarded his men as his sons, and when the Islamically rooted ruling party came to power in 2002, a rumour went around that Major General Baydar told his boys the news with tears in his eyes. A proud product of the secular republic, the old man now immersed himself in the study of the Turks' pre-Islamic past, an era he called the 'glory days'. Baydar wasn't the sort of man readily associated with civil disobedience. So what had he been doing at the Karaköy squat at six o'clock that morning?

'We know that the opposition in this country is made up of strange bedfellows,' İkmen said to Süleyman. 'I can't think why you find that odd. Deniz Baydar and General Kavaş are friends. Kavaş's son was often in the squat. There are covered women in that house. The spirit of Gezi has persisted in very disparate groups. Anyway, what were *you* doing in Karaköy at six o'clock this morning?'

He shook his head. 'One of Gonca's daughters was sleeping in a bed she shouldn't have been.'

'Oh.'

Gonca's daughters were well known for such behaviour.

'I also noticed that Uğur Bey and his squatters have flattened the land where some sort of extension used to be,' Süleyman said.

Ömer Mungun entered İkmen's office. 'Oh, are you in a meeting?'

'No, we're just talking about the Kavaş case,' İkmen said. 'You've had a conversation with Dr Sarkissian, I believe.'

Ömer sat down. 'Yes, sir,' he said. 'I received information via my sister about a possible Bloom syndrome patient at the

Or-Ahayim Hospital about ten years ago. Dr Sarkissian knows a surgeon there, who told him there was no record of such a person.'

'Who did your sister get her information from?'

'A Pink Angel,' Ömer said. 'She's a friend.'

'Mmm. They generally know what's going on,' İkmen said. 'You made a note of what was said?'

'Yes, sir.'

'Let me have it.'

'I will.'

'Inspector Süleyman was just talking about the fact that the residents of the squat in Karaköy have demolished an old extension to the side of the building.' He looked at Süleyman. 'We've no reason to think that the squatters are involved in the Kavaş case.'

'Apart from a report from an Imam Ayan that his sons, both of whom are now missing, used to give the squatters a hard time. This in itself is nothing, but—'

'Oh, wasn't this something about a boy who had an idea the Ayan kids had been taken by the squatters?'

'Yes. A Syrian kid. But it's a complete dead end. Both Mustafa and Burak Ayan are in Syria with ISIS.'

'Ah, yes. Kerim was circulating descriptions.'

'We checked the imam's phone, and he was indeed called by his son Burak from Syria. He told his father that his brother had died for Islam.'

İkmen put his head in his hands.

'I've no reason to doubt that is true,' Süleyman said. 'But of course I'm uneasy, shall we say, when I see suspicious behaviour happening in a property connected in any way to an investigation.'

'I agree with you.' İkmen looked up. 'Fortunately for us, the hacker I engaged yesterday to look into the possibility of Internet cannibal fetish activity in the city lives in the squat.'

'Oh? Who is it?'

'A young zenne, would you believe, called Gül.'

Kerim Gürsel came into the office as İkmen spoke. He looked surprised.

Chapter 17

Halide Can put her phone down. The lab technician she'd spoken to had been certain the meat she'd taken from the Imperial Oriental Hotel had been wild boar. She immediately picked her phone up again and told Cetin İkmen. She also told him her other news.

'I met a junior chef who actually liked Celal Vural,' she said.

The missing waiter had been generally avoided by his colleagues, but this chef had a different opinion.

'Vural even told him that his father was Jewish,' she said.

'Interesting. Who is this man?' İkmen asked.

'Bülent,' she said.

'Bülent who?'

'I don't know. But he and Celal were close.'

'How did you get into conversation?'

'On a cigarette break,' she said. 'I noticed this guy standing apart from everyone else and I went over to talk to him. He said he was thinking of refusing any more shifts at the Imperial Oriental now that his friend had left.'

'Left?'

'Yes, sir, he thinks that Celal has disappeared intentionally.'

'Why?'

'Hated his job and was having marital problems, apparently.'

'Well that's new,' İkmen said. 'Wife says differently. Find

out who this Bülent is, Halide. We may need to speak to him officially.'

'Yes, sir.'

Even by day, the place made him tired. It had been many years since Imam Ayan had been to Esenler bus station. He'd only ever travelled to and from the vast Istanbul terminus at night. But daytime was no better. Maybe the toilets were a little bit more sanitary, but . . .

'Gaziantep,' Radwan said. 'You got tickets to Gaziantep?'

He was looking at the wretched things, but of course he couldn't read or speak Turkish.

'Yes,' the old man said. 'Twenty hours.'

'Took me four days,' Radwan said.

The boy had hitched lifts and insinuated himself inside melon trucks to get to Istanbul. The imam didn't like to think about what he might have had to do to persuade drivers to let him into their cars.

'This will just *feel* like four days,' the imam replied.

The boy laughed. The old man had dressed him in some of Burak's old clothes, but even they swamped him. He looked exactly what he was, an undernourished displaced Arab child. And because he could only speak Arabic, everyone probably thought they were both Syrians.

The old man sat down on a bench. Their bus didn't leave for five hours. Even taking prayer time into account, that still left oceans of empty time to kill.

The only person the imam had told of his plans was the Twisted Boy's mother, Aylin Hanım. Over the years, Imam Ayan and Aylin Hanım had shared much that was painful. Her son's illness coupled with her husband's desertion had almost driven Aylin to despair. The imam had helped her in practical ways, like obtaining work for Ramazan, and offered a kind word when she needed one. But then he owed Aylin Hanım. And he would be in her debt again. She had after all agreed to look after his house and his cats while he was away.

Aylin Hanım knew where he was going and the old man knew that she hadn't approved. Not that she'd said so. She wouldn't.

'There are ISIS safe houses in Gaziantep,' the boy said.

'Oh, and what use are they to us? We want to take one of their fighters from them.'

'I know that,' Radwan said. 'You must speak to the Kurds. But if we can go to where the safe houses are, we may hear things.'

'How do you know about ISIS safe houses? I thought all your information was made up.'

'It was,' he said. 'But Mustafa, Burak and me saw things online, at Internet cafés.'

'Safe houses?'

'No. But a hospital for mujahaddin. It was in Gaziantep.'

'This was on a jihadi site?'

'Yes.'

'In an Internet café?' The old man rolled his eyes. 'And did it look like the brightest, cleanest, most wonderful hospital you have ever seen?'

'It did.'

He put a hand on the boy's arm. 'Radwan, child, these things are used to draw people in. I don't think there is any such place.'

'Yes, but—'

'Oh my God, why am I here with you?' the imam said. 'What am I doing? This is madness.' He began to cry.

Radwan, who didn't know what the old man had just said, watched him. For a long while he said nothing. When he did finally break his silence, it was to ask for some biscuits from a buffet kiosk. The old man gave him some money, and when he came back, he said, 'Radwan, I need to tell you something about Mustafa and Burak.'

Kerim Gürsel didn't dare phone Zenne Gül. Now that Gül was working for the department, his every breath would be monitored. But how had İkmen found him – in his capacity as a hacker? Gül had given that up when he'd been barely out of his teens. Or so Pembe always said.

Gül would know not to talk about Kerim. He lived in that squat they'd been investigating in connection with the cannibal incident and still the two men hadn't even seen each other. Gül was no fool, he'd keep quiet, and anyway, İkmen, Gürsel's immediate superior, knew about his unconventional personal life. It had never got in the way before. He just had to trust.

He rang a familiar doorbell and waited for a familiar person to let him in. Most police officers knew Madame Mimi. She'd had her business on Zürafa Sokak for almost fifty years. She'd even known the great Mathild Manukyan, Istanbul's greatest, wealthiest brothel-keeper. Mimi, sadly, was of a different stamp.

'Come in,' she said through a haze of cigarette smoke.

Dressed in a tattered kimono, Mimi looked every day of her almost seventy years – and a few more. Unlike her aristocratic mentor, Mathild, she was as much a coalface worker as the rest of her girls. A combination of harassment from the authorities and competition from unlicensed Eastern European streetwalkers had made Istanbul prostitution more competitive than it had ever been. Kerim was aware that Mimi might have called the department just to earn good behaviour points with the police.

'You want a drink?' she asked.

'No thanks.'

'Mind if I do?'

'No.'

She took a bottle of rum out from under the battered table that passed for a reception desk and slugged a shot down straight. When she'd finished, she said, 'One of the girls told me that Volkan Doğan hadn't been for a while. I wish I could say that I'd noticed, but I hadn't. We were throwing old newspapers out when we found the bit about him being missing.'

'Three months ago.'

'You'd be amazed at how useful newspaper can be as insulation round the windows in the winter,' Mimi said.

'So why were you throwing it out?'

'You can have too much of a good thing sometimes,' she said. 'It was beginning to make the place look untidy.'

Kerim sat down.

'So what can you tell me, Mimi?'

'Me? Not a lot. Didn't see Volkan last time he came in.'

'He was a regular?'

'Once a month, at least,' she said. 'People think that men like him don't have sex lives, but they do. He liked Raquel.'

'Raquel?'

'She's from Antakya originally. Parents were Arabs or something.'

And her name wasn't Raquel. All Mimi's girls took exotic names when they came to the brothel. If he remembered correctly, Mimi's real name was Ayşe.

'Volkan, bless him, isn't young, and neither is Raquel, which is part of the attraction,' she said. 'Raquel takes care of him.'

'Why'd you call us?'

'The paper said he was missing. Is he still?'

'I wouldn't be here if he wasn't.'

'It said he was last seen on the twelfth of April, which was the day before he came here,' she said.

'So you're saying that Raquel . . .'

'Could've been the last person to see him, yes. And there's something else, too. He told Raquel he wasn't going home.'

'He lives with his sister.'

'Yeah. Married to some army officer who's been in prison.'

'Deniz Baydar.'

'Yes. Well Volkan told Raquel that he wasn't going back there. His sister and her old man were pissing him off. He said he was going to rent an apartment of his own. He was picking up the keys the next morning. Said he'd invite Raquel round. But he didn't. Never seen him since.'

'Did he say where this apartment was?'

'Etiler, he reckoned,' she said. 'Which made it all so sad and stupid. Can you imagine someone simple like him living in a big glass and steel mansion in the sky in Etiler? Someone like Volkan wouldn't even be allowed to make deliveries to those places. And anyway, he had no money. When he comes here, he pays mostly in coins. I don't know where he gets those from. He doesn't work. I suppose his sister keeps him.'

Kerim said nothing. The sister, Defne Baydar, would have to be told all this, which wouldn't be easy. She was an aggressive woman who would probably be angry at any suggestion that her brother used prostitutes.

'Can I speak to Raquel?' he said.

Mimi looked at her watch. 'In ten minutes,' she said. 'She's with a regular.'

Speaking to Selma Vural about her husband, her children clustered on and around her lap, was like kicking a puppy.

'Celal never said that he was dissatisfied with me,' she said, crying. 'Life is hard but we carry on. Why would he say such a thing to a stranger?'

'I don't know,' İkmen said. 'Do you know this chef, Bülent, Selma Hanım?'

'I don't know anyone Celal works with,' she said. 'I don't go out. I am a good woman, Cetin Bey.'

'I'm sure you are. But if we are to find your husband, we have to know as much about him as we can.'

'Sergeant Mungun took a hairbrush when he was here,' she said. 'What else can I do?'

'Tell me the truth.'

'I am.'

He believed her. DNA tests on hair from Vural's brush were far from complete. Could it be that, rather than being dead, this woman's husband was fit and healthy and off with another woman?

'As I say, life is hard,' she said. 'Look at this place.'

The family were so cramped inside their small apartment, it looked as if it could have been burgled. There was no storage, and on walls where shelves could have been put up, the damp was so bad the plaster had rotted. This area was one of the few working-class districts left in Kağıthane, which was slated to become a transportation hub for Istanbul's new third airport once it was built.

'It's all we can afford.'

'I know.'

'And now the landlord is getting upset about the rent,' she said. 'Which I understand. I can't pay it and we have no savings. This whole block is going to be demolished in the next few years anyway. As people are evicted or leave, the landlord doesn't replace them. He'll make money. That's what Celal always said.'

İkmen sat on a rickety chair that just about held what there was of his weight.

'Do you have family you can go to, Selma Hanım?'

'In İzmit,' she said. 'But what do I tell them?'

'The truth.'

'My parents never liked Celal,' she said. 'I married him in spite of them. I have dishonoured my family.'

İkmen had seen this scenario more times than he cared to

179

remember. A woman married a man in spite of her parents, he went bad, and she, and sometimes her children too, ended up homeless.

'Have you explained the situation to your landlord, Selma Hanım?'

'Yes. But he's unwilling to help. He wants us out.'

'Even though when people move out he doesn't replace them?'

She said nothing. She didn't want to discuss what was a source of shame any further. But he could find out the landlord's name and address easily. He'd have a quiet word.

'My husband loves me and I love him,' Selma said. 'He would never leave me and the children defenceless. He is a man of honour.'

Radwan and the imam hadn't been able to sit together on the bus. The imam sat next to a young man who would later snore all night, while the boy was squashed against the window by the fattest man in the world. In common with most cheap long-distance buses, this one was overheated, and the driver had arabesk, hip hop and even some rap blaring out of his antiquated tape recorder. In his youth, Imam Ayan had read Dante's *Divine Comedy*. Now he wondered which circle of hell he was in.

Behind him, he heard the boy squeak.

'What's the matter?' he asked.

'Nothing,' the boy said. He squeaked again.

The imam looked round. The boy was squirming in his seat. The fattest man in the world looked at them both with disgust. He thought they were Arabs.

The imam said to him, 'Don't look like that!'

The fattest man in the world looked away.

'Radwan, what is the matter, boy?' the old man said.

Then he saw a hand snake out between the seats that Radwan and the fat man sat on and dig itself into the boy's groin. He

180

stood up and walked up the aisle until he drew level with the culprit. Sitting next to a covered woman, who was probably his wife, the small, weaselly man with his hand on Radwan's penis looked up at the imam and then, untroubled, looked away.

'Shame on you, son of a donkey!'

The man looked up again, and this time he reddened.

'Leave the child alone or I will have the driver throw you off!' the old man said.

The wife didn't react, but other passengers muttered. The man said nothing, just sat back and stared out of the window.

As he returned to his seat, the imam said to Radwan, 'If he touches you again, tell me and I will give him a thrashing he will never forget.'

The boy thanked him, then said, 'You're very kind.'

His words made the old man sad. He hadn't been acting out of kindness so much as decency. The boy had experienced little of that in recent years.

The music blared and the heat increased. Imam Ayan looked at his watch. Still another eighteen hours to go.

Chapter 18

Zenne Gül knew bullshit when he saw it, and this was bullshit. A supposed meet-up site for cannibals was actually a dating site for the desperate. People past their prime, the lonely, the unlovables who had finally hit the bottom of the kink barrel and were offering themselves as food to people just like them. It was difficult to find anyone who actually wanted to eat. What was interesting about this site and the other one he'd tracked down was the advertisements.

Human meat both fresh and frozen was offered for sale. No prices, no details, no names. Just a contact e-mail address, which Gül knew from experience didn't lead directly to its owner. Did these people, any more than their Western counterparts, really have human flesh to sell? How many people wanted to do that? Gastronomy had become a huge business in recent years, with people eating things they wouldn't have dreamed of consuming ten years ago. But even so, human flesh was way beyond any of that. How had someone as kind and caring as Ümit Kavaş stepped over that line?

In spite of all his worries about his father, Ümit had always seemed cheerful. He drank and smoked too much at times, and Gül had known him to be depressed, but he had always managed to stay basically positive. Maybe he hadn't known what he was eating. Inspector İkmen had said he thought that was possible. But how had Ümit got into a situation where he ate human meat? And where had he done it?

Ümit had usually hung around Karaköy when he wasn't working. But on the day he ate the meat, when he died, he'd been up on İstiklal Caddesi. Had he got it somewhere up there? Gül knew there was a small Goth scene around İstiklal, but Ümit had been a bit old for all that. Most of the Goths were kids who wore black, got tattoos and talked about becoming vampires. A lot of them enjoyed zombie fiction, but he doubted whether any of them ate human flesh.

One of Pembe Hanım's friends, an old trans woman who called herself Madame Edith, had spoken once about snuff movies. Back in the 1970s and 80s there had been, so Edith said, horror films where people actually died. Most of these movies came from America, although Edith did say that she was once asked to be in a Turkish version. The money had been good but she'd turned it down because she feared that she, as well as the unwitting victim, would be killed.

Being back in the world of the Dark Web didn't fill Gül with any sense of achievement or joy. He was doing this because it was the right thing to do, not because he wanted to be inside people's weird fantasies. Swapping hacking for dancing had been the best move he'd ever made. There was nothing healthy about grubbing around in the far reaches of the Internet.

Whenever he'd done research for Father Bacchus, he'd always ended up feeling faintly nauseous. Where did these so-called cannibals get their victims? Did they all volunteer online, like these lost and lonely souls, or were they homeless people picked up at random? As fiction it was entertaining, but in reality . . .

It was almost eleven o'clock and nearly everyone in the house had either left for work or gone shopping. Only Ziya stayed behind, throwing what still remained of the old bathhouse into a skip. Usually he was with the other biker boy, Bülent, but on this occasion he was alone. When Gül went down to the kitchen to get himself some tea, he asked Ziya if he'd like a drink too.

'Yeah, that'd be good, thanks,' Ziya said.

When Gül had made the tea, he took it out to the biker.

'Where's Bülent today?' he asked.

'Gone to get some fertiliser,' Ziya said. 'We'll grow tulips here. And roses.'

Aylin Hanım had seen that man before. He was a policeman. What was Ramazan doing talking to him?

She called her son over, but he didn't move. He looked at her, as did the officer, but neither of them came over. She had taken the decision to cover herself completely many years ago. It made her invisible, which was what she had wanted. But sometimes it worked against her. The policeman, all smart suit and shiny shoes, didn't know how to approach her.

Aylin Hanım walked over to them.

Ramazan said, 'Inspector Süleyman was asking after Imam Ayan, Mother.'

'He's gone away,' she said. 'My son is feeding his cats.'

'Yes, he said.' The officer smiled. 'Do you know where he's gone?'

'No.'

People weren't supposed to go to Syria any more. She remembered when the imam's wife had come from that country, and how shocked everyone was by her strange clothes. Some malicious types had wondered whether she was a gypsy. But no one had ever asked the imam.

'Are you sure?'

'Yes.'

'Your son told me that Imam Ayan took a boy with him, a Syrian.'

'Yes, he did,' Ramazan said. 'Radwan.'

Stupid child! Aylin didn't know whether the imam had wanted people to know he had the boy with him or not, because he hadn't said, but she suspected that he didn't.

'I don't know about that,' she said.

'Yes, you—'

'I don't!'

'Hanım, if you know where Imam Ayan and the boy have gone, you have to tell me,' the policeman said. 'We are currently investigating the disappearance of the imam's sons, and we need to speak to him.'

If she said the word 'Syria', Aylin Hanım feared that all hell would break loose. The policeman would shout at her for not telling the authorities. She couldn't say that. But she did know where Imam Ayan had taken the bus to, which was known to be a stopping-off point for Syria.

Eventually she said, 'Gaziantep.'

He wrote it down.

'To do what?' he said.

'I don't know.'

'Do you know who he's staying with?'

'No.'

'Do you have a mobile phone number for Imam Ayan?'

'No.'

'So if his cats get sick, what do you do?'

She was lying, which was a sin, albeit in a good cause. But she couldn't continue. Of course she had his mobile number! She gave it to the policeman, who thanked her. Then he said, 'You know, Hanım, that if the imam and the boy are going to Syria, they are putting themselves in grave danger.'

'Mustafa and Burak are in Syria,' Ramazan said. That boy had always talked too much!

'They may be,' the policeman appeared to correct him. 'But the imam still shouldn't go. If that's his aim, I will have him intercepted, for his own safety. When did he and the boy leave?'

'Yesterday,' she said. 'They went from Esenler.'

*   *   *

185

İkmen put his phone down and looked over at Kerim Gürsel.

'Call Gaziantep for me, will you, Kerim?' he said. 'See if you can track down an Inspector Ali Ata. I haven't seen him for at least twenty years. He could be dead for all I know. He came up here for training and we got on. He's an old bastard, like me.'

'If you go to their website . . .'

'Yes, I know,' İkmen said. 'But as you are aware, Kerim, I find that almost as painful as having a tooth removed.'

'You have your own web profile, sir.'

'Yes, and it brings me no joy. That photograph makes me look as if I've just died.'

Kerim laughed.

'Just get me Ata's number if you can, and then you can get yourself over to Etiler,' İkmen said.

'Yes, sir.'

Based on information given to him by the prostitute known as Raquel, Kerim Gürsel had an address in Etiler for the missing Volkan Doğan. No telephone number was listed for that address, but he had managed to get in touch with the landlord of the building, who was going to meet him at the property.

İkmen, meanwhile, was concerned about the call he'd just had from Süleyman. The Syrian child who had claimed that people in the Art House squat had killed his friends seemed to be on his way back to Syria with the father of those friends. Still searching for his lost sons, Imam Ayan was putting himself and the boy in the kind of danger İkmen felt he wouldn't fully understand. The boy had escaped from Syria once, and so he had to know what ISIS and the other groups controlling parts of the country were like. But from what İkmen could gather, he was fixated on getting his friends back from wherever he believed they were.

Kerim gave İkmen Inspector Ata's direct line number and then left to go out to Etiler.

When İkmen called Ali Ata, it was as if twenty-plus years hadn't happened. They laughed and they gossiped and they asked after each other's families. Then İkmen said, 'The reason I have called you, Ali abi, is because I want you to intercept a man and a boy travelling from Istanbul to, we think, Syria. One is an Imam Ayan, in his sixties, medium height, slim, grey beard. The other is a child called Radwan, a Syrian. We think he's about twelve. The boy only speaks Arabic, so this man will communicate with him in that language. The imam, we think, has a son or sons in Syria, possibly fighting for Islamic State.'

He heard Ali Ata sigh. Like him, he was an officer of a certain vintage who was finding it hard to adjust to the reality of a new and unknowable threat from the east.

'What gets into these kids?'

'Adventure, romance, religious fervour. Pick one,' İkmen said. 'We have to make sure this man and the boy don't become casualties. I've no reason to believe that either of them wants to join Islamic State or take part in any sort of terrorist activity. They just want to find the imam's sons.'

'Understood. Do you have an ETA?'

'They should pull in at midday.'

'The direct bus. OK. I'll call you when I've got them.'

'Thank you, Ali abi.'

He put the phone down. It was doubtful whether the imam or the boy would own up to wanting to cross into Syria. However, given that the imam's sons were officially missing persons, believed to be in Syria, Ali Ata could legitimately detain them. The boy was a refugee, but if the imam was with him, they could both be sent back to Istanbul for their own protection.

İkmen, now alone, locked his door, opened his window and lit a cigarette.

The meat that Halide Can had taken from the kitchen of the Imperial Oriental Hotel had been wild boar – just like the meat he'd found. Celal Vural, the missing waiter, it seemed, had probably run off to escape his dire job and dismal home life. İkmen had to think carefully about whether he needed to keep Constable Can in the hotel. Was it just as an act of spite towards Boris Myskow, his top-of-the-range friends and their spooky protectors? There was no proof that Myskow had any connection to cannibalism, and as a person under special protection, he was dangerous to be around. If Can got caught, there would be hell to pay.

How had human flesh got into the stomach of a nice, liberal man like Ümit Kavaş? So far Zenne Gül had only found what he described as 'theoretical fantasists' in the local online cannibal community. He didn't think they acted on their fantasies. But what if they did? And what if Ümit Kavaş's outward niceness had just been a cover for this and possibly for other awful perversions? Now that the investigation had divided between the Imperial Oriental and possible sexual deviance online, it was sometimes difficult to keep one's thoughts focused.

What did concern Gül was the trade in human meat, which he said he'd come across on western European sites too. He wanted permission to contact one outlet that described itself as local. Quite how these hackers knew which advertisement or site might lead somewhere significant, İkmen couldn't imagine. Were there particular tells that gave it away? He'd have to instruct Gül to go ahead, because what choice did he have? They were getting nowhere using traditional methods. They didn't even know where Ümit had been going the night he died, or where he'd been. But would a man like Ümit Kavaş buy human meat? Really? What were they missing about the character of this man?

He called Commissioner Teker, who said she'd meet him in his office. When she arrived, she looked pale. He didn't comment on it. She explained of her own volition.

'Not sleeping,' she said as she took one of his cigarettes and lit up.

'I'm sorry.'

He told her about Gül.

She said, 'I agree. But have him make contact from here so we can supervise. Maybe Kavaş had a secret kink that was at odds with the rest of his character. These people are never who you think they are. And the whole family have been through the most terrible trauma. How do we know how having a father in prison affects a person?'

'I'm not making a connection between that and human flesh-eating myself,' İkmen said.

'No.' She shrugged. 'But we don't know everything. What I do know is that General Kavaş's wife has left town to go and stay with a relative. The old man is alone.'

'The general is a brick wall,' İkmen said. 'The trouble is that nobody really knew Ümit Kavaş. Not his childhood friend Cengiz Tanır nor the people he mixed with at the squat. He mainly worked from home and socialised when he wanted to, which wasn't very much. I know it is said that people who indulge strange fantasies tend to be reclusive . . .'

'Ümit, as I recall, was sometimes spoiled,' Teker said. 'Babies born late in their parents' lives can be. But he was always a gentle, thoughtful child.'

'No dog torturing?'

'No,' she smiled. 'The only thing I think I'd say was a little left field about Ümit was his patriotism.'

İkmen frowned.

'Like his father, and my father to some extent, he was a Turkish nationalist, albeit an extremely liberal one,' she said. 'The Kavaş family have always had an almost fanatical devotion to the secular republic. My father and General Kavaş argued about it. It's why they didn't remain friends.'

'Where did your father stand?'

'He was a pragmatist,' she said. 'He believed, as I do, that those

189

who wish to live a religious life have to be accommodated and included within the system. That's what I think Ümit believed too. If we can't do that, then how can we call ourselves a democracy?'

İkmen sighed. 'I am so tired of these arguments,' he said. 'Why do we have to take sides? Why can't people just be left alone to believe what they like and pursue their lifestyles as they wish – within reason?'

She laughed. 'Within reason? What does that mean, Cetin Bey? For some, the fact that others eat pork is beyond reason; for others, the sight of people praying is anathema. Where do you draw the line?'

'I don't know,' he said. 'But someone is still missing out there. Someone, and maybe a second person, is dead. Sergeant Gürsel is following up a lead on Volkan Doğan . . .'

'Major General Baydar's brother-in-law.'

'Yes. But we can't find any Jewish connection. Or rather, we haven't yet.'

'Have you been inside Le Meridien, Sergeant?'

Kerim Gürsel resisted the urge to say, *Do I look like someone who visits high-end hotels?* But he restrained himself. Barbaros Bey, the landlord of the Etiler Diamond, the city's 'foremost residential destination', was a pleasant enough young man. By his own admission, Barbaros's father was an 'Anatolian Tiger', one of the new group of conservative businessmen to come out of cities like Konya and Kayseri. Encouraged by the ruling party, the Tigers had thrown themselves into businesses like real estate and construction with incredible energy. And while some had tarnished reputations due to poor safety standards, the Laleli Corporation, which Barbaros chaired, was not one of them.

'I never personally met Volkan Bey,' Barbaros continued. 'My agent, Erdel Bey, showed him around apartment number 12. Of course we would rather that people bought our apartments, but

190

number 12 was advertised to buy or to rent, and Volkan Bey did pay three months up front.'

'How much per month do you charge?' Kerim said.

'Seven thousand Turkish lire.'

They got into a glass lift, which would take them to floor four. It was on the outside of the building, which was also mainly glass.

'That's a lot of money,' Kerim said.

'Well, you've got Bosphorus views on one side and Le Meridien on the other. This is a prime address, Sergeant.'

But even so . . .

Apartment 12 was on the next floor up. It could only be accessed via a private lift. Barbaros entered the appropriate code and the two men stepped in.

'So does this lift take us directly into the apartment?'

'We'll get out in a lobby. Then we'll use a keycard to enter the property itself. Our residents, particularly of our prime apartments, are offered complete security. As I told you on the phone I have tried to obtain a response by ringing Mr Doğan's doorbell but to no effect.'

The lift opened in front of a wood-effect security door.

'What about facilities for the residents?' Kerim asked.

'Well, as you saw, we offer secure underground parking,' Barbaros said. 'There's a fully equipped gym on the second floor and a pool on the roof. We clean all the public areas, and for a small extra cost, residents have the option of cleaning services in their homes. Volkan Bey didn't take that option.'

He opened the door. At that point, Kerim detected nothing untoward.

The girls hadn't seen each other for a couple of days. Aysel had booked time off a long while ago in order to see her mother in Eskihisar. But now she was back and was having coffee with her friend Halide in trendy Cihangir.

'How are you enjoying the kitchen cleaner's life?' Aysel asked.

Halide put down her iced coffee and lit a cigarette. 'I will never complain about my job again,' she said.

Aysel laughed. 'It's tough, eh?'

'I'm almost beyond words.'

The garden of the White Mill Café was well known as an oasis of calm in an otherwise frenetic city. The women met there often.

Aysel leaned across the table. 'So is the job, you know, useful?'

Halide frowned. 'Not as yet.'

'Sorry.'

'It's not your fault,' Halide said. 'But you may be able to help me with something.'

'Name it.'

'Do you know anything about that chef called Bülent who sometimes does a shift?'

'Bülent Onay? Rides a Harley-Davidson? Yes, I know him a bit,' she said. 'Be careful around him.'

'Why?'

'He sucks up to Mr Myskow. Chef Tandoğan hates him.'

'What, for being a fan?'

'No,' Aysel said, 'because Mr Myskow likes Bülent and shares his recipes with him. Tandoğan is jealous. If he sees you getting too close to Bülent, he'll fire you.'

He knew that smell. As they walked through the vast lounge and into one of the three bathrooms, it was getting stronger. Why had a man on his own rented such a large apartment? Not only did it have three bathrooms, it had four bedrooms. So far it was all very high-spec indeed.

He said to Barbaros Taytak, 'I think I should go ahead on my own now.'

'Why?'

'Just do as I ask, sir.'

The landlord sat down.

The bathroom led into a small bedroom, where the smell became stronger. Kerim took a handkerchief out of his pocket. Beyond this bedroom was another bathroom, and then the master bedroom, which Barbaros Bey had said afforded stunning views of the Bosphorus.

In the second bathroom he found a few flies. Not many, which struck an odd note when coupled with the smell. This bathroom had a Jacuzzi. He opened the door into the master bedroom.

And there it was. On the bed, as well as liquefying into it, was a body. Even from across the room he could see maggots. It must have been there for weeks, if not months. Kerim put the handkerchief up to his nose and gagged. The reason so few flies remained was that a window was slightly open. He could see the Bosphorus shining in the sunlight; it *was* stunning. He made himself walk over to the bed.

The body was man-sized, and – another reason for the lack of flies – it was also drying out. No face remained. He gagged again. Every dead body was grotesque but some were more offensive than others. This one was bad.

'Sergeant Gürsel?'

Reluctantly he took the handkerchief away from his nose and said, 'Please don't come in, sir.'

'Oh.'

'Stay where you are, I'm going to have to make a call.'

'Does that mean he's dead, Sergeant?'

'Yes,' Kerim said.

And then he wondered how that awful old woman Defne Baydar was going to react when he told her not only that her brother was dead, but that he'd found out where he was from a prostitute.

193

Chapter 19

The bus pulled into the station over two hours late. Due to inactivity and the heat, the imam's feet had swollen to almost double their size. Radwan was exhausted, upset by the man who had tried to grab his privates and still traumatised by what the imam had told him about Mustafa and Burak. But they couldn't get off.

'The police are checking everyone's papers,' the imam said to the boy.

'I don't have any.'

Police officers were stationed each side of the exit. The fattest man in the world stood up with some difficulty and the imam slid painfully into his seat.

'If they stop me, I'm never going to be able to run like this,' the old man said.

'What can we do?'

The imam thought for a moment. A woman was arguing with the police about having mistakenly picked up her husband's ID card.

'Although I think you're making a mistake, you want to go home,' the imam said.

'Yes. But we want to find Burak first, don't we? To tell him. They won't stop you, will they?'

'They might,' he said. 'I missed a call from Aylin Hanım last night. Perhaps she has told people where we've gone. Now look, Radwan, you must get off the bus before me, and while I pretend

194

to look for your papers, you must slip away. It's the only way you'll get back home.' He shook his head. 'This was a mad idea. I don't know why I listened to you!'

'But won't they shoot me? The police?'

'I don't know,' he said. 'Stay with me and we will go back to Istanbul.'

'But I want to go home.'

The imam put his head in his hands.

'Well it's male. But I'll be honest, I'm taking my cue from his clothes at this stage.'

Kerim Gürsel looked at the doctor expectantly.

'What do you want me to say?' Arto Sarkissian said. 'How long has he been dead? Answer, at the moment, is a long time.'

He walked away from the bed fanning his face. The stench was overwhelming, even for the pathologist.

'Do you have any idea who he might have been, Sergeant Gürsel?' he asked.

'A man called Volkan Doğan rented this apartment.' Kerim had found that, oddly, he was coping with the smell now. 'Sixty-five years old. He was reported missing three months ago.'

'And he was here all the time?'

'Maybe.'

'God!' The pathologist looked in his attaché case for something that turned out to have a hook on the end.

'He rented this apartment without his family's knowledge,' Kerim said.

The doctor shook his head. 'These accursed blocks cut people off from neighbourhoods and life in general,' he said. 'That a man can come to a place like this and die without anyone noticing appals me. I hate these places. All this building is destroying everything that was good and decent about this city.'

'Will his family have to identify the body?'

'Why?'

The doctor was very aggressive. He wasn't usually. Kerim wondered what was wrong.

'Well . . .'

'Sergeant Gürsel, if I can't find a face, do you think they'll be able to?'

He put the thing with the hook somewhere inside the body, and Kerim looked away.

'No, this will be dental records and, maybe, DNA,' he said. 'It's not going to be a quick fix, and if you're wondering why I'm not my usual happy and optimistic self, not only is this smell worse than anything I've come across lately, but I also have an abscess on a tooth. Quite honestly, the way I feel at the moment, I just wish a passing veterinary surgeon would put me down.'

'Do you have painkillers?' As soon as he'd said it, Kerim felt stupid.

'Of course I have painkillers. I'm a doctor of a certain age.'

'Sorry.'

The doctor shook his head. 'No, I'm sorry, Sergeant Gürsel,' he said. 'It is inexcusable of me to behave in such an unprofessional manner.'

'Well, toothache . . .'

'Oh, the toothache is the least of it!' he said. 'The reality of the situation is that I have a domestic problem that this place, tragically, calls to mind. Not your fault, or even the fault of the building.' He smiled. 'Let us start again, shall we?'

'If you wish, Doctor.'

'I do.' He sighed. 'Good afternoon, Sergeant Gürsel, what do we have here?'

*   *   *

Bülent Onay didn't have a police record, but he was a 'person of interest'. As a student at Boğaziçi University, he'd been a left-wing activist, he'd been involved in the Gezi protests of 2013, and he now lived in the Art House squat in Karaköy. He also had a highly desirable Harley-Davidson motorbike.

'There were two men in biker leathers when I visited,' Süleyman said. 'One dark and the other fair.'

'Bülent is fair, sir,' Halide Can said.

'So this Bülent is close to Myskow?' İkmen said.

'No, sir, but Myskow likes him, according to Aylin. Seems odd to me that he even knows a casual chef.'

'Maybe Bülent has talent.'

'If he's replicating Myskow's recipes, then he must be good,' she said. 'What with the foams, airs and vacuum cooking, a lot of the chefs struggle with Myskow's "vision" – his word, not mine. Only Romero just gets on and does it, and Bülent. Tandoğan struggles, which is why he's so angry all the time.'

'All life exists in a kitchen,' İkmen said.

'Yes.'

'Do you know if Bülent ever works with Myskow alone?' Süleyman said. 'Maybe at these private dinners he cooks?'

'Aysel told me he has done, but I've not noticed him going up there myself,' she said.

'Do you know where else he works?'

'What, because he's casual? I don't know,' she said. 'Maybe he doesn't. He's well educated – apparently he speaks English like an Englishman – and he must have money to run the bike.'

'Mmm.' İkmen frowned. Then he said, 'And he's due in tonight?'

'Yes, sir.'

'See what happens,' he said. 'Try and have a conversation with him again, if you can. Do you think he's telling the truth about Celal Vural?'

'Why would he lie?'

'Unless he had a hand in Vural's disappearance,' Süleyman said.

Halide Can left to get some sleep before her next shift at the hotel.

İkmen lit a cigarette. 'I'm wondering how much I can ask Zenne Gül about Bülent Onay,' he said.

'Are they friends?' Süleyman said.

'I don't know.'

'Do you trust Zenne Gül?'

'I think so,' İkmen said. 'Find out for yourself. He's due here in an hour.'

'I have met him briefly.'

'Oh yes.'

'You don't feel you should go out to Etiler?'

'Kerim can handle it. He's a big boy now. I just hope the body is that of Volkan Doğan, so that at least we can clear that situation away. To be honest with you, I am avoiding Dr Sarkissian at the moment.'

'Why?'

They had always been such close friends.

'A property developer has bought the vacant plot of land next door to the doctor's house. Yesterday he was shown what they plan to build on it.'

'Is it huge?'

'Not by modern standards, no,' İkmen said. 'Ten floors of glass and steel. Residences for the rich who want modern apartment living and Bosphorus views.'

The doctor lived in what was little short of a mansion on the northern shore of the Bosphorus at Yeniköy.

'I didn't think redevelopment was allowed in Yeniköy,' Süleyman said. 'The rich live there.'

'I think you'll find,' İkmen said, 'that when money is involved, there is no protection, unless you're the right kind of rich.'

'Which is?'

'The kind that have influence in high places or an enormous amount of money to buy the bastards out.'

The imam and the policemen were speaking in Turkish, so Radwan couldn't understand them. But he could see when the old man put his hand in his jacket and began to search through his pockets. There was less than a second to make a decision.

The boy ran. He heard shouting, then a scream, and then he thought he heard a gunshot. But he kept on running. The bus station was huge and modern and he didn't know where he was going. All he knew was that he had to get home. Whoever was in Syria and whatever was happening, it had to be better than living in a place where no one understood him and most people looked down their noses. And in Istanbul, there were ghosts . . .

Radwan could hear the sound of boots on marble as the police came after him. Was the bus station anywhere near the city, or was it in the middle of nowhere like so many of them? There was more shouting. Radwan jumped over a small pile of plastic toys for sale in the middle of a walkway. If only he could understand what people were saying!

Imam Ayan had been kind to him, but once he got home, Radwan knew he'd forget all about Burak Ayan. Mustafa was dead already, and Burak had always been a crazy boy. Maybe it was because he was so small that he fell in love with ISIS. Perhaps being part of something like that made him feel bigger and stronger. Burak had always envied Mustafa. Radwan had seen how he looked at him, and Mustafa hadn't helped. He'd sometimes talked about their mother, and how Burak had clearly inherited her delicate hawk-like Arab features.

The police were gaining on him. Once he felt fingers just touch his shoulder. But he'd put on a turn of speed since then. Not that they were giving up. Radwan turned a corner, which was when a hand grabbed his arm and pulled him into a place that was dark and hot and smelled of oil.

Zenne Gül had expected İkmen to be in his office. But he wasn't.

An exotic-looking young man called Sergeant Mungun said, 'He'll be with you as soon as he can. He's with Inspector Süleyman, there's a problem.'

'Oh. Shall I come back later?' Gül said.

'No. Wait, please,' Mungun said. 'It's not a problem with you. I will bring you tea.'

He left.

Alone in İkmen's cluttered office, Gül put his laptop on the great man's desk and sat down.

Unknown to İkmen, as yet, he'd already made contact with the seller of frozen human meat and begun a conversation. The meat came, the seller claimed, from Eastern Europe. He or she further claimed that it had been obtained from a willing source. Gül had asked for more details but had received an angry response along the lines of 'Why do you need to know?'

He'd heard about willing victims before, and not just in the context of the German cannibal Armin Meiwes. Eastern Europe was frequently cited as a source for two reasons – first, the connection to the area of vampire legends; and second, because people in places like Romania were poor. The poor were vulnerable; they could be killed and not missed and then passed off as willing meat for those enthralled by the dark myths of Transylvania. But that still didn't mean the meat on offer was genuine. If it existed at all. On the Dark Web, face-to-face meetings were even more hazardous to engineer than ordinary Internet negotiated assignations. Getting close to people who claimed to be so outlandish in their tastes could put one at grave risk. Gül had heard stories of people going to meetings being robbed, raped or blackmailed. Some, it was said, had even been killed.

The office door slammed open and İkmen entered, followed by the handsome Süleyman.

'Gül, I am so sorry I was not here for you,' İkmen said as he sat down behind his desk. 'You've met Inspector Süleyman, I believe.'

'Yes.'

Süleyman shook his hand. 'Good afternoon.'

'So, Gül, tell me where we are up to,' İkmen said.

It didn't take long to get İkmen and Süleyman up to speed. Ömer Mungun came in with tea halfway through his exposition and then left.

'You feel this particular line of enquiry is useful?' İkmen said.

'Yes. I can't guarantee that it's genuine, any more than I can say that for the ads on any number of sites,' Gül said.

'What makes this one stand out for you?' Süleyman asked.

Gül thought for a moment. To say that he had a feeling about it was too vague, even if he knew that over the years he had come to trust such a notion. Was it because this advertisement had been so discreet?

'Some of these so-called human meat sellers seem to enjoy decorating their advertisements with pictures of naked women and symbols denoting devil worship,' he said. 'Anecdotal evidence I've come across in the past would seem to suggest that these are not serious. Their aim is to get people with weird kinks to come to them. Their motive is generally sexual and involves instant gratification. The quicker the better.'

He told them his theory about Eastern Europe.

Süleyman said, 'But this could still be nonsense, right?'

'Oh, absolutely. Real cannibalism is rare. It's something people claim to have done or say they want to do. All life, however odd, is on the Internet. Much of it is pure fantasy. I've not said I'll buy this person's goods, just that I'm interested.'

'OK. So what's the next step?'

'Purchase.'

'How does that work?'

'How he or she wants it to work,' he said. 'I'll almost certainly have to pay up front, and then the meat will either be delivered to me or we'll agree to meet somewhere for the handover.'

'How will you pay up front?' Süleyman asked.

'Could be via Western Union,' Gül said.

'Bit old-fashioned, isn't it?'

'It'll be that or Bitcoin.'

'That I don't understand.'

'Fortunately I do.'

'I will be guided by you, then.'

'OK. I'll be given a name, probably bogus,' Gül said, 'and if we assume the money will go by Western Union, the location of the office I'm to send it to. But this is all speculative, Inspector. Until I agree to actually buy the meat, I won't know. It's a risk.'

'Mmm.' İkmen frowned. 'How much does he want?'

'I've said I'm interested in buying two kilos,' Gül said. 'He wants a thousand lire.'

'Expensive.'

'Of course. Which is something that makes me think it could be genuine. I can get it for half that price on other sites. But if this is a real phenomenon, then whoever is selling will sell high. It's a trade that is full of jeopardy, and of course it's also a money-making scheme. The seller, if genuine, is taking huge risks.'

İkmen looked at Süleyman, who shrugged. 'All right, say you'll buy. I'll get you the money. But you must say that you want to meet rather than have the goods delivered to your home. We can set up an address, but I'd rather you agreed a meeting place that we can observe.'

'He'll almost certainly want a conversation via Skype before that happens.'

'So he can see you.'

'Yes.'

İkmen nodded. 'OK. Let me know when that is and we'll have an officer stand in for you.'

Zenne Gül laughed. 'You think?'

'What's the problem? We can brief him.'

'Inspector,' Gül said, 'those who use the Dark Web are a particular breed. We know our own, and this person will smell a police officer, trust me.'

'But I can't let you go to this meeting,' İkmen said. 'Even with back-up from us. It's too dangerous.'

'If you want to get a result, you're going to have to,' Gül said. 'There isn't time for me to teach your officer what he'll need to know.'

There was something about this police officer that made Defne Baydar's skin crawl. Courteous and polite, he was nevertheless not a classical man's man, and that made her uncomfortable. Being brought up around soldiers had made her expect a man to be as hard and emotionless as she was. And then, of course, it had been this officer who had suggested her family might be Jews.

'How did you find my brother?' she asked.

If it was Volkan. This Gürsel man said that the body they had discovered in Etiler was in a highly degraded state.

'We obtained the address from one of his friends.'

'Volkan had no friends. He was simple.'

She watched Sergeant Gürsel swallow. What did he have to tell her that he knew she wouldn't like?

'This friend, a lady, is a . . . well, a bad . . .'

'You mean she's a prostitute? I don't believe it,' Defne said. 'Deniz Bey?'

Her husband had been hiding behind his newspaper. Stupid man! 'What?'

'This policeman says that Volkan went to a prostitute. I've

203

never heard anything so ridiculous in my life.' She turned to Kerim Gürsel. 'This is nonsense. Whoever you've found in Etiler is not my brother.'

'We have his kimlik.'

'So you have my brother's identity card! So what? This man could have taken Volkan's identity when he killed or robbed him! Don't you people think of these things?'

'Yes, but—'

'Defne Hanım, of course Volkan went to prostitutes,' her stupid husband said. 'How else was he to fulfil his sexual needs?'

'I don't believe it!'

'Madam . . .'

'Believe what you like. I knew he went to a brothel,' Deniz Baydar said.

'You knew!'

He looked at the policeman. 'Place in Karaköy?'

'Yes, sir,' the officer said. 'A lady who has known Mr Doğan for many years. He planned, so she said, to entertain her at the address in Etiler. But then she heard nothing from him.'

'I see.'

'We had to get the landlord to use his duplicate key to get in. Mr Doğan had paid three months' rent in advance and had also bought a considerable amount of clothing. Do you know where he got this money from?'

Defne began to speak, but her husband interrupted her. 'Volkan inherited money from his parents,' he said. 'My wife administered his account, giving him a monthly allowance.'

'He paid his landlord in cash.'

'Then he must have saved,' her husband said.

'It's not him!' Defne said. 'Volkan had no sexual needs! His type don't.'

'Oh but they do, my dear. Everyone has sexual needs. Well, almost everyone.'

Defne left the room. How could he shame her in such a way, and in front of a stranger? Just because he was an animal who used all sorts to satisfy his lust didn't mean that everyone was like him. She understood and approved his stand on the notion of the Turks as a warrior race, but his beliefs about the nation tipped over into perversion. It had to be because he was really a Jew.

She could hear the policeman talking to him and she cringed. Deniz had known for years that Volkan went to prostitutes. Why hadn't he told the police that when her brother went missing? She found it hard to believe it was to protect her, but that was the only explanation she could find.

Chapter 20

The man looked at him and said something in a language he couldn't understand. Radwan shook his head. He was young, this man, and very dark. Could he perhaps be from the Gulf? Or Saudi Arabia? But if he was, why wasn't he speaking Arabic?

'I don't understand,' Radwan said.

Outside, in the bus station, he could still hear raised voices. The police hadn't given up looking for him. He wondered what the imam had told them, if anything.

'Why you run from Turkish police?' the man said.

He wasn't a native Arabic speaker. His accent was weird.

Radwan shrugged.

'You want to go to the caliphate?'

However he answered would determine whether Radwan got out of this small storeroom alive. From the way he was dressed, the man could be ISIS, a local Turk or a member of any number of rebel groups.

'No . . .'

'Why?'

Radwan thought for a moment and then decided that his best course of action was honesty. 'I want to go home,' he said.

'Syria?'

'Yes.'

'Is the caliphate now,' the man said, and then he smiled. 'You want to come to the caliphate?'

'Well, yes, if Syria is the caliphate now. If you put it like that . . .'

'Good. Good!'

And then the man hugged him. Radwan felt the knife in his belt touch his legs.

'You didn't ask Zenne Gül about Bülent Onay,' Süleyman said to İkmen.

'No. I decided against it.'

'Why?'

'I don't want him to be distracted,' İkmen said. 'If he's going to pursue this meat line of enquiry for us, we need him to concentrate on that. Ömer is running further checks on Onay. And anyway I have another idea . . .'

His phone rang. He picked it up. 'İkmen.'

Süleyman couldn't hear the person at the other end of the line, but when the call had finished, İkmen said, 'Gaziantep have Imam Ayan, but not the boy.'

'They were travelling together.'

'Yes, they were,' he said. 'But the kid made a run for it at the bus station and our country cousins, no doubt full of ayran and too much lahmacun, let the little bugger get away.'

Süleyman shook his head. Gaziantep was a big city; they should have been on top of the situation. But they hadn't been, and now this latest loss would just be chalked up to rural incompetence, like so many incidents in the past involving forces out of town.

'They're sending the imam back here,' İkmen said. 'He held his hands up to the charge that he was attempting to get to the caliphate. But he said the boy wasn't. In which case, why take him?'

'Oh, he was using the child's local knowledge,' Süleyman said. 'Did he mention his son, Burak?'

'Yes, he said he was planning to go in and get him out.'

'Delusional.'

'We know that. But how would you feel if it was your son?' İkmen said. 'I'd go, I'll be honest.'

'And you'd die.'

'So what? It's your child. We'll interview the imam when he gets back. Gaziantep will carry on looking for the boy.'

Süleyman said nothing. The child was as good as lost. He changed the subject. 'What's your other idea about Bülent Onay?'

'We'll see what Ömer can find,' İkmen said. 'Hopefully Constable Can will see Bülent tonight, and then, I think, surveillance.'

'Not using Zenne Gül, who is on the spot?'

'No,' he said. 'And not just because we want him to concentrate on his Internet work. I'm not entirely convinced it's a good idea to show him too much of our investigation. He lives in that house, and we can't be sure what dynamics are at play in there.'

'You said you trusted him,' Süleyman said.

İkmen laughed. 'My dear Mehmet. Haven't you realised yet that I actually trust no one?'

There was no better way of expressing how difficult it had been to get the Etiler body into a bag than that of one of the orderlies, who had said it was 'like pouring water into a sock'.

Arto Sarkissian laughed when he thought about it. Standing next to the body on a mortuary table didn't make it any less funny. Or true.

The corpse was in a very advanced state of decay brought about by time and the action of central heating. But there was something else too, which might or might not be significant. There was some evidence of what could be defence wounds on the forearms. It was as if someone had sliced them.

Could it be flesh removal for, possibly, cannibalistic purposes?

Or was it self-harm? The latter was rare in males, particularly in this older age group. But it wasn't an impossible scenario.

The doctor put plastic gloves on and began a close visual examination. The stench was dreadful, but he was accustomed to it. Few of his subjects ever smelled exactly sweet. God, the face was just liquid! There was no way that Volkan Doğan's family could see him like this. Identification would have to be via the few documents he had on him, and dental records. But who else could it be?

The poor man had been simple, by all accounts. Trying to have an independent life of some sort, he'd spent a lot of money, and now he'd died. The doctor hoped it was from natural causes. A wish for a violent death was something he reserved for the people who wanted to build next door to his house.

'You know you're no fun these days, don't you?'

Gül looked up from his laptop screen. 'What?'

Meltem walked into his bedroom. 'You,' she said. 'You're always either at work or on that thing. I thought you'd given all that up.'

Gül shut the screen down.

'I told you, I'm just fiddling around.'

'You know Pembe Hanım came by this afternoon?' Meltem said. 'But you were out.'

He'd been with İkmen. Wouldn't Pembe already have known that via her lover Kerim? Maybe not.

Meltem sat on Gül's bed.

'The boys have been working really hard on the garden today,' she said. 'Digging out the last of the old foundations and putting in fertiliser.'

'Oh.' Gül couldn't be less interested in what the macho men were doing out in the yard. It would be nice to have flowers to look at, and maybe even some vegetables to eat, but gardening wasn't Gül's thing.

'Then Deniz Bey arrived,' Meltem said. 'He was absolutely furious and wanted to see Uğur Bey.'

'What? He was angry with Uğur Bey? Why?'

'No, not with Uğur Bey, with his own wife,' Meltem said. 'He wanted to let off steam to Uğur Bey, but he was out. I sat with him in the end. Defne Hanım is convinced that Deniz Bey has Jewish forebears. She keeps on about it. And now the police think they've found her brother – dead.'

'What's that got to do with Jews?'

'Nothing as far as I know. Except that apparently the police had asked her whether her brother was Jewish.'

'*Her* brother?'

'Yes. Weird. Deniz Bey had no idea about that. He said he tried to comfort Defne Hanım but she didn't want him near her. Can't say I understand that.'

'No.'

'Anyway, the garden's coming along, and if you want to choose plants, you should put your order in now,' she said. 'The boys are going to start making beds in a couple of days.'

They talked for a while and then she left. Gül wasn't really that interested in the garden, but he did take a look out of the window before he settled down in front of the laptop again. It looked as if it had just snowed.

They were coming back for more and they were bringing friends. Thirty covers all on his own was impossible. He'd need help. He'd have to phone the little shit and make sure he was coming in. He didn't dare ask anyone else. How had a few pork chops led to this?

The little shit agreed, but he wasn't happy.

'You should never have told them what it was,' he said. 'Were you boasting, or what?'

He had been boasting. Of course he had. Boris Myskow had

the most innovative table in the world; he could and would serve anything.

He said, 'You have no cause to criticise me!'

And he didn't.

In the daytime it was strange. But at night it was eerie. A vast empty settlement of ancient stone decorated with carvings of weird beasts, half man, half lion.

'Idols,' Waheed said.

He said he came from the United Kingdom, but Radwan was suspicious. He was very dark for an Englishman.

'When we have this place, they will all be smashed,' Waheed said.

They walked up a stone staircase. It was very quiet. During the autumn and spring, people came to this place to dig up things Radwan's father had told him were from the time of the Hittites. He didn't know much about who the Hittites were, except that they were ancient people who had been in the area before Islam. The people who came were scientists who were trying to find out things about the Hittites. Radwan had no idea why.

The place the man and the boy were alone in at night was called Karkemiş. On the northern shore of the Euphrates river, it was across the Turco–Syrian border from the ISIS-held town of Jerablus. In the daytime, Radwan had been able to see the black flag of the jihadists flying over the settlement. Now it was their goal.

'Once we're in the caliphate, you'll be given a gun,' the man said.

Radwan said nothing. He'd seen enough guns to last a lifetime.

'And you can get married.'

Why? He just wanted to go home. To curl up in a corner of his house, go to sleep and not wake up. He'd try to find Burak for the imam because he'd promised to do that, but he didn't want to fight. Or get married.

The man led him into a maze of stone and brush. Occasionally they could see lights from the nearby Syrian town, but there was no light on in Karkemiş. In summer, most of those who dug went away because it was too hot. Only a few remained plus some Turkish soldiers. But Waheed knew ways through the site that they didn't, or so he said.

Radwan hadn't managed to get to the bottom of the reason why Waheed had been at Gaziantep bus station. He'd tried to explain in his limited Arabic, but Radwan hadn't understood. It had something to do with delivering things to people was all he could make out, but he didn't know what.

Watching where he put his feet in case he tripped, Radwan wondered what had happened to the imam and whether the police had beaten him. He didn't feel as safe with Waheed as he had with the old man. When they'd needed something to eat, Waheed had stolen it from a cart. Why had he done that? He had money.

Assholes!

Snouts in the trough, snuffling up their illicit pleasure. Laughing. He wanted to ask Bülent what he thought about them, but he knew. He hated the sight of them. Even the way he served them made that plain. Whacking their plates down in front of their unconcerned, overfed faces.

Boris Myskow went back into the kitchen to finish preparing the desserts. Butterscotch peanut butter cake. Nice and heavy. He hoped they had heart attacks. Why had he allowed himself to become involved with these bastards? He knew, and it made his blood freeze. It was all his own fault. He could have passed on Istanbul, easy as anything. But everyone had said it was the new place to be.

The peanut butter was like glue. Fuck it. It'd be like working with shit. It looked like shit. He flopped it in anyway and stirred. He had to give a bit of a fuck or they'd all decamp elsewhere, and then who knew what would happen to him? He'd go back to the States, he supposed. Was that so bad? He took it in to them and made a bit of limited conversation. Then he returned to the kitchen.

He saw a movement out of his left eye. If that was that fucking moron Tandoğan, he'd rip him a new arsehole. Useless prick. But then he saw that it wasn't Tandoğan, it was that girl he'd caught in the kitchen before, and she had her head in his freezer.

They laughed a lot, the boys from ISIS. Radwan didn't know exactly where they were except that they were in the town of Jerablus. His father had had a cousin in Jerablus, he remembered. He wondered whether any of these men had killed him.

They spoke in a variety of languages, but mainly Arabic, albeit a kind of weird Arabic with strange accents. He could understand, but he had to concentrate. They talked about women. Not their wives, but their 'slaves', as they called them, mainly Yezidi girls. Radwan remembered a family of Yezidis who had lived in his neighbourhood back in Aleppo. They'd been a quiet group. The father had owned a shoe mender's shop.

Waheed had given him a gun for a bit. It lay by his side now. They'd shown him how to use it and taken pictures of him with it on their mobile phones. All he wanted to do was get out. He'd asked Waheed if he knew Burak Ayan, but he'd said he didn't. He wanted to ask the rest of them, but they were so high he didn't dare. ISIS fighters didn't drink or do drugs, and so how they could be that high, Radwan didn't understand.

One of them poked him in the ribs. 'You had a woman yet, little man?'

Radwan felt his face go red.

Another man said, 'No, he hasn't. Look at him! Have you ever seen such a virgin in your life? We must get this boy married!'

He was twelve. Or was it thirteen now? Radwan couldn't remember. His mum had married his dad when she was sixteen, but his father had been twice her age. He was a kid; he didn't want to get married. He didn't even have a job.

'I'm fine,' he said.

A man with a long red beard pushed his face close. 'You some kind of homo, boy?'

'No!'

He'd heard that they threw homosexuals off buildings.

'Then you should have a woman,' the man said. 'Women raise the heat of the blood, which is good for a man of war.'

'Yes, but if he doesn't want to marry, maybe just give him a girl,' Waheed said.

'A slave.'

'To practise on.'

They were all laughing when they took Radwan to a tent behind what had been a shop. When they pulled the tent flap to one side, he saw a row of girls with frightened eyes. They pushed him in. Radwan didn't know what to do. The girls were little, like his sisters. Waheed threw what had become Radwan's gun in after him.

'If they don't do what you want, use this,' he said.

They all stood at the open tent flap, laughing.

'Get on with it!'

Radwan looked at the girls. Then he looked at the gun. Not only were the high ISIS boys looking at him, but the tent was guarded by four men whose faces were covered. Radwan needed to even out the odds.

'I can't do anything with you lot watching,' he said.

'Aww!'

'Shame!'

They all laughed. But they replaced the tent flap.

Radwan looked at the little girls and put a finger to his lips. Ever since he'd left Aleppo, everything he'd done had been wrong. Now he was at least back in his homeland. What he needed to do as soon as possible was something right.

Chapter 21

The old man shook in his chair. Whether it was because he was afraid of the law or still traumatised after his flight from Gaziantep, Cetin İkmen didn't know. Imam Ayan had never flown before and had been sick twice on the one-hour journey. İkmen sent Kerim Gürsel to get tea and water. He waited until Mehmet Süleyman had joined them and his sergeant had returned before he began his interrogation.

'I take it, Imam Ayan,' he said, 'that your recent journey to Gaziantep is indicative of your belief that your sons are not somehow imprisoned in the Art House squat in Karaköy.'

'I never thought the boys were there,' he said. 'That came from Radwan.'

'The Syrian child?'

'Yes.'

'Do you know where Radwan is?'

'I don't,' he said. 'Not now.'

'But you have a good idea?'

The imam said nothing.

Süleyman said, 'You were both on your way to Syria, weren't you? Looking for your sons?'

Still the old man didn't speak.

'Look, this can be difficult or it can be easy,' İkmen said. 'Personally I'd choose the latter course. You planned to go to Syria to find your sons, using the boy Radwan as your guide. We know this, so there's no point in denying it.'

The old man moved his head to one side in a gesture that might have been agreement.

'It's an offence to cross that border without good reason. And by that I mean that it is an offence to go and join the group who call themselves ISIS.'

'Once we knew where you were, we had to get you back,' Süleyman said.

'Not that we exactly have time for this at the moment,' İkmen added. 'But as soon as we knew what was happening, we had to act. Now look, we need to find out who you were going to meet in Syria.'

'No one!'

'We'll have to turn you over to our anti-terrorist—'

'I went to find my sons!' the old man said. 'That was all! I went to find my sons to tell them something!'

İkmen's phone rang. He excused himself and picked it up. It was Commissioner Teker.

'Can you come to my office, please, Cetin Bey?' she said.

'I'm with a—'

'Five minutes.'

He put the phone down. Süleyman, who had heard the brief conversation, widened his eyes. It had sounded urgent.

İkmen looked at the imam. 'To tell them what?'

The old man raised his arms in a gesture of submission. 'The truth.'

'The truth about what?'

'About who they are,' the imam said. 'If they know this, then maybe that will stop them pursuing this ISIS dream.'

The e-mail arrived first thing in the morning. The laptop let Gül know with a grunt. He'd had a long night and wasn't amused. The henna party he'd attended in Bebek had gone on and on, and although he had earned massive tips, he'd worked for them and was exhausted.

He looked at the computer. The meat seller wanted to Skype him. He'd suspected he would. He was asking for a time. Gül sat up in bed. He didn't have to be at the club until midnight, so he guessed that early evening would be best. But he'd have to liaise with Cetin İkmen before he sent a reply. The policeman wanted to be with him when he took the call.

Gül unearthed his phone from his clothes on the floor and dialled a number. No one answered. He let his body flop back on the bed and closed his eyes.

'My dear Zanubiya, my late wife, was Jewish,' the imam said. 'Everyone knew she was different, but because of the situation with Israel, I decided to tell people that she was Christian. I didn't want her to be hurt. You know where we live, and how sometimes certain people in that area can judge.'

'You didn't tell your sons the truth?'

'No.'

'Not even when she died?'

İkmen's phone rang, but he ignored it.

'No. They were very young. It was a long time ago.'

His phone rang again. This time he took it. 'I'm sorry . . .'

'Cetin Bey, I need to see you now,' Teker said.

'All right.'

İkmen stood. 'Something apparently requires my attention immediately. I will be back.'

He walked to Teker's office, where he found his superior in a state of agitation.

'What's going on?' He closed her office door behind him.

'Constable Can is not answering her phone, and she isn't at her apartment,' Teker said.

'How do you know?'

'She rents a room from Hatice Bayrak. She didn't return home last night, although her friend Aysel at the Imperial Oriental says she saw her at work.'

'So what do we do?' İkmen frowned. 'Can always kept in communication. This isn't good. Boris Myskow is a protected individual.'

'We treat it as an ordinary missing person investigation,' Teker said. 'Aysel Gurcanli says that she saw Can working in the kitchen until around one a.m. Her shift was due to end at two, and Aysel looked for her but was told that she'd already gone.'

'Told by whom?'

'A chef called Tandoğan.'

'Did the two women usually leave together?'

'Not always, which is why Aysel thought nothing of it,' Teker said. 'It was only when Hatice Bayrak contacted her this morning that she wondered whether something might have gone wrong. You'll have to return to the Imperial Oriental, Cetin Bey.'

'And retrace Constable Can's route home.'

'I've already asked Miss Gurcanli to come in and talk to us about that,' Teker said. 'She's on her way.'

İkmen exhaled. 'It wouldn't have been a massive stretch for our colleagues in the shady services to find out Can's identity.'

It had been a calculated risk. İkmen wondered how aware Halide Can had been of the danger she could have been in. But why would Myskow's minders take notice of a kitchen cleaner? As far as İkmen could tell, they spent most of their time sitting around availing themselves of Myskow's hospitality. He knew, though, that it was dangerous to underestimate spooks.

'We have to proceed with caution,' Teker said. 'The security services know we're still looking for Cemal Vural and they are aware of the cannibal situation. But I've not been contacted by them. I want you to interview Gurcanli, and retrace Constable Can's route home. It's not a vast distance; Hatice Bayrak's apartment is in Cihangir.

'Now I am aware you were in a meeting. Can you leave that now?'

'Yes,' he said.

There wasn't much more to say about or to the runaway imam. He would have to be turned over to anti-terrorist officers.

'Then let's advance this investigation as quickly as we can,' Teker said.

İkmen stood. 'Madam, you don't think that Can may have just gone to a club after work, do you?'

She stared at him. 'And what club would that be, Cetin Bey?'

'I don't know,' he said. But he did, and she knew it. 'Constable Can and her friend Aysel do go to clubs . . .'

'Like a lot of young women, yes,' she said. 'But if you don't know which club . . .'

'I will ask Miss Gurcanli,' İkmen said.

What Constable Can and her friends got up to in their private lives was their affair. But while she was missing, if she was missing, it was his affair too. And İkmen knew all about the rumours that had gone around about old Hatice Bayrak for years.

'I have two pieces of information for you,' Dr Sarkissian said. 'One is that Celal Vural cannot be our cannibalised victim.'

It was difficult for Ömer Mungun not to look disappointed. One quick solution wasn't too much to ask, was it?

Dr Sarkissian said, 'I feel your disappointment.'

Ömer smiled. 'Do you feel my guilt too, Doctor? How could I want an innocent man to be a cannibal's victim?'

'You didn't,' the doctor said. 'You wanted to find out who Ümit Kavaş ate on the night he died, and you hoped that it was Celal Vural because he is a missing person and therefore a mystery to be solved, and if you can identify the victim, it might

220

just lead you to his killer. But if we assume that his colleagues and his wife are telling the truth about when he disappeared, the timings were always wrong.'

'Yes.'

Ömer put the report from the forensic laboratory back on the doctor's desk.

'Bloom syndrome is rare, Sergeant,' Arto Sarkissian said. 'The probability of Celal Vural's DNA throwing it up was always remote. And yet, I repeat, I feel your disappointment. Now that Vural has been ruled out, we are back to the endless possibilities that really exist – of the victim being a visitor to the city, or a nameless refugee, or anyone.'

Ömer shook his head. 'What about the man from Etiler?' he asked, referring to the body that Kerim Gürsel had found.

'My second piece of information.' The doctor sighed. 'I think he died naturally. There are what I initially thought might be defence wounds on his arms, but I've come around to the view that they were self-inflicted.'

'Self-harm?'

'Maybe. He lived with his sister and her husband. She called me and we had what I can only describe as a challenging conversation.'

Ömer frowned.

The doctor shook his head. 'The deceased, as you may know, had learning difficulties. Which meant, according to his sister, that he couldn't possibly have possessed sexual needs and so the body could not be his.'

'Denial.'

'Of course, but also ignorance. I asked the woman how much her brother drank, and she told me he didn't. But I can see from the state of what remains of his liver that he did, heavily. If I were to bet on cause of death at the moment, I'd put my money on liver failure. I know sclerosis when I see it.'

221

'Maybe she just doesn't want to believe that her brother is dead?'

'Maybe not. But it was most certainly her brother who patronised the prostitute known as Raquel at the brothel in Karaköy, and the apartment where the body was found had been rented to a Volkan Doğan, a sixty-plus man just like my body. Now tell me, who do you think it is?'

'If we go home together, we walk along İstiklal until we reach Turnacıbaşı Caddesi, which then turns into Liva Sokak. This brings you on to Sıraselviler Caddesi, then you cross the road and go south until you hit Bakraç Sokak on your left.'

'OK, I'll get someone out there,' İkmen said. He called Kerim Gürsel.

Aysel Gurcanli came across as a light-hearted young woman who was really worried.

'I thought nothing of it when Chef Tandoğan said that Halide had gone home,' she said. 'We both live so close to the hotel – I live on Sıraselviler Caddesi – and so I didn't worry about her. And she's a police officer.'

'We can get beaten up too,' İkmen said. 'But you're right not to chastise yourself, Aysel Hanım. Can you remember where Officer Can was the last time you saw her?'

'In the kitchen.'

'Where?'

'Cleaning the floor, I think,' she said. 'It was one-ish and I think she'd not long had a cigarette break. But I didn't go with her. I know she'd wanted to talk to one of our casuals, Bülent, but he didn't come in last night.'

Bülent Onay from the Karaköy squat.

'Did Chef Tandoğan tell you why Halide had gone home early?'

'No,' she said.

222

'And was Mr Myskow in the hotel last night?'

'Yes, but I didn't see him. He was upstairs in the conference area.'

'Who with?'

'Guests,' she said.

The guests Halide Can had told him about.

'Aysel Hanım, would Halide have gone anywhere else on her way home last night?' İkmen asked.

'No. She was working for you, wasn't she?'

'Yes, but don't you sometimes go out together . . .'

'Together, yes. Do you think she went to a club on her own? I don't think so.' She rubbed her hands together. 'People don't do that.'

'Aysel, did Halide have a boyfriend?' İkmen said.

Aysel Gurcanli turned away.

He was sure they were going to chop his head off. But only when they caught him. Radwan hadn't touched any of the little girls in the tent, and so the ISIS men had laughed at him. One of them had told him he'd show him what to do, but Radwan had said he needed to relieve himself first. He'd gone around a corner and then he'd run. In the darkness it was difficult to see a hand in front of your face. But now it was daylight and he didn't know where he was. The river was nowhere to be seen, and even the town of Jerablus had disappeared. There was no one about and it was getting hot. But he still had the rifle that Waheed had given him. He carried it over one shoulder, just like the ISIS boys did. But he knew he didn't look like one of them. Even an idiot would know he wasn't a fighter.

Radwan walked up a small hill and then down the other side. He wanted a drink and something to eat; he also wanted to be able to stop squatting down to relieve himself. He had diarrhoea and was dehydrating fast. He knew that if he didn't drink something soon he would die. He'd seen that happen to small kids when he'd crossed into Turkey. But he had to keep walking.

It was about an hour later when he saw the village. A tiny settlement of stone and mud huts with a few goats and sheep running about outside. At first he didn't see any people. He thought that maybe it was deserted. Had ISIS been here? If a village like this existed in this place, there had to be some water nearby.

Then he saw a woman. Radwan dropped to his haunches. She was shooing animals out of her house – sheep. She said something, but he couldn't hear what it was. Then a small man appeared. Unlike the woman, he was dressed in black. Radwan cringed. ISIS.

The man shouted at the woman. Again, Radwan couldn't hear exactly what he said. He hit her. Punched her straight in the face. It came suddenly, and it made Radwan jump. It also made him make a noise, which caught the attention of the ISIS man, and for a moment, their eyes locked. Then Radwan was on his feet and running again. He could just hear the sound of the ISIS man coming after him.

Gül had finally got through to Inspector Süleyman. İkmen was busy – there was some sort of emergency – but Süleyman said he'd pass Gül's message on. Failing that, he'd come and be with him when the meat seller Skyped at eight o'clock that evening. Gül had been forced to nominate a time in the end. The meat seller had been very insistent. He'd said, 'You know this stuff doesn't keep for ever, don't you?'

He obviously needed to shift it fast.

Ziya was in the garden, sunbathing. Gül lay down on a towel beside him and said, 'Where's Bülent?'

He hadn't seen him for a while. Ziya and Bülent were friends and usually did lots of things together.

'Sulking in his room,' Ziya said.

'You fallen out?'

'No, he's just pissed off.'

'About what?'

'I don't know,' Ziya said. 'It's a nice day. I suggested we get on the bikes and head out to somewhere cool like Polonezköy. Be great to get away from the city and into some trees. But he told me to fuck off.'

'Why?'

'I've no idea,' Ziya said. 'Maybe it's because he did a long shift last night. I don't know when he got in, but I spotted him out here digging, and then later I saw him stomping out of Uğur Bey's room back to his own. I don't know whether they had an argument or what. But best leave him alone for now.'

'Yeah.'

Ziya had a good body. Tanned and hard, but he wore terrible shorts and always looked as if he'd just fallen out of bed after a hard night on the drink. Gül liked him, Bülent less so. Ziya put a cigarette in his mouth and lit up.

The ground was hard and hot, and Gül shifted the towel underneath his back to make himself more comfortable.

'So what was all that white stuff you put on the ground yesterday, and where's it gone now?'

It had looked like snow.

'Fertiliser,' Ziya said. 'Bülent dug it in this morning. Soil'll be rich and crumbly in a couple of weeks, then we can plant vegetables. Self-sufficiency in the city, man. It's one of the cornerstones of alternative living. All we need now's a bit of free love!'

And then he laughed.

Chapter 22

'Mr Myskow . . .'

This time Boris Myskow smiled. 'Inspector.'

'Thank you for seeing me, sir.'

'My pleasure. Or rather it would be if it wasn't under such bad circumstances.'

The two men shook hands and İkmen sat down. Myskow's office was on the top floor of the hotel and had panoramic views over the city and the Bosphorus. Like the rest of the hotel, it was decorated in nineteenth-century Ottoman baroque style.

'It was the young woman's landlady who let us know she was missing,' İkmen said. 'Then we contacted her friend, who also works here. Chef Gurcanli.'

'Oh yes.' Myskow smiled.

'She said that Miss Can went home early last night.'

'Oh?'

'That's what Chef Gurcanli was told by a chef called Tandoğan,' İkmen said.

'I see. Well I wasn't in the restaurant last night. I was hosting a function in our conference suite and so I'm afraid I don't know.'

'I'd like to speak to Chef Tandoğan,' İkmen said.

'I'm sure that can be arranged. Inspector, have you checked that the young woman didn't just leave here and not go home?'

It wasn't easy for İkmen to remain civil in Myskow's presence given their history, and when he came out with observations like that, it was even harder.

'I can assure you, sir, that all the basic work that needs to be done has been,' he said.

'Sure.'

'And just to bring you up to date, I'm afraid that we haven't managed to find your waiter yet.'

'My waiter?'

'Celal Vural,' İkmen said. 'You know, the man whose wife reported him missing.'

'Oh. Yeah.' Myskow smiled. 'That's a shame.'

'Yes, isn't it,' İkmen said. 'But we will find him, Mr Myskow, and soon.'

'You think?'

Did he look nervous, or was İkmen reading signals in Myskow's face that didn't really exist?

'Oh yes. We'll find him soon, İnşallah, as I'm sure you know people round here are inclined to say.'

Uğur İnan had to have noticed him come into the building. His studio was just above the front door. He could theoretically see whoever came in and went out of the squat. Süleyman wondered what he thought about having a police officer in the building again. The squat was, after all, illegal. Maybe Uğur believed he was having sex with the zenne. He had after all gone straight to his room.

'Do you have a name for this person who's going to call you?' Süleyman said to Zenne Gül.

'He, she, it is just "Raw", like the name of the supposed company,' Gül said. 'I call myself Cengiz, by the way. Don't know why. Just felt as if I needed a really butch name.'

Süleyman smiled. 'Do you know how he wants to be paid?'

'Not yet. But you'll need to be out of sight.'

Süleyman moved so that he couldn't be seen from the screen. The familiar Skype tone trilled.

'Here we go.'

He almost made it. Had he been able to get to the top of the hill, he would have done. But just before the summit, a hand grabbed his ankle, hard. He had no strength left.

He turned his head and looked into a pair of eyes that possessed no pity. He thought, *I'm dead.* The man pointed his gun at him and Radwan thought, *It's now.* He closed his eyes.

But nothing happened. He waited. Then he heard laughter.

'Your face!'

Radwan opened his eyes. 'What?'

'Your face,' the man said, 'a picture of terror!'

The man had uncovered his own face. It was nice, if scarred on one side, but also, significantly, familiar.

'Burak?'

He opened his arms wide. 'The same.'

Relieved, Radwan threw his gun down and ran to him.

'Where have you been? Your dad and me, we've been worried sick. Where's Mustafa?'

'You've seen my dad?'

He was dusty and tanned and looked about ten years older than the last time Radwan had seen him.

'I was so worried about you. I went to see your dad to tell him about that squat in Karaköy. I thought you were in there.'

'In the squat? Why?'

'Because that was the last place I saw you,' Radwan said. 'Outside the squat. You and Mustafa yelling at the people inside. I can still see the look of fury on their faces at the windows. But then you were gone. Why did you leave without telling me?'

'And what would you have done if we'd said we were going to do jihad?'

'I would've come with you. I could've helped.'

Burak laughed. 'You're just a kid. What are you doing here?'

'Looking for you.' He told him about the journey he'd made with the imam, and how he'd come across the border with Waheed. He didn't tell him he'd run away from Waheed.

'So where is Mustafa?' he said when he'd finished.

'Didn't my father tell you? He's dead,' Burak said. 'He died fighting the devil-worshippers in Iraq.'

He meant the Yezidis. And yes, the imam had told Radwan, but he'd wanted to hear Burak say it himself.

'He is a martyr, Radwan,' Burak said. 'And you know that in honour of my brother I have named this village we captured "Mustafaköy".

Mustafa's village. That was nice.

'Which you must now come and see,' Burak said. 'Come and tell me all about your adventures, and I will introduce you to the Brothers.'

Weirdly, he didn't once ask about his father.

Unsurprisingly, 'Raw' covered his face. In a way, Zenne Gül did too, by not putting on make-up.

There was a lot of talk about money. About relative prices and how Raw's competitors were just fucking about. There was some talk about the use of Bitcoin. Raw didn't volunteer information about where he lived. Gül was up front about his location, or rather the location of the house in Tarlabaşı that he was saying was his. A massive nineteenth-century Greek place, it had been empty for years until the department bought it. Now it just sat there, apparently inhabited by an old man who acted as its caretaker, ready for when it might be needed.

But Raw didn't want to go there.

'You come to me,' he said.

'And where are you?' Gül asked.

'Pay me, fix a day and a time and I'll text you instructions,' he said.

'I've not just got off the train from Anatolia, you know.'

Raw laughed. 'Frightened I'll jump you?'

'I'm frightened of no one,' Gül said, and Süleyman, at that moment, was inclined to believe him. 'But I'm not an idiot. Unless we meet in public, you could jump me any time.'

'But I won't. Why would I do that?'

'Oh for God's sake!' Gül said. 'To keep your meat and get my money!'

Raw laughed. 'I could.'

'So give me a plausible alternative,' Gül said. 'One that doesn't insult my intelligence.'

'Oh?'

'I've told you I live in Tarlabaşı in Istanbul. You're a Turk, I'm a Turk. How far away from me are you?'

Raw said nothing. Süleyman wondered whether Gül had pushed him too far. He imagined that real cannibals would simply be grateful to get their meat and wouldn't worry too much about whether they were going to get mugged. All he could do was trust Gül and his experience of something – the Dark Web – that Süleyman didn't know about.

'Well? I can get meat elsewhere if you prefer,' Gül said.

'What, fake meat?'

'It's not all fake and you know it.'

'Mine's the best.'

'So it's the best, so what?' Gül said. 'If you want meat, you want meat. You going to sell it to me, or what?'

There was a pause. Whether Raw sold his meat or not depended upon how much he needed the money and how desperate he was to get rid of his goods.

Eventually he said, 'I can meet you on the eight forty-five ferry from Beşiktaş to Kadıköy tomorrow evening.'

Luckily Gül didn't look at Süleyman for any sort of approval. He would have given it but Raw might have seen.

'All right,' he said. 'How will I know you?'

'You won't,' Raw said. 'But I'll know you, and besides . . .' He laughed.

'What?'

'I'll be carrying a cool box, won't I?'

Chef Tandoğan reminded İkmen of one of those borderline insane chefs on television. Usually foreign, they spent more time shouting than cooking and seemed to enjoy terrorising both their staff and their customers. İkmen always wondered what it would be like to go to one of their restaurants, wait for a chef-induced scene and then arrest one of them.

'She left, she wasn't feeling well.'

He barely looked at İkmen, this self-important little prick with his waxed moustache. Was he just being rude, or did he think that his offhandedness was fooling İkmen in some way? It wasn't.

'*Mr* Tandoğan,' he said. Not using the title 'Chef' was designed to get his attention, and it did.

'I beg your—'

'Chef,' İkmen said. 'Miss Gurcanli is a friend of Miss Can, and she didn't tell her she was unwell.'

'How do you expect me to know that?' Tandoğan said. 'The woman was sick, she went home. Maybe Chef Gurcanli was busy at the time.'

'Where was she working last night?'

Tandoğan shouted at a boy to 'Hurry up with that!' and then said, 'Here in the kitchen. Where else would she be?'

'Upstairs in the conference suite with Mr Myskow?'

'Why would she be there?'

'I don't know. You tell me.'

'She wasn't up there.'

'No? How do you know whether she was up there or not? She could've gone there after she left here.'

'Why? She was unwell!'

'Don't ask me,' İkmen said. Then he looked at Kerim and nodded.

Kerim took a piece of paper out of his pocket and held it up.

'I've a warrant to close this kitchen,' he yelled across what became a silent space.

Then he made a call on his mobile phone.

'You can't—'

'Oh, but I can, sir,' İkmen said to Chef Tandoğan.

'Yes, but Mr Myskow . . .'

İkmen leaned in close to the chef. 'His minders can't really help him this time,' he said. 'Not with two people missing. That's beyond careless, or so my boss, Commissioner Teker, thinks.'

What he didn't tell him was how unhappy Teker had been about requesting that warrant. If Constable Can hadn't been one of their own, would she have done it? And who, if anyone, had she liaised with in security services?

He didn't know, and nor did he want to.

'You'll have to let Mr Myskow know,' Tandoğan said.

'Oh yes,' İkmen said. 'I will.'

A group of officers who had been outside the hotel came in.

'But we've got customers to serve!' Tandoğan said.

İkmen ignored him.

The Brothers weren't as scary as their counterparts in Jerablus had been. But then, as Burak's men, they wouldn't be. He wasn't a bad boy, not really. Just a bit mad. As long as Radwan had known him, he'd been like that. Much more daring than his brother, who had actually been quite soft. It was difficult to believe that Mustafa was a martyr. It was weird he had this village named after him.

Women from the village, which Radwan learned had been

Christian, came with platters of rice and meat. The Brothers didn't look at them. Only when the women had gone did they fall on the food liked starved hyenas. Radwan ate what he could get hold of while Burak went outside to take food to Brothers on guard duty.

Although Burak had introduced him as a Brother from Istanbul, Radwan got the impression that his men weren't very impressed. Once Burak had gone, at best they ignored him, at worst they pushed him out of the way of the food. But Radwan didn't mind. He'd found Burak and so he could go back to the imam and tell him, and then he could make his way back to Aleppo. Except he didn't know where the imam had gone . . .

'Did you ever meet Brother Burak's brother Mustafa?' a man with grease running down his chin asked the company in general. He was a fat thing of about forty. What was he doing with a load of lads half his age?

'No,' a boy of no more than sixteen said. 'Did you, Abu Daoud?'

'No,' the man said. 'But then I've not been to Iraq, unlike Abu Jemal.'

On hearing his name, a reed-thin boy said, 'What?'

'You were in Iraq, Abu Jemal.'

'Oh yes. Sinjar. Amongst the devil-worshippers.'

'Where this supposed martyr Mustafa Ayan was,' the fat man said. There was a mocking tone in his voice that Radwan didn't like.

'I never met him,' Abu Jemal said. 'But then he was martyred.'

'You sure?'

'A lot of good men died in Iraq,' Abu Jemal said. 'What are you implying?'

'Nothing.'

Radwan looked at the fat man, who pulled a face at him. Burak was leader of this group, but this older man seemed to be dis-respecting him.

233

'All I'm saying is that I remember when Brother Burak arrived from Turkey, and I can tell you that he came alone,' he said.

A man who hadn't spoken before said, 'How do you know he came alone? Maybe his brother was sent to Iraq as soon as they arrived.'

The fat man raised his eyes to heaven but said nothing.

For a while the men just ate in silence. Radwan didn't like the fat man, Abu Daoud. His tone was spiteful, and he felt that he meant Burak harm.

Then a voice from a distant, dark corner of the room said, 'I cannot settle this matter. All I can say is this . . .'

All eyes turned to that murky corner, where Radwan saw what at first looked like a bundle of rags but was in fact a boy of about his own age. Pale and thin, the boy had only one leg, and Radwan noticed that he had a drip attached to one of his arms.

'So, Brother Salah,' the fat man said. 'What do you have to tell us?'

The child's parched lips moved into a slight smile. 'You know that I have never agreed with you, Abu Daoud.'

'I know you hate me.'

The boy laughed. 'If I had the strength to hate . . .' he said. 'No. Listen, in this matter you are right.'

'Right?'

There were eight men in that room, and they all sat up straight.

'I know this from my wife.'

His *wife*!

'She works tending the wounded in Jerablus,' he said. 'A lone Turk came over the border with a stab wound to his face. On his left cheek.'

Burak had a scar on his face. But which cheek was it, the left or the right?

Then Burak came in and smiled at him.

*   *   *

'This is fucking outrageous!'

Commissioner Hürrem Teker had known she'd have to confront Boris Myskow directly, and so she'd held herself ready for a phone call from İkmen. Now she was outside the conference suite kitchen at the Imperial Oriental, hoping that she wasn't watching the beginnings of the famous chef's first heart attack.

'Well you tell me what I should do, Mr Myskow,' she said. 'Two missing persons who were last seen alive in this building. What would *you* do?'

He moved in to whisper in her ear. Westerners didn't usually get that close. They generally didn't like it.

'Security forces are already inside this hotel, as you well know,' he said. 'Don't you think they would have noticed if I'd murdered two members of staff I barely know?'

This didn't even deserve recognition, let alone an answer, and Boris Myskow knew it. With the sort of company he kept, he could do pretty much whatever he liked, and that included selling unlicensed wild boar.

'My officers will need to get into this kitchen, as well as the one downstairs,' Teker said.

'Why? This Can woman never came up here!'

'Never? Word is she came here to clear up the day before yesterday.'

'Did she?'

'Word is that you shouted at her,' Teker said.

'Word? Whose word?'

'Word,' she reiterated. 'As in popular opinion.'

He looked confused. It was great being able to flummox such an arrogant arsehole in his own language. And there wasn't a thing his minders could do about it. Not this time.

Hürrem Teker pushed past Boris Myskow and opened the kitchen door. Then she hailed her team.

'In there,' she said. 'Leave no chicken leg unexamined.'

Chapter 23

Fatma had gone to sleep on the sofa in front of the TV. It was still banging out soap operas when her husband eventually made it home at 5 a.m.

'Fatma?'

Her eyes opened slowly.

'I'm so sorry I didn't get home last night.'

She sat up. Her long iron-grey hair looked like an explosion, but unusually for Fatma, she smiled. 'As long as you're all right,' she said. 'You must be hungry and thirsty. I'll make tea.'

She went to get up, but he stopped her.

'No, I'll make the tea. I'm already up.'

He walked into the kitchen and put the kettle on. He didn't know how the activities of the previous night had worked out. Yet more meat samples had been taken from the fridges and freezers of the Imperial Oriental, but whether they were significant or not was impossible to tell. They hadn't found any human heads, which was a mercy – in one way.

What they had found was blood. Whether that was just sloppy meat storage practice remained to be seen. Significant amounts had been swabbed on the appliances in the main kitchen, particularly the fridges and freezers. Up in the conference suite they'd had to use Luminol to highlight areas of blood contamination. İkmen thought about how cleanliness was apparently much more of an issue when it came to Mr Myskow's more exalted guests.

The kettle came to the boil and he poured the water on to tea leaves in the pot. Fatma was never going to use tea bags. In the same way that Fatma washed the floors on her hands and knees and always boiled towels even if they fell apart in the process, she was never going to use tea bags. She had her ways of doing things that were not going to change.

İkmen looked out of the kitchen window at the Aya Sofya and the Blue Mosque and wondered how long it would be before someone came along wanting to redevelop his apartment building. It was quite an ugly early 1960s lump, but his apartment was large and, significantly, he owned it. Not that ownership meant much to property developers. Or who and what a person did for a living.

Uğur İnan, the textile designer, had only moved to the Karaköy squat after his house in Zeytinburnu had been compulsorily purchased. It had been one of the last gecekondu homes in the area. Those were the days! İkmen smiled. Time was that if a man could put up four posts and a roof in one night, he could claim that land as his own. Some of these properties had been very large, well built and sophisticated. Uğur İnan's father had constructed his own gecekondu, and when he became famous, the designer had built his studio on the vacant plot of land next door. No wonder he'd set up the Art House; the uncertainty of gecekondu living was all he'd ever known. In the only interview İkmen had ever seen with İnan, he'd said that by setting up the squat, he was fighting for his life. His last stand.

'You don't want to go back to Turkey, do you?'

'No. Why?'

Burak shrugged. 'You were safe there.'

'I want to go back to Aleppo,' Radwan said. 'I want to go home.'

'Well you're in the caliphate now,' Burak said. 'So you are home.'

They were sitting on a mound of earth outside Jerablus,

237

overlooking the Turkish border. Kurdish militia known as the Peshmerga were moving into the area, and so all available ISIS fighters had been drafted in to protect the major towns and cities. They'd literally got their marching orders at two o'clock that morning.

Roused from his sleep by a kick in the ribs from one of Burak's men, Radwan had watched as Abu Daoud finished having sex with a terrified village woman and then pushed her away. Only Brother Saleh, the pale boy with the blue lips, had remained behind. Just before Radwan left, he had beckoned him over.

'Your friend Burak is not who he claims to be,' he'd said. 'I believe my wife. He came alone. I'm dying. Why would I lie?'

Radwan had not stopped thinking about the scar on Burak's cheek. It was on the left.

'But why would he lie?' he had said.

'A man with a martyred brother is a big man.'

'All I know is that Burak and Mustafa left at the same time,' Radwan had said. 'Mustafa was a strong, big boy.'

'Maybe so, but he didn't make it to the caliphate,' Brother Saleh had said.

Now, alone with Burak, Radwan said, 'How did Mustafa die?'

'I told you. He went to Iraq, he fought the devil-worshippers. He fought bravely and was martyred. Why?'

'He was my friend,' Radwan said.

'And he leads the way for us to make our martyrdoms even more famous than his,' Burak said. 'You know, Radwan, his death was truly glorious!'

And it was at this moment that Radwan knew for certain that Burak was lying.

'Is it OK if I get a bit more sleep?' he said.

Burak smiled. 'As long as you make namaz. You know that anyone who misses namaz willingly even once is an unbeliever, don't you?'

238

Radwan, like his father had, only prayed on Fridays. But he agreed with Burak so that he could get away from him. In a way, it had been fortunate that Burak and his men had moved up to Jerablus, because it meant that when Radwan made a break for the border, he wouldn't have so far to go.

A knock on the door brought Gül out of a dream where his mother was still alive and was beating his father with a yard broom. If only she'd really done that, maybe she wouldn't have died when she was barely forty.

'Yes?'

The door opened and Uğur İnan came in.

Gül sat up in bed. 'Good morning, Uğur Bey.'

He smiled. 'Good morning. Mind if I have a word?'

'Sit down.' Gül patted an empty space beside him on the bed.

Uğur İnan sat. 'Gül, I just wanted to speak to you about your new friend. I hope you don't mind.'

New friend? Who did he mean? Gül had danced from eleven the previous night until four o'clock that morning. His brain and his body were both addled. Then he remembered.

'Oh . . .'

'Inspector Süleyman,' Uğur said. 'A very handsome and charming man, and believe me, I can see the attraction, but . . .'

But if Gül said he was working for Süleyman, that could be a problem. People in the Art House didn't do authority. Gül said all that he could say.

'It's just a thing.' He smiled. 'Nothing serious.'

'Right. Because we can't get too cosy with the police, you know. We're illegally squatting this house and so one day they're going to come in here and evict us. I'm sorry, and while I'd never interfere in your private life under ordinary circumstances, I'm going to have to ask you not to bring him here again.'

'Oh.'

'See him,' Uğur said. 'I wouldn't rain on your parade for the world. I'm straight, but even I can see that he's a doll. But not here. Do you mind?'

Gül smiled again. 'No. Not at all. I shouldn't have invited him here, it was stupid. Just . . .'

'You let your heart rule your head.' Uğur patted his hand.

'Sorry.'

'No problem.' He stood up. 'I'll let you get back to sleep.'

When he had left, Gül picked up his phone. If he didn't call Süleyman now and tell him they were having a fling, he might forget. As he dialled the number, he laughed.

The pain in his chest was fucking awesome. He'd always had secrets, but this was another level – one that was going to kill him if he wasn't careful. Keeping stuff from his wife had been a walk in the park compared to this. Lying to his accountant was just something he'd always done. This was something else, and now he'd have to compound it. His guests would have to go back to chicken chasseur and he knew they wouldn't like it. Consequences could involve the cancelling of contracts, withdrawal of support, maybe even closure of the hotel. But what could he do when İkmen had barged in asking about a missing employee? A missing person was a missing person.

And yet what puzzled Boris Myskow a little bit was how quickly the cleaner had been reported missing. Didn't the police normally wait twenty-four hours before they opened an investigation on an adult? He wondered whether İkmen knew the woman somehow. Then he had a truly horrific thought that he had to banish from his mind if he didn't want his heart to fail. What if İkmen hadn't been frightened off by his friends in high places? What if he'd put that woman in his kitchen to spy on him? Nobody ever checked on such people. They could be anyone.

240

Then he remembered that one of his junior chefs was a friend of the woman.

The Twisted Boy brought the imam his lunch as usual, but he also brought his mother with him. Aylin Hanım did not mince her words. She'd stayed away when Imam Ayan had first returned, but now she had things to say.

'You're a silly old fool,' she said. 'Going to Syria! What were you thinking?'

Her son, afraid of what the holy man might say in return, left.

'You and I have lived through too much together for me not to tell you the truth,' she said. 'We did a bad thing to Zanubiya Hanım all those years ago. We did it with the best of intentions, but she had become a Muslim by then. What was the point?'

'You didn't say that at the time, Aylin Hanım.'

'No, I didn't, because you persuaded me that was what she wanted. But she was in and out of a coma, talking nonsense.'

He shook his head.

'One day she was here so her boys could see her, and the next . . .' She shrugged. 'If those boys don't know who they are . . .'

'It is my fault, I know,' he said. 'But I did what I did for the best.'

'As I said.'

'And now they are all gone,' he said. 'I have paid a hard price.'

'And yet you still owe,' she said. 'And so do I. I have been thinking about this, Imam Ayan, and I have come to the conclusion that we must go to her now.'

'To whom?'

'To Zanubiya Hanım,' she said. 'We must go to where she is and we must beg her forgiveness. It is the only way we will ever have peace.'

*   *   *

241

Everyone was out. Even Zenne Gül had left the building to go shopping. It was the first time Birgül İnan had had the place to herself in a long while. But baby Barış was hot and grumpy and wouldn't stop crying.

She took him out into the relative coolness of the garden, where they both sat on a beach mat underneath the huge umbrella her father-in-law Uğur had brought back from one of his trips to London. But still the baby cried. Eventually Birgül took him into the kitchen and put him in his high chair. Then she filled one of the large old laundry bowls with cool water and took it out into the garden. When she went back indoors to get Barış, she said, 'Let's see if a little paddle cools you down, shall we?'

It did. Shaded by the umbrella, Barış sat naked and content in the bowl and stopped crying. Birgül, her arm around his middle, lay down behind him and half closed her eyes. It was a pity the garden was such a dust bowl; she just had to hope that the boys would make a good job of planting it up. Neither Ziya nor Bülent really knew what they were doing. Only old Deniz Bey knew anything about gardens. Long ago his family had owned a cotton plantation on the Çukurova plain. He'd grown up hearing things about how to condition soil, and watering and all that stuff.

Birgül wondered where the old man had got to. He usually spent most afternoons and some evenings at the squat, where other ex-military types were wont to gather around Uğur Bey. Ümit's father General Kavaş had been one of them until Ümit died. The people who flocked to her father-in-law were a weird and diverse bunch. Birgül herself had come from a family of pious academics, but she'd rebelled when she went to university and met İsmet. Most people thought they were married, but they weren't. They'd never felt the need. Her parents considered Barış a bastard and had told her they never wanted to see him. That was their loss. But it was hers too. If and when the squat was

242

raided, they'd need somewhere to go and they couldn't all fit into İsmet's grandmother's tiny place in Üsküdar. They'd have to find somewhere to rent, which was a joke.

Rents in Istanbul were immense. The two covered girls, Meltem and Ahu, both students, would find it impossible to get anywhere they could afford. Their staunchly secular parents just about paid their university fees. They'd stop well short of funding lifestyles of which they didn't approve. And then there was Zenne Gül . . .

Birgül had just started to drift into a semi sleep when she heard Deniz Bey shouting.

'What the fuck are you doing out here in this wasteland with your baby?' he roared at her.

Birgül sat up. 'Oh, er . . .'

'This isn't a garden, not yet!'

He marched over to her and took the umbrella down.

'Silly girl! This is totally unsuitable!'

Barış looked up at the shouty man and began to cry.

'Have they given it a ridiculous name yet?' Cetin İkmen asked.

Arto Sarkissian raised his eyebrows. 'Sadly.'

'What is it?'

They were sitting in İkmen's office with Kerim Gürsel.

'The Flagship,' the doctor said.

'May they be forgiven,' İkmen said.

Arto Sarkissian shook his head. 'But I haven't come here to talk about the new building that is going to dwarf my house and turn my wife into a nervous wreck. I'm here to tell you that the body we think is Volkan Doğan, is. According to dental records . . .'

'Have you taken DNA samples?'

'Yes. But we won't know about that for a few days. And in answer to your next question, Cetin, I have requested an ethnic profile just in case Mr Doğan was secretly Jewish. I know it's probably not relevant to the Ümit Kavaş case because Doğan died naturally, but I know you're curious.'

İkmen smiled. 'You know,' he said, 'if one's oldest friend has to get himself up to his elbows in the dead for a living, I can think of no one who does that with better grace and efficiency than you. Your memory never ceases to amaze me, Arto. Do you ever forget anything?'

'My own name occasionally,' he said. 'And once my wedding anniversary. But never again. Will you tell Defne Hanım?'

İkmen sighed. 'I will take the coward's way out and get Kerim to do it. You know I've always had problems with religious types, but in their way, the old republican military elites are just as aggravating. Especially the wives. Like Ottoman princesses, some of them.'

Arto laughed.

'Why is it that everyone in this country is obsessed with being someone they're not? And why do they want to be? I'm working class and I'm proud of that. Even if I suddenly became rich, I'd still be working class because that's what I am. I can't bear the waste that accompanies being rich. I don't want Police sunglasses, in spite of my profession. I know Mehmet Süleyman wears them, but then . . .'

'He's the genuine article,' the doctor said.

'Exactly. His grandfather had a servant whose sole purpose was to help him put on his boots.'

'Full employment in those days.'

'Serfdom in all but name,' İkmen said. Then he smiled. 'You know, Arto, during the course of this investigation I have deliberately avoided going to the squat where Ümit Kavaş was a regular visitor. I know of it, I've been past it, but I've never been in. For a while I couldn't think why that was.'

'And then?'

'And then self-realisation,' he said. 'Remember when we used to dream about hitting the road when we were kids? Joining the hippies in their beaten-up old vans and going to Kathmandu?'

'Ah, yes, I think we were going to find ourselves through the medium of free love and a lot of drugs.'

'Indeed. And socialism,' İkmen said. 'Equality, fraternity, all that.'

'All good stuff.'

'Absolutely. But I got married and had the kids and you went off to university and began cutting dead people up. Wise choices and choices I wouldn't change. But I do sometimes wish we'd had a few months living the dream. Don't you?'

'Yes. But Cetin, the Art House people live their dream in dangerous times. This is no longer the 1960s.'

'I know.' He sighed. 'And there's a young man living in the Art House I need to speak to.'

'I thought your zenne came from the Art House?'

'He does,' İkmen said. 'But there's someone else I need to contact. Bülent Onay. He knew Ümit Kavaş and he works, on a casual basis, at the Imperial Oriental.'

The cemetery caretaker was a Muslim of the type the imam didn't like. He was clearly a man who enjoyed a drink, evidenced by his bright red nose and the bottle of rakı only partly hidden behind his desk. More to the point, he was a hypocrite.

'What do you want in here?' he asked the imam. 'This is where they bury Jews.'

'Do I have to have a reason?' the old man said.

Aylin Hanım, from behind her niqab, said, 'What's it to you? We want to visit a grave. Let us in.'

'You're Muslims, these are Jews. You should be ashamed of yourselves!'

Imam Ayan had lost his wife and both his sons. He wasn't in

the mood for arguments. 'I come to visit the grave of a relative,' he said. 'How dare you judge me! Do you see me judging you for your drinking!'

The man almost visibly shrank.

Once in the graveyard, the imam said to Aylin Hanım, 'Thank you for backing me up.'

'I know a bigot when I see one,' she said. 'Can you remember where it is?'

'It is burned into my memory.'

They walked past the monument to the people who had died in the 2003 bombing of the Neve Şalom synagogue and walked towards the back of the cemetery. Aylin Hanım had only been to the Ulus Ashkenazi cemetery once before, when the stone that marked Zanubiya Ayan's grave had been set many years before. It had been a private affair attended only by a rabbi, a doctor from the Or-Ahayim Hospital, the imam and herself. The world beyond those four people believed that the unknown woman who had died at the hospital had passed without a name. But the imam had met with the rabbi, who had spoken to the doctor, and money for a stone decorated with a Star of David had changed hands.

The old man kneeled on the ground when they arrived. The name on the monument was the one the imam's wife had been given at her birth: Zanubiya Klarfeld.

The imam, crying, stood up, and together with Aylin Hanım he prayed. Then he asked forgiveness and made his dead wife a promise. If their son Burak ever came back from Syria, he would bring him to this place and tell him the truth about the mother he looked so much like. Although whether he would ever tell Burak what the doctor at the Or-Ahayim had told him about his mother was something else.

Chapter 24

Aysel Gurcanli sounded anxious.

'Mr Myskow has barely looked at me before,' she told Cetin İkmen. 'Now he's asking questions about where I live, what my ambitions are and who I like to socialise with. What do I do?'

She was on a cigarette break and was obviously not entirely alone, because she was whispering.

'Keep your answers general and do not mention Halide,' İkmen said.

'But what if he brings her name up?'

That surely had to be his objective.

'Say you don't know her that well,' İkmen said. 'Say you met her in a club and that it is in that context that you socialise. You know nothing about her life outside that.'

'OK.'

But she sounded nervous. She wouldn't want to lose a job at such a prestigious hotel. Would Myskow threaten her? And if he did, what would that mean?

Meat samples from the freezers both upstairs and downstairs at the Imperial Oriental had come back clean, as in none of them were human. But there was still the issue of the bloodstains.

'Aysel Hanım,' he said, 'Mr Myskow is in no way secure. Between ourselves, he is sourcing certain meats without a licence.'

'Oh God!'

'It's all right,' İkmen said. 'I doubt you've had contact. This time we only found samples in the upstairs kitchen's freezer, where I understand you don't work.'

There was a pause, and then Aysel said, 'The freezer upstairs? There is no freezer upstairs, Cetin Bey.'

Radwan could see the border. The weird shapes of the ruined city of Karkemiş stood jaggedly on the skyline in front of what remained of the sunset. In spite of the ISIS men, he didn't want to leave Syria again. But Burak was not going to go anywhere with him. He was a big man in ISIS now. Radwan couldn't tell Burak what the imam had told him. It wasn't his place. He put his gun down and moved forward. He couldn't cross into Turkey with that, and he didn't want to.

He hoped the imam was still in Gaziantep. All he wanted to do was tell him that he had found Burak and then leave. Maybe one or more of his brothers or sisters was still alive. Until he got to Aleppo, he wouldn't know.

He felt a hand land on his shoulder.

'What are you doing, Radwan?'

He recognised Burak's voice. He'd have to make something up. But his mind just wouldn't. He said, 'I need to tell your dad that you're OK. I promised.'

'My dad?' He laughed. 'Why? He knows where I am. I told him.'

'I need to tell him,' Radwan said. 'I promised.'

'You can't.'

'Why not? I'll come back.'

'Because nobody leaves,' Burak said. 'Don't you understand? If it please God I could be dead tomorrow, and then you'd be lying to him, wouldn't you?'

At first, Radwan didn't know what to say. When the words did come, he wondered whether he should have said them. 'Your dad needs you to come back. He's got something he has to tell you.'

'What?'

'I can't tell you,' Radwan said. 'He must. Come with me.'

'No. You'll stay. No one leaves the caliphate.'

Radwan regretted ditching his gun. But it was too late now.

'I'll have to lock you up,' Burak said.

That just wasn't possible. He would go mad. 'No.'

'What do you mean, no?'

'I mean you can't lock me up,' Radwan said.

Burak shouldered his rifle.

Radwan tried to think. If he told Burak what the imam had told him, would it shock him out of what he was doing? Or would it just make him go insane with fury? He wouldn't know until he did it.

'Burak,' he said, 'your dad told me that he lied to you about your mother.'

'What do you mean?'

'She wasn't a Christian. She was a Jew,' he said. And then Radwan closed his eyes and put his hands over his ears. He neither wanted to see nor hear his own death.

The ferry was packed. They always were. Day and night they heaved with humanity, most of them trying to get seats by a window. Beşiktaş to Kadıköy was one of the major commuter routes, and so even after office hours were over it was crowded.

Zenne Gül looked for a seat as far away from others as he could get. It wasn't easy. Seconds after he'd sat down, he found himself surrounded by women carrying large bundles and children hassling for sweets. He wanted to look out of the window to distance himself from them and to avoid looking at Süleyman and his officers. The young eastern man was the closest to him, reading a newspaper.

The ancient diesel engines gathered power. Apparently new ferries were to be put into service that would be quieter and more efficient. Gül hoped they didn't replace the old ones, as he was very fond of them. Some people had said that the new ones would have fewer windows and wouldn't allow food and drink on board, which would be awful. One of the great delights of the old ferries was the way you could get a glass of tea and a ring of simit bread by the window.

The ferry pulled away from the Beşiktaş pier and began to make its turn towards Asia. Gül hadn't seen anyone with a cool box. But then it just wasn't possible to look at everyone when boarding. Getting on via the duckboards laid down by the ferrymen was not for the faint-hearted, and most people had to use all their concentration just to avoid falling into the water. But now that he was on, Gül could look around.

Arto Sarkissian was a wonderful man in so many ways. Everyone who came into contact with him liked him. Unless that person was the property developer who had bought the land next door to his house. Cetin İkmen couldn't imagine they got along. But he was really popular at the Forensic Institute. He could wind the scientific staff there round his little finger.

And he'd just done it again.

Aysel Gurcanli had been absolutely certain that the kitchen on the first floor didn't have a freezer. And yet İkmen had seen one. He'd instructed the forensic team to take samples from it. Upstairs, the use of Luminol had revealed a large area of blood-stain that had been largely cleaned away. There had been one tiny dot of crusted blood that might or might not have originated from the same sample. If they could analyse that, they would.

With Aysel's phone call, when İkmen had learned that the freezer on the first floor was apparently unknown to her, that analysis had become urgent. Cetin had told Arto, who had gone straight to the Forensic Institute with one simple instruction. Now, finally, he was calling from his mobile.

İkmen picked up. 'Arto.'

'Well, the girls and boys of the Institute have worked miracles,' Arto said.

'You have a result?'

'I do. Basic, as you requested. More tests will be performed subsequently . . .'

'Get on with it!'

'The blood inside the freezer is human.'

'Thank you,' İkmen said. 'Thank you very much, my friend.'

'Pleasure.'

İkmen put his phone down. It was important at this point not to get too anxious. The human blood in the freezer could have got there as a result of a cut finger. Although because it was at the outer edge of a large stain highlighted by Luminol, was it part of that or just a coincidental artefact?

As a tiny lone blob, it wasn't enough to go back and challenge Myskow with. Or was it? The next step was genetic profiling, which meant that if the blood had come from Celal Vural or Halide Can, they would know. İkmen thought that perhaps Commissioner Teker should be aware of this, and so he called her.

He'd missed the possibility of meeting a cannibal on a ferry because of this blood.

Five minutes of the twenty-minute-long journey had already gone, and Gül could only see one person with a cool box. It was a woman. What was more, it was a very traditional-looking woman, bundled up in lots of heavy clothes and a headscarf. But then he looked again, because there was something unusual about her.

She was wearing sunglasses.

Not only did country women like this one rarely wear sunglasses, it was also almost dark. Had she been a hip young

251

thing, this would have made a difference. There was a man standing up reading a book with sunglasses on. But then he looked like an underwear model.

Gül looked at the woman, and after a few seconds she appeared to look at him. He expected her to come over. But she didn't. Was she even the right person?

The woman looked away. Maybe not. Then after a few seconds she got up and went outside to the outer deck. Gül followed.

'You're lying.'

'I'm not,' Radwan said. 'Ask your dad. Phone him now. I swear to God—'

'Shut up!'

Radwan opened his eyes in time to see Burak put his gun on the ground and take his phone out of his pocket.

'Move a muscle and I'll kill you,' he told Radwan.

The boy stood like a statue while Burak punched a number into his phone. The sky was beginning to darken, and with little light pollution from the largely destroyed villages in the area, it would soon be as black as death.

The time it took for the imam to answer seemed like for ever. But when he did, Burak got straight to the point. 'Radwan tells me I am a Jew. Tell me he's lying.'

Radwan couldn't hear what the imam said, but whatever it was, it took a long time. It only ended when Burak said, 'I'm not coming back, and making up lies about my mother won't change my mind.'

What would happen when Burak ended the call? Radwan looked at the gun on the ground and wondered if he could reach it before Burak. Then he saw the young man looking at him and decided that he probably couldn't.

'You want him to come back?' he heard Burak say. 'No one leaves the caliphate, old man.'

He ended the call, dropped the phone on the ground and picked up the gun.

'Well?'

'Well what?' Burak said.

'Did he . . .?'

'He told me lies to get me to return home, and then he asked that I let you go.'

'Me?'

'He's back in Istanbul. He wants to give you a home there, with him.'

'My family . . .'

'Are dead and you know it,' Burak said. 'But as you heard me tell the old man, no one leaves the caliphate, and so I can tell you now that I'm not letting you go.'

But if Burak had spoken to his father, was there any reason for Radwan to stay?

'So you'd better escape,' Burak said.

'What?'

Burak turned his back. There was no one else about. For a moment Radwan didn't know what to do. Then he ran.

The woman was a man. Short and fat, he said he came from Raw, although Gül strongly suspected that he was the meat seller.

'I got your payment.'

He hadn't asked for any ID. But then if he was Raw he'd seen Gül on Skype.

'I need to see the meat.'

Süleyman had told him he had to do this. Buying an empty cool box wasn't a crime. But what did human flesh look like?

The man grunted as he put the box down on the floor and opened the lid. Inside were bloodied plastic bags containing things that resembled chops.

'It's definitely . . .'

'From Eastern Europe as we discussed,' Raw, or whoever he was, said. 'Do you want it or what?'

Gül could see that eastern officer out of the corner of his eye. He was leaning against the rail looking at the Asian shore as it got closer. He had to accept the meat before they could arrest Raw.

'Yeah,' he said.

The man closed the lid of the cool box and gave it to Gül.

'Nice doing business with you,' the man said.

And then they were not alone any more.

Chapter 25

The old woman didn't cry. In fact she appeared to be quite composed. But Kerim could see that she was struggling with the news he'd just given her.

'My brother was a worry, I won't lie to you,' Defne Baydar said. 'A child-man. The ignorant used to say that my mother must have been frightened by a djinn when she was pregnant. But Volkan was just damaged.'

'Is your husband home?' Kerim Gürsel asked.

'No.' She shook her head. 'But I don't need him.'

'Where is he?'

'With his friends in Karaköy, in a squat of all things,' she said. 'Now that our government is, it seems to me, at odds with pretty much all sections of society except one, those who fear what is happening to this country are a strange and diverse group. And you may tell your superiors I said that, Sergeant Gürsel, I no longer care. Better people than I have been accused of treason.'

If Kerim was right, İkmen would be arriving at the squat at any moment. When he left the Baydars' apartment, he called him.

'He's at work,' Ziya said.

Police made him nervous, and so he was sweating.

'Where?'

The policeman, İkmen, had come mob-handed with a load of uniforms and was looking around the place in a way that Ziya didn't like.

'Don't know.'

'I'm aware of the fact that he sometimes works at the Imperial Oriental Hotel,' İkmen said. 'But he isn't there. I've been there already.'

Ziya felt even hotter.

'Where else does he work?'

'I don't know. It's all casual stuff, you know.'

The policeman shook his head. 'No, I don't know,' he said. 'Which is why I'm asking you. Where's Uğur Bey?'

'Oh . . .'

'Well?'

He was talking about things to Major General Baydar. Uğur Bey was worried. Now he'd be even more concerned.

Where the border was exactly was a good question and one that Radwan couldn't answer. But once in amongst the ancient ruins of Karkemiş he assumed he had to be back in Turkey. This was bandit country, where borders were porous, and so he couldn't assume that he was safe until he cleared the area completely. He still had some of the money the imam had given him on the bus for food and drink. He didn't know if it would be enough to get him back to Istanbul, but when morning came, he'd soon find out. The good thing about this area was that a lot of people spoke Arabic. If he got on a bus, someone would tell him where it was going and how much the fare would cost. Then, when his money ran out, he'd have to walk or beg, but he'd get to the city even though he knew that the ghosts of his family were waiting for him there. There was nowhere left to go.

Burak had disappeared, leaving Radwan alone in the dark. He'd gone back to ISIS and his life as a big man in the caliphate. Only dying could ever top that. A little boy like Burak had to have been waiting all his life for such an opportunity. Radwan wondered if he even believed what the imam had told him about his mother. But it didn't matter. Burak was going to die and that was what he wanted. Had his big, handsome brother wanted that too? There was no way of knowing. All Radwan could work out was how he felt and what he had to do. He'd have to learn to live with his ghosts and he'd have to learn to speak Turkish. Beyond that, he didn't know what lay in store for him or why the imam wanted him back. He'd felt that the old man had liked him, but he didn't know why.

Maybe the imam just wanted a child, even if that child wasn't his own.

It was a gunshot that finally brought Radwan out of his reverie. This was followed by a tremendous pain in his forearm.

'As long as people contribute towards the household budget, I don't ask them where they get their money,' Uğur İnan said. 'Bülent is a very talented chef. He's in demand all the time.'

Cetin İkmen looked at the slim, dignified figure of Major General Deniz Baydar, who sat beside İnan, but he didn't speak to him. When he got home, according to Kerim, he'd find his wife resigned to her brother's death. There'd be nothing for him to do.

'Why the interest in Bülent, Inspector?' İnan asked. 'Or is this simply about shaking this place up a bit?' He smiled.

Now İkmen had a choice. He could wipe the smile off Uğur İnan's face or he could just leave him guessing. That said, even if he told him what he knew, would that make İnan's bonhomie fade? He thought, *What the hell?*

'Uğur Bey, we have been monitoring events at one of Mr Onay's places of work, the Imperial Oriental Hotel, for some time. This is in connection to a missing waiter. But one of the pieces of information that has come to light during the course of that investigation relates to Mr Onay.'

'Really?'

'Yes.'

Aysel Gurcanli had spent the time she wasn't being questioned by Boris Myskow well.

'There's a second-hand freezer in one of the Imperial Oriental Hotel's kitchens that came from this house,' İkmen said.

'From this house? I don't think so.'

'No?' İkmen sat down without being invited. 'Uğur Bey, did you and others here in the squat not demolish an outhouse?'

'An old bathhouse, yes.'

'Which contained a freezer?'

'Well, yes, it did, but that went for scrap.'

'Where?' İkmen asked.

'Where?'

'Where was it sent for scrap? And by whom?'

'I don't know. Some men came and took it . . .'

'Bülent was the one who organised it, Uğur Bey,' the major general cut in. 'Remember?'

Uğur İnan frowned.

'So Mr Onay will know which company came for the freezer?'

'Yes,' Deniz Baydar said. 'But what they did with it after that is not known to us. Maybe they sold it on to the hotel.'

'Mmm.' Except that Bülent Onay had been seen delivering the freezer by one of Aysel Gurcanli's co-workers, a girl called Serra. Bülent, with whom Serra had once had a brief fling, had even asked her to open a door for him and his good-looking biker friend Ziya, who had been helping him with the appliance. Not that either of them had said who or what the old freezer was for. Or where it had come from. And Aysel had been of the opinion that Serra had been hurt by Bülent, so maybe she'd had an agenda regarding her old flame.

Or maybe not.

'I'd like to see where the freezer was kept when it was here,' İkmen said.

'The bathhouse,' Uğur İnan said. 'Which is no longer there . . .'

İkmen smiled. 'I know,' he said. 'But I'd like to see where it used to be, please.'

'It's pork.'

'Not human flesh?' Süleyman held up a piece of meat wrapped in a plastic bag for the man to see.

'Do I look crazy to you?'

Süleyman didn't answer. Dressed as an elderly country woman, thirty-six-year-old Cüneyt Civan, AKA Raw, did not look like the average man on the street.

'It's pork. Test it,' Civan said.

'I intend to. Where did you get it?'

Civan said nothing.

Süleyman shrugged. 'We'll find out,' he said. 'So you may as well tell me. You told the man you tried to sell human flesh to that your supplier was in Eastern Europe. Is that where the pork comes from?'

Again Civan said nothing.

'You know, just because most people are Muslim in this country doesn't mean that you can't buy pig meat . . .'

'I know that!'

He was a testy little bastard. He'd been caught in the act of trying to sell something he'd advertised as human meat, had been found out and was now angry. Süleyman knew that whatever else he said, Mr Civan would ultimately blame someone other than himself.

Süleyman leaned back in his chair. 'Tell me about it.'

'About what?'

'About your scam,' Süleyman said. 'Some of your meat has already gone for testing, so don't try to lie to me.'

'It's pork, like I said.'

'And why pork?'

259

'Because it's the closest meat to human flesh. Looks and smells the same. So I'm told.'

'Who told you?'

He sighed. 'It's the wife,' he said. 'Her habit, her problem. I never wanted this!'

'"This" being?'

He sighed again. 'Look, I never knew there were so many weirdos in the world until I met her.'

'Your wife?'

'She's Romanian. Legs up to her neck, a body you could drown in. Pity about the heroin addiction. We married, and the next thing I know I'm in debt to three local dealers.' He shook his head. 'I nearly killed the bitch when I found out! I'm just a fucking cab driver, you know? Then her brother comes over from Bucharest, so I've another addict to accommodate!'

Süleyman was slightly satisfied that he'd been right about this man.

'It was Nicolae's idea.'

'Your brother-in-law?'

'Yeah. There's a whole online trade around Romania and the Dracula legend. All sorts of things from straight souvenirs to weird stuff like human blood and Dracula's ashes.'

'Fake.'

'Most of it. Pigs, like I said. I don't know whether the real fucking crazies out there on the Net know it's fake or not . . .'

'But you market it as genuine.'

'Well wouldn't you? I can make a few hundred lire from curious Muslims just with the pork, but I can make a few thousand from a pervert who wants to eat human flesh. And where's the harm? I give them pig so they don't have to go out there and kill some innocent on the street to get their kicks. So a pig died! So what!'

Süleyman smiled. This little shit was completely unaware of what he'd done. But not for long.

'Laws governing the sale of goods are not my forte,' he said, 'but I know you've broken a few.'

'Yeah, well . . .'

'You've also encouraged and facilitated an act of perversion at a time when we have reason to believe a real consumer of human flesh may be at large in this city.'

'A real cannibal? I don't know anything about that,' Civan said. 'I'm not into all that!'

'Yes, but you know people who are.'

'No I don't!'

'That isn't what you told your customer, is it?'

'Well what do you think I'd tell him?' Civan said. 'Sorry, friend, this is the first time I've done this.'

'Our investigator said your operation was very professional.'

'Yeah. Thanks to Nicolae. If you want to know how "Raw" came about, and why, you'll have to ask that bastard.'

'Oh, and you're going to give him to me, are you, Cüneyt Bey?'

He thought about it for a moment. But only a moment. 'Why not?' he said. 'What's he ever done for me except get me into trouble?'

'So Nicolae . . .'

'Oh, he's not in the country at the moment,' Civan said.

'Where is he now?'

'He's in Romania. Buying up pork.'

There was still a plug socket next to the place where the freezer used to stand outside the kitchen.

'Why did you demolish the old bathhouse?' İkmen asked.

'It was a health hazard. We had rats,' Uğur İnan said.

'You're very near the Bosphorus here.'

'The foundations were rotten. The rats were coming into the house. My son has a baby, I couldn't take the risk.'

'Of course not.'

Whoever had demolished the bathhouse had done a good job. Barely a stone remained to indicate where it had once been, and the earth beneath had been flattened.

İkmen looked up at the huge tattooed biker, Ziya, and said, 'Do you recall which company came to take the freezer away?'

'No . . .'

'Shame. Because you see I have a problem with this story I have been told about you and Bülent delivering a freezer to the Imperial Oriental Hotel.'

'We didn't. It went for scrap.'

'I don't disbelieve you,' İkmen said, 'but I can't disbelieve the other story I've been told either. Do you see?'

Nobody said anything.

İkmen continued. 'So if you could find out who took this freezer away for scrap, it would help me enormously.'

He saw the major general narrow his eyes. He was thinking, *Here we are again, the government persecuting me via the police.* Or was he?

Uğur İnan put a hand on İkmen's shoulder. 'I'm sure we can do that, Inspector,' he said. 'When Bülent comes back, I'll ask him. We must have some paperwork somewhere. None of us knows where Bülent is at the moment. He may be out clubbing for all I know. Can we leave this until the morning? I'm sure he'll be back before dawn, whatever he's doing.'

İkmen made him wait for an answer, then he said, 'OK.'

'Good.'

Once he was back in his car, İkmen called Kerim Gürsel to ask him how he'd got on with the major general's wife. He also asked him if he wanted to get some overtime in.

Chapter 26

Gül had hardly slept. After his debrief at police headquarters, he'd been taken home to the squat, where a lot of people had still been up. Too tired to think straight, he hadn't paid any attention to what they were doing, but as soon as he'd got into bed, their voices had kept him awake. He couldn't work out what any of them were saying, but he knew anger when he heard it.

He'd taken a sleeping pill. But that had only served to make him even more restless, and so in the end he'd smoked a bit of dope. That had given him two hours' sleep. But it hadn't been worth it. Awake now, he felt wrung out and wretched. Not even a cold shower could revive him. And there was no one to talk to. Whoever had been up in the night was sleeping in. Even the girls, Meltem and Ahu, were still in bed.

Gül thought about the cross-dressed cannibal man and what Inspector Süleyman had said about him. Gül had been his first customer, and yet the operation had seemed professional. Could Gül have been wrong about Raw? He leaned on his windowsill and looked out into the street.

The man, Cüneyt Civan, had needed money to pay his wife's debts to drug dealers. A common story, even if his solution to it was uncommon. How did people think these scams up? He'd been a hacker for years and so he knew how people did these things, but not why. Just the thought of eating human flesh made him gag, and yet there was a market. Transgression was always attractive to certain people, and cannibalism was one of the ultimate manifestations of that.

The police had been pleased with him. Süleyman had told him that because of his actions, an illegal trade in Eastern European pork had been unearthed. Sadly, no real cannibals had been encountered, but then how many of them really did exist? He'd helped Father Bacchus get material to create fictional monsters, but Gül had to admit that they were in all probability based on pure fantasy. Even on the Dark Web people lied.

Gül had been aware of a man in the street below for some time, but he hadn't paid him any attention. But now the man turned and Gül saw his face. It made him smile. What on earth was Pembe Hanım's handsome beau Kerim doing outside the squat so early in the morning?

Then he remembered what Kerim Gürsel did for a living and he frowned.

Denial had always been Boris Myskow's default position. That was what his therapist said. But this time his lies seemed convincing even to him. He had to go back to New York to personally take control of a failing restaurant on Madison Avenue. That was what he'd told his head chef and what he told himself.

Of course his private party guests wouldn't like it, but he couldn't help that. The spooks who protected him said that if he was worried about the police, he needn't be. But what did they know? He'd told them nothing, and as far as he was aware, they'd witnessed nothing either.

Once he was back in the States, he could sort things out. He'd sell the Imperial Oriental – to hell with Istanbul's trendiness. Somehow he'd got involved in this weird country in ways that had turned sour, and he wanted out. If they banned him from ever coming back, then so what? Gastronomy was huge in the States, and new hot spots were coming on stream all the time.

Spain was massive, and if he went there, he'd be able to use as much pork and boar as he liked.

Boris didn't put much more than a few suits, a couple of pairs of shoes and his insulin in his suitcase. The rest of it could go to hell. He left room number 9, where he'd just spent a sleepless night, and went down and asked the concierge to get him a taxi. He didn't say where he was going or why, and she didn't ask.

Of course even he had to wait, which was a ball ache. He didn't want to sit down, but he made himself do it. Wandering about the lobby like a nervous jackrabbit was freaky. But then the taxi came and he picked up his suitcase.

Out on the street, he waited for the taxi driver to open the door for him. It only took a second. But in that tiny space of time he saw a man he hadn't expected to see, and it made him hold his breath.

Cüneyt Civan had told them everything. How and why he'd become 'Raw', how he'd accessed the cannibal scene and when his brother-in-law Nicolae Popescu was going to return from Romania with a consignment of pork. But they still didn't know who Ümit Kavaş had eaten on the night he died, or why, and Mehmet Süleyman was beginning to wonder whether they ever would.

His phone rang.

'Süleyman.'

İkmen entered his office and quietly sat down.

'Inspector, it is Imam Ayan,' the voice on the other end of the line said.

'Oh, good morning.'

'Good morning, Inspector. I am calling you because I have heard again from my son Burak.'

Which meant that by some miracle the kid was still alive.

'He has seen young Radwan.'

265

'In Syria?'

'Yes. But he's making sure that the boy comes back here. I'll gladly take him in. I'm asking, Inspector, whether you can alert your colleagues on the border to help the boy. He tried to persuade Burak to come home, and although he failed, I owe the child a debt. Can you help me?'

The last thing Turkey needed was another Syrian refugee, but if the imam was going to give the boy a home, at least he wouldn't be on the street.

'I'll put out an alert,' Süleyman said. 'But what of your son?'

He heard the old man sigh. 'My son is lost. Radwan told him what I should have told him many years ago, but rather than piquing his curiosity, it turned him still further against me.'

'Told him what?'

'About his mother, my late wife,' the imam said.

'What about her?'

'It was only when the boys began to grow that I realised that my Zanubiya had passed the disease that killed her on to Burak. He was small and thin, just like her; I could see it in him from the age of twelve. Mustafa was like me, but . . . There was a complication.'

'Which was?'

'Which was that if I told them the truth, they would also have to know that their mother was a Jew. Radwan, may God bless him, just came out with it. "Your mother was a Jew." It was his way of trying to shock Burak into coming home with him.'

Süleyman began to feel light-headed. 'This disease,' he said, 'was it Bloom syndrome?'

There was a moment's silence, and then the imam said, 'Yes. How did you know?'

Süleyman said, 'Sir, can I ask you to come in to police head-quarters, please?'

'Yes, but—'

266

'I'll send a car,' he said. 'Now.'

When he'd finished talking to the imam, Süleyman told İkmen.

'Mmmm.' İkmen frowned. 'Meanwhile, I have a problem with a freezer.'

'The one at the Imperial Oriental? With the bloodstains?'

'Yes,' he said. 'Anecdotal evidence has it coming from the Karaköy squat via the chef Bülent Onay, but Uğur İnan denies it. He told me last night that it went for scrap.'

'Where?'

'He doesn't know,' İkmen said. 'But he promised to have a word with Onay, who organised the disposal. He wasn't home last night and neither was he at the Imperial Oriental. So we'll see.'

'Are you going back?'

'Yes,' İkmen said. 'I'm told that there's been a lot of activity inside the squat all night, but no sign of Onay.'

'How do you know?'

'Kerim had some valuable overtime,' he said. 'I was going to ask if you wanted to come along. But now you must talk to the imam.'

'I may join you later,' Süleyman said. 'I get on rather well with Uğur Bey, although he thinks I'm having an affair with Zenne Gül . . .'

İkmen laughed. 'You will have to disabuse him of that notion now you have your cannibal.'

'Fake cannibal,' Süleyman corrected. 'But you're right to make the offer, Cetin. After all, the young Syrian boy the imam wants us to get back to the city for him was convinced that his son Mustafa died in the Art House squat.'

What was she supposed to do all on her own? She'd called her husband's mobile every hour all through the night, but she'd just got his answering service. Had he finally managed to have his way with one of those young girls at that squat? Defne Baydar shook her head. Surely if she found her husband repulsive, so would a pretty young girl? It wasn't even as if he had any money. Not any more.

The police were going to release Volkan's body to her at midday. But what could she do with it? Organising funerals was men's work. She tried Deniz's mobile again, but to no avail.

What he did in that house full of perverts and communists she couldn't imagine. But they had to like him because he spent so much time there, spouting off about ancient Anatolia, no doubt. Hippy types were into all that animism business. Anything pre-Islamic was trendy. Although not religious herself, Defne found that noble savage stuff disgusting. If nothing else, Islam had civilised the early Anatolians – and they'd needed it.

She looked at her watch and then rang her husband yet again. Again she got his answering service.

He'd been shot by an ISIS fighter with bad aim. The bullet had made a terrible mess of Radwan's left arm but it hadn't killed him. Burak had killed the shooter.

Radwan had been just a few metres from the Turkish border when he'd been hit. Burak, who had watched him from behind a sand dune when they'd parted, hadn't reckoned on one of his colleagues being in the vicinity. He'd shot him without a thought.

Once inside the strange, darkened terrain of Karkemiş, Burak had helped Radwan to stagger to a group of huts and then left without a word. Radwan wondered how he was going to explain his dead colleague. But he'd probably just say that he'd been shot by a Kurdish sniper and they'd all declare him a martyr and that would be that. Why Burak had saved his life was beyond Radwan.

It was several hours later that the door to one of the huts had opened and a man had come out. He'd smoked a cigarette and was just about to go back inside when he saw the boy. He'd come over to him immediately, speaking a language that Radwan couldn't even make a guess at. Then he'd taken him inside the hut and woken up other people, who were equally unintelligible.

Later, a doctor had appeared who had been able to speak a little Arabic. He'd told Radwan that the people who had taken him in were Italian archaeologists. That had been many hours before. Now he was in a hospital, about to have an operation to remove the bullet, and he was scared.

One of the many problems associated with being stuck in an airport waiting for a flight was that it made you buy shit. So far Boris had bagged three different types of perfume for his mother, some crap for wrinkles for his wife, a giant Toblerone and a large bottle of Bacardi. He felt like necking the rum. Why couldn't he get a direct flight to New York? Changing in London with a two-hour layover was fucked up. But it had been all he'd been able to get at short notice – and it had cost him a shitload.

Boris sat down when he got to his departure gate. No one else had arrived, but he didn't care. What else did he have to do but sit? And think?

At least he wasn't as anxious as he'd been before he'd left the Imperial Oriental. The police wouldn't be coming for him once they caught up with the man he'd seen in the foyer. And they would catch up with him, because he wasn't exactly being discreet. He'd just marched straight back in to his previous life, so it seemed.

Boris Myskow wondered where he'd been, even though he really didn't give a shit.

Chapter 27

It was actually the afternoon by the time İkmen and Süleyman arrived at the Karaköy squat. Kerim Gürsel, whose eyes were an alarming shade of pink, greeted their arrival with a smile. Finally he could leave the café opposite the squat and go home. What confused him a little bit was that his superiors, plus Ömer Mungun, were accompanied by a small squad of uniformed officers. But when İkmen, Süleyman and Mungun went in, they remained outside.

İkmen looked at Uğur İnan. 'Did you manage to track down Bülent Onay or the paperwork for the freezer, or both?'

İnan smiled and gave him a receipt for the item from a company called Kelebek Metals of Kartal.

'Thank you.'

Uğur İnan said nothing. İkmen read the receipt. 'Very nice.'

He'd waited for Süleyman to finish interviewing Imam Ayan, as he had already spent a considerable amount of time first with Arto Sarkissian and then with Commissioner Teker. Requesting powers under the circumstances he had cited had not been easy. He'd had to do a lot of explaining.

'So did Mr Onay come home and give you this receipt?'

'Yes.'

'I see. And he's out again now?'

'Yes.'

İkmen paused before he took the document he'd obtained from Teker out of his pocket. Whether he deliberately did this for dramatic effect he didn't know. But he did it.

'I've a warrant to search these premises,' he said.

'A warrant! Why? Over a freezer? I've given you the receipt,' Uğur İnan said.

'Yes, sir,' İkmen said. 'And now I'm serving you with a warrant.'

'But why?'

It was a hot day and everyone was sweating anyway, but was Uğur İnan sweating just a little bit more?

'I can't tell you that, Mr İnan,' İkmen said.

'Can't or won't?'

Until now, Major General Baydar had stood silently by İnan's side. But this was too much. 'This is harassment,' he said. 'I will call my lawyer.'

'Call your lawyer if you like, sir,' İkmen said. Then he turned to Ömer Mungun. 'Go and open the door for the search team, Sergeant Mungun.'

'Yes, sir.'

The old soldier took a phone out of his pocket and dialled a number. 'This is outrageous!' he said.

'I had problems.'

'What problems?' Chef Tandoğan threw his arms in the air. 'Your supervisor? You caused trouble. You're not wanted here. Get out!'

Aysel Gurcanli was shocked to see Celal Vural back in the Imperial Ottoman. She'd been convinced he was dead. But now he was back and Halide Can was missing. What was going on?

'This place still owes me money,' Vural said. 'For that last week.'

'Oh, so we have to pay you even when you fuck off with no explanation . . .'

'Things happened.'

'What happened? Your old mother die? Your cat?'

'It's none of your business.'

'The police have been looking for you,' Tandoğan said. 'Your wife . . .'

'Don't talk about my wife!'

'Your wife has reported you as a missing person!'

'Oh.'

So he hadn't even been home? Aysel felt herself cringe. What an arsehole!

'Well you may say "oh",' Tandoğan said. 'Now get out of my kitchen! You'll get no money from me!'

'Yes, but—'

'Get out!' he screamed. 'Fucking coming here in designer clothes and asking for cash! Fuck off!'

For once Tandoğan was right. Celal Vural did look very smart and well groomed, which was unusual for him. How had he got that way?

Aysel took her phone out of her pocket and called Cetin İkmen.

'I had a bad feeling about your boyfriend,' Uğur İnan hissed.

Gül had only just woken up. Shaken into consciousness by his sort-of landlord, he sat up and said, 'What boyfriend? What do you mean?'

Uğur İnan pulled Gül's duvet on to the floor, exposing his nakedness.

'Uğur Bey!'

'Get up,' he said. 'Get up and either get out or persuade your boyfriend Süleyman to stop searching this house!'

Gül didn't know what he meant. Why was Süleyman searching the squat?

'He's not my boyfriend,' he said as he hastily put on a pair of briefs.

'Oh, come on . . .'

'Honestly! I swear! I've been helping him . . .'

'How?'

Gül had never seen Uğur Bey like this before. He'd always been laid-back and cool. But he could hear unfamiliar voices in the squat and the sound of heavy hands knocking on doors.

'I used some of my old skills,' Gül said. 'You know . . .'

'Hacking. Hacking what?'

'I can't tell you,' he said. 'But it's nothing to do with this house, I swear.'

'Then what is it to do with?'

'I told you, I can't—'

Uğur İnan grabbed him by the throat. 'The police are all over the house and the garden,' he said. 'Tell me or I'll tell everyone it's down to you!'

'It isn't! And anyway—'

'And anyway nothing,' Uğur said. 'What have you been doing for the police, Zenne Gül? Tell me!'

Gül expected Uğur İnan to laugh when he talked about cannibals. He expected him to tell him to get the hell out of his own fantasies. But instead he sat on the zenne's bed and said nothing.

Gül, unnerved by Uğur İnan's silence, went to his window and looked outside. There were two police officers in the garden. One carried a spade.

Kerim Gürsel had hoped for more sleep, but when İkmen told him that the missing waiter from the Imperial Oriental had turned up, he tipped himself out of bed and went to see Aysel Gurcanli at the hotel. He found the place in uproar.

'Mr Myskow has disappeared,' Aysel told him. 'It's said he took a taxi to Atatürk airport. I don't know if that's true.'

Kerim called İkmen. Then he said, 'You're sure it was Celal Vural you saw?'

'Positive.'

It took him some time to get through the traffic to Kağıthane.

A lot of what impeded him was construction vehicles. The Vurals' tiny apartment block was dwarfed by newer, more ostentatious buildings, for which there seemed to be an endless appetite. Before he'd even knocked on the door, he heard a woman crying.

'Yes?'

Celal Vural wasn't a distinctive-looking man. But he was wearing nice clothes and he did have an expensive haircut.

'Celal Vural?'

'Who are you?'

'Police,' Kerim said. 'You were reported missing, sir.'

'Well I'm back now,' Vural said. 'No harm's come to me. Everything's OK.'

The crying continued, occasionally punctuated by a childish voice asking, 'What's going on?'

'Where have you been?' Kerim said.

'Away.'

'Away.' Kerim looked into the tiny, dark apartment and saw a small snot-nosed child staring at him with frightened eyes. 'Away where?'

'That's my business,' Vural said. 'Now—'

'Ah, but it's not just your business, sir,' Kerim said. 'You were reported as a missing person. We need to know where you've been.'

Celal Vural sighed. 'I stayed with a friend.'

'Who?'

'A friend. I don't think I need to tell you more than that, do I?'

'Depends who the friend was,' Kerim said. 'If your friend was a criminal, well . . . You know your wife was very worried about you? If you were with a friend, why didn't you tell her?'

Maybe Celal Vural was about to answer and maybe he wasn't. But he didn't get the chance. Amid a whirl of paisley fabrics and a torn headscarf only just on her head, Selma Vural ran up

274

beside her husband and pushed him aside. Her face was wet not only with tears but also with blood from scratches down her cheeks. Had Vural attacked her, or had she done it to herself?

'He didn't tell me because he was with a woman!' she screamed. 'A whore he met at that hotel!'

'Watch your mouth!'

He raised his hand, but Kerim caught his wrist. 'I'm sure you don't want to assault your wife, do you?'

'No. Who said I—'

'He only came back to see whether he could get more money from his employer,' Selma Vural said. 'So he can run back to Ölüdeniz and his woman!'

'Is this true?'

Celal Vural sniffed. 'My private domestic life is my own affair,' he said.

'Not when you abandon your family,' Kerim said. 'What do you intend to do now, Mr Vural?'

'It's—'

'He wants a divorce,' his wife said.

Kerim heard one of the children murmur, 'What's that?'

'So he can marry some child he met while she was on a shopping trip with her mother.'

'A child?'

'She's not a child, she's eighteen!' Vural said.

'Eighteen? Fourteen? What does it matter?' his wife said. She turned to Kerim. 'She comes from some rich Kurdish family from Diyarbakir. My stupid husband followed her and her family down to the coast. Spent all our money impressing this . . . child!'

'She's—'

'Mr Vural, do you intend to go back to this lady or—'

'As soon as I'm free, I'll marry Nazdar, as if it's your business,' Vural said.

Selma began to cry again.

Vural looked at her with disgust. 'So as you can see,' he said to Kerim, 'this is a domestic issue. I'm safe and well and there's no need for further police involvement.'

He was right. Now it was between Celal and Selma, however distasteful that might be. Vural was clearly the sort of man who was short on conscience, but then maybe his life of poverty had finally ground him down to a place where any chance of escape had to be taken. It was still a vile thing to do to his wife and children.

'You know you will have to provide for your dependent children,' Kerim said.

'When I marry Nazdar, I'll take them with me.'

It was then that the slight figure of Selma Vural attacked her husband with her nails.

Kerim Gürsel considered letting her tear him to pieces – he deserved it – but he also knew that a nasty piece of work like Celal would use such an act against her. He pulled her off and said, 'Don't let him goad you. Please!'

Celal, laughing, went back inside the apartment to be with his children. Kerim heard him say, 'Yes, Mama went mad, didn't she?'

Selma looked up into his eyes and then began crying again. Kerim Gürsel took a card out of his pocket and pressed it into her hand.

'Here are my numbers,' he said. 'Contact me. If there's anything I can do . . .'

'There isn't.'

She pulled away from him. Inside the apartment, the children began to cry. Their father raised his voice.

'If he lays a hand on any of you, call me,' Kerim said.

She looked down at the ground, a hopeless expression on her face.

'I mean it,' he said. 'He has betrayed and impoverished you.

He deserves to suffer for that, hanım. He is in the wrong, not you.'

It was so hot, smoking outside was impossible unless it was in the shade. Cetin İkmen and Mehmet Süleyman stood underneath the porch over the kitchen door. Noises of both the search and discontent because of it came from inside the Art House. But the two men were fixated on what was happening in the garden.

'The most likely scenario is the official version,' Süleyman said. 'We have to accept that.'

'I do,' İkmen said. 'But what I also accept is that every ISIS death is a propaganda tool.'

'But the imam has spoken to his other son in Syria, and he says his brother died in battle. Why would he lie? Burak Ayan didn't like these people any more than his brother did. Surely if they killed him he would want them punished?'

İkmen shrugged. 'I see that,' he said. 'But I don't think that what Burak Ayan says can necessarily be relied upon. This war against ISIS – and if we're serious about it, it will have to become a war – is one of smoke and mirrors, on their part.'

'What do you mean?'

'I mean they are not what they seem.'

'I think we know that.'

'Do we?' İkmen said. 'If we put aside the money this group makes from its donors, from the sale of archaeological artefacts, oil, gas and, some say, illegal drugs, what do we have? A relatively small group of mainly young men and women, many of them from the West, who have been groomed. This is religion with extras. I wish I'd thought of it.'

'Cetin!'

He laughed. 'Joke. Did you never hear that quote from the founder of Scientology, L. Ron Hubbard, about how the quickest way to get rich is to invent your own religion?'

'No.'

'He said it, trust me,' İkmen said. 'Older men are the real forces behind ISIS. You've seen that picture of Burak Ayan. For a tiny lad like that, what's not to like about people who will make you a man? And now we know that he probably has Bloom syndrome . . .'

'But it's his brother we're looking for, and he was apparently normal.'

'Ah well, let us see,' İkmen said.

'I need to go to the café. I need coffee.'

The voice came from inside the kitchen. İkmen turned. Uğur İnan was marching away from him.

'Ah, Mr İnan . . .'

He stopped.

'I'm sorry, but you can't leave these premises,' İkmen said. 'Not until the search is complete.'

'Yes, but—'

'No,' İkmen said. 'No exceptions. If you need liquid for rehydration purposes, then I'll send one of my men out to buy water. But you've got water here.'

İnan looked at him for a moment and then walked away.

When he'd gone, Süleyman said, 'I must say, the work they've done out here has intrigued me. We Turks love our gardens, but we're not exactly gardeners, are we?'

İkmen smiled. Every plant he'd ever owned had died within a month. That was Fatma's area.

'I thought it had to do with being environmental and green and all that,' Süleyman said. Then he frowned. 'Cetin, what do you think you might find here?'

'I don't know,' İkmen said. 'But I'm sure I'll find something. Getting that phone call from London will help, I feel.'

Chapter 28

Was it raining, or was it just in his head? Boris Myskow looked out of the aircraft window and saw grey tarmac and early evening sunshine. OK, so summer had to be possible even in the British capital. Not that it was relevant. He didn't have time to leave Heathrow Airport before his flight to the Big Apple. But it didn't matter. Now that he'd left Turkey, he was cool.

When the aircraft came to a halt, he got up and took his bag out of the overhead locker. He was only transiting so there'd be time for a drink. Boris felt quite buoyed up. Leaving Istanbul had been totally the right thing to do. Sometimes you just had to cut your losses, especially when things got too complicated. There was always a certain amount of schmoozing that had to be done when one was working in a new territory, but Turkey had been ridiculous. He'd never really got those men he'd been advised to pander to. OK, they'd made sure he'd made money by getting all their friends into the hotel, but there'd also been a political dimension he'd never understood. And the pork thing had just been *insane* . . .

Boris thanked the British crew, who smiled indulgently as he deplaned. He put his bag on his shoulder and began to walk up the ramp and into the airport. But then a hand stopped him.

'Mr Myskow?'

The voice was British, its owner a large man holding something up for him to see.

'Yeah?'

'Police,' the man said.

Boris's good humour evaporated.

She'd sat out there – with Barış. Birgül İnan put a hand up to her mouth and shook her head. Her husband, İsmet, tiptoed away from their sleeping baby and joined her at the window.

'What's happening?' he asked.

'They've found something,' Birgül said.

'What?'

'I don't know, but look, they've put one of those tents up.'

İsmet peered down into the darkening garden. 'One of those tents?'

'That the police use to cover dead bodies,' she said.

'Dead bodies? Why would there be a dead body in our garden?'

'I don't know,' Birgül said. 'But there was a lot of shouting earlier. That's what made me come over to the window. Those two detectives ordered that tent erected and then they went inside and spoke to your father.'

'Did you hear what they said?'

'No. Your dad came upstairs and I heard him go to his room.'

İkmen ended the call and put his phone back in his pocket. Sitting across the Art House's kitchen table from Mehmet Süleyman, he said, 'The Metropolitan Police will hold Myskow in custody overnight and then put him on a plane back here in the morning.' He shook his head. 'One piece of positive news, I suppose.'

Süleyman put his cigarette out. 'What was she doing here?' he said. 'There's no way this was on her route from the hotel back to her apartment.'

'Unless she was brought here.'

In spite of having been buried deep underneath the Art House's garden, the body of Constable Halide Can had not degraded to the extent that she couldn't be recognised. Luckily for the police, the probable cause of Can's death had not involved her face. It was the back of her skull that was smashed to a soil-drenched pulpy mess.

'Do you think the untouchable Boris Myskow killed her?' Süleyman said.

'Why?'

'Because he found out she was a police officer? He has tried to run . . .'

'Why would he be frightened of a police constable with the spooks in his corner?' İkmen said. 'No, this is either a lot more complicated than it looks or very much simpler. And at the moment, to me, it looks like the latter.'

'Why?'

'You saw the back of Can's head,' İkmen said. 'That's either the work of a lunatic, someone in the grip of terror or the result of something really heavy falling on her head.'

'If it had been an accident, it would have been reported . . .'

'Which leaves us with a lunatic or a very frightened person.'

'Myskow?'

'Maybe,' İkmen said. 'But we can start interviewing everyone in the house now.'

'Except for Bülent Onay.'

'Yes,' İkmen said.

Ömer Mungun came into the kitchen and placed a large holdall on the table. He looked exhausted.

Süleyman said, 'Give you a bad time?'

Ömer sat down. 'Makes me wonder whether other nationalities are so wedded to their phones.'

'Ah, the romance between the Turk and his mobile phone!' İkmen smiled. 'Our technicians will have a busy time with that lot. How's the mood, Sergeant?'

'Subdued. They know we've found something, but if Uğur

İnan has told anyone else, he or she is keeping it quiet. The guy with all the tattoos is a bit wired.'

İkmen looked down at his list of residents. 'Ziya Yetkin. Friend of Bülent Onay. Does he know where Onay has gone?'

'He says not,' Ömer said.

'Then we'll need to speak to him more formally. According to Uğur İnan, Onay came back here briefly last night. Except we know he didn't, because Kerim was watching the house all night. Be interesting to see what his room-mate can tell us about that.'

'Sir,' Ömer said. 'About Constable Can . . .'

'You must all be upset,' İkmen said. 'I know I am. Losing a colleague is one of the worst things we have to experience in this job. Sadly, it comes to almost all of us at one time or another.'

'Yes, sir.'

'But if it's any consolation, Commissioner Teker herself has taken on the awful task of informing Can's family.'

'Is Dr Sarkissian . . .?'

'Yes, he arrived about fifteen minutes ago,' İkmen said.

When Ömer had gone, Süleyman said, 'Cetin, I do hope you don't blame yourself.'

'What do you think?' He lit a cigarette.

'You shouldn't,' Süleyman said. 'You sent Can in there, at Teker's suggestion, as a way of investigating a missing person case without treading on the security service's toes. It made perfect sense.'

'Yes . . .'

'It did.'

İkmen said nothing. Süleyman knew there was nothing he could or would say that would make him feel any better. Then İkmen laughed.

'What's funny?'

'What's funny, Mehmet, is that the missing person I sent Can to the Imperial Oriental to track down has not only reappeared but has turned out to be a complete bastard.'

Süleyman shook his head. He'd heard Kerim Gürsel's account of his doorstep interview with Celal Vural. 'But he's a win, Cetin,' he said.

'Crime statistics.'

'We've found Vural and Volkan Doğan . . .'

'And our own Halide,' İkmen said. 'But we haven't found Mustafa Ayan, have we, Mehmet?'

'No. If indeed Mustafa Ayan is here in Turkey for us to find.' İkmen nodded.

Ali, the photographer, was almost as hot and sweaty as Arto Sarkissian. Why, the doctor wondered, were these tents so small?

Halide Can had met her end by sustaining repeated blows to the back of her head. Exactly what the murder weapon was had yet to be determined, and so the next stage in his investigation had to be removal of the body to the laboratory. He'd phoned Cetin İkmen to obtain permission to remove the corpse. He didn't need to see her again and he had enough on his hands with the residents of the Art House, who all had to be under suspicion.

It nevertheless struck the doctor as odd that any of the socially conscious people in the squat should do anything violent. Once Ali had finished photographing the scene, he called his orderlies in to lift the corpse and place it in a body bag. They were good lads who worked well together and were always respectful, but he still felt the need to supervise. He always did.

The two boys came in and put the bag down on the ground.

The doctor said, 'I'd like to retain the soil on the body. Just take her as she is.'

'Yes, Doctor.'

Poor Halide Can was covered in earth and many of the creatures that lived in it. She'd not been placed, but dumped. Chucked

into a hole, her legs wide apart in a way that had upset Cetin
İkmen. It didn't please the doctor. Did her open legs signify
sexual assault?

The boys lifted her out and put her in the body bag in one
smooth movement. They didn't need supervision. Arto watched
them take her out of the tent. Forensic investigators would follow.
He put his instruments and his paperwork back in his briefcase
and prepared to leave.

But, as was customary for him, he took one last look at the
crime scene. Of course forensics would have found what he saw
as soon as he had gone, but Arto was glad that he managed to
see what had been underneath Halide Can's body with his own
eyes. Otherwise he might not have believed it.

They were all being taken to police headquarters. Even his son,
his daughter-in-law and his grandson. Uğur İnan looked at Deniz
Baydar but said nothing. What was there to say? The old soldier
had come to his room so they could talk, but neither of them had
said a word.

To Uğur, Baydar looked stoic and calm. He probably wasn't
inside. But Uğur also acknowledged that at least the old man
didn't look like him. Because he both looked and felt mad.

The police had found her. When İkmen had called him out to
the garden, it had been the first time that Uğur had seen her.
What a mess!

Now this wait. He'd watched all sorts of people arrive and
go inside that tent they'd erected over her. But now she was
gone, which meant that it was all about to get an awful lot worse.

He was watching İkmen go back inside that tent again when
there was a knock on his door. A voice said, 'Mr İnan, can you
come downstairs, please?'

Baydar looked at him as he rose to his feet. Uğur knew that
there was nothing in the old soldier's expression that said 'do

this'. He knew that what he did next was entirely up to him. He couldn't face İsmet. It was impossible.

Uğur İnan walked over to his door, turned and then began to run.

Cetin İkmen said, 'What is it?'

Arto Sarkissian shook his head. 'I don't know.'

İkmen peered down at the place where Halide Can's body had been.

'Flesh?'

'I think so,' the doctor said. There wasn't a lot that could make him feel squeamish, but the sight of what appeared to be a pile of rotting meat had turned his stomach. The stench was appalling.

'Get the boys back in here with a bag and we'll have it analysed,' İkmen said.

Arto was about to call his orderlies back in when the ground moved slightly underneath his feet. 'Oh God,' he said, 'not now.'

Istanbul had been waiting for its next big earthquake since the last one in 1999. Both İkmen and the doctor had lived through several quakes over the years, of varying degrees of strength. But now this one, if it was an earthquake, seemed to have stopped.

Then he heard someone yell.

'Oh for God's sake!'

He pulled the tent flap to one side and saw one of his uniformed officers running across the garden.

'What's going on?' he said.

But the officer didn't answer.

İkmen couldn't afterwards recall whether he saw the body on the ground first or whether he heard the voice. But from the window of Uğur İnan's room he distinctly remembered Deniz Baydar saying, 'What a ridiculously excessive thing to do!'

* * *

He had finally left her. And what timing! How was she supposed to organise Volkan's funeral all on her own?

Nothing had been done. Nothing!

Defne Baydar walked in circles. She didn't even know any imams. What was she supposed to do? The whole thing was ridiculous. Volkan had never had any notion of a god.

She sat down. They'd always had an arrangement, herself and Deniz. He did what he wanted and she never asked questions. He never bothered her for sex, which was something she was grateful for, but to actually leave . . .

That had never been part of their domestic arrangement. But ever since he'd started going to that awful squat, he'd been even less in evidence than before. Prison had driven him mad. And when he'd come out, he'd easily found an audience for the ideas that had been festering in his mind for years. All sorts were dissatisfied with the status quo. Not all of them were entirely savoury. But Deniz Bey had never cared much who listened to him, as long as someone did. He'd always loved the sound of his own voice.

Defne stood up again. All the men she knew were his friends, so she couldn't call any of them. And anyway, they'd be useless. They'd just reassure her that Deniz Bey would be back soon and that everything would be all right. They were good at fairy tales.

İsmet İnan wept. The police doctor had thought he'd detected signs of life, but he hadn't. Uğur İnan was dead. That stupid old soldier, Deniz Bey, was protesting his innocence to İkmen.

'He just ran,' the old man said, 'towards the window and then out to his death.'

'You've no idea why?'

'Why should I?'

'You were with him in his room for at least two hours,' İkmen said. 'You were the last person to see him alive.'

'Yes, I know, but we didn't talk. What was there to talk about? There is only so much state-sponsored persecution a person can stand. I take it this will mean that the Art House will close?'

'Human remains have been found underneath the garden,' İkmen said.

Human remains! How had they got there? İsmet experienced a level of unreality he couldn't handle. Not only had his delightful, talented, liberal father apparently committed suicide, but there was a body in the garden and he and his family were about to lose their home.

Why had his father killed himself? İsmet stopped crying and looked Major General Baydar in the face. 'This is your fault,' he said. 'Ever since you and all the other old fossils started to come here, it's been less a protest squat and more a holding pen for the delusional!'

'İsmet . . .'

'Don't try to get round me, Deniz Bey!' İsmet said. 'Ümit Kavaş was a friend. When he started visiting, everything was fine, but when he brought you people . . .'

İsmet stopped talking as the crying took over again.

İkmen put a hand on the young man's shoulder as the police doctor supervised the erection of another small tent, this time over his father's body.

Chapter 29

None of them had called him, not even Uğur. Bastards!

He'd known that something was going on because of the call he'd got from Ziya the previous night. But things had clearly developed. Now the squat had police all over it and Bülent Onay knew he was entirely separated from his stuff for ever. He couldn't go back inside now. The cops were loading people into minivans and taking them away. Unless he was really lucky, that had to mean they'd found the woman – and maybe the rest of it too. Not that they'd know what it was.

Bülent pulled his hoodie down so it almost hid his eyes. The only place left for him to go was the hotel. Unless someone talked, and no one would, Myskow was entirely in the clear. Whoever had killed the woman had dug her grave in their garden and thrown her body in. Everyone had been able to see that the garden of the Art House was being dug over for weeks. Why wouldn't a bad person use it to hide a body? That was the story that had been agreed, and if they all stuck to it, they'd be OK. Except that . . .

No, he wasn't going to think about it. He was going to be positive. At the very least, Boris Myskow would let him stay at the Imperial Oriental for a while until he sorted himself out. Boris did, after all, owe Bülent.

'Tell me about the other members of the squat,' Süleyman said.

'Tell you about them? Tell you what?'

Zenne Gül was confused. One moment he'd been Süleyman's golden boy, and now he was a suspect. But he knew nothing about the body they'd found in the garden!

Panicking, he blurted, 'I've known Meltem all my life. My mum used to work for her mum. She got me a room in the squat when I needed to move really badly.'

'Because you were uncomfortable in Fatih?'

'Yes, you know this, Mehmet Bey,' he said. They'd talked about the religious people, the homophobia . . . 'Meltem is religious, you know. And Ahu.'

'Ahu Kasap.'

'Yes. But their parents didn't want them to cover, and they were part of Gezi and—'

'Gül, slow down,' Süleyman said. Then he smiled. 'You've said you know nothing about the body in the garden . . .'

'Do you know who it is? Who is it?'

Süleyman held up his hand. 'Slow again, please.'

Zenne Gül took a deep breath.

'In answer to your question, I do have a good idea who this person is, but until we have an official identification, I can't say. Gül, apart from Meltem Baser and Ahu Kasap, can you tell me anything else about other members of the community?'

'Everyone knows . . . knew Uğur Bey.'

Gül didn't know how Uğur İnan had died, only that he was dead. On the way to police headquarters, nobody had spoken. It was shocking and terrible. It was made worse by the fact that their last conversation had been an argument and it had been about the arrival of the police. Uğur Bey had blamed Gül for bringing his 'boyfriend' Süleyman into the house. Had the implication of that anger been that Gül had somehow allowed Süleyman to see or hear something he shouldn't?

'I met Uğur Bey at Gezi,' Gül said. 'Although I came to the

squat much later than anyone else, that was where Meltem, Ahu and I met him and his friends.'

'Who were his friends?'

'Ziya and Bülent and poor Ümit Kavaş,' he said. 'And İsmet and Birgül.'

'What about Major General Baydar?'

'He was still in prison,' Gül said. 'All those military men only started visiting once the Art House had been established for some time. I don't know when. Before I arrived.'

'Why did these military types visit the squat?'

'I don't know,' Gül said. 'They all talked to Uğur Bey. There was a lot of booze. Ziya and Bülent, if he was around, joined in too. And Ümit. Political stuff, I think.'

'Squatters and soldiers?'

'That was Gezi, though, wasn't it? People from all sorts of places and backgrounds coming together for a common cause.'

'Against a—'

'I'm not saying a common enemy, Mehmet Bey,' Gül said. 'But there are unusual alliances now. I heard that Ümit didn't like Major General Baydar much. He tolerated him. But then Ümit didn't actually live with us. He was always polite to the soldiers. Because of his father, I guess.'

'When did you last speak to Uğur Bey?'

'Midday,' he said. 'Today . . .'

'Yesterday.'

It had just gone midnight.

'Yesterday. He came to see me in my room. Inspector İkmen had already spoken to him and he was angry. He accused me of bringing you into the house so that you could find out things about us or see something you shouldn't. I don't know, that's what it felt like.'

'You've no idea what I was supposed to have found out or seen?'

'No,' Gül said. 'But Uğur Bey was furious and that didn't happen with him too often.'

'Have you been aware of any unusual things happening in the house over the past few weeks?'

'Only the demolition of the bathhouse,' he said. 'Ziya told everyone we had rats. I thought it was a bit extreme to demolish it. We could have put down poison.'

'There was a freezer in the bathhouse, wasn't there?'

'Yes, but I never used it. I don't know that it actually worked.'

Halide Can's parents lived in the far north-east of the country, in the city of Trabzon. But there was a brother in Gaziosmanpaşa, and so it was he whose sleep was disturbed by a knock on the door in the early hours of the morning and who was asked to come and identify the body of his sister. While waiting for Murat Can to arrive, Arto Sarkissian prepared samples for DNA testing from the rotting and putrid pile of flesh that had been hidden by Halide Can's body. In order to get close to what remained of whoever it was, he had to mask up, which even in the laboratory made him feel as if he was boiling alive.

As he slowly picked his way through skin, fat, muscle and sinew, Arto, while concentrating on the job at hand, listened to Israeli superstar Ofra Haza's *Yemenite Songs* on his iPod. He didn't understand the words of what were modern adaptations of sixteenth-century rabbinical texts, but he loved the tunes.

Only very small bones remained inside the flesh. Effectively butchered, it inevitably called to mind what he had found in Ümit Kavaş's stomach. But where had those bones gone? Had they been boiled up for stock maybe? In spite of Ofra Haza's beautiful voice, Arto's stomach turned. How did one actually perform what had to be the ultimate human taboo? How had an apparently nice man like Ümit Kavaş done so? Had he even known what he was eating? And if he hadn't, then who had? And why had they given him human flesh in the first place?

Although the restaurant service was still closed, they were in full cleaning and reordering mode. Without Tandoğan, Chef Romero couldn't make himself understood and was about to go into a Latin-style meltdown. Zerrin claimed to have last seen him outside Mr Myskow's office – presumably looking for menus or something. As far as Aysel Gurcanli knew, Myskow was still missing.

It was hot in the Imperial Oriental's kitchen. Given the situation, everyone was nervous, confused, and accidents were happening all the time. If someone didn't do something about the situation soon, at the very least Romero would have a stroke. Aysel finished cleaning an oven and then asked Haydar, a very junior pastry chef, to cover for her. He wasn't happy about it, but he agreed.

Aysel took the lift upstairs. It opened just in front of Myskow's office, and she was too tired for stairs. Nobody had said that Myskow had returned, and the police hadn't called her back, so Aysel just opened the door and blundered in.

Later she would wonder what, if anything, she might have heard from inside Myskow's office had she stopped outside to listen. But now it was too late to go back.

Aysel screamed. It wasn't like her, but it just came out.

Her colleague, Bülent Onay, dashed towards her with the knife he'd just used on Chef Tandoğan, and held it at her throat.

'After Mr İnan fell from the window, you were heard to say, "What a ridiculously excessive thing to do",' Cetin İkmen said. 'What did you mean by that?'

'I thought that was self-evident.'

There was much that Cetin İkmen shared with old soldiers

like Deniz Baydar. They usually had a secular outlook on life and they had little time for irrational flights of fancy. But they could also be deeply prejudiced and not just against religious orthodoxy. Baydar looked at İkmen and saw a scruffy, undisciplined oddity. İkmen could see it all over his face.

'The man threw himself out of a window,' he continued. 'Don't *you* think that's excessive?'

'That depends why he did it,' İkmen said. 'Or *if* he did it.'

Baydar glared at him. 'What do you mean?' he said.

'I mean we only have your word that he threw himself out,' İkmen said.

'You think I pushed him?'

'I don't know. Our forensic team will analyse the room where the incident happened, and the body will be examined for signs of violence.'

'We were friends,' Baydar said. 'Why would I kill him?'

'I don't know,' İkmen said. 'Why did we find a female body in the garden of a house that you, by your own admission, frequent often?'

'How should I know?'

'Because according to some of the other residents of the Art House, you're always around,' İkmen said. 'You and until recently, I imagine after his son's death, General Kavaş plus other military gentlemen . . .'

'Well we have to meet somewhere!' he said. 'If we meet in the street or even in a café, we're always under surveillance.'

'You think?'

'I know!' he thundered. 'Uğur Bey kindly tolerated us because in many ways he shared our discontent. Our perspectives were very different, but there was a sympathy there, and a friendship. We first met years ago, when Uğur Bey designed the fabrics for the officers' mess at Selimiye.'

Major General Baydar had been with the First Army Corps,

which was stationed at the Selimiye Barracks in Üsküdar.

'What do you talk about at these meetings you have with other military men?' İkmen asked.

'Trying to root out sedition, are you?'

'I'm trying to find out who killed the woman in the garden of the Art House, and why Uğur Bey is dead,' İkmen said.

There was a moment's silence and then the major general said, 'I don't just meet with other military men, as you put it. The Art House is a very sociable place, as I'm sure you know. People meet and talk there in a spirit of freedom of ideas and brotherhood.'

'You know there are homosexual—'

'We cannot agree on everything, that wouldn't be democratic!' Baydar said. 'Our views differ, we debate.'

And yet İkmen wondered what Baydar would do if he ever got into deep conversation with Zenne Gül. But according to Gül, that wouldn't happen. Baydar rarely so much as glanced at him. He was far more interested in the girls who lived in the house.

'What do you talk about in a spirit of freedom and brother-hood?'

'Everything,' Baydar said. 'Politics, history, art . . .'

There was a knock on the door, which opened, and a constable entered the interview room.

İkmen said, 'Yes?'

The constable whispered in his ear. 'You have a call, sir. It's urgent.'

'What is it?'

These so-called urgent calls were often far from even vaguely important.

'An incident at the Imperial Oriental Hotel,' the constable said.

Without the presence of Boris Myskow? This didn't feel good.

İkmen stood up and motioned for Ömer Mungun to rise.

'I'm sorry, we'll have to resume this interview later,' he said to Major General Baydar. 'Something has come up.'

'What?'

'I don't know yet,' he said. 'But it's not good, Deniz Bey. That's all I can tell you.'

'I don't want to hurt you!'

'Then why are you?'

Aysel Gurcanli struggled against the thick tape that pinned her to Boris Myskow's chair.

'I need to get out of here and I need to do it without worrying about you,' Bülent Onay said.

'Why were you in here with him?' She looked at the body of Tandoğan, who lay across Myskow's desk in his own blood.

'He disturbed me.'

Bülent went over to the window, looked out, then came back.

'Doing what?'

'I needed cash,' Bülent said. Then he placed a strip of tape over Aysel's mouth.

She watched him pick up the knife he'd used to kill Tandoğan, and a rucksack, and walk towards the office door. Had anyone heard her scream? Noises of all sorts happened in hotels, but surely a scream was different?

Bülent opened the door quietly and left. Aysel knew that she was bound tightly to the chair and so would it make any difference if she struggled to free herself? She tried it for a few seconds, but it was painful and so she stopped.

And then the door opened and she began to make grunting noises to attract attention. When she saw who had just arrived, though, she began to cry. Bülent Onay ran over to her and put his knife to her throat once again. He was followed by other men, including Cetin İkmen.

Chapter 30

İkmen down sat on one of the chairs in front of Boris Myskow's desk.

'Hello, Bülent,' he said to the young man sweating heavily and holding a knife to Aysel Gurcanli's neck. Who else could it be but Bülent Onay? He'd been seen in the hotel kitchen. People had described his appearance as 'mad'.

'I will kill her,' Bülent said.

'Under what circumstances?' İkmen lit a cigarette. Oddly, there was an ashtray on Myskow's desk, just beside the dead body. Americans didn't smoke, did they?

'You have to let me go.'

'Oh. So you want a helicopter to the airport and a flight to South America?'

'I . . .'

'You know it's not happening, don't you, Bülent? That's fantasy,' İkmen said. 'As you can see, I have a group of officers with me who are all armed. The only way you're getting out of here alive is by surrendering to us. Sorry.'

For a moment, Bülent didn't react at all. Then he said, 'It all got out of hand.'

'What did?'

'It was an accident.'

'What was?'

'All of it,' he said.

İkmen looked at Aysel Gurcanli. Her face was red and her breathing laboured. 'Are we going to talk, Bülent?' he said.

He ran his fingers through his hair. 'I don't know. I just want to go, you know?'

'Yes. But we've ruled that out, haven't we?' İkmen said.

In his agitation, Bülent could still harm Aysel – or himself.

'Let Aysel go and we'll give talking a go,' he continued.

He had entirely underestimated Bülent, who clutched Aysel Gurcanli tightly to his chest. İkmen regrouped. 'All right,' he said, 'keep hold of Aysel but tell me about the body I've found underneath that of Halide Can.'

Bülent breathed. 'We killed a boy,' he said.

'By accident?'

'Yes.'

'OK, and "we" are?'

'Uğur Bey, Ziya, Ümit Kavaş and me.'

'Why?'

'Because he was a horrible kid!'

İkmen began to feel cold. 'When?'

'Weeks ago. He and his brother and another kid kept on coming to the house and shouting abuse. Throwing stones . . . Months it went on for! Then it was really hot one afternoon and we . . . Uğur Bey, he lost it!'

'His temper?'

'Ziya, too. There were only the two brothers that afternoon. We caught them and dragged them inside. We meant to humiliate them . . .'

'But?'

'The little one just soaked up his punishment like a sponge. The bigger one . . .' He looked down for a moment and then said, 'His heart stopped. I don't know why.' He shook his head. 'His brother saw all of it but he didn't show anything. No emotion.

I thought at the time it had to be because he was in shock, but . . . Ümit said we'd have to call the soldiers, Deniz Bey, even his own father.'

'Did you?'

'Yes,' he said. 'Ziya put the little kid in the toilet downstairs and locked him in. Everyone else was out but we knew they'd be back soon. Deniz Bey came.'

'And what did he do?'

Bülent put the hand without the knife up to his head. 'Oh man!'

He appeared to be in pain. İkmen let him have a moment. Poor Aysel Gurcanli was very uncomfortable, but he didn't think she was actually in danger. Bülent was clearly the one suffering – for whatever his sins had been.

'He said we should kill the other kid too,' Bülent said. 'Uğur Bey went *mental*!'

'And?'

'He wouldn't have that!' Bülent said. 'He went and talked to the boy. Tried to explain how it had all been an accident and that if he wanted to call the police he could. Deniz Bey meantime's just losing his mind at what he saw as the "hippy" stupidity of it all. I thought that someone else was going to die that day, and I don't necessarily mean the kid. But it was the kid who ended it.'

'How?'

'So this is where you don't believe me,' Bülent said.

'Maybe.'

'The kid said that he and his brother had been on their way to Syria. He didn't say why and no one asked. He had a ticket for a bus to Gaziantep. He said if we just let him go, he'd say nothing about his brother. Not to you or his family or anyone.'

'And you believed him?'

'Of course we didn't! He had to be lying. Who wouldn't want to get their brother's killers put away?'

'Did he ask for money?'

'Oh yes, that too. It was Uğur Bey who made the compromise. I mean, as he said to the rest of us, a kid like that was going to Syria only for one reason.'

'To join ISIS.'

'Of course. Both kids had been full of holy advice for us for months. He was that kind of boy. And later we all agreed that he was also the kind of boy who hadn't had a lot of love for his bigger, better-looking brother. Like a cross between a toddler and a malicious old man he was, with arms and legs like sticks. I hated him. Who trades their own brother for a lift to the Syrian border and a handful of euros?'

'Who gave him a lift?'

'Ziya. I think he thought it was getting him away from the aftermath, but it didn't. When he came back was when it all really kicked off.'

İkmen raised an eyebrow.

'We had to get rid of the body.'

İkmen knew what was coming, but it made it no less of a shock. Getting rid of bodies was always a problem for killers who valued their liberty. In the past, he'd found them hidden in ancient monuments, burned, buried, dismembered and even embalmed. But never this . . .

'Deniz Bey has this belief that the early Anatolians ate the flesh of their enemies,' Bülent said.

'So you ate the boy.'

'Part of him. If we'd eaten all of him, then we wouldn't have needed to involve anyone else.'

'Like who?'

'Mr Myskow,' Bülent said.

Bülent had never even thought about eating human flesh. But then until he became a chef in the city he'd never thought about making lime into foam or dehydrating tomatoes. He'd always cooked his mother's food. Basic but beautifully presented dishes from the Black Sea region. Then he'd worked for Myskow and discovered he had a talent for really weird modern food.

That bastard Tandoğan had been all about 'pushing the boundaries of gastronomy'. Except he didn't have the talent to do it. Romero did, and he made exceptional food for the restaurant. But not good enough for Myskow's special guests. Only Boris and Bülent were able to cook for them, because they wanted it really weird. Or so they thought.

Bülent knew many of them by sight. All good citizens and responsible businessmen, they'd started small with modest amounts of alcohol. The spooks who minded them just turned away. But pig meat had been a big step.

'The boy died in the old bathhouse,' Bülent said. 'We put his body in the freezer and locked it.'

'Had the freezer always been locked?' İkmen asked.

'No. But no one had used it for years; it was filthy.'

Deniz Bey had wheedled. He'd said it would make them true Anatolians, that it was an act of protest against the current status quo, that it was honourable.

Eventually Bülent said, 'When you don't know what to do about something, anything becomes possible.'

He moved the knife just a fraction of a centimetre away from Aysel Gurcanli's face. He didn't want to hurt her accidentally, and talking about this might make his hands shake.

'If we ground the bones down for fertiliser, buried the guts and intestines – which would rot easily – we could . . .'

'Consume?'

'I cooked it. I did it well but I didn't like it. I didn't do it for the challenge or anything like that! You've got to believe me. I couldn't finish it. On my mother's life. Only Deniz Bey enjoyed it, although he encouraged Ümit to eat, which he did. Poor Ümit, accustomed to taking orders from soldiers, I suppose. But not even Deniz Bey thought it would kill him.'

'It didn't,' İkmen said. 'He had a heart attack.'

'So why did you come sniffing around?'

'Because it isn't every day you find human flesh in a corpse's stomach,' İkmen said.

'Which was why we had to demolish the bathhouse, grind up the bones and . . . There was so much of it!'

He wanted to cry. He'd just killed a man and he wanted to cry. How fucked up was that?

'We couldn't eat it, not again. Not after Ümit. We couldn't bury it. None of us had the nerve to do so. What if we were seen?'

'You buried the intestines.'

'Which could have come from any kind of animal,' Bülent said. 'Try doing that with a human leg.'

'Boned, it wouldn't—'

'We couldn't do it! You people were coming to the house and we were going nuts, OK?'

'OK.'

And there was something else. Bülent lowered his head. It was shameful. It was fucking weak and low and gutless. 'I wanted Myskow to be in debt to me,' he said. 'I needed that.'

'What do you mean?' İkmen said.

'You know how taboo pork is amongst the faithful,' he said. 'I know plenty of so-called Muslims who drink, but none who eat pork. Myskow's guests are prominent people . . .'

'Who?'

He laughed. 'You think I can tell you and live?' he said. 'I doubt *you'd* be allowed to live if you found out!'

İkmen said nothing. Bülent wondered what he was thinking. He was well known for his lack of piety. But did he actively have it in for those who practised their faith?

'I told Myskow that if he didn't help me move the body, I'd make sure that his arrangement with the boar hunters came to light,' Bülent said.

'Yes, but he in turn would know that you had killed a child,' İkmen said.

'He would. He does. Anyway, I didn't kill the kid. I didn't!' Bülent said. 'But I knew that Boris Myskow had a weakness. We cleaned the old freezer and installed it in the first-floor kitchen. Myskow would keep it there until the heat was off, and then we'd take the body away again – somehow. Except I knew that wouldn't happen.'

'Why?'

'Because Myskow is crazy,' Bülent said. 'People have no idea what he puts in some of his most exclusive, most innovative dishes.'

'What do you mean?'

'OK, for example, he has a starter called caviar on sturgeon thins, which is dressed with a caper and lamb's kidney foam. People comment on the slight ammonia scent that pervades the dish, but that's the essence of lamb's kidney, right? Wrong. What he decants into his "essence" isn't lamb's kidneys, it's human piss.'

İkmen frowned. 'Why?'

'Because he's pushing the boundaries of gastronomy. Anything can be food. That's his belief. It was mine too, which was how we came together professionally.'

'Yes, but he employed Chef Romero as his second in command. Why not you?'

'Because Romero has an international reputation. I'm just some Turkish guy,' Bülent said. 'Romero knows nothing about this, unlike Tandoğan.'

They looked at the body across the desk.

'So why didn't he work with Tandoğan?'

'Because he was shit,' Bülent said. 'He shared Myskow's philosophy but he couldn't innovate and he couldn't cook.'

'And so . . .'

'And so I knew that Myskow wouldn't be able to resist the urge to cook with human meat,' Bülent said. 'I knew he'd cook it for his special guests and eat it himself. I wanted him and the scum he cooked for to be as damned as I was.'

'We didn't find any human flesh on these premises,' İkmen said.

'No,' Bülent replied, 'but that woman did.'

'What woman?'

'That Halide Can woman.'

'My officer.'

It took a few seconds to filter through. A police officer had died. There would be no mercy, no redemption. But then as soon as he'd put human flesh in his mouth, that had been impossible. Bülent loosened his grip on Aysel Gurcanli, put the knife down on the desk and cried. Through his tears he said, 'Myskow killed her. He slammed the freezer door down on her neck!'

The Kurds let their women fight alongside their men, uncovered. It was haram. Burak Ayan pulled the straps on the side of his vest tight. Then he put on the heavy fragmentation jacket filled with nails, steel balls, pins and screws. He'd teach those Kurdish bitches a lesson when he detonated his vest.

The Brothers were in good spirits as they drove through the night, laughing at how Burak's small stature would bring out the natural mother in the Kurdish girls. Burak had always hated being small. People had compared him unfavourably to Mustafa his whole life, but this time would be different. Mustafa had 'died' somewhere in Iraq and his death had to be glorious because he was Burak's brother. But Burak's demise would be better. Taking out a battalion of Kurdish whores would be an event that would live for ever in the minds of all those who heard about it. And he'd go to Paradise.

Or would he? Did what he was about to do now wipe away what he'd allowed to happen to Mustafa? He'd used him. And although he hadn't planned to do so, when the opportunity had arisen, he'd taken it. He'd allowed bad people to get away with murder. Wouldn't doing this atone for that? Yes. But he knew that his father would disagree. And his father was an imam.

One of the Brothers had told him that it said in the Koran that women had to be covered in burqas and wear gloves on their hands all the time. Burak knew that was wrong. Why was he following these people?

Outside the car, he could see very little. Brother Imad said that the Kurdish lines were only about five kilometres away now, but there was no sign of anyone or anything. There was no light.

Mustafa had just died. Burak had always thought his brother was much stronger than him. It had been a shock. That was why he'd done what he'd done, because of the shock. Yes. And he was doing what he was doing now because he was no Jew. Why would his father, who was a religious and learned man, marry a Jew?

Brother Imad laughed for no particular reason and Brother Jawad said, 'Just outside the door to Paradise now, Brother Burak!'

Burak smiled.

The deep thud as the Kurdish mortar bomb was detonated made them all look at each other. It was the last thing any of them did.

Chapter 31

The flight from London to Istanbul was usually a breeze. But being cuffed to a bobby the size of a tree was an uncomfortable experience. They'd both eaten their economy-class plastic airline meal and the cop had allowed Boris to have a cup of coffee. But no booze. It did little for his nerves. The British police cell had been bad enough, but what would its Turkish equivalent be like? Did they still torture people by hauling them up by their ankles and then beating the crap out of their feet with a stick?

When they landed, everyone else got off except Boris and his minder. The crew remained on board and then, after about half an hour, he heard footsteps on the stairs outside the aircraft. They were still on the tarmac, in a distant part of the airport; whoever they were had to have come out in some sort of transport.

All the Turkish cops – there were four of them – wore plain suits and wraparound shades. They looked like the *Men in Black*. The tall, slim one was familiar.

'Mr Myskow?' Mehmet Süleyman said.

The British bobby answered for him and unlocked the handcuffs. The bobby, a DC Caulfield, and Süleyman shook hands. As the three other Turks re-cuffed Boris and escorted him down the aircraft stairs, he heard Süleyman say, 'We're very grateful.'

Yeah, Boris thought, *I bet you are.*

* * *

'I'm sorry, Defne Hanım,' Kerim Gürsel said. 'I don't know when your husband will be released.'

'My brother's body lies unburied!' the old woman said. 'I have no one to help me! What can I do?'

In spite of her high-handed behaviour towards him in the past, Kerim felt sorry for Major General Baydar's wife. Her brother's corpse was still awaiting burial and she didn't know what to do without her husband.

'What is my husband accused of?' she said.

When she'd opened her apartment door, it was clear she hadn't slept. Her eyes had been red, her face pale, and she'd almost burst into tears when Kerim had told her why he had come. Apparently she hadn't known if her husband was alive or dead.

'I can't discuss your husband's case,' Kerim said.

'Why not?'

'I can't,' he said. 'Defne Hanım, you say you didn't know where your husband had been . . .'

'He disappeared!' she said. 'Switched his phone off!'

He'd been at the Art House when the body of Halide Can had been discovered, and although he hadn't yet been implicated directly in her death, the pile of flesh she had been found lying on was another matter. Had Baydar, Ümit Kavaş, Uğur İnan and that biker, Ziya, really eaten human flesh?

'I think you should bury your brother,' Kerim said.

She flung herself down into a chair and put her head in her hands. 'And how do I do that, young man?' Defne Baydar said.

Boris was pissed that he had to rely on this Turkish clown. But his attorney from the States was on his way, and so all Mr Emre had to do was hold the situation. He wasn't doing very well.

'You don't actually know who the blood sample found on the inside of my client's freezer belongs to,' Emre said to Cetin İkmen.

'DNA matching can't be done overnight,' the policeman said. 'As I know you are aware, Lütfü Bey.'

The idiot lawyer smiled at him. His only saving grace was that he could speak English.

'But we have a witness too,' İkmen said.

'Oh?'

Boris closed his eyes and it all came back to him. Bülent had tried to stop him, but he'd just gone into a blind panic. Smashing the lid of the freezer down on her neck.

Again and again and again.

It was his word against Bülent's. But Bülent was a Turk. They'd believe him – until Ralph arrived from the States. Boris Myskow sat back in his chair.

'Yes,' İkmen said. He looked Boris straight in the eye. 'You like to cook with unusual ingredients, Mr Myskow.'

Lütfü Emre frowned.

'Shall I detail some of them?'

Boris felt himself flush. Should he have told Lütfü Emre? He'd told no one except those who understood. Like Bülent Onay.

'Human urine,' İkmen said. 'That's part of a starter, I believe. Then we have a dessert called Miracle, designed to cure all and any bodily disease. You use a certain type of water in that, I believe, Mr Myskow. Can you tell me where that water comes from?'

Boris felt his heart begin to hammer. If Emre were religious, would he be offended? He was a Muslim. No.

'Lourdes,' he said.

'So-called holy water from the shrine at Lourdes,' İkmen said.

'What shrine?'

'It's a Christian shrine in France, Lütfü Bey. Your client has been using water from a sacred spring at Lourdes to make a cream pie that can allegedly cure cancer.'

'I've never said that!' Boris said. 'I've never claimed—'

'Then why call it Miracle?' İkmen said. 'Why only give it to your most prestigious guests and why charge the weekly wage of an ordinary man for it? I am told that you are an innovator, Mr Myskow. But that is disingenuous, as is your use of human blood.'

'That's a lie, I've never—'

'Did Mr Cihan Özlü know that you gave him and his friends human meat instead of wild boar?' İkmen said. 'And yes, Lütfü Bey, I do mean Mr Cihan Özlü the economist.'

Boris began to sweat. How had İkmen found out about Özlü and his friends? Weren't they supposed to have been protected by the spooks that followed them around? He looked at his lawyer's face, which was white.

'I'm not saying anything until my attorney arrives from the States,' he said.

Up until that point, the cop called Süleyman had been silent. Now he said, 'That's your choice, Mr Myskow. But you need to know that you have to stay here until he arrives.'

Boris looked around the interview room and then closed his eyes.

'Bülent Onay is, behind all his grief, a rational man,' İkmen said as he lit up another cigarette. 'Which is why he'll serve a long sentence.'

İkmen and Süleyman had come out from the Myskow interview and were standing in the car park.

'Can cannibalism be described as rational?' Süleyman asked.

'As a method of disposing of a body, yes,' İkmen said. 'At least that's what I think.'

'It's not madness?'

'And what's that?' İkmen said.

Süleyman smiled. One of his ex-wives had been a psychiatrist,

308

and so he knew something about the debates that routinely raged around what was and wasn't insanity.

'Bülent and his companions accidentally killed Mustafa Ayan and then didn't know what to do with his body.'

'And his brother let them get away with it,' Süleyman said. 'That's what I don't understand.'

İkmen shrugged. 'Going to join ISIS, so who knows what he was thinking? Too involved in the cause to care about his brother? You have to be part of that to understand in any way, I think.'

Süleyman sat down on the wall surrounding the car compound. 'But we've only got Bülent's word.'

'As yet,' İkmen said. 'But Aysel Gurcanli positively and freely identified economist Cihan Özlü, so we know the rough composition of the group that came to Myskow's dinners.'

'No, I mean that no one else – Deniz Bey, Ziya, Uğur İnan, none of the other "killers" – has admitted anything.'

'But Bülent did.'

'You gave him no choice.'

'I did,' İkmen said. 'He could have released Aysel Gurcanli and said nothing. He chose to confess. Or rather, he broke down when I told him that Halide Can was a police officer. From then on, I believe he felt he had nothing to lose by owning up to everything. We could both see the body of the chef he'd murdered on the desk, and I blew his "helicopter to the airport" fantasy away as soon as I entered that room. Hostage films featuring offenders obtaining transport to airports should, in my opinion, be banned.'

Süleyman smiled. Then he said, 'Why would anyone want to cook with urine? Why would people eat such things?'

'In both instances I think it must be because they can,' İkmen said. 'Why climb Everest when you can sit on your arse and watch someone else do it on TV? Answer? Because it exists and because human beings need to both achieve and transgress.

Ban cannabis and people will make bonzai; limit cigarette smoking and they will fetishise food and die of obesity. My kids go out for meals and pay colossal amounts of money for two tomatoes whipped into a foam by some celebrity. I'd want a full main course and a drink for the same price. Gourmet food is as much a vice as alcohol and drugs.'

'But we all have to eat.'

'Yes, but not like *that*,' İkmen said.

İkmen's phone rang. He took it out of his pocket and answered. It was Commissioner Teker.

'Is it true that you're waiting for Myskow's lawyer from the States?' she said.

'Yes, madam.'

There was a moment of silence and then she said, 'That's absurd.'

'Mr Newman is on his way here from the airport,' İkmen said.

'What?'

'Myskow called him from London,' İkmen said. 'He took a night flight.'

'Oh. Oh, I see. Let me know when he arrives.'

'Of course.'

İkmen ended the call. 'I sometimes think,' he said, 'that she believes I'm an idiot.'

Süleyman laughed. 'Oh, that is far from the truth and you know it! Teker just likes to have her finger on every pulse, and that includes yours.'

İkmen smiled. He was right. Commissioner Teker was very liberal in what she allowed her officers to do on their own recognisance. Just as long as she knew all the details, all the time.

Meltem and Ahu walked slowly out into the sunshine and the waiting arms of Zenne Gül. None of them said a word until they got away from police headquarters and out of Fatih district altogether. Back in Beyoğlu, Gül settled the girls into a comfortable corner of the beautiful little garden at the back of the Café Lumière – one of their favourite places. Once enlivened by coffee and omelettes, they began to talk.

'They wanted to know what I was doing on all these dates and at various times,' Meltem said.

'Yes, but you keep a diary, so all you had to do was look it up. It was terrible for me,' Ahu said. 'I never know what I'm doing.'

'But they let you go,' Gül said.

'Us, yes,' Meltem said. 'And Birgül and the baby. But I think everyone else is still there.' She leaned across the table towards Gül. 'What happened to you?'

'They questioned me,' he said. He wondered how much he should tell them about his work on behalf of the police, and then decided that to say nothing was probably the best option.

'They must have been satisfied . . .'

'Yeah.'

Ahu shook her head. 'Do you really think Uğur Bey killed himself?'

'I don't know.'

'Deniz Bey was with him when it happened,' Meltem said.

'He gives me the creeps!'

Meltem looked at Ahu. 'Deniz Bey?'

'Yes.'

'Why?'

'Always there, listening. What's an old soldier like him doing around us?' Ahu said.

'Politics . . .'

Ahu shrugged. 'He looks at girls in a bad way,' she said.

They all paused to drink coffee, and Gül lit a cigarette.

'The body in the garden was a woman, wasn't it?' Meltem said.

'I think so.'

311

Gül knew that it was. He also knew that the body of the woman wasn't all that the police had found. Inspector Süleyman had not told him much, but he had confided that other remains had been discovered in the garden, and that maybe a link existed between these finds and the cannibalism they'd been investigating.

How could *that* happen in *his* garden? Gül, in spite of the summer sunshine, felt chilled. Could Uğur Bey have killed himself because he had eaten human flesh? He'd been almost insane with anger at Gül when he'd come to speak to him about Süleyman. Could he really have done that? Could Bülent? Ziya? Deniz Bey?

'If we can't go back to the squat, where can we go?' he heard Ahu say.

That was a good question.

'I'm not going home,' Meltem said.

'We should find a place together,' Ahu said.

'What? All three of us?'

Gül laughed. 'No, you girls stand a much better chance without me.'

'Maybe, but . . .'

'I've places I can go,' he said.

If worst came to the worst, he could sleep behind the bar at the club for a few days. But Gül knew people. Pembe Hanım, because of her affair with Sergeant Gürsel, wasn't an option, but there was always Madame Edith. An elderly drag queen and Edith Piaf impersonator, Madame lived in a rat-scented dive in Tarlabaşı. On one side lived a prostitute who specialised in S&M, and on the other a whole crowd of dying bonzai addicts. But Edith was kind and she'd give him a home in a heartbeat.

What was more worrying at this stage was what was going to happen to the squat movement if it was tainted by something as horrifying as murder. Would all the Art House residents lose their credibility, and would this find in the garden mean that every other squat in the city would be investigated by the police?

'You took the boy Burak Ayan to the Syrian border.'

'No.'

Ziya Yetkin was scared, big and butch as he was. Ömer Mungun could see nothing but fear on his face.

'That's what Bülent Onay told us,' Ömer said.

'No he didn't. He wouldn't.'

'Wouldn't what?' Ömer said. 'Tell us what you did?'

'No!'

'No, he wouldn't tell? Think that much of him, do you?'

Ziya shook his head. It was obvious he'd become lost in the exchange and now fell silent.

Ömer sat back in his chair. 'You're a man who uses the road,' he said. 'So you know as well as I do that we have traffic cameras these days.'

Although he'd requested footage from Gaziantep, he didn't know whether he'd actually get it. But a photograph of Yetkin's motorbike at Taksim on the right day at a plausible time had been located – and he, or whoever was driving, did have a passenger.

'I've got pictures of your bike.'

'Not me riding it.'

'You have a passenger,' Ömer said.

'That wasn't me riding the bike.'

'Then who was it?'

'I don't know.'

'You don't know!' Ömer folded his arms across his chest. 'I can't believe that. It's your bike, right?'

'Yes.'

'So you'd know if you lent it to anyone.'

Ziya said nothing.

'And if it had been stolen, you would have reported it. Valuable machine like that.'

He shrugged.

Ömer shook his head. 'Bülent has confessed,' he said.

'No he hasn't.'

'Wouldn't it have been better to say "confessed to what"?'

Ziya looked at the floor. Then he said, 'I didn't kill anyone.'

'Maybe not. But according to Bülent, you helped to conceal a murder.'

Again Ziya said nothing.

Ömer leaned forward across the table. 'You know,' he said, 'I don't think you instigated any of this. I think that was someone else. And although you may have concealed a crime, that's not as serious as instigating it. Judges like an offender who comes forward with information of his own volition.'

Süleyman, standing at the back of the interview room, nodded his agreement when Ziya looked up at him.

Chapter 32

'What's he like?' Cetin İkmen asked.

'He looks every inch the successful New York attorney,' Commissioner Teker said. 'Told me he's not leaving here without his client.'

'What did you say?'

'I said, "We'll see." What else could I say?'

İkmen smoked. 'Bülent Onay saw him kill Halide Can with the lid of the freezer,' he said. 'Which is consistent with the injuries on the body and that sample we now know is Can's blood.'

Arto Sarkissian had pushed the forensic team to match Halide Can's DNA record to the blood sample from the freezer, and they'd done it.

'But it's still Onay's word against Myskow's. Both their prints are on the lid of the freezer. Maybe Onay killed Can when he saw her just about to discover human flesh in the freezer,' Teker said. 'Myskow will blame him.'

'Mustafa Ayan's remains were moved to the squat and buried after Can was murdered.'

'With her body.'

'Probably, yes. They were buried with it. By that time, both bodies had to be hidden wherever they could be and as far away from the hotel as possible.'

'Myskow is going to find it hard to deny that the boy's remains were in his freezer. There is no sense to Can's death unless she found something she shouldn't. Myskow is guilty of something.'

İkmen shook his head. 'What about the spooks?'

'Not heard a word,' she said. 'We won't until just before Myskow's involvement is about to become public.'

'What then?'

'I don't know,' she said. 'I assume that Cihan Özlü plus other prominent citizens will be protected. After all, they only ate—'

'Human flesh,' İkmen said. 'Don't you think they'd like to know about that?'

'We only have Bülent Onay's word for it,' Teker said. 'I was going to say "boar", actually. No crime has been committed by them.'

'Except one of deception,' İkmen said. 'Nice, clean-living, pious men . . .'

She smiled. 'How many people do you want me to imprison for hypocrisy, Cetin Bey? Do we have enough prisons? Myskow gave private parties. No one needs to know who attended, even if he is convicted of Can's murder.'

'Don't they?'

'No.'

İkmen put his cigarette out and stared at the wall.

The two men looked into each other's eyes, while Kerim Gürsel stared at them from across the room.

'I will tell you everything,' Major General Baydar said. 'Provided my request is fulfilled.'

'I can't do that,' Mehmet Süleyman said.

'Not even to arrive at the truth?'

'Not even for that. I don't know who you think I am, Major General Baydar. For that matter, I don't know who you think *you* are that you can ask me to allow you to kill yourself.'

'I can't go back to prison,' he said. 'That's it.'

'Even if you've committed a crime?'

'Have I? What?'

316

Süleyman said, 'You were allegedly instrumental, with others, in the murder of a young boy. You then either assisted in or instigated the disposal of the body. Tell me that's not true.'

He looked away. 'You all just want me back in prison,' he said.

'No. That's absurd. Don't contradict yourself! If you have nothing to hide, why did you offer to tell me everything in exchange for me letting you kill yourself?'

The old man looked momentarily confused, and then he said, 'It was a bad day when this country abolished capital punishment.'

'In order that you could take the facts about your involvement in this case to your grave?' Süleyman shook his head. 'I have thought many things about our military over the years, Deniz Bey, but I have never, until this moment, imagined they were craven.'

Baydar, infuriated, sprang from his chair.

Boris Myskow had his US passport in his hand.

İkmen looked at it. 'You won't need that, Mr Myskow.'

'He will.'

The other voice belonged to a large man with unnaturally brown hair. To İkmen, Ralph Newman rather resembled the late President Ronald Reagan, which was unfortunate, as he'd never liked him.

'Mr Newman.' He smiled. 'I'm sorry, but waving a US passport about like some sort of magic talisman will not work, and it will irritate me. Please ask your client to put it away.'

But he didn't. İkmen thought, *Oh God, he wants to have a stand-off.*

Then he saw Myskow put the document away.

The attorney shook his head slightly, disappointed in his client.

'Right. I want you to tell me what happened the night Constable Can died, Mr Myskow,' İkmen said.

'I . . .'

'My client was serving his guests,' Newman said. 'That's all.'

317

'Your client, who served human flesh . . .'

'Prove it.' Newman leaned back in his chair, making himself comfortable. 'Mr Myskow served wild boar to some dignitaries who shouldn't have been eating pig. So what? Mr Myskow is himself Jewish; he understands about the pork ban. Muslims and Jews have that in common, right?'

'Observant Jews and—'

'Right, observant,' Newman said. 'My understanding is that these dignitaries should be observant. In fact, if they were found not to be observant, that wouldn't be good for them or you, Inspector.'

'What such people do is not my affair,' İkmen said. 'My only concerns are who killed my officer and who may have killed a young boy called Mustafa Ayan.'

'Who's that?' He looked at Myskow, who shrugged.

'Oh, he was nobody,' İkmen said. 'Just a young misguided boy we think may have provided dinner for some people, including your dignitaries.'

'They're not mine,' Newman said.

İkmen looked at Boris Myskow. 'Did you eat the meat Bülent Onay asked you to take care of for him?' he said.

Newman answered for him. 'No.'

'I'm aware of the fact that *you* didn't eat it, Mr Newman,' İkmen said. 'I want to know whether your client did.'

'He didn't.'

'Didn't he?' İkmen sat back in his chair, mirroring Newman's stance. 'I'd like Mr Myskow to tell me,' he said. 'And as a non-observant Muslim, I'd like to ask Mr Myskow, a non-observant Jew, whether he's eaten wild boar.'

'Of course he has.'

'Has he?' İkmen looked into Myskow's eyes, which shifted uncomfortably. 'Not sure I'd like people to know I eat pork, if indeed I do.'

318

'You just said you're not observant.'

'Yes,' İkmen said. 'But pork is a taboo in this society. Just like it is in Jewish society. Tell me, Mr Myskow, do you taste the pork products you cook for people?'

'Of course he does!'

'Do you?' İkmen said.

Boris Myskow looked away.

Mehmet Süleyman straightened his jacket. The old soldier hadn't been able to do much more than grab his lapels before Kerim Gürsel had pulled him away. No one had been hurt, although part of Süleyman had wanted to beat Deniz Baydar. The old military elites had no time for the sons of the Ottomans like Mehmet Süleyman, and they both knew it.

Süleyman cleared his throat. Then he said, 'To clarify, Major General Baydar, I was not being disrespectful to the military class per se. I have nothing but admiration for our armed forces. What I was questioning was your refusal to tell me the truth without conditions. That, I trust you will agree, was craven.'

'So why didn't you lie?' the old man said. 'You're a policeman! You all lie, don't you? Lie! Tell me you will allow me to die and then put me in a cell with a watcher making sure I don't kill myself! Tie my wrists together, blindfold . . .'

He stopped. Had he been a non-military man, he would probably have cried. But instead he took a breath and said, 'You will not understand.'

'I will not understand what, Deniz Bey?'

'The world before your family took this country and made it weak,' he said.

'I don't think anyone can accuse Sultan Süleyman the Lawgiver of weakness . . .'

'When he sat his troops outside the gates of Vienna in 1529

and was too afraid to attack?' Deniz Baydar said. 'The bones of our ancestors were crying out for real men to protect the earth they were buried in.'

'An attack on Vienna at that point was inadvisable . . .'

Everyone knew that the failed Siege of Vienna had marked a turning point in Ottoman imperial power. After that, the empire had gone into decline.

'Our ancestors drank the blood and ate the flesh of their enemies,' the old man said. 'That was why they were strong. It's only when you have no religious or moral strictures to hold you back that you can truly conquer. We lost that. We became weak and superstitious, bound by rules that limit us. Look at us now! We call ourselves Turks? Hah!'

'So if we drank blood and ate flesh . . .'

'If we freed ourselves from these constraints, we could be great, yes,' he said. He leaned across the table. 'I was put in prison for opposing a weakness that only Atatürk has been brave enough to stand up to. And to see his work destroyed . . .'

'Mustafa Kemal Atatürk created the Turkish Republic; he did not urge people to cannibalism. He wanted to modernise, not go back to the Stone Age.'

Deniz Baydar shook his head. 'You don't see it, do you?'

'I don't see how killing and then eating a boy not much more than a child can make anyone a better person.'

'He was infected with ISIS ideology,' Baydar said. 'He was the enemy. He had to be obliterated.'

Süleyman paused before he answered. According to Bülent Onay, Mustafa Ayan had been killed by accident. Was Onay lying, or was Baydar?

He said, 'How did the boy die, Major General Baydar?'

'Of course I eat pig. I eat everything,' Boris Myskow said.

'Human flesh included?'

320

He looked at İkmen, his lip automatically curling. 'I didn't say that. I eat pig. I have to, I'm a chef.'

'Yes, but do you advertise that fact?' İkmen said. 'Do you let people know that you, a Jew, eat pork? Would you tell your mother? Would you even like her to know that about you?'

'I don't live with my mother any more.'

İkmen rolled his eyes. 'That's irrelevant. Would you want her to know you eat pork?'

'No.'

'No, of course not. You'd not tell her that any more than you'd tell her you cook with urine, would you?'

Myskow said nothing.

'I can't prove that either you or those who attended your soirées ate human flesh,' İkmen said. 'But I'm reliably informed that there's a disease called kuru that one can get from consuming human meat. It's usually fatal, so we will see in the fullness of time.' He smiled. 'What I do know for certain is that my officer Halide Can is dead, and that either you or Bülent Onay killed her. We will have to see what your guests say about who was where and when on the night of her death.'

'You'll never get to speak to them,' Myskow said.

'Your comment on the sometimes peculiar nature of Turkish society is noted,' İkmen said.

Myskow was sweating heavily.

'I also have a . . . well, what is it? A pile of flesh? Remains, shall we say, that were buried with my officer. I believe that these belonged to a boy called Mustafa Ayan.'

'Never heard of him.'

'Yes you have,' İkmen said. 'From me. I will know whether or not that flesh came from that boy once DNA testing is complete. Mustafa's father has provided a sample for comparison. Imagine how he felt when one of my constables arrived at his door yesterday.'

'I know nothing . . .'

'Of course you don't,' İkmen said. 'That boy was just a piece of meat to you, wasn't he?'

'Inspector İkmen!'

'What do you want me to say, Mr Newman?' İkmen said. 'Quite honestly, whether or not your client ate human flesh, or even if his high-up Turkish friends joined him, is irrelevant to me. I want to know who killed that pile of flesh that Halide Can saw in his freezer, and who killed her because of it.'

'I didn't.'

'Well Mr Onay says that you did, and he has nothing to lose. Why would he lie?'

'I never had a functioning family,' the old man said. 'My parents were estranged, I was sent away to school. My first exposure to comradeship was in the army. I loved my men and they loved me, and when I was discredited and put in prison, my life collapsed. When I was finally released, the only people I could mix with were others like myself, military men with criminal records, and then latterly my old friend Kavaş's son, Ümit. Via him I met the Gezi/squatter crowd. I'd met Uğur Bey before when he designed fabrics for our mess at Selimiye. Odd people, but we had much in common.'

'Dislike for the government,' Süleyman said.

'To put it mildly.' Major General Deniz Baydar smiled. 'Strange though they were, it was like having a family again. They listened, they sympathised. I know my wife nurtures the idea that I was attracted to the young girls who live in the Art House, but it wasn't that. I like to talk and to listen, and Uğur Bey and his people let me do that in the certain knowledge that no one was going to report me to the authorities for sedition or some such nonsense. They became the closest thing to family I have had since the army, which was why I became so infuriated by the arrival of those ghastly children hurling abuse outside the building.'

'The Ayan brothers and a Syrian refugee.'

'Burak and Mustafa,' he said. 'Everything I hate about the new pious. Small-minded, joyless, intolerant.'

'Just as the military were intolerant of religion?'

'Do you want me to tell you my story or not?' Deniz Baydar said. 'My price is lack of criticism from you.'

Süleyman said nothing.

'Day after day they persecuted the Art House,' Baydar continued. 'We didn't report it to you because you wouldn't have done anything. What would be the point? But then they went too far.'

'How?'

'Don't know where the other boy was, but the two brothers got in. We were all up in the communal living room.'

'Who?'

'Uğur Bey, Bülent, Ziya, Ümit and myself.'

'Doing what?'

'Talking. We heard noises from downstairs. The two boys had got in through the old bathhouse.'

'What were they doing when you saw them?'

'Stealing or attempting to steal food from the kitchen,' he said. 'The smaller of the two had a knife, a real one, not a kitchen knife. Little bastard waved it in my face.'

'Why?'

'It's a good Islamic act to take from scum like us, apparently. According to the child with the knife. Never seen such hatred in a face. Tiny little thing. I got the knife away from him easily. Then the other boy ploughed in.'

Süleyman frowned.

'Protecting his brother, I suppose. I suppose you could also say that what happened next was an accident. The boy flung himself at me. Could I have pulled the knife out of his way? I don't know. All I do know is that I didn't have to twist it.'

'But you did.'

'Yes,' he said. 'They'd both screamed and shouted about going to join this caliphate in Syria. I couldn't believe such things coming out of Turkish mouths. I wanted it to stop. I wanted them to stop.'

'So in contrast to the statement taken from Bülent Onay, you are saying that you murdered Mustafa Ayan,' Süleyman said.

'Yes. Bülent is a good man, but far more egalitarian than I. It was at his suggestion that we all agreed to shoulder the blame should our act against these boys ever surface.'

Kerim Gürsel sat down next to his superior. 'Why break ranks now?'

'Because short of killing myself, I cannot think of any other way to get out of here with some kind of honour,' the old man said. 'That Bülent has killed a fellow chef pains me, but I cannot let him take the blame for the awful child's murder too. That was me. It was I who suggested we needed to dispose of the body in the way that we did, and it was I who suggested we kill the boy's brother.'

'Burak Ayan.'

'Yes. What a vile little rodent he was!'

'Why didn't you kill him, then?' Kerim asked. 'Did the others persuade you out of it?'

'None of the others wanted to do it,' he said. 'But that boy was clever – and I imagine psychopathic.'

'Why do you say that?' Süleyman asked.

'Because when his brother lay dying, he just left him. Not a tear in his eye or a last word of comfort. Then when his brother was dead, he cut himself a deal. He did it so quickly, it made me wonder whether he'd planned everything that had happened. It started out that he wanted us to pay for a train to take him

to Ankara and then he'd get himself to Gaziantep and on to
ISIS. He wanted a more comfortable trip than he'd get on the
bus and he wanted our money. I countered with Ziya driving
him to the border, watching him cross and leaving him. He went
for it.'

'You delivered him to ISIS.'

'Yes, we did. Had I taken him, I would probably have killed
him. But Ziya is basically a good man; they all are. Or were.
For the record, Uğur Bey jumped to his death. I didn't push him.
He too was a good man.'

'Who ate human flesh.'

'Out of necessity, yes.'

'So who also ate Mustafa Ayan?'

'All of us. Myself, Ziya, Ümit, Uğur Bey and Bülent.'

'Who knew about this?'

'Ümit's father.'

Süleyman sighed. 'And what did you all think of the meat
you consumed, Major General Baydar?'

'Bülent boned it, we used those for fertiliser. He cooked it
too. It was really rather nice.'

'And yet, sadly, it seemed to disagree with Ümit Kavaş,' Süleyman said. 'Must make you wonder about your thesis that the
flesh of your enemies can make you stronger, don't you think,
Deniz Bey?'

It was difficult to decide who was the harder to crack, Boris
Myskow or his lawyer. The chef was admitting to nothing and
his time in detention was running out. Çetin İkmen checked his
e-mail to see if there was anything from the Forensic Institute
about the DNA tests on the unknown flesh, but there was nothing.
He felt for the imam, but there was nothing he could do for him.
Because Major General Baydar had confessed to the murder
of Mustafa, the unknown remains were almost certainly those

of the missing boy. Now all that was needed was to establish exactly who had killed Halide Can.

As he walked past Commissioner Teker's office, he saw that she wasn't alone. A man was with her. İkmen didn't know him, but he was dressed very smartly and appeared to be in deep conversation with his boss. Teker, for her part, looked furious.

Chapter 33

A soldier had killed Mustafa. The imam came from a generation who had been brought up to trust the military. He cried. The Twisted Boy put a piece of bread, cheese and salami in front of him for his breakfast, but he didn't want it. The DNA comparison, which he didn't understand, wasn't back from the laboratory yet, but the police said that the body they'd found in the garden of the squat was ninety-nine per cent certain to be that of his son.

Poor Mustafa. All his life he'd been led by Burak, who had demanded and received his loyalty. So much bigger and stronger, Mustafa had always protected Burak. Had he been protecting him again when he was murdered? And why and how had Burak managed to escape? Why hadn't he run home? And why had he told him that Mustafa had died in Iraq? The police had given him so few details, and he'd heard nothing from Burak. There had been only silence from the Syrian boy too. Radwan. Where was he? Weren't the police supposed to be looking for him?

Cetin İkmen stood aside to allow Boris Myskow and his lawyer to pass in front of him. The chef, smiling, held up his US passport. They both got into a car, provided by Teker, to take them to Atatürk airport. The whole performance made İkmen feel sick. Teker owed him an explanation. He walked back into the station and found her in her office, waiting for him.

She offered him a seat, but İkmen stood.

'What happened?' he said.

'Bülent Onay confessed to the murder of Halide Can,' she said.

İkmen lit a cigarette. 'I know that,' he said. 'What I don't know is why.'

Teker's office door was still open. She asked İkmen to shut it, but he ignored her. She said, 'Inspector, you are not supposed to smoke—'

'I don't give a shit!' he said. 'Onay told me that Myskow killed Halide Can. He killed that chef, Tandoğan; we talked over his body . . .'

'Well he lied.'

She stood up, shut her office door and locked it. Still İkmen didn't sit.

'No, he didn't.'

'Yes he did.' She sat behind her desk. 'He confessed last night.'

'Who to?'

'To me.' She looked him straight in the eye.

Try as he might, he couldn't see so much as a flicker of deception in her expression.

He smoked. 'Who was that man I saw with you last night?' he said.

'That's not your concern.' She looked down at her desk.

'Well I'll give him this, he was a smart spook,' İkmen said. 'Not like the scruffy, desperate little bastards I see occasionally. Must have come from way up . . .'

'Inspector, if you are referring to the security services . . .'

'They were looking after Myskow. You and I discussed it,' he said. 'I know one of those when I see one. What happened? Did he go in to Bülent Onay and frighten the shit out of him? Promise him something? What?'

'As I told you, Cetin Bey, I—'

'Bülent confessed,' İkmen said. 'Baydar likewise. Uğur İnan killed himself. These are not people without consciences . . .'

She stood, furious. 'They ate a human being,' she said.

'I'm not condoning that. I just want the right person to be punished for the right murder. I don't want the guilty walking away.'

'The guilty are being punished.' She sat again.

'But is one guilty person walking away?' İkmen said. 'One guilty person who maybe knows too much about certain people?'

She didn't speak.

Finally İkmen sat. 'So you say nothing, which to me is most eloquent,' he said. 'I expected better from you.'

Her face reddened. 'Cetin Bey, you overstep your boundaries!'

'And you, Hürrem Hanım, have collapsed like a rotten tree. Where is Onay? I want to speak to him.'

'He's been transferred to prison.'

Of course he had. 'Which one?'

They stared at each other. Eventually İkmen said, 'I see.'

'No you don't,' she said. 'You see only a commissioner of police. You're a good man, that is all you would see.'

'What else am I supposed to see?'

'A woman in a man's job. A woman committed to getting other women into men's jobs. A person struggling to accommodate dissenting voices in a climate like this.'

And he did see all that. He knew better than most what it was to balance on a knife edge. But he knew something else, too. 'When you hold the devil's hand, Hürrem Hanım . . .'

'Oh, I expect him to bite me, Cetin Bey,' she said. 'But for some idiotic American who makes food out of piss . . .'

'I'm not worried about Myskow,' İkmen said. 'He and his conscience can tear each other apart for all I care. But Bülent Onay . . .'

She shrugged. 'No one but Onay and Myskow will ever know what really went on in that kitchen the night Halide Can died. And that includes you and me.'

329

'Maybe not,' he said. 'But don't you think that, given the existence of doubt, it is a bit unfair to put one man in prison while allowing the other to drift away to a penthouse in Manhattan?'

He got up and began to walk towards the door. 'Know what I hope?' he said.

'What's that, Cetin Bey?'

'I hope that Myskow did give the great and the good human flesh, and I really hope they get a Prion disease.'

'A Prion disease?'

'Transmitted via meat,' he said. 'Including human flesh. Brings on a form of dementia. We know the body carried Bloom syndrome. Maybe they'll all get that. I don't know, I'm not a doctor.'

He left. He was too furious to carry on talking to Teker. Whether she'd been bullied or tempted by real or figurative gold was irrelevant; she'd done a thing she shouldn't have done whilst trying to convince herself it was for the general good. It wasn't. How he would ever have found out who really had killed Halide Can, İkmen didn't know. But he did know that he should have been given the right to try.

He looked at his watch and decided he didn't care what it said, he was going to have a drink.

Later, he would wonder why he had acceded to the demands of a felon. Major General Baydar was a murderer who would almost certainly die in jail, and yet Mehmet Süleyman felt he owed him something. Maybe it was to do with growing up in the 1970s, when the military were treated almost like royalty.

Outside the soldier's cell, he said to Ömer Mungun, 'I don't know why he's asked to see me, but I want you to watch him. He's suicidal, and although he's had everything that could harm him taken away, I still don't trust him.'

330

'But what could he do, sir?'

'I've no idea, but this class of elderly officers is very honourable.'

'Yes, but he's done the decent thing by admitting to the murder of Mustafa Ayan.'

The custody officer opened the cell door and the two men went in.

The old man was standing by his bunk with his hands in his pockets. He'd always been thin, but now, with no belt to secure his trousers, he was having trouble keeping them up.

'Deniz Bey, you wanted to see me,' Süleyman said.

'I want to tell you something, Inspector.'

'What?'

The old man looked at Ömer Mungun. 'Can't we be alone?'

'Sergeant Mungun is my deputy,' Süleyman said. 'He goes where I go.'

'But what I have to say is personal, and not a little embarrassing. It isn't for the ears of a young man.'

'Sergeant Mungun may be young, but he is a man of the world,' Süleyman said.

Deniz Baydar sighed. 'Well, may I whisper to you?' he said. 'The young man can stay, but if I could just tell you . . .'

Süleyman knew it was wrong. But he also knew how the military felt about morality, shame and guilt. It wasn't that much different from the way their religious opponents felt. He also wanted to get whatever this was over with. İkmen had called him. He was in his favourite bar in Sultanahmet and needed to talk before he drank himself into trouble.

'All right,' he said. He looked at Ömer and then went over to the old man. 'What is it?'

Deniz Baydar was almost the same height as Süleyman, so neither had to bend or stretch to get close.

'Well, it is like this . . .'

331

His voice was soft, and so Süleyman moved slightly nearer.

'Can you hear me?'

'Yes.'

'Good.'

An arm like a metal cord pulled Süleyman close. He heard Ömer Mungun gasp. And then there was pain. And blood.

Ömer Mungun had rarely employed his gun. He certainly hadn't used it to beat a man. Now it was slippery with the old man's blood.

Süleyman, his hand pressed against the side of his face, yelled, 'Leave him! No more!'

Deniz Baydar lay at Ömer's feet. In contrast to Süleyman, he didn't put a hand to the wound he had sustained from the stock of the young man's pistol. His eyes looked perfectly calm.

'Get the custody officer,' Süleyman said.

Ömer banged on the cell door, not once taking his eyes off Deniz Baydar.

Blood trickled between Süleyman's fingers as he tried to hold what remained of his cheek up to his face.

When the custody officer unlocked the cell door and saw blood on the floor, he said, 'What's this?'

'Prisoner bit Inspector Süleyman. Call a medic,' Ömer said.

The man left.

Now that pain had replaced shock, Süleyman groaned. Ömer wanted to go to him, but he didn't dare take his eyes off Baydar. What was he? Crazy? Had he actually developed a taste for human flesh? Could he no longer control himself?

The old man moved, and Ömer raised his pistol.

'Don't!'

He looked at Süleyman.

'It's what he wants,' Süleyman said.

'What?'

'Isn't that right, Baydar? Beaten to death in police custody would serve your myth of martyred honour well, wouldn't it?'

The old man laughed to begin with. Then he cried, and when they took him out of there and cuffed his hands and shackled his feet, he screamed.

When the duty doctor finally arrived, Mehmet Süleyman passed out.

The bedroom was like a cross between something from a Disney fairy-tale cartoon and a whorehouse. Basques and other female fantasy wear hung from the doors of a white rococo wardrobe trimmed with faux gold leaf. The bed, a four-poster of vast size, was festooned in so many cushions and throws it was almost impossible to see its occupant.

Cetin İkmen sat on a chair covered in red velvet and put the bottle he'd been drinking from down on the empire-style bedside table. Then he lit a cigarette.

'I assume I can . . .' He waved a limp hand in the general direction of nothing in particular.

'Mmm.'

Drugged but still in pain, Süleyman could do little more than grunt.

İkmen resumed his story.

'So Myskow has gone back to America, never, I imagine, to return, and Bülent Onay will die in prison,' he said. 'Myskow's famous guests will not be named at Onay's trial. Bülent, you see, killed Halide Can to cover up the fact that the freezer he'd given Myskow had contained the body of Mustafa Ayan, which he sought to hide. You'd have thought Myskow would have noticed, wouldn't you?' It was pure sarcasm. İkmen was good at it.

'You're drunk,' Süleyman murmured.

'Yes. It's been a long time since General Cognac and myself had a really good time together . . .'

'You shouldn't drink brandy.'

'I know.' He smoked. 'My wife will be very upset. But how can a man retain his sanity in a country where one can pay fifteen lire for a tomato just because someone famous has made it into some sort of slime? And why is that person able to do anything he wants? He should be in a cell just for the tomato! Will you be scarred for life?'

Süleyman didn't answer. He'd been to hospital, where he'd had stitches, been given shots, painkillers and antibiotics. Now all he wanted to do was sleep.

'This country has gone mad,' İkmen said. 'People adopt positions they are unable to shift from, and money infests everything. I thought Teker was above that. But you can't trust anyone, because everyone is looking after his or her own back all the time. Fear, that's what it is. We're Turks, and your biting soldier is right in that we are a warrior race. A warrior race that has lost its nerve. But he's wrong about religion. Religion's got nothing to do with it. It's money that's hobbled us, money and the modern world of connectivity, which is another way of saying paranoia. We watch each other, all the time. We hit first because we're afraid of what will happen if we don't get that first punch in. I don't blame Teker. She just did what anyone would do, she watched her back. Doesn't make it any less appalling.'

Süleyman made himself half sit up. He didn't need a drunken İkmen at his bedside, but Gonca had let him in the house and so he was stuck with him.

'Major General Baydar has confessed to the murder of Mustafa Ayan, and we have the other accomplices to the offence in custody,' he said.

İkmen performed a slow handclap and then drank from his bottle again.

'We also have a confession from Bülent Onay, so at least Constable Can's family may have peace . . .'

'Peace!'

'Cetin . . .'

'Peace in a country where youths run away to a pointless war in Syria, where a brother can use his sibling's death to, what is the expression, big himself up?' He shook his head. 'I wonder whether the Ayan brothers would have gone off to join ISIS if Burak Ayan hadn't had Bloom syndrome. What if he'd been just the carrier instead of Mustafa? I wonder whether it was his physical frailty that made him so desperate to prove himself.'

'Maybe he really believed ISIS propaganda. Maybe his brother did too.'

'We'll never know,' İkmen said. 'The good imam let that computer into his home and he lost his sons to it. When will people learn that a computer is as dangerous as a car? Would you leave your child alone with your car when its engine is running? You wouldn't. ISIS squeezed into that bedroom and spread their propaganda, and now here we are.' He drank from his bottle again. 'Here we are.'

Chapter 34

Three weeks later

Radwan was playing. The imam had found the train set his father had bought him when he'd been to Germany in the 1950s. To his delight, it still worked, and now the Syrian boy was watching the clockwork engine pull into a toy station called Berlin. Bizarrely, it looked like something from a Grimm fairy tale.

The police had brought Radwan back to him. Finally. He'd been shot, but he'd told the imam that Burak had saved his life. Imam Ayan didn't know whether Radwan was telling the truth or not, but he chose to believe him. Burak, wherever he was, had been a good boy once. He'd been raised with a sense of decency even if that had been eroded in recent months. He had been jealous of his brother, which was a weakness, but how could he not have been? He didn't know that his stature and his poor health were legacies of a disease he wasn't even aware he had. The imam knew he should have told both his sons. But the fear of revealing their mother's ethnicity had stopped him, and that had been wrong. Zanubiya had been a Jew, and by never acknowledging that, he had brought misery to his sons and shame on himself.

He'd taken Radwan to her grave and they'd both laid stones, as was the Jewish custom. The stones marked a visit from the living and were a sign that the deceased had not been forgotten. She never had been. Her boys, for all their faults, had loved their mother. The imam just wished that he could turn the clock back so that he could tell them who she really had been.

But God in His mercy had sent him the child, who played in what had once been Burak and Mustafa's bedroom. The police still had the computer he had bought them, and the imam was not in any hurry to have it back. Radwan, the war child, had told him he had no interest in computers. The imam felt that he would take him at his word.

'You're still the handsomest man in Istanbul,' Gonca said.

She sat down on the bed behind Mehmet Süleyman, watching him as he looked at his own face in her dressing table mirror. She knew he hated the jagged bite mark on his left cheek.

'And it will fade,' she said.

'I know.' But he frowned.

'It's a battle scar. You should be proud.'

'I was bitten by an old man who wanted to die,' he said.

'A cannibal,' she said. She wound her arms around his shoulders. 'You are a lion. My lion.'

But he said nothing.

Gonca knew that it wasn't just Mehmet Süleyman's vanity that was silencing him. A terrible crime had been committed in the golden city on the Bosphorus. It threw the divisions and tensions that had risen to the fore in the past few years into stark relief. At the axis between the old secular elites, religious fundamentalism and the threat to the far eastern border of the country by forces no one really understood, a boy had been killed and eaten by other human beings. Süleyman had seen a lot of horrific things during the course of his career. But never anything like this. But then nor had anyone. Gonca kissed the back of his head and then called to her grandchildren to come in from the street.

Who knew who might be lurking outside in such dark times? In front of their computers in their bedrooms she knew they would be safe.

All but two of Cetin İkmen's five sons had performed military service. Though none of them had become professional soldiers, Fatma İkmen had insisted they all be photographed in uniform. And although Orhan, Sinan and Bülent had all finished their service a long time ago, she dusted their pictures every day.

Arto Sarkissian had seen her do it many times. He knew she was proud of them, but he never commented for fear of embarrassing her. Good Muslim women didn't do boasting.

'I see Anatolia Gold's share prices have slipped,' he said.

The İkmen apartment was clean but chaotic, as usual. While Fatma dusted, Cetin was in the kitchen treating the cat for fleas. No one ever stood on ceremony when Arto visited. He was family.

'I should think so,' Fatma said. 'You have to be able to trust what producers say is in their food. They upset a lot of people, not to mention losing us all money. I had to throw half my tin cupboard away.'

'You threw food away?'

'Well no, not really,' she said. 'I got Kemal to take everything up to Beyoğlu. There's a priest over there who feeds the Syrian refugees. A lot of those are Christian. Pork is filthy, as you know, but if you feel you can eat it . . .'

Cetin came in and sat in his chair.

'Get scratched?' Arto asked.

Marlboro the cat could be a handful, and Arto had heard various yowls and screeches from the kitchen.

'No,' İkmen said. 'Just made him swear.'

'Tea?' Fatma asked.

338

İkmen smiled. 'Perfect.'

She went to the kitchen.

'So how are you feeling?' Arto said.

İkmen had taken two weeks' annual leave after the Karaköy squat had been closed down. He'd watched his colleagues board up the windows and put metal screens over the doors. A boy wearing an ISIS T-shirt had stood across the road laughing until the owner of the café had chased him away. He was no more wanted in Karaköy than the police. Istanbul had always been a city of discrete quarters, but now, İkmen felt, parts of it were ghettoising. And that wasn't healthy.

'Ready to go back to work?'

İkmen shrugged. 'What else is there to do?'

'You don't sound very enthusiastic.'

'I'm not.'

'You found out who killed Mustafa Ayan, and why.'

'But not Halide Can.'

The two men sat in silence. Boris Myskow had put the Imperial Oriental up for sale. Apparently he was in negotiation to buy a new restaurant in Madrid. The gourmet dining caravan had moved back to its heartlands in the West.

'Well the forensic investigations are at an end,' Arto said. 'So Imam Ayan may bury his son's remains.'

'That's good. I heard that Defne Baydar finally managed to bury her brother too.'

'Yes.'

He'd seen İkmen despondent before, but never this deeply.

Arto said, 'You know, Cetin, I can't think of any society that isn't undergoing some level of fragmentation at the moment. The riches globalisation can bring set us at each other's throats. That ghastly building that is being constructed next to my house is, I believe, destined to be occupied by wealthy foreigners. The developer will make a fortune. But I doubt it will be his last.'

339

'Greed,' İkmen said. 'Why be a millionaire when you can be a billionaire, eh?'

Arto smiled. 'It has always been the way of things, but now it has accelerated. How are you with Teker?'

İkmen lit a cigarette. 'Still angry, but I'll put it behind me.'

'Will you?'

He smiled. 'Oh yes. But if Mr Myskow misbehaves himself now he's in Spain, I will be on the phone to the Guardia Civil.'

'She won't like that.'

'I don't care,' İkmen said. 'The only reason that man is free to inflict piss and blood and whatever other mad stuff he chooses to call food on his customers is because he knows people. He knew people back in the States, he got involved with prominent people here, and that's the entire reason why he walks free.'

'You don't *know* he killed Halide Can . . .'

'I don't know that Bülent Onay did either,' İkmen said. 'And I may never know now, and that offends me. Halide's family should know for sure who killed her.'

'We do not live in a perfect world.'

'No, but we should do our best to get as close as we can to perfection. Isn't that the point of being alive?'

Arto sighed. 'For some.'

'Oh yes, I forgot,' İkmen said. 'For others there are different reasons, aren't there? To enforce their ideas by raping women and cutting people's heads off.'

'Or eating people.'

İkmen shook his head. 'No winners in this war of attrition, eh, Arto?'

'Between the secular and the religious? No,' he said.

Fatma came in with glasses of tea and plates of börek and olives.

'But we do always have good food and drink,' Arto said as he took his glass from Fatma and put it down on the coffee table.

And this time Cetin İkmen smiled properly.

'Ah yes, but it is *real* food and drink, my dear friend. Made with love by a real person.'

Fatma said, 'Well I should hope I'm a *real* person.'

İkmen took her hand. 'I can assure you that you are.'

'Oh, well that's good.'

He closed his eyes and launched himself into the music. Hot, sweaty but exuding the smell of the rosewater he had mixed with his body oil, Zenne Gül could feel his heart pounding as the excitement of the moment grew. He was dancing. In spite of all his recent trials, the loss of his home, of his good friend Uğur Bey, and in the face of so much horror in the world, he was still in the city and he was still dancing.

Madame Edith had let him move into her rat-scented hovel. Tarlabaşı was a good neighbourhood. Full of bonzai addicts it might be, but all Gül could feel for them was pity. And there were others he could build friendships with – Gezi protesters, trans girls, gypsies, even an old soldier in a basement underneath a brothel. Although perhaps old soldiers were best avoided . . .

Gül opened his eyes. Green, red and pink lights played across his slim body and illuminated the audience at his feet. He recognised many of the faces. The club was one of Istanbul's foremost gay venues, but a lot of audience members were girls. Meltem and Ahu had been here once, long ago. Gül wished they'd come again. In fact he wished that everyone he loved was in the audience. That way he would know they were safe and happy.

But then he saw a face that didn't bring him joy. He didn't know who the man with the neat designer beard right slap bang in front of him was, but he knew his type from his eyes. Those boys who had hurled abuse at everyone in the old squat had possessed eyes like this man's. They looked at him with disapproval and disgust, and Gül felt a chill run through him. He glanced away. When he became brave enough to look down again, the man with the frightening eyes had gone, replaced by a joyful and outrageous drag queen. It was almost as if he had never existed.

Gül continued his performance and lost himself in the music.